'An unusual, engrossing story full of excitement and shocks'

*Primary Times*

'Extremely descriptive and exciting – I couldn't put it down!'

*Chicklish*

'After turning the 412th page, I was left wanting to know more. I would recommend *The Dragons of Ordinary Farm*'

*Fantasy Book Review*

'Expert storytellers Tad Williams and Deborah Beale take readers on an extraordinary adventure'

*Books on Board*

# THE SECRETS OF ORDINARY FARM

## TAD WILLIAMS
### & DEBORAH BEALE

Quercus

First published in Great Britain in 2012

Quercus
55 Baker Street
7th Floor, South Block
London
W1U 8EW

A CIP catalogue reference for this book is available
from the British Library

ISBN 978 1 84916 574 7

1 3 5 7 9 10 8 6 4 2

Printed and bound in Great Britain by Clays Ltd, St Ives plc.

FOR MISS ISABEL LAPIDUS

*A star among critics*


AND FOR MATT BIALER &
LENORA LAPIDUS

*A little bit of night-time reading, with love*

# PROLOGUE

## CALLING HIM LIKE A DOG

'Hurry! Make faster magic, boy.' Mr. Walkwell sounded grumpy, but that was no surprise: Mr. Walkwell didn't like Colin much and made that clear to him nearly every day. 'The children will be here in a few hours and Gideon wants everything to be ready.'

Colin Needle made a face but didn't say anything, only bent closer over his laptop. Thunder rumbled above the distant hills. The sky felt hot, heavy, and close. *The children this, the children that* – he was so sick of hearing about them! Everybody at Ordinary Farm except Colin and his mother seemed to think Lucinda and Tyler Jenkins were something wonderful, but really the two were nothing but troublemakers. In just a few weeks last summer the Jenkins kids had managed to ruin all of Colin's careful plans to improve Ordinary Farm, and now they were coming back for another summer's stay. Lucinda and Tyler, Tyler and Lucinda – he was tired of hearing their names and tired of everyone on the farm making such a big show out of their return visit.

The sky growled again. A single fat drop of rain fell on Colin's screen. The weather had been strange all spring and didn't show any sign of changing, the days as hot as they always were at this time of the year but also damp, overcast, and even sometimes stormy. Colin Needle had never been to a tropical country, but he imagined it might be a little like the weather around this part of California lately.

Ragnar had finished installing the complicated new gate on the adobe barn and now he wandered over, wiping either sweat or rain off his forehead with his wide forearm. 'Why aren't you finished, Needle?' the great Norseman demanded. 'We have done all the hard part, boy! Just cast your spells so we can go and get ourselves something cold to drink.'

'It's not magic and they're not spells,' Colin said through clenched teeth. 'I'm trying to hook the new security gates and fences up to a computer network so we can do everything from a distance. I already explained it all several times.'

'You told me your flat box makes things work by invisible lightning that flies through the air,' said Ragnar. 'What is that if it is not magic?'

Colin scowled. Nobody else at Ordinary Farm

knew anything much about electricity or computers, let alone wireless networks – most of them had been born centuries before such things existed. Even his mother, who had learned enough to use the internet and keep her experimental and household records on a computer, still could not come close to what Colin himself could do. Some day Gideon would be gone and Colin Needle would be in charge. Lucinda and Tyler Jenkins would have to do exactly what he said, then – if he even allowed them to visit the farm.

And his own mother, frightening as she might be, would have to do what he wanted . . .

A deep, rasping snarl from the far side of the barn made Colin Needle jump in fear. Ragnar laughed and slapped his thigh; he had made it very clear that he didn't like Colin any more than Mr. Walkwell did. 'Don't jump out of your skin, boy! It's just the manties saying they are tired of their cage. They want to come out and play with you!'

'Very funny,' Colin said, but he was shivering. 'Those things are killers.'

'And who made Gideon think so much about protecting the farm?' Mr. Walkwell gestured to the sliding electric gate they were struggling to finish. 'Who was it who brought Gideon's enemies here onto our land?'

'Leave me alone, will you? I *said* I was sorry! I've said it a thousand times!'

In truth, Colin thought Gideon's new obsession

with security was the most intelligent idea the old man had come up with in years, but that didn't make him want to spend any more time around these imprisoned monsters than he absolutely had to. There was something about their orange eyes – something so cold and *knowing* . . . 'You said their cage is secure, right?' he asked the two men. 'Right? Then get out the way and let me try this.' Colin clicked the 'OPEN' button on his screen. A few yards away the motor whined for a moment. Then the heavy metal barn gate rattled as it began to slide to one side on its small wheels. It really was a *little* bit like magic, Colin Needle thought proudly. The manties heard the noise and began grunting and barking inside the barn. Colin was very grateful the savage things were caged behind heavy steel bars: their long yellow teeth, clawed fingers, and curiously intelligent but emotionless eyes had haunted more than a few of his nightmares lately.

A brief flurry of rain spotted the dust and splashed warmly on Colin's neck. He opened and closed the gates a few more times to make certain he had set everything correctly, then shut down the program while Ragnar and Mr. Walkwell finished with the last details.

Simos Walkwell whistled to him, a sound that made Colin bristle – calling him like he was a dog! 'Needle,' he said, 'take the end of this metal rope and hold it as I roll the rest up.' Mr. Walkwell didn't seem to sweat even in the most sweltering weather, but he pulled off his hat and ran his fingers through his hair as he examined the loop of plastic-covered wire cable in his hands. He hadn't sanded down his horns in several days and they looked like tiny tree stumps growing just above his temples.

'It's not a metal rope,' said Colin, 'it's wire. The word is *wire.*'

The old Greek barked a humourless laugh. 'You knew what I meant. Now make yourself useful, boy. Hold the metal rope and close your mouth. Both things will help.'

Colin swallowed a bitter response. *You'll see,* he thought. *I really will be in charge of this farm one day, no matter what you or those stuck-up Jenkins kids think. And when that happens, everything's going to be different. Very,* very *different.*

The summer storm had already drifted off to the other side of the valley as its last damp traces vanished into the dirt. As the thunder died away Colin could finally hear the sounds coming from the barn on the other side of the new gate – the restless noises of large, hungry creatures waiting to be released.

# CHAPTER 1

## COLD-WAR FARM

'I can't believe you came to pick us up, Uncle Gideon!' Fourteen-year-old Lucinda Jenkins turned to her younger brother. 'Isn't this great? We're back!'

For once, even Tyler wasn't trying to pretend he was too cool for everything. 'Yeah,' he said, grinning. 'It's definitely great.' It was amusing to see his sister so thrilled – this from a girl who thought even *Planetoid*, the best video game in history, was 'lame'. In fact, Tyler was feeling pretty happy himself; even the unusually damp weather seemed exciting.

Uncle Gideon looked happy to see them too, which made a nice change from long stretches of last summer when he had acted as though he regretted inviting them to his very special farm. Gideon Goldring looked healthier than he had last year as well – he was even wearing something other than his normal working

6

costume of pyjamas and a bathrobe. His white hair was uncombed as usual, of course, but very clean, and his skin was tanned as though he had been spending time out in the sun.

'And it's good to have you two here!' their great-uncle said, laughing. 'Now, hurry, children! We have a long drive ahead of us and everyone's waiting to see you.'

Simos Walkwell, Gideon's right-hand man – or at least with his hat and boots on he *looked* like a man, though Tyler and his sister knew better – nodded and might have even smiled a little, but broad emotional displays were not his style. He tossed both big suitcases up onto the wagon bed as if they were no heavier than sofa cushions then hopped up onto the driver's bench. Lucinda scrambled up into the bed of the cart, Tyler right behind her.

Lucinda was so excited she couldn't stay quiet. 'Wow, it's great to be here! How is everybody – and how are the animals? Ooh, how's the baby dragon? Your last letter said she's big now!' Uncle Gideon's last letter had also been months ago. Lucinda had been driving her brother crazy since then. 'Is she all right?'

Gideon chuckled. 'Yes, child, yes, all the animals are fine. All the people too!'

Mr. Walkwell swung back up onto the bench and clucked his tongue. Culpepper the cart horse snorted, then pulled the wagon into a broad turn across the main road. A few townsfolk on the opposite sidewalk looked up and one or two even waved. It was clearly another slow Saturday in downtown Standard Valley.

Gideon lowered his voice. 'You didn't tell anybody at home anything, did you? About the farm?'

'No, Uncle Gideon!' both children cried at the same time, and Tyler added, 'We wouldn't do that. We promised.'

'Darn right.' Gideon settled back on the bench. 'Because that is the first rule. In fact, that's almost the only rule I have!'

*Not quite true,* Tyler thought, amused. *You've got a few of them. Don't ask too many questions about the animals. Don't ask questions about the Fault Line, where the animals come from. Don't ask about what happened to your wife, Grace. And definitely don't ask why you have a witch for a housekeeper . . . !* But of course Tyler didn't say any of that. He had made it through an entire amazing, wonderful, incredibly dangerous summer at Ordinary Farm last year and the one thing he had learned for certain was that when Gideon Goldring was in a good mood it was better just to keep your mouth shut and enjoy it.

And their great-uncle really was in a good mood, as though he had missed the children almost as much as they had missed Ordinary Farm. Tyler hadn't spent his school year counting the seconds until they could return in quite the way his sister had, but he had definitely been looking forward to this. He had been worrying about it too. So many secrets – so many crazy, dangerous secrets!

*And now it all starts again,* he thought. Ten whole weeks. Anything could happen!

'Wow. We're really back.' Lucinda stared down the sloping road to the valley floor. 'It was so hard to wait!'

'Does it look the same?' asked Gideon. 'As you remember it?'

'Better. When can I see the dragons?' Tyler knew she was dying to talk to them, as she had found out she could do at the end of last summer – she had talked about little else all the way down on the train today. 'Can I stop in and see them now, Uncle Gideon? Before we go to the house? The reptile barn's just over there, and we're so close . . . !'

Mr. Walkwell grunted in disapproval, but Gideon was still in a good mood. 'I suppose so, just for a minute – *if* you promise to stay out of trouble . . . !'

'I will, I will! Oh, thank you, Uncle Gideon!'

The old man was smiling. 'Just don't tell Mrs. Needle. She doesn't like me changing the schedule.'

'She doesn't like anything with a pulse,' Tyler said under his breath, but he knew that at this moment Lucinda wouldn't have cared even if Patience Needle was riding toward them on a broom.

After they had descended from the hill road they crossed a wooden bridge over a creek, then followed the line of the new and impressively tall wire fence

9

that ran around the outside of the property. Tyler also couldn't help noticing the signs reading 'DANGER – ELECTRIC FENCE.'

'Is it really electric?' he asked.

'Not enough to kill anyone,' said Gideon. 'Just to keep unwanted visitors from climbing over. And if they try it some other way, well . . .' He pointed to a small dome-shaped object on the top of a fence post. 'We've got cameras – they work at night too!' Gideon chortled. 'Much less work for Mr. Walkwell to guard the property now. Isn't that right, Simos?'

'I didn't ask for this.' Mr. Walkwell sounded unhappy. 'My ears and my nose are still better than any seeing-box.'

'Yes, but even you can't keep track of what's going on across the whole valley at the same time.' Gideon seemed amused by the overseer's grumpiness. 'This will be good for you, Simos. You're not getting any younger.'

'Pericles said that to me too.' Mr. Walkwell turned back to watching the road as it ran along beside the fence. They were approaching a large gate that was definitely another new addition.

'He never knew Pericles,' said Gideon in a stage-whisper. 'Pure exaggeration.'

Since Tyler didn't know the guy either, he could only shrug. 'So that's the new gate?'

'One of them, yes.'

'But *why*?' Lucinda sounded alarmed and Tyler

couldn't entirely blame her. The hills and the valley hadn't changed at all, but here was something that definitely had, a ten-foot-tall gate of steel and heavy timbers. Tyler thought it looked like the entrance to a fortress . . . or a prison.

'I told you in the letter I sent over the Christmas holidays,' Gideon said. 'Told you we couldn't have you visit until now because we were making some changes. Well, this is one of them. We've got new fences and gates for the whole farm – in fact, we've got a whole new security system!'

'Kind of weird,' said Lucinda. 'It looks like . . . like . . . '

'East Berlin,' said Tyler, who had just finished the Cold War in his American-history class.

Gideon shook his head emphatically, happy mood now gone. 'Don't be stupid! The Berlin Wall was meant to keep people in. I am protecting myself against people who want to creep onto my property and steal my secrets. Not the same at all!' He glared at the children. 'Or have you forgotten what happened last summer?'

Tyler decided it might be a good time to stop talking about the gate. 'No, Uncle Gideon.'

'Of course not, Uncle Gideon,' said Lucinda. 'We get it.'

Tyler looked along the fence, which stretched as far as he could see in either direction. 'It . . . umm . . . looks very secure.'

Gideon laughed harshly. 'It had better! Do you know

how much it cost to build fences and mount cameras around ten thousand acres? It took most of the money that Ed Stillman tried to use to bribe Simos! And that was quite a lot of dough!'

Except that money hadn't really been a bribe, Tyler knew. Billionaire Ed had brought it to purchase a dragon egg from Colin Needle, a crime against Ordinary Farm that Tyler and Lucinda had helped prevent, then also helped to hide from their great-uncle.

Now Gideon climbed down from the cart and punched some numbers into a keypad beside the fence. A lock clicked open and the heavy gate rolled to one side on little wheels. After they had driven through it slid closed again by itself.

'That's to make sure no one leaves it open by mistake,' Gideon said. 'Wonderful improvement – and there are others you haven't seen yet! We're really set now. Just let Stillman's mob try to sneak in here without us knowing about it!'

Even Lucinda had finally fallen silent. As they turned toward the reptile barn, the tall shadow of the gate stretched a long way down the road in front of them.

# CHAPTER 2

## A Flaming Loogie

As they pulled up in front of the barn, Lucinda thought she heard someone calling them. Mr. Walkwell must have heard it too, because he turned to look off in the direction of the farmhouse. A strange object was approaching them, something odd and upright trailing a cloud of dust.

'Oh, crud,' said Tyler. 'Him.'

Colin Needle rode unevenly toward them across the dirt, jouncing up and down on the seat of a plain, old-fashioned black bicycle.

Tyler laughed. 'Hey, nice ride, Needle! Is that your mom's bike?'

'Oh, it's good to see you too, Jenkins,' said Colin with a tight and completely unconvincing smile as he bumped to a halt beside them. 'Hi, Lucinda,' he said to her. 'Welcome back to the farm.' He sounded like he actually meant that part.

Lucinda thought Colin was taller and thinner than the previous summer. He was also dressed in an old, ill-fitting coat and matching trousers; with his hair mussed by his riding he looked like some kind of wheeled scarecrow. 'Hi, Colin,' she said. 'You look nice in your suit.' It wasn't entirely true, but Lucinda wanted to start the summer being friendly this time – she was convinced that Colin Needle wasn't all bad. Tyler snorted, but Colin and Lucinda both ignored him.

'Thanks.' Colin quickly turned to Gideon, as if he was embarrassed now to meet Lucinda's eye. 'My mother saw you heading over here and she wanted me to remind you that Sarah's worked all day making us all a hot meal but it won't stay hot for long.'

'Saw us? She must have been watching through my binoculars!' Gideon turned to Tyler and Lucinda. 'Meaning we had best hurry up, I suppose.' He sounded as pleased as a small boy to be bending the rules. 'Before Patience loses her patience!'

Even Lucinda on her best behaviour couldn't pretend that was a great joke, but she chuckled as best she could. 'Come with me, Colin,' she said. 'I'm just going in to see the dragons. Come along! I'll be quick.'

Colin, who was beginning to get off his bike, suddenly stopped. 'Ummm . . . no, thanks. You go on. I'll wait here.'

'Don't be silly! You can tell me what you've been doing since last summer.' Lucinda almost took his arm, but thought better of it. She wanted to be nicer to the tall, awkward boy this year, but she didn't want to give him any ideas. 'Come on!'

Colin reluctantly – *very* reluctantly – joined the small group as Mr. Walkwell pushed open the heavy door.

The air was at least as hot inside the massive barn as it was outside, but it was also full of the musky smell of wild beasts. Lucinda did her best to not to let the stink bother her – after all, this was what she had been wanting for months, the way a little kid wants a special doll for Christmas.

Meseret, the adult female, lay stretched in her enclosure with her wings folded against her body, big as a city bus, beautiful and awful. Lucinda could not hold in an excited squeak at seeing her. Meseret was like something out of a children's storybook, all thick leathery scales and knobs and whorls of bone, something that should not exist in the real world . . . but there she was. The eyes with their slit pupils watched them all and gave away nothing.

*Can you hear me, Meseret?* Lucinda did her best to speak with her thoughts. *Do you remember me? We flew together!* Although to be perfectly fair, an observer on that night last summer might have thought Lucinda had been dangling helplessly from Meseret's harness. *Do you remember me? I'm Lucinda!* She had tried to convince herself not to expect too much at first, but Meseret's gigantic, uncaring silence pained her anyway. *Remember? I helped save your egg!*

'Man, look at this! The little one's here too!' called Tyler, and Lucinda reluctantly turned away from the big dragon.

'You wrote in your Christmas letter that you named her Desta,' she said to Gideon.

Her great-uncle nodded. 'It's an Ethiopian word for "Happiness". My wife Grace once had a puppy with that name that was very dear to her . . .'

Desta didn't look much like a puppy, or in fact like a baby of any kind, at least compared to the tiny thing that had hatched in the farmhouse kitchen last summer. The young dragon was now as big as a small horse. In most ways she was a smaller, more slender version of her mother, but her overall colour was a sandy brown instead of drab grey-green, with rosettes of brick red and a frill of pale olive spines down her back. Desta's scales, some as big as Lucinda's hand, others as small as a sliver of her pinky nail, glinted and shone as the muscles moved beneath the skin.

The young dragon was watching Lucinda and Tyler too, but she mostly looked as if she wanted to go back to sleep. '*So* cool,' Tyler whispered.

'Is anything wrong with her?' Lucinda asked, staring at the straps around Desta's middle. A chain connected the arrangement to a large ring set into the concrete floor of the pen, close to the pile of straw she was using for bedding. 'What's that thing she's wearing?'

'Harness,' said Gideon. 'Have to keep it on her right

now. She'll learn to fly soon, you see. Don't want her leaving the property by surprise.'

'She must hate it.'

'Don't sentimentalize the animals,' her great-uncle said. 'That's a mistake.'

Meseret suddenly growled, and although the mother dragon was some distance away from her, Lucinda could feel the slow, rumbling sound through her feet.

'Why'd she do that?' Lucinda asked. 'Is she all right?'

'Perfectly all right,' said Gideon. 'She's probably just hungry . . .'

Meseret raised her vast head and swivelled it from side to side, nostrils flaring, as if she smelled something.

'Gideon . . .' said Colin, 'maybe we should . . . maybe we ought to . . .' Lucinda couldn't help noticing that the older boy sounded genuinely frightened. 'I'll just . . .'

A strange loud noise made Lucinda jump, a wet *pop* like a starter's pistol held underwater. Colin Needle jumped, shrieking in surprise and pain. 'Owwww! Oh, help, it's hot! It's *burning me*!'

Lucinda spun to see Colin jumping and thrashing wildly. Something thick and sticky was running down his jacket – something that *smoked*. An instant later, Colin's jacket burst into flame.

Luckily Mr. Walkwell was only a few yards away.

The wiry old Greek moved with such incredible speed that Lucinda had just opened her mouth to shout for help when he wrestled off Colin's burning jacket and threw it aside. He shoved the pale, whimpering boy onto the floor, then rolled him back and forth to make sure he was no longer on fire. For long moments after the flames were out he kept Colin down on the ground. The black-haired boy lay trembling violently, his breath hitching.

'Is he all right?' Lucinda asked. 'Colin, are you okay?'

'It is not bad,' said Mr. Walkwell. 'His mother will give him something for the burns.' He didn't sound too worried.

As Mr. Walkwell and Gideon helped the tall, pale boy out of the reptile barn, Tyler crept up next to Lucinda and quietly said, 'Well, I guess dragons don't forget that easily, huh? Desta's mom hasn't forgotten who stole her egg.'

'Don't be mean, Tyler!' What he had said finally sunk in. 'Wait a minute – you mean Meseret? Was that her? What did she do?'

'I guess she still remembers Colin from last summer. She *spat* at him from twenty feet away! Hawked a big one.' He rubbed his mouth to hide his grin. 'A flaming loogie.' Thunder rumbled softly in the distance. The storm seemed to be moving away.

Lucinda was not amused. In fact, she felt a bit sick inside – all this from trying to be friendly . . . ! 'Poor

Colin. He didn't want to go near the dragons but I made him do it . . .'

'He's fine, Luce. Anyway, he deserved it – just ask Mama Dragon!'

But this was most definitely not the way Lucinda had wanted to start the summer.

# CHAPTER 3

## INTO MOUNT ZION

The side trip to the reptile barn had led them a different route from the one they usually took back from town. Tyler found it interestingly strange to approach through the centre of the farm, past outbuildings and barns, instead of seeing it across a distance from the road in the hills. From the hillside the buildings came into view below like a fleet of strange painted wooden spaceships, all red and yellow and tan and white, but their approach this time made the house and its connected structures rise up before them like a vast sea of sawtoothed roofs and towers – an entire toy city made by drunken Christmas elves and plunked down in the middle of a dusty California valley.

'Look, Luce!'

His sister looked up. 'Oh, yeah,' she said. 'We're definitely back.' She had been trying to comfort Colin, who was huddled near them in the back of the wagon, eyes red and jaw clenched. Tyler didn't think the older boy's injuries were as bad as he was making them out to be.

Lucinda gave him a warning look as the cart horse pulled them past the old grain silo. The tall grey structure looked like a haunted house out of a scary movie but was actually only an empty wooden building that covered the farm's greatest secret – the Fault Line, a gateway to other times and places, discovered by Octavio Tinker. Tyler didn't know what Lucinda's look meant and didn't much care: she had her dragons and he had the Fault Line. In fact, as far as Tyler knew, he was the only person in the world who could walk into it and out again safely without the help of any machine or device. Did she really think he was going to ignore it all summer?

A crowd of people was pushing through the front door of the farmhouse and out onto the covered porch, a group of smiling, familiar faces waiting to greet them. Even before the wagon rolled to a stop the farm folk were hurrying toward them.

'You are here! That is good, very good!' cried Sarah the cook as she wiped her hands on her apron, her ruddy cheeks even ruddier than usual because she had been cooking. Tyler took his hug from her with good nature, although she nearly squeezed the breath out of him – Sarah was short but strong. She was also serious about hugging: a moment later she had captured his sister too and squeezed her until she squeaked. Sarah's kind spirit filled the house and was responsible for much of what was homey and welcoming about strange old Ordinary Farm.

Pema, a quiet young woman from long-ago Tibet, and her near-opposite, Azinza, from Africa, tall, dark, and regal, followed closely after Sarah with hugs of their own.

'We missed you,' Azinza told Lucinda. 'It was too quiet here after you went away.'

'But not so quiet today, it seems.' Sarah had seen Gideon lead Colin past them and into the house. 'What happened to him?'

But before Lucinda could answer, most of the rest of Ordinary Farm's inhabitants were upon them. Ragnar the Viking, a blond, bearded grandfather built like a professional wrestler, came at them with a big grin and surprised Tyler by pulling him into a rib-cracking embrace. Kiwa, Jeg, and Hoka, the Mongolian herders whom the Jenkins kids had named the 'Three Amigos', hovered smiling, holding gifts they had made, a bracelet for each of the children woven from long strands of hair.

'Horsehair?' Lucinda asked.

'Not horse,' said Kiwa, the oldest. 'Unicorn. From tails, manes. They leave on fence and bushes.'

'Wow,' said Tyler. With Jeg's help he tied his onto his wrist. The braided hair was surprisingly thick and heavy, shiny as platinum wire.

'That's so cool,' said Lucinda, examining hers. 'Thank you!'

The last person to come forward was Ooola, the girl Tyler had rescued from the ice age, cleaned up and wearing a dress but with long curly brown hair that looked as if it hadn't caught up with modern brushing techniques. Ooola took Tyler's hand and pressed it carefully to her forehead. Tyler smiled at her, but he wasn't quite sure what the gesture meant. 'It is good to see you,' she said, looking at him shyly through surprisingly long lashes. She then seemed to remember something else she had to do and scuttled back to the kitchen, leaving Tyler a bit confused.

Of course, a huge celebration banquet had been prepared to welcome them back – *'eine Feier,'* as Sarah named it – and soon the children were led to the table. Tyler decided it was entirely reasonable and polite to honour the work the cooks had done by dedicating himself completely to food for the rest of the day. As he walked along the table where the dinner had been set out he found roast chickens, juicy inside their crispy skins, enchilada casserole with homemade corn tortillas, several kinds of salad, and great big bowls filled with grilled artichokes and summer beans. Sarah had also prepared a speciality dish called *Sauerbraten,* a sort of beef roast with fruit and cabbage. Tyler approached that one cautiously, but after a few sample bites he went back and helped

23

himself to a huge serving. Something about Ordinary Farm made him hungrier than he almost ever was at home.

Later, as evening turned to night, Sarah brought out beer for the adults and a pitcher of strawberry lemonade for the others, then settled her wide, warm self between Tyler and Lucinda. 'How you two have grown!' The mistress of the kitchen looked Lucinda up and down. 'So big now! Woman very soon, yes indeed!' Lucinda blushed. 'And you, Tyler. You are much bigger!'

Tyler laughed. 'Oh, I've got a while to go before I catch up with Ragnar.'

Sarah nodded. 'Yes, poor Ragnar, he works so hard on all Gideon's fences and gates.' She shrugged.

'What do you think about all that?' Tyler asked the cook. 'All the new fences and security?'

'Oh, me, I don't know anything.' Sarah clearly didn't feel comfortable talking about it. 'If Gideon says we need, then we need. He works so hard to keep us safe here! And he is still so sad his wife is gone.'

'Poor man,' said Lucinda. Gideon's wife, Grace, had disappeared decades ago, but the mystery was still unsolved. 'He must miss her so much!'

'But you help him, Tyler!' Pema, the little Tibetan woman, had come up quietly. She blushed when everyone turned to her, but bravely continued. 'I mean, when you find his wife's necklace last summer.

He always carries it! Always around his neck. When he is sad, he reaches up and –' she stroked an invisible something at her throat – 'like so. Makes him not so sad.' She pointed. 'Look,' she said. 'He is doing it now.'

Tyler turned to look at Gideon, some distance away. He was indeed stroking the locket's gold chain at his neck, but that wasn't what caught Tyler's attention: his great-uncle was speaking to Mrs. Needle, the first time Tyler had seen her since their arrival. The witch – to him she would *always* be the witch – was dressed in her usual prim, timeless way, long dark skirt and white blouse buttoned right up to her slim throat. She seemed to feel Tyler's gaze, because she suddenly looked up; for a moment he saw what he felt certain was icy hatred in her eyes, but then it vanished like a mist and she smiled at him in a way that appeared almost natural.

'Welcome back!' she called.

Tyler turned away, his stomach clenching. Lucinda gave him a warning look.

'And how is our Mrs. Needle these days?' he asked.

Sarah made sure the Englishwoman wasn't looking before she scowled. 'She is what she is.' Like almost everyone at Ordinary Farm, Sarah was a refugee from the past, a medieval woman with very, very firm ideas about witches. 'But she holds Gideon's ear and he trusts her. Please do not make her angry.'

'Why would we want to make her angry?'

Sarah shook her head. 'Just be careful, children,

please! She doesn't like you and she is a bad enemy to have.'

Evening had fallen. Bats were swooping over the garden, snatching up moths and mosquitoes. Country hours ruled Ordinary Farm: those who had not left to take care of after-dinner chores were beginning to drift toward bed. Gideon had retired half an hour earlier. Caesar, the old black man who did handyman work around the house and insisted on taking personal care of Gideon Goldring, suddenly began to sing a song, his cracked voice full of longing for something Tyler couldn't quite understand.

> *'Oh, let me fly, now, let me fly!*
> *Let me fly into Mount Zion,*
> *Lord, Lord.'*

The song was exactly right for the mood: or perhaps it was how Caesar sang it . . . Even Mr. Walkwell tapped a hoof. Ooola the ice-age girl stood in the middle of the floor swaying and twisting her fingers in her thick brown hair.

> *'I jes wanta get up in the Promised Land—'*

A hard hand fell onto Tyler's shoulder: he jumped in surprise.

'Good evening, children,' said Patience Needle.

'Lovely to have you with us again. Now it's time for me to show you to your rooms.'

'How's Colin?' asked Lucinda. 'Are his burns okay?'

The woman's expression did not change. 'He is nearly well already. Burns are easy for me to heal. Now come with me.'

Tyler fought to keep his voice friendly. 'It's okay. We remember how to get to our rooms, Mrs. Needle.'

Mrs. Needle smiled thinly. Her pale face gleamed like the moon in the frame of her black hair. 'But you don't have the same rooms this year. Now, come along, children, it's getting late. Say goodnight to everyone.'

The main house at Ordinary Farm was a labyrinth of wooden floors, dusty, faded carpets, flickering light bulbs in empty halls, and countless locked doors, but it was clear that Mrs. Needle was indeed leading them somewhere different from where they had slept last year. For long minutes she glided before them like an apparition, holding a battery-operated storm lamp, then stopped at last in a corridor Tyler didn't recognize.

'Here you are, children.'

'Isn't this in . . . your part of the house ?' Lucinda asked.

'Yes, Lucinda,' the housekeeper said in her crisp way. 'It's near my retiring room – my office, as you'd call it. That's why I know you will be comfortable here. Sleep well.'

'Why can't we stay in our old rooms?' Tyler asked.

'Because the decision has been made,' she said, her voice less friendly than before. 'I can keep a closer eye . . . pardon, I mean I can *take better care of you* here.'

The assigned bedrooms stood side by side and both looked out over what was perhaps a courtyard – it was too dark now to tell for sure, although one thing Tyler could make out was that they were several floors above the ground. Mrs. Needle snapped on the overhead light in first one room and then the next, revealing both to have dark wood panelling and flowered wallpaper from another century. The only modern thing in either room were the children's suitcases, apparently brought up earlier. 'Get ready for bed, now,' the Englishwoman said. 'It is late.'

Tyler brushed his teeth and returned to his room. He wasn't thrilled about having to change rooms – it had been hard enough to learn his way around the ever-confusing farmhouse the first time – but he was too tired and too full to worry about it. He was just thinking about wandering over to Lucinda's room to discuss this eventful first day when he heard the lock in his door click. By the time he had jumped up and run to it he could hear Lucinda thumping on her own door in surprise and protest. Tyler rattled the knob but it wouldn't turn and the door wouldn't budge.

The witch had locked them in.

# CHAPTER 4

## LIZARD JERKY

Angry but very tired, Lucinda sat on her bed and did her best to ignore Tyler banging around in his room, thumping the walls and door in frustration.

Okay, so they'd been locked in. She didn't like it either, but they couldn't do anything about it tonight, so why wouldn't her brother just let her go to sleep?

Tyler's room finally went quiet. Lucinda took a book out of her suitcase and settled back against the pile of pillows to read, an old novel of Mom's called *The Singing Tree* about a Hungarian family during the First World War. The story was good and she was tired enough just to fall into it, so when someone knocked on her window it startled her so much she screamed and dropped the book.

It got weirder. Tyler was hanging upside down at her window like a huge bat, waving and grinning.

'You idiot!' she said as she jumped up to shoulder open the ancient window so he could climb in. She looked down. 'It's like three floors to the ground! You could have broken your neck!'

'You sound just like Mom,' he said. 'There's ivy all over the walls outside – it's totally grown into the bricks, really easy to climb.' He sat up, his hair all kinds of wild and looking enormously pleased with himself. 'Nobody's going to lock *me* in.'

Lucinda found herself almost admiring his total irresponsibility. 'You're insane,' she said. 'How are you going to get back?

Tyler sank to the floor and stretched out on his back. 'It was pretty awesome, really. There's a big moon tonight – plenty of light for climbing. And this house . . . ! I forgot how big it is. It just goes on and on – crazy, gigantic big . . . !' Tyler's eyes narrowed. 'What's that?'

Lucinda sighed. It was like having a young dog around – sniffing, scratching, digging, chewing, always into something. 'What's *what*?'

'That.' He pointed at the ceiling above her dresser. 'That square up there. Looks like a trap door or something.'

'Yeah, well, check it out tomorrow, Dora the Explorer. I'm tired.'

'No, really.' He sprang up and pulled out a couple of the dresser drawers. 'Here, help me. Keep this from tipping over . . .'

'Tyler, no!' But it was useless, of course – he was already clambering up the dresser, making it sway ominously. She hurried forward just in time, wincing as she heard the wooden drawers creaking and protesting under his weight. When he reached the top of the dresser Tyler reached up and poked the rectangular ceiling panel once, then poked it again. It gave a little.

'I knew it!'

'Knew what? That there was a heating duct up there?' But Lucinda was a little intrigued in spite of herself. Tyler pushed the wooden panel up and out of the way, exposing darkness. 'Eew,' she said. 'Probably full of spiders.'

'Give me your flashlight, Luce.'

'Where's yours?'

'I dropped it when I was climbing on the roof.'

Lucinda sighed. 'Good going.' She found the dopey pink flashlight Mom had given her and passed it up to Tyler. He gripped it in his teeth, then pulled himself up into the space above until he could rest his upper body on the edge and only his legs dangled down. 'What do you see?' she asked. 'Don't let any spiders crawl down or I won't be able to sleep in here.'

His voice was muffled. 'Yeah, that makes sense. You're on a farm with dragons as big as a jet plane and you're worried about ordinary house spiders?'

'Spiders are creepier than dragons. What's up there?'

'Mostly heating pipes or something . . . and insulation and empty boxes.' He sounded disappointed as he rattled things around.

'Don't make so much noise!' she hissed up into the dry, old-smelling air above her head.

Tyler's face appeared in the opening. 'It's a big space, Luce. An attic.' He vanished, returned to his inspection. A long moment passed. 'Wow. Actually there's a lot of stuff stacked right behind that heating-pipe thing over there . . .'

He fell silent. Lucinda listened for long moments, heart pounding. He was doing a good job of being quiet – too good. 'Tyler?' she called.

'I found a cool-looking box up here, Luce. It's like wood, and it's got . . . labels all over it.'

'What do you mean, labels?'

'You know, like someone sent it from far away. Come stand under the hole and help me get it down.'

Despite her very strong desire not to handle anything that might have spider webs on it, Lucinda got on a chair and reached up, squinting her eyes in case anything jumped off at her. The box, when Tyler slid it down, was smaller and less heavy than she'd expected, about the size of an overnight bag, made out of pale, thick wood with rusted metal corners; Lucinda just managed to avoid getting scratched by the metal as she took it. Tyler jumped down.

'What is it?' There were labels all over it. The labels

were in English, but the names all looked very exotic – the sender seemed to be someone named Koto. Lucinda couldn't even guess what kind of name that was. 'Wow – look at this label,' Tyler said. 'This box came from Madagascar!' He pulled his knife out of his pocket. 'Swiss Army to the rescue!' He began hacking through the thin metal bands that held the box closed.

'Don't cut yourself,' she said, but Tyler ignored her; a few moments later he was prising up the lid of the small crate. When it popped free, a smell rolled out like nothing Lucinda had ever smelled before, dusty and dark and rotten-sweet, confirming every prejudice she had against this venture.

'*Ooh*, gross!' She gasped. 'What is *that*? Don't touch it, Tyler!'

*That* was something shrivelled and possessed of little legs folded up against a long, dried-out body. Tyler lifted it off the top of the nested paper. 'Awesome. It's a lizard!'

'Yech. It's lizard jerky, is what it is.'

Tyler actually waved it in her face, like he was four years old.

'*Stop!*'

Luckily the lizard had been dead and dried long enough that it had almost no smell, but Lucinda still didn't want to touch it. She watched as Tyler set it aside and began digging through the scrunched-up paper. 'The rest of looks like it's all plants,' he said, holding up some kind of bulb with little bits of dry soil still clinging to its tiny roots. 'And seeds in glass jars – this one has a note on it that says, 'Unknown *Sarracenia . . .*' Tyler was digging busily in the paper now, and suddenly she flashed back to him as a very small kid, seeing in her mind's eye the way he used to excavate in the just-opened cereal box for a free toy, and how crazy that used to make their mother: '*Pour it out in a bowl, for God's sake. Don't stick your dirty hands in there!*'

Tyler tossed something at Lucinda – a bundle of letters, held together with an old rubber band that broke into pieces as she grabbed for the letters. They scattered all over the floor.

'Clumsy,' said Tyler, which made Lucinda fume. She picked one up and was startled by what was written on it.

'''*Doctor Grace Goldring . . .*''' she said. 'Wow! Did you know Gideon's wife Grace was a doctor?'

Tyler shook his head. 'But this stuff is mostly seeds,' he said, disappointed. 'Some powdery, mushroomy stuff, and a couple of bugs in, like, test tubes . . .'

'So she was a biologist . . .' said Lucinda, impressed. 'A scientist.'

Tyler stopped abruptly, his hand sunk deep in the packing materials, and for moment Lucinda was scared that the poisonous spider she'd been worrying about all along had bitten him. Then she heard it too – a key turning in the door of her room.

Lucinda looked at Tyler, who stared back at her, wide-eyed. '*Just a minute!*' Lucinda shouted. '*Don't come in!*'

Tyler was shoving everything he'd pulled out back into the wooden crate. Lucinda frantically tried to gather up the letters, dropping several in her haste, but there was no time: the door banged open.

Mrs. Needle stood in the doorway, slender as a pointing finger. Her eyes widened when she saw the crate and its contents on the floor, but her face otherwise remained an emotionless mask. 'I might have known. The first day and already you two are causing trouble.' She called over her shoulder: 'Colin!'

Her son walked in. The boy who had just endured a horrid dragon-snot burn looked fine now, just as his mother had claimed. He gave Lucinda a look as he walked into the bedroom that she could have sworn was pure embarrassment.

'You locked us in!' Tyler said accusingly.

'And you not only got out, you made what must have been a very dangerous excursion to get here,' snapped Mrs. Needle. 'What did you do, child, climb out the window? Do you know how foolish that is?' She stared down at the crate. 'And what is this?' She looked up to the open panel in the ceiling. 'Incorrigible. A few hours back in the house and you are already burglarizing the place, rifling through things that don't belong to you . . .' She shook her head. 'Colin, gather this all up and carry it to my office.'

He already had the papers in his hands. 'The lizard too?' he said, sounding wary.

'Yes, of course the lizard – goodness only knows what kind of important scientific specimen it might be.' Mrs. Needle sighed. 'As for you two, I am sure Gideon will have something to say to you both in the morning. Tyler, back to your room.'

'You're not my mom,' he said quietly, but for once that was as much resistance as he was willing to offer. Colin led him out.

*Great,* Lucinda thought as Mrs. Needle locked the door behind her. She threw herself back on the bed, miserable. She wanted to pound her heels on the floor like an angry toddler. *Here less than a day and we're in trouble again.*

# CHAPTER 5

## NOT INVITED

All year Colin had been very careful to stay away from the dragons. What happened in the reptile barn proved him right, although it had hurt too much for him to enjoy his moral victory. Yes, his fears were now confirmed: dragons *remembered*. The beasts had too much freedom, that was the problem. Meseret should be muzzled like a dangerous dog, and her mate, Alamu, shouldn't be flying around the huge property unsupervised. It was all just another example of why someone sensible – someone like Colin himself – should be in charge.

As he was thinking these and other sour thoughts over breakfast, his mother appeared in the kitchen doorway. 'Colin, go to Lucinda Jenkins's room and make certain there is nothing left in that crawl space – I cannot trust those children to tell me. If you find anything else, bring it straight to me. *Straight* to me.'

Colin nodded and went without complaining, an act he occasionally put on, like an old T-shirt he could pull over his head and later just drop on the floor. It was easier and more sensible than arguing, since he had never won an argument with his mother and doubted he ever would.

Lucinda's room was empty of Jenkins kids, which was a relief. After an awkward climb onto the dresser and up into the crawl space yielded no further discoveries, he trudged back down to his mother's office to tell her the news. She didn't seem surprised. She was already carefully unpacking the shipping crate, setting out its contents on her big table in neat rows of jars, tubes and crumpled foreign newspapers, and making notes on a lined pad.

'That's fine, dear. Run along and help the others now – I'm sure Gideon can find something for you to do. I'll be busy until lunchtime but I'll see you then.'

'I thought maybe I could work with you – help you sort through this stuff . . .'

'Oh, no, Colin. Thank you, but you'd just be in the way.' She hadn't even looked up.

He kicked the banister as he went down the stairs and hurt his toe. Why was it that every time Tyler and Lucinda Jenkins showed up, things immediately went bad for Colin Needle?

\*

Blazing early-morning light filled the open front door, throwing much of the rest of the entry hall into darkness. A little hot, fresh air blew in, disturbing the dust motes as they drifted in the light.

Gideon was up and wearing his going-out clothes, which meant he'd pulled a pair of trousers over his pyjamas. His white hair looked as if he'd just pulled a pair of pants over that as well – it stuck up like wispy grass. The master of Ordinary Farm also had the hearty, pleased-with-himself air that Colin disliked – what he thought of as Gideon's 'great man' personality, when he acted as if everything he said and did was being noted by historians. What the old man was really like, Colin thought, was the movie version of the Wizard of Oz – a humbug, full of speeches and hot air.

But when Gideon abruptly turned to Colin his scowling face looked more like Oz the Great and Terrible. 'What's this I hear about you and your mother locking Tyler and Lucinda into their rooms?'

Surprised, Colin swallowed hard. 'Mother wanted to keep them out of trouble, with all the changes to the property and everything. Especially Tyler.' He couldn't hold Gideon's sharp stare. 'It wasn't my idea.'

'I think you and your mother sometimes forget who owns this farm,' the old man said sternly. 'You can tell her there will be no more locking *anyone* in. As for the changes to the property, we're going on a little tour right now.'

Colin frowned. He hated the idea of spending

time with Tyler Jenkins, who seemed to be even more obnoxious than last summer, if such a thing was possible. Lucinda wasn't so bad – in fact, Colin had been almost looking forward to seeing her – but he really didn't want Gideon to think he was going to spend the summer babysitting those two. 'I'm supposed to be working in the library, Gideon . . .'

'The library?' Tyler had just appeared on the stairs. 'Why?'

'He's doing some work for me.' Gideon's hand stole up as if it had a mind of its own, reaching toward the locket he wore hidden under his pyjama shirt – his wife's locket that Tyler Jenkins had brought back to him, which Colin knew was the whole reason the old man had sent him to the library. 'And now that we're talking about it, Master Needle, I haven't seen any results, considering all the time you spend over there instead of doing your regular work.' The old man shook his head. 'I'm losing patience, lad.'

'That's not fair . . . !' Colin felt his cheeks get hot and bit back the rest of his angry reply. 'I'm doing my best, Gideon. The books are all out of order . . .'

'What's Colin doing in the library?' Tyler was not going to let it go.

'That's none of your business!' Colin said. 'You've only been here a day . . . !'

'Now, let's have no more of this silly fighting,' Gideon said, growing cheerful again as other people argued. 'Young Colin's just doing some research for me. You'll hear about it later. Right now we have a tour to take!'

'Can we see the unicorns?' Lucinda asked. 'And Meseret and Desta again?'

Gideon laughed. 'Maybe, if there's time. Come along, everyone. I want to show you some of the features we've added since last summer – you might call it the new, improved Ordinary Farm!'

'But Gideon, what about my work?' Colin asked.

The master of the house looked at him without much kindness. 'You might as well get to it, lad. I wasn't inviting you to join us.'

He led them out, leaving Colin Needle alone in the entry hall with his face red, smarting as if someone had slapped him.

# CHAPTER 6

## A DOZEN ORANGE EYES

After everything that had happened the night before, Tyler thought it was wonderful to be out of the house, away from the Needles, and rolling across the farm with Uncle Gideon and Mr. Walkwell. They picked up Haneb outside the Sick Barn. The shy little animal keeper nodded to the children and might even have said hello, but he spoke very quietly as always, keeping his head turned away to hide the scars on his face.

They headed out toward the pasturelands, the horse-cart rattling up and down the dirt roads and through the golden hills. Beyond the hills the valley was fenced by mountains, dark purple shadows against the sky in every direction Tyler looked. Even the air smelled different here in Standard Valley, wild as ocean air, full of mysteries.

As Lucinda had requested, their first stop was the unicorn pasture, where they found Ragnar already pouring feed into a huge trough. He summoned the animals with three loud whistles and they appeared over the rise less than a minute later, a spiky, thunderous cloud of dust and horns. Tyler, Lucinda, and Gabriel sat watching from the cart while the Norseman, Mr. Walkwell and Haneb worked with the creatures. A foal was corralled and given a shot of antibiotics. Several others had their delicate hooves inspected, cleaned, and trimmed. Shy, scarred Haneb gently felt the stomach of one skittish, expectant mother.

'Her time coming soon,' he announced.

'Well, that's something to look forward to!' said Gideon. He settled back against the seat. 'Ah. What a fine day. This is heavenly!'

Lucinda said, 'Can we go see the dragons next?'

He frowned. 'I told you, we'll see. First, we truly do have to talk about security, if only for your safety. You've seen how hard we've been working to improve things since you were last here. Many things have changed.'

'How many fences are there now?' Tyler asked. 'And are all of them, like, electrified?'

'There are three,' Gideon said. 'One around the very outside of the property, one around the main buildings, and one just around the house itself.'

'How come so many?' What Tyler really wanted to see was what would happen if someone tried to climb

43

over one, but he felt sadly sure that wouldn't be part of any demonstration.

'It will be easier to explain once you see the rest of our precautions,' Gideon told them, his good spirits returning. 'And it was all possible because of that money Stillman left here last year! Half a million! Even if he's a billionaire, I bet that still hurt!' The old man let out a sudden cackle. 'I'll bet he's kicking himself. He tried to ruin me, but it only made me stronger!'

'Has he tried to do anything else since then?' said Tyler.

'He never stopped,' his great-uncle growled. 'He seems to have a new plan every week. Right now he's trying to buy all the properties along the border of Ordinary Farm – throwing money at my neighbours like the soulless pig that he truly is. He wants to surround me! Do you wonder I'm trying to protect the farm?'

As the wagon creaked and bumped back toward the centre of the property, where they could again see the jumbled silhouette of the farmhouse, Tyler found himself coming back again and again to Uncle Gideon and Colin Needle. What was Colin doing in the library for the old man?

It hit him just as they made their way past a row of huts that might once have been workers' cabins.

*The necklace*, he thought. *He's wearing Grace's necklace. And where did I tell him I found it? The library –*

44

*which was partly true.* He had not told his great-uncle the rest of the story, how he had been given the locket by a woman Tyler was certain had to be Grace Goldring herself, a woman lost in a strange, backward version of Ordinary Farm on the far side of a magical washstand mirror Tyler and Lucinda had found in a little room off the library. *Gideon's got Colin trying to figure out how Grace's necklace got into the library.* Tyler doubted Colin would ever guess what had really happened, but knowing that the pale, unpleasant boy had been given free run of the library bothered Tyler. A lot.

Gideon cleared his throat as they reached a little wooden bridge over the stream that ran through this part of the property, only a few hundred yards from the house itself. 'Now,' he said, pointing at the water, 'I know you've seen this before, but do you know what it's called? It's Kumish Creek – that's an Indian name. Course, the creek recedes a bit as the summer goes on, but even in mid-August it's more than wide and deep enough for a man to go down the middle in a canoe or even swim it. It runs all the way from the hills outside of the valley almost to our farmhouse door.'

'Why don't you just make it run through a pipe or something?' Tyler asked.

Gideon scowled. 'Oh, Lord, what would I ever do without children to point out the obvious? Because, boy, if we meddle with the creek it might flood the Fault Line chamber, which is just a few hundred yards away, over there. So we had to find another way to defend it.'

With Tyler smarting a little at his great-uncle's rebuke, the cart rolled on over the little bridge before Mr. Walkwell pulled it off the road and reined up. They could see the dark water better now that the sun was behind them. The creek was muddy green and brown with bumps of light in it where it splashed over rounded, multicoloured stones, and was surprisingly noisy.

'It's all the spring rain,' said Gideon as they pulled to a stop. 'We've had a wet year.' The cart had come to a halt under some leaning alders, just at a point where the earth turned to shale and reedy grasses. 'So here is our first new line of defence,' he said.

Tyler stared out across the reeds to the river. 'I don't see anything.'

'Don't worry, you will.'

Lucinda let out a little moan of worry beside him.

'Not unless we tell them we are here, Gideon,' said Mr. Walkwell.

'Ah, of course, silly of me. Do the honours, will you, Simos?'

Mr. Walkwell bent down and found a large rock that Tyler would have had trouble even lifting, then flicked it with one hand into the river where it disappeared with a loud *blurp*.

'You see,' Gideon said, 'even if they're half a mile away they feel the vibrations. Even with as strong a

46

current as the Kumish has. I think they must have some kind of special gland – platypuses do, you know, and the two species are related.'

'I don't get it,' said Tyler. '*What* feels the vibrations?'

'Sssshh.' Gideon held his fingers to his lips. He pointed toward the far side of the river, where something was making the tall reeds shiver and bend. Whatever it was slipped into the water without ever once showing itself clearly, then could be seen moving beneath the surface, quickly and silently. It was very large. 'Here it comes . . .'

Lucinda's fingers were gripping Tyler's sleeve. 'Uncle Gideon,' she said, 'you're scaring me.'

'Oh, I'm sorry, child.' He didn't sound like it. 'I am just very proud of them. They're creatures right out of Aboriginal myth – bunyips.'

'*Bunyips?*' said Tyler with a snort of laughter. 'That sounds like some kind of Japanese kiddie anime.'

'Don't sass me, boy, and don't take these creatures lightly!' Gideon's anger was swift as a summer storm: a moment later he had recovered himself again. 'Yes, bunyips. I suppose it is a funny name. Legendary swamp demons – but they're quite real. From Australia. And even more fascinating, they're *monotremes*.'

Something rose in the centre of the creek, out of a dark spot where the bottom dropped away. The water bulged and then a broad, flat brown head emerged, a few twigs and limply streaming grasses snagged in the

47

creature's bristling, thorny pelt, its eyes all black and big as saucers.

'It's huge!' Tyler said, his heart speeding. It was one thing to see something that big behind bars in a zoo, quite another to find it staring at you from open water a few yards away. 'Bunyip. Is it going to come out?'

'Not if we stay out of the water . . . but I wouldn't get too close, anyway,' Gideon said. 'They're all male, very territorial. This one came because he felt the splash. They'll swim half a mile to attack one of their rivals and protect their territory, like bull crocodiles. Make a tremendous noise when they're fighting – they roar like elephant seals! We hear it, come and save the poor fool, then give him one of Patience's forget-your-own-name potions . . .'

'What's . . . what's a monotreme?' asked Lucinda. She had backed right against the far side of the wagon seat.

'Same family as the echidna and the platypus,' Gideon said cheerily. 'They're the only poisonous mammals, and the only mammals that lay eggs – very weird critters. But *my* bunyip was a hundred times bigger than any modern monotremes and has been extinct for thousands and thousands of years.'

For just a moment the thing in the river splashed upward instead of sideways, rising a little way out of the water. Lucinda gave a shriek of dismay and Tyler jumped in alarm too. The creature was big as a hippo but shaggy or maybe prickly – Tyler thought its silhouette looked a little like a giant porcupine – and its blunt, huge-eyed head ended in a short trunk with wiggling fingers at the end, like the snout on a star-nosed mole.

The bunyip slid back into the water, a large, flat island rippling its way back across the river to disappear into the crackling reeds.

'Wow,' Tyler said.

'You bet!' agreed Gideon, smiling broadly. 'Don't you feel safer just *looking* at that magnificent animal?'

They left the creek behind, following the line of the innermost fence away from the farmhouse. Mr. Walkwell, who as usual had not said twenty words all morning, suddenly narrowed his ageless brown eyes and said sternly to Tyler and Lucinda, 'You must behave now, children. Remember, there are beasts on this farm who can repay impatience with blood or even death.'

'I know,' said Tyler. 'We just saw one, right?'

Mr. Walkwell went on as if Tyler hadn't spoken. 'Hear me! No games where we go next, Tyler Jenkins.'

'Hey,' said Tyler, 'I'm all grown up now.'

Mr. Walkwell made a noise that Tyler couldn't quite convince himself was a grunt of agreement. Lucinda's face had gone quite pale. In fact, she hadn't looked very comfortable since the creek. 'Do we have to do this?' she asked.

Gideon had his hat tipped low to keep off the worst

of the sun. Eleven o'clock in the morning and it was already very hot. 'People would pay thousands just to see what you're going to see next. We have amazing things on this farm – taking care of them and this place is a sacred trust.' As Tyler watched, one of the old man's hands reached up to his throat and Tyler guessed he was fondling his wife's necklace again.

'Uncle Gideon, where's Zaza?' Tyler asked suddenly. 'The flying monkey. I haven't seen her yet.'

The old man waved his hand vaguely. 'She's around somewhere,' he said, but he was thinking about something else. For someone who basically owned the most astounding zoo in the world, Gideon Goldring sometimes seemed almost indifferent to the individual animals, especially those that weren't a new project . . .

Mr. Walkwell punched in the numbers at another gate and it slid open to let them through. Within a few moments they crested a rise and saw a large tan brick building sitting by itself in the middle of an otherwise empty dirt lot. Its shiny metal roof stood out dramatically above the earth-coloured walls.

'Is that building new?' asked Lucinda.

'No, but the roof is. We had to fix it up for our new guards!'

'Guards?' Lucinda looked relieved but still confused.

With relish Gideon said: 'Yes, the "manties", as Colin calls them. Our manticores.'

'Manticores!' Tyler was impressed. 'But you said last summer they were vicious.'

'They are,' said Mr. Walkwell, as the wagon pulled up beside the building. 'Come along, follow me – don't hang back!'

'It's so much cooler in here!' said Lucinda as they all entered the barn. She was trying to sound cheerful, but her voice was even more nervous now and Tyler could guess why – the place stank with the sharp, nose-burning urine of predators.

'Cool, yes. It's the adobe,' said Gideon. 'It keeps the temperature down. People have used it around here for years.'

Most of the barn's interior was taken up by a huge cage, which extended up to the new metal ceiling and ran along most of two walls. The cage floor was covered in sand and sticks. At the centre a pile of large concrete blocks formed an artificial jumble of boulders.

'Enough,' said Gideon Goldring. He had lowered his voice. 'No more talking now. Simos, go and bring them out.' He turned to the children. 'They're usually sluggish during the daytime. They're night hunters.'

Tyler watched avidly as Mr. Walkwell made his way around the two walls of the cage on his deceptively delicate hoofed feet, whistling a series of repetitive notes and keeping well away from the bars. Lucinda hung back near the door, her eyes wide and her face making it clear she would rather be somewhere else. Even Tyler, who normally enjoyed anything spectacular or dangerous, was beginning to feel anxious.

'Hurry them up, Simos,' said Gideon after Mr. Walkwell had been walking back and forth whistling for half a minute or more. 'We don't have all day.'

Walkwell gave him a look, but took a long metal pole off the wall and reached it through the bars to rap sharply on one of the concrete blocks. The first manticore emerged a moment later, sloping out into the open as leisurely as a sullen teenager.

'Whoa!' said Tyler. 'They were *tiny* last summer!'

'They did grow up fast, didn't they?' said Gideon.

Two more followed the first. Once out in the open the manticores sat on their haunches, pale tan faces half-hidden in the ruff of mane, watching the visitors with their surprising orange eyes. Each one was the size of a full-grown lion, but it was something else about them that made the children stare.

Lucinda's voice was very shaky. 'Their faces . . . they look like . . .'

'They look almost human, don't they?' said Gideon. 'Manticores are a sort of simian, I think – like a giant baboon, but their faces are more like those of apes. But tan instead of black-skinned, like gorillas or chimpanzees.' He laughed.

'They're horrible,' Lucinda said.

'I'm disappointed in you, child,' said Gideon with a frown. 'These are amazing creatures. My goodness, these are more wonderful than the dragons! You have no idea how hard it was to raise so many to adulthood!

We've been struggling with them all year – several of them died when they were small. And just training them to take simple commands – here, I'll show you.' He stepped to the bars and whistled in much the same way Mr. Walkwell had. The manticores turned to watch him. Six had now come out of their artificial den. He whistled again and they slowly drew closer, then lay down on the sand in front of him with obvious reluctance, twelve orange eyes watching his every move. Only the bars stood between Gideon and the weird, manlike faces.

'Oh,' said Lucinda. 'Oh. They have such big teeth . . . !'

'The old stories claimed they had rows and rows, like sharks,' said Gideon, grinning rather impressively himself. 'Now, up, you lot! Up!' He raised his hands in the air: the bright orange eyes and the expressionless, masklike faces watched him. Slowly the manticores began to rise to their feet. 'Do you see? They know who's the master!'

Mr. Walkwell was watching intently, standing very close to the bars: Tyler suddenly saw the monster nearest him had fixed the old Greek with its tangerine-coloured stare. Its tail twitched. Could it reach him through the bars with those jagged-nailed hands? It was so still, so watchful . . .

'Mr. Walkwell!' he cried, sensing something, and at that same instant the manticore leaped forward, silent as air until it slammed heavily against the metal bars. But Mr. Walkwell had already stepped back out of reach.

'Hee-hee!' laughed Uncle Gideon. 'Keeping you awake on your hooves, eh, Simos?'

Mr. Walkwell only shook his head.

Gideon said, 'Well, obviously this is all too distracting for the manties. They'll never behave properly with all these new smells and people. We'd best get on now.'

'What . . . what are you going to do with them?' Lucinda asked as they climbed back into the wagon. Back out in the sun, Tyler found himself sweating.

'We let them out at night, of course. They roam between the two fences here on the property. If one of Ed Stillman's spies gets over the outer fence, or even tries to parachute in . . . !' He let out a breathless laugh. 'He'll be begging us to save him when the manticores come after him, I'll tell you that much.'

*Or not begging for anything, because he'll be dead,* thought Tyler. *How are you going to deal with that, Uncle Gideon?* But of course he didn't say anything.

'The new, improved Ordinary Farm!' crowed Gideon. 'There you have it!'

Tyler looked at Lucinda. He could see on her face that she was even less comforted by these so-called improvements than he was.

# CHAPTER 7

## COMMUNICATION PROBLEMS

Some things about Ordinary Farm hadn't changed at all. One of them was the hard, hard work.

As the long summer days passed, Lucinda and her brother quickly fell back into the farm's routine – they had no choice, because at Ordinary Farm everyone had to do his or her share, most definitely including the two young visitors. Feeding the animals meant following daily schedules that could not be broken – '*A sea-goat doesn't care if you didn't get your own breakfast,*' as Gideon liked to say, '*he just wants his.*' The bleating capricorns could be snappy when they were hungry too, and they fought over each fish, so that some days they had to be taken out of their pool and fed individually. The dragons needed twice-weekly deer carcasses and the unicorns had to have their daily fodder and supplements. And the bonnacon's cage had to be cleaned out every day, which – since the buffalo-like creature's dung burst into flame once it was out in the air, then lay smouldering for hours – was absolutely no one's favourite job.

Lucinda and Tyler spent much of their day tending to the smaller creatures in the reptile barn and elsewhere, taking some of the load off Mr. Walkwell, Ragnar, and the others who also had to care for the big animals. But even the small animals could be a lot of work. The jingwei, white Chinese birds with long tails, had got loose from their cage in the reptile barn some weeks before, and each day they did their best to fill the biggest water trough, Meseret's, with small stones, swooping down in turn to drop pebbles with a *plink, plink, plink* that went on all day as if someone was using a tiny hammer. Each afternoon Lucinda or her brother climbed into the trough and removed them all, but the jingwei could fly in and out through the empty spaces in the vast barn and so they always found more.

'The Chinese believed this bird was a drowned princess trying to fill the ocean so no other would ever lose her life there,' Gideon informed them, frowning at a rising island of stones near one end of the trough. 'Mythological or not, I wish we could get them out of the reptile barn. They're a dang nuisance!' But the beautiful, fast-moving jingweis refused to be caught, so every day one of the children went swimming in Meseret's greasy trough and shovelled out the stones so she wouldn't swallow too many of them and get her insides plugged up. Dragons didn't even notice things that small going down.

Even after feeding time was over many other chores awaited: Lucinda and her brother spent three long, hot afternoons on the farm whitewashing a new barn for the unicorns. Five hornless, staggering foals had been born that spring, and Gideon wanted the young ones and their nursing mothers to have a place they would be safe from summer storms.

And of course Gideon's greater concern for security added to the workload as well: the electric gates and fences that kept strangers out and animals in had to be checked regularly to make sure they were secure – even a branch across the fence could shut down a large part of the system.

Lucinda was thrilled to be back on Ordinary Farm, but the chores were hard and she was equally happy when Sunday rolled around, her first free day since they'd arrived. Spared for once from early egg duty, it was hard even to drag herself out of bed. Only the threat, relayed by Tyler, that all the breakfast things were going to be cleared and washed in ten minutes finally drew her downstairs, where Azinza gave her some eggs, a fruit muffin, and a glass of milk. She had forgotten the notebook she meant to use for dragon-communication observations, so after returning the plate to the kitchen she plodded back upstairs to get it.

A few minutes later, as she made her way down one of the back staircases, notebook in hand, she heard voices coming from the room full of pictures of Gideon's wife – the 'Grace Shrine', as she thought of it. The first voice was clearly Gideon's, then, quieter but just as distinct, the cool tones of Patience Needle. Lucinda paused, her heart suddenly beating fast. What were the two of them doing in the seldom-used parlour? And what if they thought she was spying on them? For a moment Lucinda considered turning around and heading back the way she'd come.

*But that's not fair!* she thought. *I haven't done anything wrong. Beside, they're probably talking about bills or something, anyway.*

She slowed as she reached the parlour door – she was feeling a bit curious now about what the two might be discussing so far from the rest of the household.

'. . . But I do *not* approve, Gideon.' That was Mrs. Needle, and she sounded angrier than usual, her voice with a hard, piercing ring like metal. 'With all due respect, you are not a young man.'

'I assure you, Patience, I'm far more aware of that than you are,' Uncle Gideon told her. 'These days, even my aches have aches. You're right – I probably don't have very long left to me. That is precisely why I'm going to do this now.'

Something in his tone and what he said frightened Lucinda badly. Was Great-uncle Gideon sick? Dying? He upset her sometimes, made her frustrated and even angry, but she couldn't imagine the place without him.

Apparently Mrs. Needle felt the same way. 'You're in no danger, Gideon. In fact, you're quite healthy for a man your age. But what would become of this place if . . . if something *did* happen to you now? An accident, perhaps? Before the children are really ready? Are you certain you want to see the lawyer and change everything without thinking about it a bit longer . . . ?'

Gideon sounded amused but not cheerful. 'I *have* been thinking, Patience. That's why I don't want to wait any longer. The children would have all the help they needed – Simos to look after the animals and the land, and you to keep an eye on the business end of things. And of course you and Colin will always have a place here, no matter what. So I can rely on your help if such a day ever comes, can't I, Patience?' Lucinda thought she heard a little edge in his voice, as though he was giving her a test of some kind. What were they talking about? She couldn't make sense of it. Were she and Tyler the children they were talking about? And why a lawyer . . . ?

'Of *course*.' Mrs. Needle said it very quickly. 'Of course you . . . they . . . would have my help, Gideon. I would hope by now that goes without saying.'

'Goes without saying, of course.' Gideon sounded pleased. He cleared his throat. 'But before we discuss the details, I need a glass of water. I'm dry as a bone . . .'

'I'll get it for you,' said Mrs. Needle, her chair

scraping on the floor. Lucinda heard the housekeeper's footsteps and realized she had only seconds. She looked around, but there was nowhere to hide nearby. With no other alternative, she simply turned and bolted back down the hall in the direction she had come.

Lucinda didn't stop until she reached the entry hall, where she threw herself down on one of the old velvet stools that stood against the walls and tried to get her breath back and listen for pursuit, but for half a minute she heard nothing but her own pounding heart. Finally she could think clearly again.

*He must have been talking about this house*, Lucinda realized. *This farm. About what happens if he dies. The children – that must be us!* She paused as the thought finally showed itself – a huge thought, a huge surprise.

*Giving us this farm someday. That had to be what Uncle Gideon was talking about.* That much seemed unmistakable. But like everything else important that happened here, they had only learned about it by accident or spying, by listening to whispers in back rooms.

But what did that mean? Had he really forgiven them for all the times they'd screwed up . . . ? *Then someday the dragons – Desta, Meseret – and all the other animals will belong to us*, Lucinda thought in sudden excitement. *To us!*

She couldn't wait to tell Tyler.

60

Lucinda had two complicated gates to open, pass through, and then lock behind her, and plenty of time to think during the long walk, so some of her first excitement began to wear off before she reached the reptile barn.

What if something happened to Uncle Gabriel and she and Tyler *did* inherit Ordinary Farm one day? Suddenly that seemed such a huge thing that she felt overwhelmed. It wouldn't just be having a giant farm to run, although that would be challenge enough for anyone, let alone kids their age. And as strange, wonderful, and dangerous as they were, it wasn't even the dozens of different kinds of mythical animals that were suddenly worrying her: Lucinda had helped with them enough to know it could be done (although it took a lot of work and money.) The thing that suddenly frightened her was that whoever inherited the farm from Gideon would also inherit all the farm folk as well, because Gideon Goldring's farm was a refuge for misplaced *people* as well as creatures. Every single one of the farm's inhabitants except for Gideon himself had come from another place, another century – some, like Haneb and Ooola and Mr. Walkwell, from nearly forgotten ages of the distant past. Gideon had plucked them all from their original eras at the moment of what had seemed like their certain death, hoping that way he would cause minimum upset in the flow of time. The farm's inhabitants might sometimes resent Gideon and his high-handed ways, but he had saved the life of every one of them, and now they were all stuck in the modern world with no way to go back home and no way to prove they belonged here.

The responsibility was terrifying and Lucinda decided she didn't want to think that much right now. Time enough later once she'd found Tyler and told him about it. She hurried the last yards to the reptile barn, anxious for the distraction.

She didn't linger, but trotted to the back of the cavernous barn where the dragons were housed. They were by no means the place's only exotic residents, but Lucinda wasn't much interested in flying snakes and poison-breathing basilisks.

Meseret was lying on her side in her huge pen like an airliner docked for service, one fiery eye half open and following Lucinda as she approached. The baby dragon was harnessed in her own pen a short distance away. As Lucinda approached, little Haneb waved in his usual bashful way, scarcely looking up from the cheerful chore of shovelling dragon poop. Full-grown dragons like Meseret didn't eat very often, but when they did, they pooped out piles the size of a sports car. Haneb wore a bandana over his face as he shovelled the ill-smelling black and green mess into a wheelbarrow. Gideon had told her that after it had been properly treated dragon poop made safe and excellent fertilizer – they even used it on the farm's vegetable patch.

That had been more about the subject than Lucinda had wanted to know, and it had also put her off greens for days.

*At Ordinary Farm, even the salad has secrets . . . !*

She pushed away her worries about the conversation she had overheard between Mrs. Needle and her great-uncle. *Hello, Meseret,* she thought. *Can you hear me? Do you remember me?*

The golden eye stared, blinked slowly, stared.

Lucinda tried to remember how it felt the first time she had made the dragon understand her – the first time she and the huge creature had shared thoughts. *I rode on you, do you remember that?* 'Rode' was a bit of an exaggeration, of course – 'held on for dear life' would have been closer to the truth. *I helped you get your egg back – do you remember?* Lucinda let her gaze slip over to Desta, curled on sand and hay. *I helped bring back your daughter.*

Meseret's immense yellow eye blinked again, then closed and stayed that way. The dragon wasn't going to talk to her, that was clear, but whether she just didn't want to do it or Lucinda had lost the knack, there was no way to tell. Lucinda shrugged and moved over to Desta's much smaller pen.

'Not too close to them, Miss,' called Haneb as he trundled his wheelbarrow past. 'Remember what happened to Master Colin.'

*Of course I remember,* she thought. *It was my fault.* 'I'll be careful. Neither of them would hurt me, Haneb.'

That was called 'wishful thinking' and she and Haneb both knew it; still, the small man nodded shyly at her and went on his way. 'Just . . . careful, please, Miss.'

She turned to the baby dragon, who was watching her with the same seeming disinterest as her mother had shown. 'Hello, Desta,' she said, both out loud and in her thoughts. She remembered the day the baby dragon had been born, how excited they had all been when she pecked her way out of her leathery egg, and tried to make those memories into pictures so Desta could 'see' them too, but the dragon showed no signs of noticing.

Lucinda continued her efforts for most of an hour, talking with both her thoughts and her voice, trying everything she could think of and making notes about each failed approach, but it was like calling over and over in the centre of an empty room: nothing came back to her but echoes. The dragons seemed happy to ignore her. At last she gave up and stood by the rail of Desta's pen, fighting back tears. She had looked forward to this so much all year, had got through so many boring classes with the knowledge that this was ahead of her – that once again she would have the chance to be special, to be Lucinda, the Girl Who Talks to Dragons! Had it all just been an accident, a fluke?

'Don't feel bad, Miss,' Haneb said. 'They are not

friendly. They are dragons. But the little one . . .' He hesitated. 'With the little one – there is a secret . . .'

Lucinda sniffed and quickly wiped her eyes. She was ashamed to have Haneb see her feeling so sorry for herself. 'A secret . . . ?'

'So she like you better. To . . . touch her. To be her friend.'

Lucinda's heart jumped. Ragnar had once told her that Haneb had come to Ordinary Farm with Meseret and Alamu when the dragons were younger than Desta was now, that they all came together from the ancient Middle East. Was he finally going to share the secret of communicating with them? Magic words? Some special hand movements? 'Yes? Haneb, tell me! Please!'

The animal handler looked at Desta, then turned toward Lucinda in that odd way he had, looking at her only from the corner of his eye. 'She . . . she likes carrots.'

# CHAPTER 8

## OLD FURNITURE

Really weird things were going on with the farm this year – Tyler could feel it. Probably the strangest was that Lucinda had overheard Gideon talking to Mrs. Needle about what might happen if he died – she was certain their great-uncle had been saying that that he wanted to arrange things so that Tyler and his sister would inherit the farm! And Mrs. Needle had actually gone along with that, or at least appeared to, but Tyler didn't for a second think that if something really happened to Gideon things would go so easily: the witch was not just going to give up on grabbing the farm for her son Colin.

But if she couldn't change Gideon Goldring's mind, what else could Patience Needle do? She didn't even legally exist in this century – it wasn't as though she could take Gideon to court and sue him.

Tyler had also been thinking about what Colin was really up to in the library. Tyler had told Gideon he'd found Grace's locket there, of course, but on a farm with so few people to do so much work, would Gideon really send a healthy young man to sit in the library for months just in case another locket appeared out of thin air? And why had they been talking about books? What did books have to do with Gideon's missing wife?

The locket *hadn't* just appeared out of nowhere in the first place, of course, but Tyler couldn't admit that without giving up the secret of the washstand mirror, the gateway he had discovered that led to another, strange version of Ordinary Farm, a place where Tyler was certain Gideon's wife Grace was still trapped.

Tyler scowled. Just a couple of small lies had made things really complicated. It didn't seem fair.

Tyler took a bite from his peanut-butter sandwich and spread what he called the Octavio Files across the bed – all the fragments of the great inventor's notes and journals he'd been able to collect last summer and had just fetched from their hiding place, a pile of ripped, water-stained and mouse-chewed fragments small enough to fit into a single old cigar box. It was the first time this visit he'd had a chance to look them over and he wondered if they would make more sense now. He'd tried to pay closer attention at school the last year, especially in science and maths, but the kind of things Octavio Tinker wrote about in his journals – *crystallometry* and *dipolar coupling* – just hadn't seem to come up much in Mr. Ortolani's sixth-grade Earth Sciences class.

In his early notes Octavio kept going on and on about the need to create a device that would enable someone to steer their way through the Fault Line. Later on, Tyler knew, Octavio had actually invented such a thing (with some help from Gideon Goldring, apparently) and named it the Continuascope. Tyler himself, however, had gone through the Fault Line safely and come out again without any such gadget. Had that been a one-time accident, or was Tyler himself some kind of mutant freak, like out of a comic book? He had wondered about that since last summer, and now something in one of Octavio's long, boring, and hard-to-make-out scribbles jumped out at him like a jack-in-the-box:

> *I am beginning to believe that some people, like myself, might have a natural sensitivity for the Fault Line – an inbred ability to discern between its close-packed strata and perhaps even MOVE from one to another . . .*

*Strata.* Tyler went and found Lucinda's school dictionary to look it up; it meant 'layers'. It was only one sentence, but it felt like dynamite in his brain. Octavio was saying that some people could steer their way through the Fault Line even without a machine like the Continuascope! That made Tyler's hair stand on end. Octavio Tinker was saying some people might have a built-in sensitivity to the Fault Line – people like Octavio himself.

*And maybe like Tyler Jenkins too . . . !*

Octavio had bought this land a long time ago, and had built his endless, crazy house in part to distract people from the Fault Line that he had found here. Maybe Octavio had even found this place because he had that 'natural sensitivity'. And Tyler was Octavio's descendant – a blood relative through his mom's side of the family.

Octavio Tinker had discovered the crazy time-hole, the Fault Line, and built his farm around it. Tyler had proved he could travel through the Fault Line by himself. And now Uncle Gideon was thinking of making Tyler and his sister the ones who would inherit the farm. It was all fitting together as if it was meant to be!

Tyler couldn't bear to sit in his room by himself any longer. He pulled on his shoes and hurried down the stairs, totally psyched to find Lucinda so he could tell her the latest news.

He looked around all the obvious places in the house but he couldn't find his sister. He guessed that she was off annoying the dragons on the other side of the farm, but he went out to have a quick look in the

69

gardens behind the house just in case – she sometimes liked to wander around there.

Ooola, the girl he had brought back from the ice age, was out in the middle of the vegetable patch, down on her knees as though she was pulling weeds.

'Hey, Ooola,' he called, 'have you seen my sister? I'm trying to find her.'

She thought about it very carefully, then shook her head. 'I do not see her.' She smiled. 'Will you come to help me, Tyler? I am picking up slocks!'

'Slocks?' He wandered nearer to peer over the fence. Ooola was kneeling by a patch of sunflowers, each bloom bright as a tiny sun. As if to make an argument against such colourful good cheer, the old abandoned greenhouse stood by its lonely self at the distant end of the garden rows, like a tomb with picture windows.

'See?' The cavegirl held out an aluminium pie pan filled with gross, shiny little blobs. 'Many slocks I find!'

'Oh. You mean "slugs".'

'Slogs, yes. They walk here from all over, these slogs!' she said. 'Many and many following! Like the deers that run all together in my home.'

'Herds of slugs – I get you.' Tyler wasn't quite certain what she was so excited about – there were lots of slugs in the garden, so what? Wasn't that where slugs liked to hang out? Tyler liked Ooola, but she also made him a little nervous: he thought she might have sort of a crush on him because he'd rescued her from a bear. He also didn't want to spend his day in the hot

70

summer sun picking up gooey slugs. 'Sorry, Ooola, but I can't help right now. I have to find Lucinda.'

She looked disappointed, but smiled again. 'Is okay, but tell Gid-ee-on – lots of many slogs!'

When he looked back, she was waving at him. 'Wait, Tyler! Something is remembering!'

'I know, many lots of slugs!'

'No!' She shook her head vigorously. 'Remembering to *me*! When I am lying down looking at slogs, I hear someone walking. Maybe your sister. Going that way.' She pointed to where the path curved away from the vegetable garden, past the old greenhouse toward the outer gardens and the library. Tyler had a strange moment of jealousy. Lucinda hadn't gone to hang out with Colin Needle, had she? He thanked Ooola and trotted off in the direction she had indicated.

Tyler had a bigger surprise as he reached the ancient, mostly overgrown rose garden and the path that led through it to the library: something dropped out of the upper branches of a tall tree, flapping and brushing against his hair so that he jumped in surprise and covered his head with his hands.

'Zaza!' he shouted in delight when he realized who was swooping around him in wide circles. 'Zaza, come here, you crazy monkey! I missed you!'

They had a long conversation. Tyler was the only one talking but Zaza contributed enthusiastically, mostly with ear-pinches and nose-nips. The little grey-winged monkey was clearly happy to see him. He wondered why she had stayed away from him so long. Maybe she didn't know where his room was this year.

As he reached the library Zaza jumped up into the air and flapped her way up to the roof where she settled and folded her finger-wings around her like a cloak, telling him as clearly as if she'd spoken it that she was going to wait outside while he finished whatever errand was taking him into the spooky old building.

Tyler walked through the open front door without knocking – he had as much right to be there as his sister, didn't he? – but slowed within a few steps because he heard voices, and neither of them was Lucinda's.

*'Because, Colin, if you wait for Gideon to understand what's best for the farm, you're going to wait forever.'* That was Mrs. Needle, her voice angry but also as cold and controlled as what came out of a soft-serve ice-cream machine. *'And we will have lost our home. Because Gideon Goldring is a fool.'*

*'That's not fair, Mother,'* Tyler heard Colin say. He wasn't arguing with her exactly, but he wasn't agreeing with her either, which was a point in his favour, Tyler thought. A very small point, but a point. *'Gideon promised there would always be a place for us here . . .'*

*'Yes! As servants! Is that what you want, Colin? To be a servant to the Jenkins children in your own home?'*

Tyler had been backing toward the open door, but now a breeze pushed it closed behind him with a sudden and surprising bang.

'*Who's there?*' An instant later Patience Needle had appeared from around the corner. 'What are you doing here, Master Jenkins?' She had wiped the emotion from her voice, but her eyes looked like furious black pinpoints. 'Were you eavesdropping?'

'N-no!' Tyler stammered. She was a small, slender woman – smaller than Tyler now that he had grown a bit – but she still frightened him very badly. 'No! I just came to . . . to look for my sister . . .' He swallowed. Better to act as though he hadn't heard anything. 'Is Lucinda here?'

'Perhaps she is doing something useful,' Mrs. Needle said, her emotions now completely disguised again. 'As Colin has been doing – which is why I brought him his lunch.' She smiled. It looked like the last thing a small furry creature might see before it got swallowed. 'I didn't know you were coming, Tyler, otherwise I would have brought you something as well.' She turned and called over her shoulder, 'Don't work too hard, Colin, dear!' She swung back to Tyler. 'I wish he'd get out more,' she said with almost convincing sweetness. 'Perhaps the two of you could have a game of catch.' She showed her tight smile once more, then stepped past him and out the library door, leaving behind a hint of chill and the scent of something flowery.

A game of catch? With Colin Needle? That was such a bizarre thought Tyler wondered if the witch was trying to psych him out somehow. *Yeah, or maybe we could shoot some marbles together . . . !*

Inside the library Colin looked up from the encyclopedia table, which was cluttered with books and notebooks and his laptop computer. In fact, it looked as if the older boy was staking a claim here – like he thought it was his library now. It was all Tyler could do not to sweep all his stuff off onto the floor.

'Research, huh?' he said. 'Yeah? Research on what?'

'None of your business.' Colin's eyebrow rose. 'And what are *you* doing here, Jenkins? I wouldn't have thought you were much of a reader.'

'Oh, you wouldn't?' It was true, but he was never going to admit it now. He didn't even want to tell Colin Needle he'd come looking for Lucinda – that just made it seem even more like the skinny jerk belonged here and he didn't. Tyler strolled past the table, trying to sneak a look at the books spread out there, but Colin leaned over, covering them with his arms.

'Do you mind?' the dark-haired boy said in his best adult manner. 'I'm working, Jenkins. Can't you go play somewhere else?'

'Actually, I've got things to do here, *Needle*. But I'll try not to disturb you.'

Tyler wandered around in the stacks for a while but he couldn't concentrate. Colin and his mother must have been talking about the same thing Lucinda had overheard. Mrs. Needle had said, '*Is that what you want, Colin? To be a servant to the Jenkins children in your own home?*' Tyler had to admit the idea amused him – Colin dressed up like a butler, scuttling around at Tyler's every order – but did she really think that's how it would be?

For a moment, and only for a moment, he even felt sorry for Colin Needle. What must it be like, to have a mother who thought that way, acted that way . . . ?

*Yeah, but his mother doesn't follow him around all the time forcing him to be a creep,* Tyler decided. *He does most of that all by himself.*

Tyler sauntered over to the huge painting of Octavio Tinker. The mad scientist's expression was as maddeningly amused and secretive as ever. As always, the founder of Ordinary Farm seemed to be staring at the retiring-room door across from his portrait. Tyler hadn't been near the magical washstand mirror since this summer's visit had begun and suddenly he wanted very much to see it again. He looked around in case Colin was paying attention, but the pale boy was bent over his books once more. Tyler casually walked across to the retiring room and stepped in, wondering if he would again see a world different from his own reflected in the washstand mirror, but instead he saw . . . nothing.

The mirror was gone.

In fact, the entire piece of furniture was gone: all that remained in the retiring room was the dusty bed and an angular shadow on the wallpaper that showed where the washstand and its magic mirror had stood.

Tyler felt as if he had been punched in the stomach by a heavyweight fighter. It took him a full minute or more to calm down enough to walk back out into the library. 'So what happened to that sink in there?' he asked as casually as he could, but he could hear a quiver in his voice.

Colin barely looked up. 'What sink?'

'In that room. Across from the picture of Octavio. There used to be a sink there.'

Colin made a face – the great man interrupted by small minds. 'My mother took it over to her room. She said it was an antique and it should be taken better care of.'

It was all Tyler could do to bite his lip and stay silent. *Mrs. Needle has the mirror*. The mirror that led the way to Grace. She must know the truth! Or at least she must know there was something special about it – he didn't believe that 'antique' story for a second.

Tyler was so angry and frightened by this news that all he could think of was to get back outside into the open air. The washstand mirror had been taken by the witch, and Colin Needle was squatting in the library like a bandit. It was all bad, impossibly bad.

'Tired of books already?' Colin said as Tyler went by. 'Off to play?'

'Shut up.' He shouldered the door open.

'That's just like you, Jenkins,' the older boy said. 'You don't try to understand this place at all, you just mess about with things. You don't understand the true genius of someone like Octavio Tinker. You wouldn't know a Continuascope if you saw one. But *I* would –

76

I've been learning all about them. In fact, I might just make one . . .'

With that horrifying threat echoing in his ears, Tyler let the door fall shut.

Zaza came down to accompany him, sporting and fluttering, clearly pleased to be with him again no matter how downhearted Tyler himself might feel, how listlessly he might trudge back toward the farmhouse. But when they got to a certain point she leaped up, spread her wings, and disappeared without a backward glance. When he turned from watching her fly the first thing he saw was the distant glitter of the old greenhouse, flashing its underwater colours in the afternoon sun.

# CHAPTER 9

## KINGAREE

Lucinda was beginning to appreciate travelling by horse-cart – the only wheeled vehicle Mr. Walkwell would ever use. Rattling along through the open air made her feel so vital, so connected – as if nature itself was flowing through her. Mr. Walkwell, horns and goat-legs hidden for the trip into town, held the reins loose but taut, almost talking to the horse Culpepper through the leather straps.

When he saw her watching the old man gifted her with a quick, careful smile, something she hadn't seen much. The sunlight was golden, the day not too hot, and the air filled with the smells of eucalyptus and warm yellow dust. Things even seemed to be going well at the farm this year – why wasn't Mr. Walkwell happier?

'Is everything all right, Lucinda?' asked Colin Needle. 'You seem very quiet.'

That sounded like sincere interest, which surprised her a little. 'I'm fine. Just enjoying the ride. Do you think it's going to rain?'

Colin looked up at the bruise-grey sky. 'Maybe. Gideon says there hasn't been weather like this since 1983 – they had floods then! But it won't rain anywhere near that hard this summer, I don't think.'

1983 was well before Lucinda had been born. She was impressed. 'Have there really been a lot of storms here this year?'

Colin smiled. 'Oh, yes – thunder, lightning. The week before you came it was almost like being in a war – *boom, crack, boom!* Sarah said the world might be ending!' He laughed and Lucinda found herself laughing with him. They both fell silent again, but this time it was a comfortable silence.

When they reached downtown Standard Valley (such as it was) Mr. Walkwell tied Culpepper and the cart to a hitching post outside the store. Colin stood up. 'I have to go over to Rosie's for something. Shall I meet you somewhere?'

The old man looked up, squinted, and said, 'You can do what you wish, Master Needle. Just be back here in an hour.'

'Where are you going?' Lucinda asked, then immediately regretted it. Surely secretive Colin Needle wouldn't take kindly to being quizzed about his plans. But to her surprise Colin only grinned.

'I'm going to Rosie's to use their wireless connection.'

Lucinda couldn't help laughing at the idea of the ancient diner with its glowering owner as a fancy internet cafe. 'Wi-Fi? You're kidding, right?'

'No. Rosie lets me use it when I'm in town and I help him with his accounting software.' Now Colin laughed too. It sounded quite ordinary and pleasant. 'Yes, even Standard Valley is finally stumbling into the twenty-first century.' He climbed down, threw Lucinda a little goodbye salute, then walked off toward Rosie's, cradling his laptop as carefully as a bundle of dreams.

Lucinda picked up a large bag of carrots at the grocery store, then decided it wasn't big enough – they were for a dragon, after all! – and dug down to find a larger one. When she had paid for it she headed back to the feed store, where Mr. Walkwell was talking sourly to the clerk about the horrors of machinery. Bored, Lucinda stared out of the window at the main street and wondered when they were going to see the Carrillos again, the kids from the farm next door. She and Tyler had first met them here in Standard Valley last year, on another of Mr. Walkwell's shopping trips, and they had all become friends. She thought it was a little strange they'd been back on the farm so long and still hadn't heard anything from Carmen and the rest. She and Tyler would have to find a way to contact them.

Mr. Walkwell was still denouncing the dangers

of steam power to the confused counter clerk when Lucinda finally gave up and wandered outside into the hot grey afternoon. The air smelled like rain but none was falling yet. She briefly considered going over to join Colin at the diner but felt reluctant to do that – what if he thought she had a crush on him? Which, though he occasionally acted almost human, she most definitely did *not.*

She wandered away from the centre of town instead. It didn't make for a very long walk – past the few stores and the train station until the only buildings around her were board houses with small fenced front yards.

As Lucinda turned at the furthest houses and started back, someone stepped out of the shadows at the front of the train station, a tall man who angled toward her with long strides. By the time she had reached the centre of the block the stranger was walking beside her.

'You – child,' he said. 'Stop and talk to me for a moment.'

Every instinct told Lucinda to run; only the fact that they were standing in the middle of the town's main street in the middle of the afternoon with people watching them from outside the diner gave her courage to stand her ground. The towering stranger had to be nearly six and a half feet tall, she thought, with the easy physical grace of a young man, but his face was tanned and hard as old leather. His hair was black, as were most of his clothes and his wide-brimmed hat.

He looked more like a gunslinger out of a western movie than a farmer . . . a man out of time . . .

A sudden understanding felt like icy fingers on her neck: this man *did* look like someone from another time, like someone who had stepped out of the Fault Line. Suddenly she was terrified.

'I saw you and Simos Walkwell roll into town,' the stranger said in a slow, confident drawl. 'Are you staying out at the Tinker farm? Gideon Goldring's an old friend of mine.'

Lucinda just stood, mouth working helplessly.

'You don't have to be afraid of me, child.' He showed her a flash of teeth. 'I'm not your enemy.'

It was hard to swallow down the lump in her throat enough to make words. Something about this man made him seem as though the day itself had created him out of dust and summer heat. 'I'm s-sorry, but I'm not supposed to talk to people I don't know . . .'

'Of course you're not,' he said. 'Smart girl. But I'm no stranger – just ask Gideon and the rest. Tell them you saw Jackson Kingaree. Tell 'em I said I'll be coming by real soon to catch up on old times. Can you remember that?'

Lucinda nodded.

The tall man bent over. Lucinda could smell liquor on his breath. His smile seemed like a trick he'd learned without understanding it, a dog taught to shake hands. 'I'm glad to hear it, child. We'll talk again one day, you and I – that's a promise.' He straightened and walked past her, his coat brushing her hand as softly as a bird's feathered wing. His boots clicked on the sidewalk as he walked around the corner of the train station and disappeared. A drift of raindrops, light as flower petals, sprinkled her face and hands and made dark spots on the street.

Lucinda let out the breath she had been holding so long she had become dizzy, and then she ran.

'Never go near that man! *Never!*' Mr. Walkwell was so upset he nearly knocked over his cup of coffee. Inside Rosie's, heads turned at every table.

'He came up to me in the street.'

'Next time you see him, do not talk – run away. He is evil.' The old man shook his head and growled, a startlingly inhuman sound.

For just the briefest moment Lucinda remembered Mr. Walkwell dancing on his naked hooves along a hillside beneath the night sky, a wild creature come from elder days. *We're surrounded by legends and fairy tales!* she marvelled yet again. *And monsters too.* 'But who is he, this . . . Kingaree?'

'He came out of the Fault Line, of course,' said Colin Needle quietly, eyes still on his laptop screen. 'Like we all did, in one way or another.'

'What?' Lucinda was distracted by this. 'But you said you were born here, Colin.'

'I was. My mother was pregnant when Gideon brought her here.'

Lucinda wondered, not for the first time, who Colin's father had been; neither of the Needles ever talked about it. 'But if that man came out of the –' Colin looked up at her sharply, so Lucinda mouthed the words – '. . . *Fault Line* too, why doesn't he live at the farm?'

'He did – for a while,' said Colin. 'But he didn't like the rules.'

Mr. Walkwell looked around to make sure no one in Rosie's was listening to their quiet conversation. 'No more talk about him until I have spoken to Gideon.'

'Kingaree came with old Caesar,' Colin whispered to Lucinda as they followed Mr. Walkwell out of the diner. 'That's all I know.'

'With Caesar?' She couldn't put ancient, sweet-tempered Caesar together with Kingaree – with that face full of sharp edges and violence. As they approached the wagon she looked nervously up and down the street, seeing Kingaree's menacing form in every shadow. As a result, she stared right at Steve Carrillo standing in front of the general store with his popsicle for several seconds before she recognized the husky boy.

'Steve!' she shouted. 'Oh, wow, Steve! It's me, Lucinda! We're back!'

He waved and then called to someone inside the store. A moment later Carmen Carrillo, his older sister, came hurrying out onto the sidewalk. She saw Lucinda and ran toward her, Steve following, and they met in the centre of the street to exchange hugs and excited greetings. Colin watched them embrace for a moment, then walked on toward the wagon without saying anything.

Carmen was taller and had lost weight – she looked quite glamorous, Lucinda thought, but Steve seemed like he might have put on a few pounds. 'I missed you guys so much!' Lucinda said. 'I was wondering when we'd get to see you! Tyler's back at the farm. He'll wish he came along, now.'

'Yeah, Alma's back at our place,' Steve said of the third and youngest Carrillo child. 'She's sewing stuff this year and she hardly ever comes out of her room.'

'She gave up wood carving?' Lucinda asked. 'That's too bad!'

Steve laughed. 'Naw. She still carves too. And does clay sculptures. Her room is more cluttered up than mine!'

'Not possible,' said Carmen. 'Wow, great to see you, Luce. I shared your emails with Steve and Alma.' She smiled. 'Well, not *everything* . . .'

'Thank you! How are you guys?'

An odd look crossed Carmen's face, sliding like a shadow. 'Okay, I guess. Kind of. We're having a lot of weird trouble with that guy from last year.' She looked around but the small street was all but empty. 'The one who landed on your farm in his helicopter.'

'Edward Stillman?' Lucinda suddenly felt a chill. This new guy Kingaree, the crazy rich guy – what did the universe have against Ordinary Farm? 'What kind of trouble?'

'He keeps offering our folks money,' said Steve.

'He's buying up land all around your property,' Carmen explained. 'So of course he wants our farm, because we're right next door.'

'He's offering tons of money too,' Steve said. 'We heard our mom and dad talking about it. They don't want to sell . . . but it's a lot of money. My dad keeps trying to talk to your uncle Gideon about it, but your uncle won't ever call him back or anything. Dad even went over to see him but Gideon wouldn't even come out to that big old crazy gate he built. Have you seen that? Oh, right, you must have.'

Lucinda smiled, but her joy at seeing two of her friends had soured. Stillman back, and now this Kingaree hanging around. What next?

'Hello, you bad children,' Mr. Walkwell greeted the Carrillos, but without his usual sly good cheer. 'Lucinda, we must go back. We have things to discuss with Gideon.'

'Tell him my father really needs to talk to him, Mr. Walkwell,' Carmen said. 'Please. It's important.'

The wiry old man looked overwhelmed in a way Lucinda had never seen before. 'I will tell him, of course. But Gideon Goldring does what he wants, always. Come, Lucinda.'

'Bye, guys!' she shouted when she'd climbed aboard the wagon, next to silent Colin. 'See you soon, I hope!'

'Come for the Fourth again!' yelled Carmen. 'That was totally fun last year!'

To Lucinda's surprise, Ragnar was waiting for them out by the new gate. The big Norseman did not smile as they came in, only held the gate open and waved the cart through, then closed it by hand afterward and secured it with a bolt.

'What's wrong with the gate?' Colin asked. 'It should open and close by itself.'

'The invisible lightning is gone,' Ragnar said. 'Your mother turned it away, or off, whatever you say. Until we know what is happening.' He was clearly agitated. 'Did Gideon go with you? Did he stay in town?'

Mr. Walkwell seemed as surprised by this as Lucinda. 'No. Gideon was here when we left. He did not go with us.'

Lucinda was beginning to feel really frightened. She looked at Colin but he seemed as confused as she was. 'What's going on?'

'We cannot find him,' Ragnar said. 'We have been looking everywhere since just after you left this morning. Everyone on the farm has been searching and we have looked in every place we can think, all through the house, the barns, the hills, the pens.' He shook his head. 'But Gideon has disappeared. He is gone.'

# CHAPTER 10

## LEAVING THE GARDEN

'. . . And he was so scary, Tyler!' Lucinda whispered. 'Like . . . like the *devil* or something!' His sister couldn't stop talking about Kingaree, the mysterious Fault Line escapee, but although Tyler was impressed and even worried by her experience, it seemed like the least of their problems just now.

The farm folk were assembled in what Tyler and Lucinda called the Snake Parlour – the big front room with the stained-glass window of Adam and Eve being tricked in the Garden of Eden, the serpent running all around the picture as if to draw a noose around them with its body. Tyler couldn't help wondering whether gathering beneath a glowing picture of Satan was really the best choice at such a time.

The rain that had pattered on his window and the roof a short time ago was gone and already the day was growing unbearably hot again. Everyone was talking at once and everyone sounded frightened – and no surprise: Gideon was not just their protector but the only thing that connected most of these people to the present century. Tyler couldn't even imagine what Sarah and the Mongolian Amigos and all the others must be feeling.

Mrs. Needle stood in the middle of the room, frowning, her face hard as carved ivory. 'You must all be quiet and listen now,' she announced. 'Do you hear me? Silence!'

'Why? You are not Gideon!' cried Hoka, one of the Amigos. 'You are not the master of the house!' His two silent companions looked impressed that he would talk back to Mrs. Needle, but they also looked as if they wished he hadn't done it.

Colin Needle had a strange look on his face too, Tyler thought – a bit green around the gills, as Tyler and Lucinda's mom liked to say. *Guilty conscience about something?* Tyler wondered.

'Hush, all of you!' Mrs. Needle's voice was sharper this time. 'Don't be foolish. Nobody is claiming to be the master here. But someone must take charge . . .'

'Then it should be Simos,' said Ragnar loudly from the doorway. 'Walkwell has been here longer than any of us. He has always been Gideon's right hand.'

Mrs. Needle rolled her eyes in disgust. 'This is not about who is in charge, it is about finding Gideon.'

'Have you searched the whole house?' Tyler

demanded. 'It's miles long! Why are we wasting time blabbing? Gideon could have fallen down somewhere where we can't hear him calling . . . !'

A lot of the others murmured in agreement, but Mrs. Needle was not having it. 'Of course we have searched the house, Master Jenkins, and since it is large and full of unused rooms we will continue to do so. Leave that chore to those who know the place – myself, Sarah and her kitchen help, and Caesar . . .'

One of the 'kitchen help' suddenly rose from her seat. It was the tall African girl Azinza, swaying like a tree in the wind.

'I saw Gideon in a dream!' she cried.

'Oh, for goodness sake!' hissed Patience Needle. 'This is quite out of order. Sit down now, you foolish girl . . . !' She turned away, leaving Azinza open-mouthed. 'Nobody has seen Gideon since supper yesterday. Caesar says his bed was not slept in. We will organize into groups. The women will search all through the house while the men—'

'But I tell you I *saw* him!' cried Azinza. 'I saw what happened to Mr. Gideon!'

Mrs. Needle turned on her with cold fury. 'Enough of this foolishness!'

'You have no right to stop her speaking,' said Ragnar, moving up beside Azinza. For a moment he and Mrs. Needle stared at each other, and the hatred between them made the hairs stir and lift on Tyler's neck. At last Mrs. Needle waved her hand in disgust and turned away. 'Go on,' the big man told Azinza. 'Tell what you saw, girl.'

'This is *not* foolishness,' she said, but she could not quite look Patience Needle in the eye. 'My people used to come to me for my dreams. They called me *goddess*.' She shook her head angrily, her eyes still bright with tears. Tyler felt sorry for her. Gideon might have saved this young woman's life, but he had also pulled her away from everything she knew and believed. 'Last night I had a strong, strong dream,' she began. 'A *telling* dream like the kind I used to have back home. A great creature with many fingers – as many fingers as the apple tree outside has branches – held Mister Gideon. It hurt him and he fought against it, but he was not strong. And then he . . . he . . .' Azinza's face crumpled. 'He began to melt away . . . !'

She tried to say more but could not. Weeping, she let little Pema help her to a chair. Babble and upset filled the room.

Mrs. Needle turned on Ragnar. 'There! Are you happy to fill these frightened people's heads with such nonsense?' Whatever order there had been a moment ago was gone. Everyone in the Snake Parlour was talking at the same time.

Lucinda sidled over to Tyler. 'I'm scared,' she whispered. 'Where could Gideon have gone?'

'I can think of a few places.' He was thinking about the washstand mirror and the shadowy world on the other side of it, but he wasn't going to talk about it out loud: Lucinda was the only other person in the house who knew. Still, could Gideon have got into it somehow? Did it have something to do with Mrs. Needle taking the washstand mirror out of the library?

*What better place to hide someone you don't want found?* Tyler thought. *Just knock them out and shove them through the mirror . . . !*

The more he thought about it, the more reasons he came up with that it might be true. But how could he tell the others when he'd been hiding something so important for over a year . . . ?

His thoughts were interrupted as a sudden quiet fell on the room. Mr. Walkwell stood in the front doorway, his narrow, bearded face grey with dust.

'I have been down to the Fault Line,' the farm's overseer announced. 'The bad news is there is no sign of Gideon there – the lock is still on the outside, but I opened it and went down to look and found no recent marks or footprints. I suppose that is also the good news, because if he had entered the Fault Line there would be nothing we could do to follow him. It has now been locked again. No one else go near.'

'Time to begin the search, then!' said Ragnar before Mrs. Needle could say anything. 'Hoka, Jeg, the rest of you men, come with me.'

'What if we don't find him?' Lucinda asked. The faces of the others showed that they had been wondering this too.

It was Ragnar who answered. 'That is too hard a

question for today, child. While we search, things will go on as they have. Mr. Walkwell will run the farm, Mrs. Needle will . . . will see to things in the house.'

Patience Needle favoured him with a poisonous smile. 'Thank you for giving me permission to do my job, Ragnar Lodbrok.'

'Enough arguing.' Mr. Walkwell broke his silence. 'Back to searching. Search everywhere again. Gideon is old and he might be hurt. Waste no time.' He turned and walked out the door, hooves clicking on the wooden entry-hall floor. Most of the men of the farm followed him – but where, Tyler wondered, was Colin Needle? He spotted him a moment later, talking urgently to Lucinda, which bothered Tyler more than it should have. He didn't want the pale young man being friendly to his sister. It was just . . . creepy. Creepy and wrong.

'Hey, Needle,' he called. 'Needle!'

The older boy shot him a resentful look. 'What do you want, Jenkins? I wasn't talking to you.'

'I think your mother knows something about Gideon disappearing – something she isn't telling us.'

'Tyler,' Lucinda said warningly, 'don't—'

He ignored her. 'Don't lie to us, Needle. You know she had something to do with it, don't you?' Tyler took a step nearer; to his satisfaction, Colin took a step back.

'Just shut up, Jenkins!' said the older boy. 'You don't know *anything*. You're busy ruining everything while people like me are trying to *save* this place.'

'Stop it, both of you!' Lucinda cried, but Tyler was just getting started.

'Oh, *sure*,' he said. 'Save the farm . . . like when you tried to sell Meseret's egg to the person Gideon hates most in the world? When you pretty much gave away the secret of this place? Yeah, you really care . . . !'

Tears actually came into Colin Needle's eyes. He balled his fists and for a moment Tyler thought the older boy might take a swing at him, but instead Colin turned and hurried out of the Snake Parlour toward the front door.

Tyler stared after him. 'What's *his* problem?'

'You're a creep, Tyler Jenkins,' Lucinda said. 'He came to me for *help*! He wanted someone to listen to him! And he might have had something important to say about Gideon, but no, *you* had to be . . . you had to . . .' She turned and stomped out of the room, headed for the kitchen. As the door fell shut behind her, she shouted back, '. . . a big creep!'

'Huh?' Tyler said it out loud, even though he was now the only person left in the room. 'I don't get it. What did I do?'

# CHAPTER 11

## WEREGILD

'Oh, sweet! Careful now . . . !' Lucinda laughed a little nervously as Desta took another carrot from her hand. Lucinda had just discovered to her astonished delight that Desta's long tongue was as blue as a summertime sky. 'Will it stay that colour?' she asked.

Ragnar looked down from the landing above, where he was hosing out the cockatrice cages. 'I do not know. Her mother and father are not that way, but they might have changed – I don't remember what colour tongues they had as young worms.' He laughed. The sound startled the displaced cockatrices, which hissed at him from their temporary wire cages.

'Where is Haneb today?' Lucinda asked. 'I thought he was the one who took care of the dragons.'

Ragnar shrugged as he swept the water toward the drain in the concrete floor. 'Simos has taken him and your brother and others to walk the hills and canyons. There are many trees and deep spots there which could hide . . . someone.'

*A man's body,* he had almost said. Because now that he was three days missing, Ragnar, Lucinda, and everyone else knew Gideon Goldring might very well be dead. A cloud of fear hung over Ordinary Farm.

Lucinda swallowed hard. 'Ragnar? What if Uncle Gideon doesn't come back? What if we never find him? What . . . what happens next?'

*Who will get the farm?* That was what she was really asking. *Who will take charge of this strangest, most wonderful place on earth?*

When the Norseman had all the creatures back in their cage he latched the door, then pulled off the hood of the hazard suit he wore to protect himself from the creatures' poisonous saliva. He clanked down the stairs to join Lucinda as the cockatrices stepped awkwardly around the puddles, hissing at each new outrage to their familiar home – sawdust and sand now clean and new, their droppings washed from every surface.

'What happens if he's really gone?' she asked again.

'Here you make a testament, yes?' Ragnar asked her. 'A . . . will? Writing down how your treasure will be shared after you are dead. But first someone – one of the city chiefs, what are they called . . . ?'

She thought for a moment. 'Police? Government?'

'Government, yes. They will send someone, as

96

Gideon always warned us. And how can we let that happen? How can we explain anything about this place? No, child,' Ragnar said seriously, 'believe me, it will be much better if we find Gideon alive. Much better.'

Ragnar stood now and watched, shaking his head, as Desta wrapped her sky-blue tongue around Lucinda's last carrot and pulled it into her mouth. The dragon crunched contentedly, her long teeth flashing as her jaw opened and closed, then eyed Lucinda to see if there were any more. Haneb had been right – Desta definitely liked carrots.

*No more today.* Lucinda tried to make each thought clear and individual. *That's all. But I'll bring you more carrots soon. Would you like that?*

For a moment the amber eyes bored into her, then the dragon, small but still bigger than Lucinda, turned and walked away in awkward dragon fashion, stilting on its back feet and the elbows of its folded wings. But just before Desta pulled herself up onto her nest of straw and old mattresses, Lucinda caught a whisper of happy, greedy thought, faint as a breeze through branches. It was wordless compared to her own, but still had a meaning she could understand.

*Yes. More. Bring more.*

For a moment Lucinda thought she'd imagined it, then her heart seemed to spread wings inside her chest.

*

As the cart rolled along Lucinda watched the hills shimmering in the mid-afternoon heat. 'Do you think that creepy Kingaree guy has anything to do with Gideon disappearing?' she asked suddenly.

Ragnar shook his big shaggy head. 'I do not believe it, but it could be so. He is a crafty, wicked man.'

'Everyone keeps telling me that – okay, I believe it! But what did he do?'

Ragnar stayed silent for a while as the horse slowed to a stop beside Elliot's Lagoon, as Gideon sometimes called it. The sea serpent who lived in the small lake didn't need regular feeding – the water just had to be restocked with fish twice a year – but Mr. Walkwell and the Norseman made a point to check in on Elliot every couple of days. Just now, though, Ragnar wasn't even looking at the water.

'Things were better before the fire,' the big man said suddenly.

'The fire that burned down Gideon's laboratory?'

He nodded his head. 'Grace had been gone for several years. Gideon used his shiny toy almost every day to go into the Fault Line and search for her, but he would not admit that was what he did.'

'Shiny toy . . . You mean the Continuascope.' The thing Tyler was always going on about.

Ragnar nodded again. 'He called it "collecting". He never found Grace, but instead he brought back animals . . . and people. I was one of the people he collected. It was a madness – but it was a kind of madness I understand.' Ragnar curled the reins into a loop in his massive hand. 'I had a friend once in my old country whose family was killed by raiders from down the coast. From that moment on my friend was a dead man too, but still walking. He swore he would kill two of the raiders for every one of his that had been taken from him. He put aside the blood-gold we call "weregild" so his neighbours and relatives would not have to bear the burden of what he planned to do, then gave away everything else he had, sang his death-song, and set out in a small boat . . . I hear he killed thirteen of the raiders' tribe before they brought him down, one less than the two for each of his he had promised.' Ragnar abruptly laughed. 'I am sure that his spirit is still angry about that!'

'That's a horrible story!'

'Is it?' He seemed surprised. 'I fear I don't understand this place very well, this time. But after Grace was lost, that was how Gideon's spirit was – like my friend's, restless and angry.

'In that first year or two Gideon brought back many animals and many people – Patience Needle with her son in her belly, Sarah the cook, Kiwa and his cousins. Haneb came with two small dragons during that time – he was only a child, but already his face was scarred. And Gideon found me too. And of course the other animals! Gideon told me that before she vanished Grace had begged him to help her use the Fault Line to save some of the animals that had been lost from

99

the earth – the great worms, the one-horns, all of them – and so after he lost her Gideon did his best to fill the farm with all the animals they had discovered together.

'Then one wild night Gideon came back from the Fault Line with a ragged bloody stranger – that was Caesar. We all hurried out to welcome Gideon back, but then we heard a great baying from the Fault Line cavern – I swear for a moment I thought Gideon had brought back the Fenris Wolf itself! I thought the end of days was at hand!'

For a long moment the bearded man grew silent, as if seeing that night again before his eyes. 'It was not the great wolf, though, but only a dog,' he said at last. 'But, gods, what a dog! A monster thing that rushed out after Gideon and Caesar and would have pulled them both down and killed them. But Simos was faster. You should have seen him, child! Do you think I am strong? Walkwell seized that dog with one hand around its neck and threw it so far away that it did not rise after it had fallen.

'And then Kingaree appeared, tall and dark of face as Loki the mischief-maker himself. He scarcely looked down at the dog's body as he passed, but stared only at Gideon and Caesar. I did not speak English well then – I had only been speaking your tongue for a year – but I understood what he said next: "*You have something of mine.*"'

'What was he talking about?' Lucinda asked.

Ragnar was squinting against the sun. A rolling, silvery something appeared for a moment at the centre of Elliot's Lagoon. He shook his head. 'He meant Caesar.'

'What?'

The big man shrugged. 'I do not know the history of this land well, but I know there was a time not long ago here in America when they still had thralls – what you call "slaves". Caesar was a slave who had escaped. Kingaree was the man who was trying to bring him back.'

'Oh, no! What happened? Why did Gideon bring someone so terrible back to the farm?'

'He didn't – not by choice, anyway. Gideon had made one of his devil's bargains to help Caesar escape his pursuers, but somehow the Fault Line stayed open longer than usual and Kingaree followed them back. At first Kingaree would not believe what had happened, but at last he came to see the truth.'

'Then what?'

'Gideon promised Kingaree that if he behaved himself he could live on the farm too and be safe . . . but that was bargaining with the devil himself. Jackson Kingaree stayed only until he had learned what he could. Then, on the night of the laboratory fire, he slipped away. We have not seen him since – at least not until you met him in the street. Me, I hoped we would never see him again.'

Thinking how close she had been to this Kingaree

made Lucinda feel queasy. 'Why is everyone so scared of him?'

Ragnar shook his head – firmly this time. 'You do not need to hear any more stories. All you need to know is to keep away from this man. If you ever see him again, tell Simos or me as fast as you can. Or Gideon.'

Lucinda's heart fell further. 'Tell Gideon? Sure, if we ever find him. If this Kingaree guy hasn't killed him or something . . .'

Ragnar clicked his tongue and flapped the reins. Culpepper began to pull the wagon back onto the road, leaving Elliot and his broad silver pond behind. 'Do not underestimate Gideon Goldring, child,' the bearded man said. 'You already know how stubborn he is. Well, Gideon is also stronger and more determined than you can guess.'

# CHAPTER 12

## ERGODICITY AND OTHER BIG WORDS

As Colin Needle walked toward the library he watched the male dragon Alamu flying in long, lazy circles a few hundred feet above the house as if enjoying the sight of Colin's mother's sprawling gardens. A little afternoon sun peeked through the heavy clouds, glinting off the creature's coppery scales and shining through the grey membranes of his wings – the only brightness Colin had seen in hours. A storm was moving in on the valley, a swell of thunderheads crouched above the furthest hills like an angry genie. Alamu glided low, then swung high into the air again.

*Electric fences are all well and good,* Colin thought, *but what if Ed Stillman and his men are camped out there on Springs Road taking pictures with a telephoto lens right now? It's going to be hard for him to miss an actual dragon flying around.* His stomach flopped in queasy discontent: just one more thing to worry about.

The billionaire Stillman had double-crossed him last summer, but what felt worse was that Colin had fallen for the man's lies – in fact, he had been as gullible as the Jenkins kids. That still didn't sit well. Now Ed Stillman was just one more apparently permanent problem. *Somebody* was going to have to solve these problems and save Ordinary Farm. Gideon Goldring was gone, maybe dead; Colin's mother was busy picking up the slack of Gideon's absence; and Walkwell and Ragnar and the Jenkins children were no use at all. Only Colin Needle could solve the farm's problems and make everything work again.

The sad thing, though – the truly infuriating thing – was that only Colin himself seemed to understand that.

In the library Colin sat among the papers and books piled on his table and felt something like despair. Almost every weekday for two months he had been sitting here, keeping an eye out for another Magic Necklace Drop (as he sarcastically thought of it), and had filled the time studying everything he could find about the science of the Fault Line (because none of his plans for the farm would work if he couldn't use the Fault Line.) And what did he have to show for all that work? Piles of physics books he could barely read, let alone understand, because they were full of crazy terms like *ergodicity* and *Poincaré Recurrence Theorem* and *Loschmidt's Paradox*, terms that Colin couldn't make much sense of. Still, he had worked his way through all of them, making plenty of notes at first, but as it became clearer and clearer that the science was far beyond him he had mostly given up. Despite what he'd said to Tyler Jenkins, Colin knew he was never going to make a Continuascope on his own; he had only threatened it to make his enemy worry.

As for finding Grace, he didn't think he was going to have any luck with that either. She had disappeared so completely on that night twenty years ago that almost everyone on the farm assumed she'd somehow wound up in the Fault Line. But if she had, why should her golden locket turn up here in the library, a thousand yards away from the silo and the strange phenomenon hidden beneath it? Gideon only had Tyler Jenkins's word that it had actually come from the library, but the old man had still stuck Colin here, lonely as a lighthouse keeper, waiting for some other memento of Grace's to show up, all on Tyler Jenkins's dubious say-so . . .

A new and startling thought came to Colin, an idea so astonishing that for a moment he forgot to breathe. The Jenkins brat had already been in the Fault Line once and travelled to the ice age – by accident, he had claimed – then walked back out again no worse for wear, the cavegirl Ooola trailing after him like a lovesick puppy. But what if that *hadn't* been an accident? What if Tyler had found a Continuascope of his own – perhaps some early prototype of Octavio Tinker's? If so, then he might have found the locket somewhere in the Fault Line and just *pretended* that it had come from the library, to keep everyone fooled . . .

But if Tyler Jenkins had his own Continuascope, why was he always asking questions about the whereabouts of the old one? That didn't make sense. Colin knew that if *he* had a Continuascope, he'd be in the Fault Line every chance he had.

So much was happening, and it was so hard to make sense of it all. The Jenkins kids were back on the farm; Gideon had disappeared; Kingaree had returned – could all these things happening at the same time really be coincidence?

Thunder rumbled over the distant hills. Colin Needle decided he was tired of secrets. It was time to talk to the one person who almost certainly knew more than she had told him so far . . . about everything.

His mother stood in front of the elaborate old Victorian washstand. The pretty, black-haired woman in the mirror looked back at her, expression thoughtful and pale face sombre. She was so beautiful! Looking at her now, Colin couldn't believe he had been about to tell Lucinda Jenkins that he suspected her of knowing more than she was saying about Gideon's disappearance. Yet – his mother might have a temper, but he felt certain she would never do anything to harm the man who had saved her life . . . !

She extended a finger and her nail touched the surface of the glass with a soft click. She moved her finger and then touched the surface again. The same click. Colin watched her, both repelled and fascinated. 'Tell me, Mother,' he said at last, 'why did you go to the trouble of having this thing hauled up the stairs and installed in here?'

'I'm not entirely certain.' She gazed thoughtfully at her own reflection. 'It feels . . . strange to me. Older than it looks. But perhaps you're going to tell me differently?'

He was sure she was teasing him – mocking him. 'What do you mean, Mother?'

She flicked the mirror with her nail again – *tik, tik, tik.* 'I seem to remember that I asked you to bring me anything you could find about the piece or its acquisition in Octavio Tinker's papers.'

'There's nothing. I told you that already.'

'I hoped you had come to tell me you were wrong, Colin. That you found out something about it. Because it intrigues me, and I am seldom if ever wrong about such feelings.' She gave the mirror another dreamy stare. 'Something . . . there is *something* . . .'

'I came to ask *you* some questions, Mother. Still no news about Gideon?'

A sharp, annoyed stare. 'Why on earth are you asking me? Do you think I would hide it from you

107

if we heard something? Really, Colin, just when I have so much extra work to do.' She stared at him for a long, silent moment. It was all Colin could do not to turn away from his mother's hard, fierce eyes, but there was something in her face he had seldom seen before. It took him a moment to recognize the unfamiliar expression: she was anxious. But why? Did his mother know something about Gideon Goldring's disappearance after all?

'You're worried, aren't you, dear?' she asked, more lightly than before. 'It's not good for you to brood about things, Colin. We're all worried about Gideon.'

Something about the casual way she spoke upset him. 'Really, Mother? All of us?'

Her lip curled in a snarl. She looked so angry he took a startled step back. 'What is that supposed to mean? You do say the most incomprehensible things sometimes. I'm glad you're going out for the evening tomorrow. It will be good for you.'

It took him a moment to realize what she'd just said. 'Going out? What do you mean?'

'Oh, didn't I tell you? The people on the next farm over, those . . . Spanish people . . . asked you over for their holiday celebration. Surely you remember that tomorrow is July the Fourth. Independence Day, don't they call it?'

'The Carrillos? They invited me?'

'Of course. They sent us a letter and it said, "The

children are invited." Like it or not, you are still one of the children, so of course you are expected to go.'

Colin found it very hard to believe the Carrillos wanted him at their Fourth of July gathering. 'I don't want to go to their stupid party.'

'Nevertheless you will go – I insist, Colin. We owe them several favours. Also, before he disappeared, Gideon was rather rude about not answering Mr. Carrillo's questions, so we must do our best to be polite to them. I want you on your best behaviour.' She turned back to the mirror, gazing at it again as though it was a magical picture that showed her heart's desire. 'Oh, and would you please go tell Caesar he may come up for his physic? I'm brewing his special tea.'

Colin was walking downstairs toward the kitchen when he suddenly realized that he hadn't asked his mother any of the questions he'd planned to ask. He also realized that going to Cresta Sol dairy farm for the evening tomorrow had nothing to do with the Carrillos at all, except that they provided a useful excuse: it was his mother who wanted him gone. He had no idea what she planned to do, but he was certain she didn't want to do it in front of him.

Thunder boomed again, and outside the window a flash briefly turned the sky white. Lightning, and not very far away.

Another son would have felt disturbed by his mother's secrecy, and might even have marched back upstairs to argue about it, but Colin Needle was used to being inconvenient, to being kept in the dark, and he was also used to doing what Patience Needle wanted him to do, or at least appearing to do so.

He would go to the Carrillos' – but nothing on earth, not even his beautiful, cold, clever mother, could make him enjoy himself there.

# CHAPTER 13

## A FREE MAN IN PENNSYLVANIA

The more Tyler thought, the angrier he got.

'What's *with* this place? Are they all crazy?' He was having so much trouble paying attention to what he was doing that he dropped his flashlight. The batteries he had been loading popped out and rolled across the floor. 'That Kingaree's a slavery guy? What if he'd tried to kill you? They never tell us anything about anything – we always have to find out for ourselves!'

'They're all from the past, Tyler! They don't belong here and they'd be in trouble if people found out they were here. Of course they keep secrets.'

Tyler scowled: he'd thought Lucinda was getting better about pretending things were fine when they obviously weren't. 'I don't care if they're from Magic Happy Land, Luce – *they* invited *us*! Dropped us into the middle of all this and didn't warn us about any of this dangerous crazy stuff. Dragons! Billionaires with helicopters and guns! Crazy . . . slave-whippers from the Civil War days! And now Gideon's gone, so we're the only people in this whole place who even legally *exist*.'

For perhaps the first time ever, Tyler was beginning to wonder if they really did belong at Ordinary Farm. As if to emphasize this thought, thunder boomed in the nearby hills.

Then he thought of Colin and his creepy mother again and his heart filled with anger. 'No, it's not *us* who don't belong here . . . !' he said.

'What are you talking about?'

'Never mind.' He had been planning to go back out and look for Gideon until the evening meal, but instead he put down the flashlight and stood. 'Come on. Maybe this Kingaree guy you met really *does* have something to do with Gideon disappearing – and if he does, I know who might have some answers.'

The women in the kitchen were just starting supper. Tyler noted the good smells with approval, but he was in too much of a hurry to appreciate them properly. However, a little bit of something to take along might not be a bad idea, he thought . . .

'He is upstairs,' Pema told them. 'In Gideon's study.'

'Meanwhile, if you touch that bacon, *Junge*, you will be beaten,' Sarah warned him. Defeated, Tyler led Lucinda up the stairs.

Caesar looked up from dusting. With Gideon

Goldring now missing for almost a week it was hard to know how much cleaning of his study was really necessary, but Caesar regarded it as his personal job to take care of both Gideon and his rooms, and it seemed he would continue doing it whether Gideon was around or not.

'Hello, children,' he said. 'Are you looking for something?'

'For you, Caesar. Could we ask you some questions?'

The old man laughed, showing very white teeth. 'I suppose you can.' They were not his own teeth: Mr. Walkwell had found them for him in a church jumble sale in Standard Valley, and although they didn't fit tremendously well, Caesar was very proud of them. He had lost most of his own at a young age.

*Weird that we know that about him but didn't know he was a runaway slave*, Tyler thought. 'Did you hear that Lucinda met Jackson Kingaree? He came up to her in town and introduced himself.'

Caesar's expression grew more distant, but he kept his smile. 'Oh, I heard, yes. Terrible thing.'

'We want to know more. About Kingaree. We think he might have something to do with Gideon's disappearance.'

Caesar looked at Tyler for a long second more, then turned away to dust a spotless shelf. 'I can't talk now, children. Too busy.' His voice hitched. 'I'm just too sad about Mister Gideon.'

'Just talk to us, Caesar – please!'

'*Tyler, leave him alone!*' Lucinda whispered, but he ignored her.

'Nobody tells us anything around here. What happened?' Tyler was doing his best to keep calm, but he was tired of everyone avoiding his questions. 'Please, Caesar. Did Gideon make a deal with Kingaree? And if he did, why did Kingaree leave the farm?'

Caesar turned suddenly. His smile was gone and his face looked as stern and hard as a wooden mask. 'Why did Kingaree leave? Because he's a devil, that's why. Because like the Good Book says, the devil needs the whole world to roam in, to go back and forth doing his mischief.'

'Ragnar told me . . .' Lucinda obviously did not want to say it – as if it was a dirty word. 'He said you were Kingaree's . . . slave.'

'That ain't true!' Caesar shook his head. 'But it ain't Ragnar's fault – he's from far, far back and don't know any better. Yes, I was a slave once, in South Carolina, but to a better man than Jackson Kingaree. Still, don't nobody want to be a slave even for a kind master. I earned my freedom and went north to live in Pennsylvania. Then one day I was at the market in Charlesville and Kingaree and his gang of slave-chasers snatched me up like I was nothing but an animal, even though I was in free territory and a free man. He was going to carry me quick over the border to Maryland . . . it was a slave state then . . . Oh, sweet God . . . !'

114

Lightning whitewashed the sky above the mountains outside the window – a summer storm was on its way; thunder followed moments later. Tyler saw that Caesar was shaking so hard that his long, lean body was swaying like a windblown tree. The old man felt for the chair – Gideon's empty chair – and sat down. 'I'm sorry,' Tyler said. 'I didn't mean . . .'

'You didn't know any better, son. You children don't know nothing about how things were in my day, 'less they teach it to you in school. But back then you had to know because it was the way of the world – what everyone tell you: "Never tease a strange dog. Don't look white folk in the eye, especially white women. Watch out for the slave-catchers."' He laughed, but it was a cracked, unhappy sound. 'Yes, that devil Kingaree took me. Then when his wagon lost a wheel and I wouldn't walk in chains to Baltimore, he beat me. I said he might as well kill me right there because I wasn't ever going back to the south. He damn near did.' He looked at Lucinda. 'I beg pardon for my salty language, Miss.'

Lucinda only shook her head. She was pale and Tyler thought she looked as if she was close to crying.

'I got away from him though,' Caesar said. 'The Lord was bound to keep me free, and He made sure those shackles were just a little too big for me. After a while I got out of 'em.' He lifted his arms and pulled back his sleeves. Both wrists were badly scarred, covered with streaky grey bumps. 'I got away into the woods just before we come to the Susquehanna ferry. Kingaree and his dogs and men, they come after me. They were shootin' too. One way or another, they weren't going to let me go home again.' He took a shaky breath. 'But then Mister Gideon come out of nowhere, just like the Lord's angel. Asked me if I wanted to get away from all this. Don't take much to guess I said yes.' Caesar laughed; it was shaky but less bitter this time.

'What was Gideon doing there?' asked Tyler.

'Looking for a Thunderbird – that's what he told me later.' Caesar shrugged. 'At the time I wasn't asking nothing – those dogs and all were right behind me. So Mister Gideon took out this strange thing looked half like a trumpet, half like the insides of a fancy pocket watch. He waved it around and started fiddling with it. Just then, Kingaree's biggest dog come charging out of the trees with Kingaree right behind. Mister Gideon made some kind of big, sparky, burning hole in the air and tugged me through it. Stretched me like nothing you'd ever seen – like string through a knothole!'

'Wow!' Tyler's heart was beating hard just hearing it. 'But somehow Kingaree came through too.'

Caesar nodded. 'Maybe that was the good Lord's plan – bring that evil man here, where he couldn't catch any more poor coloured folk and drag 'em into slavery. Still, I can't help wishing that He woulda dropped Jackson Kingaree in the ocean instead.'

'That's so terrible!' said Lucinda. 'I'm sorry, Caesar.'

'Weren't your fault, child. Even your granny and your grampy weren't born back then. Eighteen and forty-eight, that was – long time ago.' He sighed. 'We'll just pray that Kingaree doesn't come around here – or that if he does, he does it when Mr. Walkwell's back to catch him at it.'

'How long did he live here on the farm? And why did Gideon let him leave?'

'Wasn't anything so simple. Kingaree disappeared the night of the big fire. I admit that for a while I was hopin' he got burned up.'

'The fire in Gideon's laboratory?' Tyler tried to keep his voice even. The last Continuascope had been destroyed in that disaster. 'Did Kingaree have something to do with that?'

'Could be.' Caesar shrugged. 'Mister Gideon always thought so, but it didn't make no sense to me. Why would he burn up that laboratory instead of the house where all the people were?'

A thought was tugging at Tyler. 'To make it *look* like the Continuascope was destroyed?' His heart was suddenly racing even faster.

Lucinda eyed him with something like alarm. 'Tyler . . . ?'

'No, think about it. He knew that Gideon would never let him get away with the Continuascope – all these years and Gideon still hasn't been able to build another one! So maybe Kingaree set the fire so Gideon would think the Continuascope was gone for good.'

Caesar shook his head. 'That's what some of the folks round here thought too – especially Mister Gideon. He was sure that Kingaree had stolen that thing! He kept Mr. Walkwell out guarding the Fault Line every night for weeks and weeks. But Kingaree never came, thank the Lord. Now why, children, if he had Mister Gideon's device all those years would he wait until now to come back? And announce it to a little girl? Beggin' your pardon, Miss Lucinda.'

'Yeah, it doesn't make a lot of sense.' Tyler was still frowning when he noticed a shadow out of the corner of his eye. He turned to see Colin Needle leaning in the doorway of Gideon's office, his thin arms crossed over his chest and a look of sour amusement on his face.

'Up to mischief again, Jenkins?' the tall boy asked.

'Needle! What are you doing? Spying on us?'

'You wish.' Colin straightened so that he could look down his nose at Tyler. 'I have business here, as it happens.' He turned to Caesar. 'My mother wants you to come and take your willow-bark tea. Also, she said she's worked up some more mint-oil salve.'

Caesar nodded. 'Ah, that is a blessing. I've been missing it. My hands have been playing me up something fierce.' He turned back to Tyler and Lucinda. 'You children excuse me – Mrs. Needle's medicine tea works best when it's hot and fresh.'

After the old man had made his way out of the room Colin lingered behind. 'I don't really expect your brother to stay out of trouble,' he told Lucinda, 'but if

118

he keeps on poking and spying into old problems he's going to drop you into trouble as well. I'd hate to see that happen.'

'What's that all about?' Tyler said after Colin had left. 'Does he think he's protecting you from me? Dude, I would so like to punch him right in his skinny face!'

Lucinda gave him a hard look. 'Cut it out, Tyler. He's not so bad – not like his mother. I think he was just trying to do me a favour.'

'He was listening in on us, is what he was doing.' Tyler snorted. 'Calling *me* a spy – how long do you think he was standing there listening to us talk to Caesar? Listening to us talk about Kingaree? And the Continuascope! I told you, he's trying to make one!'

Lucinda shook her head. 'Don't worry about it. If Gideon couldn't make a new one, Colin Needle sure can't do it on his own.'

It was a good point, especially since Gideon had actually helped Octavio make the first one. 'Yeah, but he's up to something, and I don't like him sneaking around, listening in on us. I'm going to figure out what he's doing and then he's really going to know what trouble is!'

'Oh, man!' Lucinda rolled her eyes. 'Sometimes I think Colin's right about you, Tyler.' She turned and headed up the stairs, the noise of her footsteps for a moment as loud as the approaching thunderstorm.

'What?' he shouted after her. 'Wait! What's that supposed to mean?'

# CHAPTER 14

## SOY CAPITÁN

The summer storm had been a powerful one, with lightning and drum rolls of thunder in the night that had set the house shuddering, but it was gone by morning. Now the sky was clear and the hills bright with detail beneath the sun. Even the ground smelled rich and new.

'Did you hear all that last night?' Lucinda asked her brother. 'It was hard to sleep.'

'Saw some lightning,' he said. 'Pretty cool. Thought it might hit the house . . .'

'It *did* hit the house,' Colin Needle said in his most bored, superior voice. 'Probably about ten times. That's why we have a lightning rod on the roof.'

Lucinda was relieved that her brother only rolled his eyes in disgust and turned away from Colin. It was bad enough they were all so worried about Gideon. She wanted today to go well.

Mr. Walkwell was driving them to the Carrillos' Fourth of July party, so of course they were travelling by horse-cart. Before heading off to Cresta Sol dairy farm, though, he took them to the unicorn pasture so he and Ragnar could fill the unicorns' trough. The graceful creatures came down from the hills to feed, but they were skittish: when Ragnar approached a young unicorn who was limping, she spooked and ran. The rest of the herd followed and soon had all but vanished from sight, a shrinking white cloud skimming across the dry, golden grasses.

'Perhaps it is last night's storm,' Mr. Walkwell called to Ragnar. 'But something is bothering them, that is sure.' He looked at Lucinda, Tyler, and Colin as if they might somehow be to blame. 'All the animals are strange today.'

'Yes, it's not just that one foal, Simos,' the Norseman said. 'There are at least three of them, maybe four, who are wobbly on their feet. I fear we may have some pest among them.' Ragnar walked up the nearest hill carrying his binoculars, trying to get a better look at the foals. He seemed worried, and no wonder: if some disease infected this herd, every single unicorn left in the world might die. The thought of all that beauty just being swept away made Lucinda's eyes blur with tears.

'Maybe Poseidon makes an earthshake soon,' Mr. Walkwell called after Ragnar. 'That frightens many creatures. Often animals can sense what the gods plan long before men can guess.'

'The gods – of course, all this must be their doing!' Colin smirked as he said it, but Lucinda wasn't so sceptical. After all, if the farm's overseer was a faun, or a satyr, or whatever he was – something that wasn't supposed to exist – who was to say that Zeus and the other Greek gods weren't real too?

'Do you really think the gods are angry with us?' she asked.

Mr. Walkwell gave her a sourly amused look. 'The gods are always angry about something.'

'What are we going to tell the Carrillos about Gideon?' Lucinda asked as Ragnar finally turned and began to make his way back down the hill toward the wagon.

'You? Nothing,' said Mr. Walkwell. 'I will talk to Hector Carrillo myself. As for any others that might ask questions, Gideon is gone and you do not know any more than that, so do not say any more.'

'It's none of their business anyway,' Colin said. 'Those people already know too much about our farm. Don't tell them anything.'

Tyler stirred beside Lucinda. 'It's not your farm, Needle; it's Uncle Gideon's.'

'Easy for you to say, Jenkins. You have another home.'

Lucinda heard the very real pain in Colin Needle's voice and it surprised her. The older boy actually sounded worried, even frightened. Tyler was so certain Colin and his mother were up to no good – but what if he was wrong?

Ragnar and Mr. Walkwell were talking at the front of the wagon, but so quietly that Lucinda could scarcely pick out the low murmur of their voices from the constant buzzing of the cicadas in the tall grass. After the wagon had bumped along slowly for nearly half an hour, during which the hot day pressed on them like a sweaty hand, Colin Needle nodded off to sleep and Lucinda let her own eyes fall shut as well, enjoying the warmth and the wagon's motion. She hadn't felt this relaxed in a week – not since the day Gideon had vanished. Then Tyler spoke up suddenly, as if continuing a conversation they had already begun, and Lucinda suddenly found herself very much awake.

'Hey, Ragnar, you said that guy Kingaree burned down the lab, right?'

Ragnar made a growling noise. 'I said nothing like it. I only said he vanished the night Gideon's laboratory was burned.'

'Well then, what makes you so sure he *didn't* do it?'

Ragnar would have answered, but Mr. Walkwell interrupted. 'Enough of this foolishness,' he said. 'Kingaree is a very bad man, but he had nothing to do with that fire.'

Tyler was not about to give up so easily. 'How do you know?'

'I know Kingaree did not set the blaze,' said Mr. Walkwell, 'because I saw the tracks of the one who did.'

Beside her, Colin's eyes remained closed, but Lucinda thought the tall boy had become very still, as though he was now awake and listening.

'You saw footprints?' Tyler asked quietly.

'I said "tracks",' Mr. Walkwell told him. 'Clawed tracks, made by Alamu, the male dragon. And the ashes of the place stank of dragon-flame.'

'But . . . but . . . I've never heard anybody say that before!' Tyler sounded positively outraged by this new information. '*Alamu* burned it down? Why didn't anyone tell us?'

'Because I did not speak about it until now, child. To protect Gideon.'

Lucinda could hear her brother struggling to keep his temper. 'Sorry, but I don't understand . . .'

'As long as he thought Kingaree had stolen the Continuascope, Gideon could believe he might recover it.' Mr. Walkwell tugged the reins and Culpepper turned into the narrow road that led to the Carrillos' farm. 'But if Gideon knew the dragon had burned the place down and his Continuascope was almost certainly destroyed and forever lost . . . well, I feared he would despair and give up hope completely – so I kept it a secret. Losing Grace had already been a crippling blow to him.'

That was all he would say, but it was enough to

make Tyler shut up for the rest of the trip. Lucinda didn't mind at all.

By the time the wagon reached the Cresta Sol Dairy Farm gate no one had spoken for a while. The white iron and painted cartoon sun looked so bright against the grumpy grey sky that Lucinda felt herself cheering up. All these old secrets and sad stories – but surely things would get better! Gideon would come back – she had to believe that. And today, at least, there would be food, friends . . . and fireworks!

They clopped down the long gravel driveway and into the huge dirt front yard. Carmen was already visible, standing in the shade of the porch shading her eyes with her hand, watching for their arrival. She waved, then the door next to her burst open and out came Steve and Alma, the youngest child, who turned back toward the house. 'Mom! Dad!' shouted Alma. 'Look who's here!'

Hector and Silvia Carrillo came out too, Silvia wiping her hands on her apron. Ragnar couldn't wave because his arms were full with the two cases of beer that were his contribution to the feast, but he bellowed a greeting. 'Hello, Master and Mistress Carrillo! It's good to see you again!'

'And you, Ragnar, and Simos – and you too, children,' said Mrs. Carrillo, but she looked distracted. 'Where's Gideon? We thought he was coming. We asked specially for him to come.'

'Uh-oh,' said Tyler quietly, and turned to Steve Carrillo. 'Come on, you and me might as well get out of here before the manure hits the fan.'

'Why?' Steve seemed a little annoyed. 'What's going on?'

Lucinda's heart was sinking. Everyone had been so nice last year – why couldn't things be the same? Mr. Walkwell was walking toward the Carrillo parents as if he had to perform a very unpleasant chore, but before he reached them Carmen grabbed Lucinda's wrist and dragged her away, around the house to the patio and festivities in the backyard.

Half a dozen Carrillo relatives, mostly women, were setting things up on picnic tables covered with red, white, and blue paper tablecloths. 'My dad's angry,' Carmen told her quietly. 'He needs to talk to your uncle real bad, but Mr. Goldring won't answer any of our messages.'

'It's . . . complicated.' Lucinda didn't want to say more than she was allowed. 'Gideon's . . . well, he's gone.' She held out the roses she had brought wrapped in a newspaper, cut by Pema from one of the gardens behind the house just that morning. 'Here.'

'Aren't those pretty!' said a voice behind her. Lucinda turned to see Carmen's Grandma Paz standing there, a tiny, round woman with a casserole dish in her oven-mitted hands. 'Ah, yes, you are Lucinda from next door, of course. I am glad to see you are still alive!'

Carmen said, 'Grandma!'

The old woman shook her unnaturally red-haired head. 'Don't blame me for telling the truth. That is a bad place. No one should bring children there, but that young Gideon fellow was always too sure of himself.'

'Young . . . ?' said Lucinda, surprised, but Carmen was already pulling her away.

'Let's put those flowers in a vase.' As they went into the house Carmen leaned close. 'Don't let it bug you. She's always like that – although she's worse with you and Tyler.' Carmen's eyes grew wide. 'Is that the witch's kid who came with you?'

'What? Oh, Colin, yeah.'

'I hardly recognized him. He's not quite as geeky as he used to be. In fact, he looks almost human.' Carmen laughed. 'Come on, before my grandmother comes back and starts praying over you. I've got something to give you.'

In her room Carmen produced a small box and held it out to Lucinda. 'Go on, open it!'

Inside, nestled in tissue paper, lay a charm bracelet, a collection of silver crosses and clovers and hearts and even a tiny horse with wings.

'Oh, Carmen, it's beautiful! Thank you so much!'

'My aunt gave it to me for my birthday, but I already have one like it that I've had for years.' She grinned, pleased by Lucinda's reaction. 'Glad you like it. Now come look – I totally have to show you this note a boy in school sent me, trying to be all suave and ask me out. It's such a crack-up!'

*

The food was excellent and so was the company – Carmen was lots of fun and Lucinda wished they lived closer to each other during the rest of the year – but she still felt restless and worried. Things felt different to the way they had the year before, when it had been one of the nicest days she'd ever had anywhere. For one thing, it was clear that Carmen's parents, Hector and Silvia, weren't very happy, and they spent a lot of time talking quietly with Mr. Walkwell. Ragnar took part in some of these conversations, but after a while he just went off by himself and began drinking beer in serious quantities. Watching him, Lucinda was glad they were driving back in a very slow horse-cart.

'Hello and thanks for nothing,' Tyler said in her ear as she was standing in line for pie; it made her jump.

'What's your problem?'

'You and Carmen ran off and stuck us with Colin Needle . . . and Alma.'

'What's wrong with Alma? She's sweet.'

'She just follows me around like a puppy dog. She tried to hold my hand!' Tyler said it with such outrage that it was all Lucinda could do not to laugh out loud. 'And Colin, all he does is complain about how stupid Steve's games are, or how loud the music is.' Tyler threw his hands over his ears as someone turned the mariachi-style music up even louder. 'He must be loving this . . . !'

It was a song Lucinda recognized – '"La Bamba"!'

Carmen ran up. 'Leave your boring brother here with my boring brother. Let's go jump on the trampoline!'

Surprised, Lucinda laughed and let herself be pulled out of the house and into the front yard.

'I'm going to send Colin out to join you!' Tyler warned.

> '¡Yo no soy marinero!
> Yo no soy marinero, soy capitán
> Soy capitán,
> Soy capitán!'

'Ba, ba, bamba . . . ! Ba, ba, bamba . . . !' Lucinda sang as she and Carmen bounced up and down beneath the low grey sky. Her new bracelet jingled merrily, and her feelings came together with the music and her own clumsy but energetic jumping and became something like joy: it was proving to be a good Fourth of July after all.

Carmen stopped bouncing and swayed to a stop. 'Whoa, who's that?' She stared out across the empty front yard.

Lucinda looked up to see a distant figure stumbling past the cow barn. Whoever it was looked unwell, rolling like an old drunk. In fact, it looked a bit like Great-uncle Gideon – an old mad invalid with his robe billowing.

It *was*, she realized a moment later. It really was Gideon.

# CHAPTER 15

## ONE FREAKY FOURTH

One moment Tyler and Steve Carrillo were loudly explaining to Colin Know-Nothing Needle how full of bull he was – that video games not only didn't make you stupid, they improved your hand–eye coordination; they even used them to train the United States Army! – then the next moment everybody was running around yelling, 'Call a doctor!' and, 'Somebody tell Hector!' Tyler heard his sister shouting the name 'Gideon' and he and Colin both jumped up at the same time and ran toward the front yard.

Gideon Goldring, looking sick and exhausted and very thin, was crouched in the late-afternoon sun, surrounded by Lucinda and Carmen and Alma and a growing crowd of other Carrillo relatives. As Lucinda gave Gideon a drink from a bottle of water someone had brought from the kitchen, Mr. Walkwell and

Ragnar suddenly appeared around the corner of the house at a run.

'Where did he come from?' Ragnar demanded.

'He just . . . he just showed up,' Lucinda said. 'He came across the fields.'

Tyler heard something else above the babble of voices, a thin, high-pitched cry in the distance. Colin Needle, who had been staring down at Gideon with his mouth hanging open, looked up and then shook his head like someone waking up too fast. 'Hang on – that's my *mother* . . . !'

And indeed another shape was bumping across the fields toward the Carrillos' house, half-walking, half-trotting – Patience Needle in her old-fashioned clothes, waving her arms and shouting, 'Don't touch him!' Tyler realized he had never heard the witch raise her voice before. 'Don't!' she cried as she hurried toward them. 'You must leave him alone!'

Gideon was so pale that his skin was almost green, his forehead damp with sweat. '*Won't*,' he suddenly said, pulling away from the bottle so that water splashed onto his chest. He tried to grab at Lucinda's arm but his eyes, though wide, didn't seem to see anything, and his hands were twitching too much for him to control them. '*Won't . . . go . . . back . . .*'

'Back where, Gideon?' Ragnar asked. 'Where have you been?'

But the old man was lost in some world of his own, head rolling from side to side as he struggled to get up. 'You can't . . . !' he said, smacking at the hands of those who were trying to restrain him. 'Let go of me, you damn . . . *monster*!'

'We have to take him to a hospital,' said Hector Carrillo.

'*No!*' Mrs. Needle all but screamed. She staggered over and knelt beside Gideon, holding his head with one hand while feeling his wrist and forehead. 'No hospital! He will be fine. I know how to help him. We need only get him back to the farm. I have medicines there . . . special things . . .'

'You're crazy if you think I'm going to let you drag this man away – this *sick man* – before he's even been examined by a doctor.' Mr. Carrillo stood up. 'Ragnar, Simos, put him into my truck.'

'Shouldn't we call an ambulance, Dad?' Carmen asked.

'I can get him to the clinic at Liberty in twenty . . . twenty-five minutes,' Hector told her. 'It'll take at least that long to get an ambulance out here.'

Mrs. Needle gave him a glare that could have stripped paint, but Mr. Carrillo just stared back at her with calm authority; Tyler couldn't help being impressed. 'Then I will go too,' she said at last. 'I found him wandering at the farm and chased him all the way here. I will not leave him so easily.'

'Don't let her!'

Tyler looked at Lucinda in surprise. 'Luce . . . ?'

But his sister was already pulling on Mr. Carrillo's

132

arm. 'Don't let her. I'll bet she's the one who did this to him! Gave him some kind of . . . of *potion* or something. And she's probably the one keeping Gideon from answering your calls too. She probably doesn't even tell him – that's what she did to us last year.'

'How *dare* you!' Mrs. Needle rose to her feet and stood over Lucinda, her face white and her expression so furious that even Mr. Carrillo took a step back. 'How dare you talk like that in front of strangers, Lucinda Jenkins! What a terrible thing to say!'

'They're not strangers to us! They're our friends!' His sister looked terrified but determined. Tyler felt real pride in her.

'You tell 'em, sis,' he said.

Patience Needle let her gaze linger on Lucinda a moment longer, then turned to Mr. and Mrs. Carrillo, the anger now wiped from her face. 'Everyone has been worried for Gideon. He's been missing for days. You can see how upset we all are. I've been his doctor for years, more or less. Please don't let the words of a frightened, confused child keep me away from him.'

'But how did Gideon get past the fences?' Mr. Walkwell demanded.

Mrs. Needle drew herself up straight. 'I turned them off when I saw him stumbling along in the distance like a madman, of course. Did you think I would let our employer be fatally electrified?'

Mr. Walkwell snorted, but he turned and began trotting back toward Ordinary Farm. 'Then I must make the fences work again before . . . before any more trouble happens.' Lucinda guessed he would shed his boots as soon as he was out of sight. On his naked hooves he could run like the wind.

For a long moment Mr. Carrillo's gaze had been resting on Lucinda: now he turned to the housekeeper with a hard smile. 'Yes, I suppose you can come with us to the hospital, Mrs. Needle. But we'll need to take more than one car. Might as well take all the kids too – they can see the fireworks in Liberty.' He turned to his wife. 'Silvia, where's your brother . . . ? Ah.' He waved to a man with a beard whose tattoos Tyler had admired earlier. 'Jaime, you have your van, right? You bring the kids and follow me.'

Ragnar and Mr. Walkwell had been talking quietly. 'I will come too, Hector,' the Norseman said. 'And Simos will go home and make certain things are well there because he does not like driving in cars so much.'

'Where could he have been?' Tyler shouted to Lucinda over the noise of Jaime's stereo, which was blaring Mexican heavy-metal music, something Tyler hadn't even known existed. 'We looked everywhere! Do you think Gideon was in . . . you know . . . the Fault Line?' If he could hardly hear himself, he realized, there probably wasn't too much danger Jaime was listening to their conversation from the front seat. 'I wonder what Mrs. Needle knows about it. I'll bet she and

Colin had him knocked out somewhere. Drugged or something.'

Lucinda frowned at him. 'That's not fair!' she shouted. 'Colin was just as surprised as we were. I was watching him!'

Tyler had his doubts – he had already decided Lucinda was too soft on Colin Needle. 'Then if he's so shocked, why isn't he here? Why isn't he coming to the hospital?'

Lucinda shook her head. 'He is! He's in the truck with Mr. Carrillo.'

Tyler made a face. 'Oh, he's too good to ride with us, huh?'

His sister glared at him. 'You are totally a jerk, Tyler Jenkins,' she said. Which was, of course, totally unfair.

The town of Liberty was what Standard Valley would like to be when it grew up, Tyler decided. Not that Liberty was big – it was probably less than half the size of Tyler's and Lucinda's hometown, but it was big enough to have a Fourth of July parade, which was just ending, and also big enough to have a fire department, several schools, and a movie theatre, none of which could be found in Standard Valley. Tyler saw all this as Jaime followed Mr. Carrillo through town toward the clinic, a generic-looking building with a red tiled roof that if it had been a bit smaller could have passed for a fast-food restaurant.

Hector Carrillo and his passengers had beaten them

there. Ragnar, Colin, and Mr. Carrillo were already in the urgent-care waiting room.

'My mother's filling out the forms,' Colin said. 'She knows all the information – the insurance and all that.'

'You have insurance?' Tyler wondered how people from the past could manage that without birth certificates or whatever normal folk had.

Colin gave him a look of contempt. '*Gideon* does.'

Mr. Carrillo walked over. 'Look, why don't you children go out and see a little of the town. Jaime, go with them, will you? It'll be dark soon – they have fireworks in the park. Carmen, you have your phone?'

'Got it, Papacito.'

'Good. Check back in with us in an hour or so.'

Ragnar walked to the door with them, his bearded face very stern and serious. 'Don't worry, children. Gideon will be well again. I will make certain of that.' Tyler hoped for the doctors' sakes that they didn't make the big man angry.

They walked with Jaime back into the middle of town. Tyler had forgotten what it was like to see so many people, or at least to see so many people he didn't know. Living on Ordinary Farm was a bit like living on a ship out on the ocean – in this case, an ocean of farmland. Every now and then you took a lifeboat into Standard Valley and drank a milkshake at the diner or met up with the Carrillos, but the rest of the time you saw nothing but the same people day

136

after day. But here in Liberty, even though the Fourth of July parade was over it still felt like a parade, this seemingly endless stream of faces – kids, grown-ups, old people, folks laughing and drinking and eating, people shouting greetings across the main street to neighbours and friends.

'Uncle Jaime,' said Alma, 'take us to the North Pole! Please!'

'You just had dinner,' he said. 'And dessert too!'

'Please. I want Peppermint Bark!' she said, at which point Tyler realized they were talking about an ice-cream store.

By the time they got to the park they were sucking the last of the melted ice cream through the bottoms of their sugar cones. Carmen phoned her father, who said that Gideon was doing much better, that he was making sense now even though he didn't seem to remember anything from the last few days. Her father said the doctors were calling his condition 'heat prostration'.

Tyler thought that was all well and good, but it didn't really explain where the old man had been for almost a week.

It was nearly dark and people were still streaming into the park. Carmen, Alma, and Steve went to get drinks. Uncle Jaime had bought himself a beer and was sitting on the grass happily drinking it and talking to a woman he seemed to know. Lucinda leaned over to Tyler. 'Look what Gideon was holding,' she said.

She held out her hand. Tyler stared at the dark fibrous strands, hard to make out in the fading light.

'What are they?'

'I don't know. Some kind of plants, I think. He was hanging onto them like they meant something important.'

Tyler shrugged. 'But what made him crazy? That's the real question . . .'

Lucinda wasn't listening any more. She was staring over his shoulder, her eyes wide as the silver dollar on Uncle Jaime's belt buckle. '*Tyler! It's him!*'

'Who? What are you talking about?' He half-expected to see Gideon running toward them across the park grass, bathrobe flapping, pursued by doctors and nurses, but saw only an undifferentiated crowd of people loitering around the edge of the grass, waiting for the fireworks to begin. 'I don't see . . .'

'There.' She leaned in close to him. 'Don't stare, don't point. There, by the fountain. It's that man Kingaree.'

Tyler had never seen him, of course, but Lucinda's description of him as looking like a bad guy in a cowboy movie had stuck in his mind, so he had no doubt which one she meant. The tall, thin man in the long black coat – a strange thing to be wearing in summer weather, even at night – was talking to a round-faced man in more modern clothing, a beige sports coat. Even as Tyler watched, the tall man looked around as if concerned someone might be eavesdropping. Then he grabbed the man in the sports coat by his elbow

138

and marched him toward an open-sided gazebo in one corner of the park.

'They're going to that building over there,' Tyler said, jumping to his feet. 'Come on – we can go around and through the trees on the far side. We'll be able to hear what they're saying . . . !'

'What? Are you *crazy*?' Lucinda shrank away. 'I'm not going near that guy . . . !'

'What if he's the one who kidnapped Gideon? What if he's looking for him now?' Tyler couldn't believe his sister would go all girly on him at a time like this. 'Come on!'

Even as he led her around the edge of the grass, past all the people sitting on blankets staring up at the sky expectantly, she was still trying to talk him out of it. 'What about Carmen and the others? What about Jaime? Shouldn't we tell them—'

'We're only going to the other side of the park. Grow up, Luce!'

He hurried them through the trees and over a low picket fence until the gazebo stood only a couple of yards away. Lucinda looked absolutely miserable, so Tyler decided that he wouldn't climb the tree after all, although it would have let him shinny out on a branch until he was right over the roof of the building. Instead he moved as close as he could while still being ready to run at a moment's notice, until he could hear voices. He guessed that the high, slightly nervous tones belonged to the man in the beige coat.

'. . . Just don't understand it, that's all.'

'There is nothing to understand, Mr. Dankle.' *That* was Kingaree, Tyler had no doubt – a voice as menacing as a scorpion poised to sting. 'I have given you good American money already. To earn the rest of it, you will come when you are called and do what you are told.'

'Of course, of course! Haven't I helped you like I said I would?' The man was almost squeaking. 'I just have to think about . . . I have my reputation . . .'

'Listen to me, lawyer.' Kingaree's sudden words were like the crack of a gunshot. 'I have killed better men than you with my bare hands, so I would advise you *not to make me angry.*'

It was dark now, but Tyler could see Lucinda's pale face and staring eyes beside him. He prayed she didn't lose her nerve and make some noise that would give them away.

'Remember,' Kingaree went on, 'you are in this thing far too deep to start getting any pretty sensibilities now. When it is time I will call for you, and you had best be prepared to come with me. It will be at night. I suggest you keep your evenings free for the next few weeks.'

'What do you mean? When are you coming?'

'I do not know that, Mr. Dankle. But believe me, when the hour comes, you will be among the first to know. And you will do what you are told. *Do you understand me?*'

Dankle must have nodded, because suddenly Kingaree walked out of the gazebo and set out along the path at the edge of the park, his coat billowing like the wings of some great black bird. He strode past the seated families just as the first fireworks burst in the sky overhead, great, glittering, spark-dripping flowers of gold and red. People shouted in pleasure. Nobody except Tyler and Lucinda saw the tall man go – they were all too busy watching the fire in the sky.

# CHAPTER 16

## SEARCHING FOR ORDINARY

Hot sun. Chores to do. Animals to feed. Maybe a nap before dinner if she was lucky and got her work done early. Lucinda wouldn't have gone so far as to say things were back to normal, but as she and Tyler hiked across the fields toward the reptile barn she realized that for the first time in several days she didn't feel frightened.

Their great-uncle Gideon was still in the hospital but he'd be coming home today. The doctors at Liberty Medical Center still didn't know what was wrong with him, but Ragnar said Gideon was almost himself again, even though the period of his disappearance remained a blank.

'Okay, so what's he doing?' Tyler said. 'I still don't get it.'

Lucinda had been admiring her new bracelet, the

gift from Carmen, which made a very nice companion for the unicorn-hair one the Three Amigos had given her. She shook her head. 'Who? Doing what?'

'Kingaree! What's he up to with that Dankle guy, that lawyer?'

'How should I know? And what makes you think it has anything to do with us?'

Tyler stared at her. 'Duh! He's a really bad guy and *he came out of the Fault Line.* Everything about him has something to do with us, or at least with the farm.'

Lucinda frowned. The only problem with the new bracelet was that when she lowered her arm it slid all the way to her hand and the charms interfered with picking things up. She pushed it up her forearm until it felt snug. 'That doesn't mean it's anything to do with all the other stuff going on – Gideon and everything else you're obsessed with: Alamu and the fire and Octavio's Crazy-o-scope.'

'*Continuascope.* Yeah, that's the other thing.' Tyler frowned, trying to get his thoughts in order. 'Okay, so Gideon disappears, and just at the same time Kingaree comes back after all these years. Meanwhile, Colin's all "I'm researching the Continuascope"' – he did a terrible imitation of Colin's careful speech – 'which has been missing since the night of the laboratory fire. Which is also the night Kingaree disappeared. And you're telling me it's all coincidence?'

'I'm not saying it's *all* coincidence . . .' she began.

'So shut up, then.' But he smiled to show her he

143

was mostly kidding. For a moment she remembered both why she loved her little brother and why she often wanted to kill him. 'See, it would make sense that Kingaree stole the Continuascope and set the fire to cover up. But Mr. Walkwell says no – he says Alamu the dragon burned the lab down.' He grabbed his head like it hurt. 'Man! Am I missing anything?'

Lucinda smiled. 'Just your sanity.' She could see the reptile barn in the distance now and her heart rose a little. *I'm coming!* she thought, trying to send the idea ahead like a beam of light. *I'm bringing carrots!* A moment later she realized what she was doing – accusing her brother of being crazy while she tried to talk to a dragon with her mind.

'What are you laughing about?' Tyler didn't wait long for an answer. 'Anyway, something's missing here. I don't know what it is, but there's totally something missing. Why would Alamu be hanging around the lab? Why would he burn the place down?'

'Maybe it was the only way he could get somebody to shut up.'

For a moment Tyler actually looked puzzled, trying to make sense of what she'd said. Then he stuck his tongue out at her – something he hadn't done for a few years. 'Oh, yeah, thanks, Luce. You're a fat lot of help.'

Desta knuckle-walked on her folded wings and rear legs toward the front of the pen, head turned sideways as she slyly watched the bag of carrots in Lucinda's hand.

*I know you see them*, Lucinda told her – or at least thought at her. It was hard to tell sometimes how much of Lucinda's meaning Desta was receiving. *Yes, they're for you, greedy girl!*

*!* It was scarcely more than a wordless impulse, but it had meaning and Lucinda understood it clearly: *I want!*

Haneb trundled past with a wagon full of carcasses for Meseret, who was sleeping underneath the banks of sun lamps that helped to keep the reptile barn even warmer than the California summer outside. 'She wait for you, the young one,' he said. 'She know what time you here.'

'But I don't come here the same time every day,' Lucinda said.

Haneb shrugged. 'She know when you come, still. Very smart, the *illujankan*.' The strange word sounded like he was getting ready to spit. He smiled a little, embarrassed again, and translated. 'Dragons.'

'How do you know so much about them?' she asked, and held out the first carrot for Desta. The blue tongue curled, gently tugged, and the carrot disappeared from Lucinda's hand. *Good*, she thought. *Good girl!*

'I . . . I come with them. From where I was.'

What Ragnar had said was true, then. 'Will you tell me about it?'

He gaped at her, his one visible eye wide, the other

148

hidden by his curtain of hair. 'I have work. Sorry, Miss Lucinda. The big one must be fed.' He gestured to the wagon and the deer carcasses that were already drawing flies on this hot day. 'I have work.'

Which, Lucinda could tell, *really* meant: 'Please don't make me talk about it.' Ragnar had said he was already scarred when he came to Ordinary Farm as a child. 'Of course, Haneb, I'm sorry . . .'

'Oh, man,' Tyler said loudly. 'What are *you* doing here?'

She turned to see Colin Needle, who had stopped many yards away from Lucinda and the others, as if a deadly swamp lay between him and them.

'Don't start with me, Jenkins.'

'No, really, every time I turn around, there you are. You spying on us?' Tyler walked toward Colin, his hands dangling down at his sides, shoulders back, chest out.

'Stop it, Tyler.' *Boys*, thought Lucinda. *Always posturing.*

*Yes – males. So foolish, so fierce.*

For a moment Lucinda thought someone had said it out loud – a deep, resonant voice with a bass hum like a church organ. Then she realized it was in her head, and *only* in her head, and that it hadn't been words but only ideas. *Meseret?* Lucinda asked. *Is that you?* It was the first time she'd had a real communication from the big dragon since the night they had flown together.

146

*Well,* you *flew,* Lucinda corrected herself. *I mostly screamed and hung on. Do you remember?*

A faint impression of amusement touched her, followed by something much more harsh – an angry thought that scalded like acid. *Night they stole my egg. Night* that *creature stole my egg.* Meseret clearly knew who Colin was. The massive dragon stretched, suddenly restless in her harness, and the heavy industrial fabric creaked.

*But she's here now,* Lucinda thought hurriedly – she didn't want to see Colin Needle burned to ashes. *Your baby, your egg, she's alive and safe. See?*

*Carrots.* This nudging thought drifted over from Desta. *Have more. Give!*

Tyler and Colin were still staring each other down. 'What are you babbling about now, Jenkins?' the older boy said. 'Do you think I *want* to be here? With these monsters?' He cast a quick, fearful look toward Meseret. 'I was sent to get you. Personally, I'd be happy to leave you to your little games and your –' he looked from Lucinda to the baby dragon – 'animal friends.'

*He could be nice if he wanted to,* Lucinda thought. Every now and then he showed it. Why did Colin Needle always turn back into such a creep?

*Angry.* It was feelings that came to her, not words, and they came from Desta. *Frightened. Tangled.*

Lucinda almost dropped the bag of carrots. It was the first time she had ever had anything but the

147

simplest communication from Desta, anything but childlike greed, pleasure, or discontent.

'It's about Gideon,' Colin continued sullenly. 'My mother called to say they're bringing him home from the hospital. If you really want to be off doing something else when he comes back, fine, be my guest. But it will look pretty bad.'

*Desta, tell me that again,* Lucinda thought, but the dragon was distracted now by the carrots in Lucinda's hand. After a few more fruitless attempts to communicate, she gave Desta the last of them as Colin watched.

'Huh. She really does like you.' The tall boy sounded a little wistful. Of course, it was his own fault if the dragons didn't like him, Lucinda thought – he had kidnapped Desta when she was in her egg, after all. But to be fair, he hadn't known there was a live baby dragon inside.

'You look nice today, Colin,' she said, trying to be pleasant in turn. Tyler, who had been ready to slug the older boy a moment before, stared at her in disgusted disbelief. 'Very dressed up.'

He seemed surprised by the compliment. 'Thank you. Well, since it's Gideon's first day back, I thought . . .' He stopped abruptly and shook his head as though he had caught himself doing something dangerous. 'Anyway, I'll wait for you outside. I don't really want to be set on fire today.' He backed toward the entrance.

'I guess we'd better follow him,' said Lucinda. She

had one last carrot for Desta, but had to dig deep into her pocket. When she found it and extended her hand, the charm bracelet slid down and clinked to a stop around her wrist.

Desta lunged so swiftly that Lucinda barely even saw her move, striking like an angry rattlesnake, but instead of grabbing at the final carrot the dragon's long teeth snagged in Lucinda's bracelet and snapped it loose from her wrist. The bracelet dropped into Desta's pen even as Lucinda staggered back, shocked by the sudden attack.

*Desta, no!* she thought as forcefully as she could, angry but also fearful that the young dragon would swallow the bracelet and harm herself. *Don't you dare!* But Desta ignored her, moving toward the shiny thing as though nothing else existed in the world.

*I said NO!* It happened so quickly Lucinda didn't understand it for a moment: the young dragon jumped back as if burned, then crouched down, hissing as though she had been struck. But it wasn't just that Lucinda's angry thoughts had scared her.

*I made her do that,* Lucinda realized. *I made her move back just with my thoughts . . . !* It hadn't felt good at all, forcing the young dragon away from the bracelet against her greedy will, but somehow Lucinda had reached out and . . . and made her do it.

*Wow,* she thought. *What just happened?*

While Lucinda and Desta stood staring at each other, the alarmed dragon's fins erect and quivering at the sides of her head, Haneb leaped forward and pulled the silver bracelet out with the handle of his rake, then shoved it into Lucinda's hand as if it was stolen property. 'Hide it, or else she will try again to take it. Don't bring things like this here.' He sounded cross, as if Lucinda had done something very foolish.

'Things like this?' She stared at the young dragon, who was pretending not to care, but whose orange eyes stared hungrily at the silvery object as it disappeared into Lucinda's pocket. 'What do you mean?'

*Stop why? Scare Desta! Pretty. Love that.* The smallest dragon was sulking.

'Dragons like all shiny things – silver and gold and metal and glass.' Haneb gently steered Lucinda further back from Desta's fence. 'Alamu is worst bad of all. His nest must be full of all shiny things he find or steal.'

Lucinda didn't even resist as Haneb hurried her and Tyler out of the barn. She wasn't worried about the bracelet, which could be fixed, but she was *very* excited about what else had happened.

*The dragons were talking to me!* she thought. *I was really learning something about them! But how did I make Desta move like that? It was like she was . . . a puppet or something . . .*

Colin Needle was waiting for them outside. He looked so pathetic on his own that Lucinda said, 'You missed all the excitement. It wasn't quite the same as Meseret spitting fire at you, but Desta just tried to pull my arm off!'

150

'Don't, Luce,' said Tyler in a sharp, warning tone that made her angry – what right did he have to stop her talking to Colin?

'Well, she did! She grabbed this bracelet on my arm. Haneb said that dragons love shiny things – that they'll steal them any chance they get . . . !'

'Lucinda, stop . . . !' Her brother was obviously upset.

She turned on him. 'No, *you* shut up, Tyler Jenkins! I'm tired of you telling me what to do.' She half expected to find Colin looking at her gratefully because she'd stuck up for him, but instead the older boy was staring at her brother. Tyler stared right back at him, both of them showing their teeth and glaring like puppies playing tug-of-war with a toy.

*Boys!* she thought again. *Meseret was so right . . .*

Strangely, Hector Carrillo and all three Carrillo children were waiting out in front of the farm's main gate when Lucinda and Tyler and the others from the house pulled up in the horse-cart. Lucinda couldn't help wonder who had told them Gideon was coming back.

'I offered to drive Gideon home from the hospital,' said Mr. Carrillo, patting the fender of his truck, 'but your Mrs. Needle wouldn't hear of it. "Too much trouble," she says. "We'll just take a cab."'

'She's not *our* Mrs. Needle,' growled Tyler. Still angry, Lucinda shushed him. Colin was standing only a short distance away, craning his neck to look for Gideon – or was it his mother he was waiting for so anxiously? Colin might be a strange, difficult boy, Lucinda thought, but Patience Needle was a complete nightmare. How could anyone expect the poor kid to be normal?

They saw the plume of dust from the farm road long before they saw the cab, but soon it appeared, a white-and-red smear against the brown of the hills. A few moments later the car pulled up beside the tall fence and the gate. It took a little while for big Ragnar to unfold himself from the back seat, then more time to help Gideon out while Mrs. Needle paid the driver. Judging by the look on his face as he pulled away, Lucinda guessed she hadn't given the man much of a tip, if any.

Gideon looked small and unwell, but what was worse was that he almost didn't seem to notice what was going on, letting Ragnar help him but scarcely even looking up as the folks from the farm gathered around. Mr. Carrillo stepped forward with his hand extended.

'Nice to see you back, Gideon,' said Hector. 'I hope when you've had a few days to recuperate we can have that conversation I've been waiting for.'

Gideon looked down at Hector Carrillo's hand as if he didn't know what it was, then turned away and continued trudging toward the gate.

'He is still not well,' Mrs. Needle said – not

apologizing, but in a tone that suggested Mr. Carrillo should know that and should leave him alone. 'I'm sure he will be happy to speak to you when he's feeling better.' She hurried after Gideon as the old man shuffled toward the gate on Ragnar's arm, as though she could not bear to be separated from him for long.

'Wow,' said Carmen Carrillo. 'He looks *weird*. I thought somebody said he was better.'

Mr. Walkwell looked troubled. 'I apologize for Gideon, Hector,' he said. 'Ragnar said he was much better, but now he seems ill again. Perhaps the ride made him that way. Those cars are foul things.'

'Yes, but *somebody* has to talk to me soon, Simos,' said Mr. Carrillo. 'Stillman's calling me every day. I can't wait forever. I've been begging for Gideon to deal with this for months!'

Mr. Walkwell pulled him aside for a quiet conversation. Colin and the other farm folk stood watching as Ragnar lifted Gideon onto the wagon, then followed after as it creaked back toward the house, all of them on foot this time as though walking behind a funeral procession. The thought made Lucinda shiver.

'So what's going on with him, anyway?' Steve Carrillo asked. 'Dude, he looked like a zombie.'

'He didn't even look like himself,' said little Alma. 'Like the real Gideon is lost in there somewhere.' She hugged herself as if the hot day had made her shiver.

Mr. Carrillo returned, his conversation with Mr. Walkwell finished. He did not look happy. '*Vamonos,* kids,' he said. 'In the truck. We're not going to get anything done here today.'

Lucinda waved as they drove off, but the Carrillo kids just looked embarrassed. As Mr. Walkwell turned the cart back toward the house, Lucinda realized her brother had been silent nearly the whole time since the reptile barn – Tyler hadn't even said anything to Steve Carrillo or asked what he was playing on his GameBoss.

*That proves it,* she thought gloomily. *The world really is coming to an end.*

# CHAPTER 17

## THE FAMOUS AND ANCIENT BOTTLE-CAP HOARD

According to Mr. Walkwell, the male dragon, Alamu, was around the night of the laboratory fire and had probably even caused it. Octavio Tinker's Continuascope had been gone since then. Jackson Kingaree had also disappeared that night, but hadn't shown any sign of having the Continuascope then or since. And Haneb said dragons, and especially Alamu, loved to collect shiny things for their nests. The Continuascope had been *very* shiny.

*Elementary, my dear Watson,* Tyler thought. Find Alamu's nest, find the Continuascope. More important, make sure *Colin Needle* didn't find it, because if Colin got hold of Octavio's invention he'd be able to use the Fault Line. He'd be able to travel back and forth through time. In fact, Colin might even find a way into the washstand mirror world to rescue Grace, and then

Gideon would put *him* in the will instead of Tyler and Lucinda.

The biggest problem, of course, was that Lucinda had opened her mouth and started babbling about dragons and shiny things and what Haneb said *right in front of Colin Needle*. Yes, if someone forced him, Tyler would have admitted that he loved his sister, but right now he didn't *like* her very much. Colin might be a total jerkwad but he wasn't stupid – he would definitely be thinking the same things as Tyler was.

So it all came down to two questions: where was Alamu's nest, and how could he get to it before Colin did?

Almost halfway through his second summer on the farm now, Tyler knew better than to walk around asking people where Alamu kept his hoard. He didn't want to talk about it to Lucinda either, even if he hadn't been angry with her, because he knew she would have a fit at the idea of him going anywhere near a dragon's nest. His sister was the kind of kid who always waited for the grown-ups to fix things. They *didn't*, of course, which was why she was grumpy a lot. Tyler had figured out a long time ago that if you wanted something you had to do it yourself: if he was hungry for cookies, he scavenged money from under the sofa cushions and went and bought some at the store, because Mom sure as heck wasn't going to bake any. But finding double-stuffed Choco-Marshes in the grocery aisle had to be easier than finding a dragon's nest in a farm the size of a state park.

It turned out to be a good time to ask questions. With Gideon back at home, people were bustling in and out of the house all day long and Tyler had plenty of opportunities to talk to the farm hands. Kiwa, one of the three Mongol herdsmen and the one who spoke the least English, still managed to tell Tyler a few things he hadn't known, and his fellows Jeg and Hoka were even more help, letting Tyler know all the places that Alamu seemed to frequent. Even Ragnar had useful information to offer.

'Of course he spends a lot of time around the reptile barn because that is where his mate and her child live,' he told Tyler, 'and he comes there when we put food out as well, but he also spends many warm afternoons in the sun on that rocky hill there.' The big Norseman pointed to a distant granite face, a shiny smear along one of the hills that fenced the valley. 'Why do you write down these things, boy? You are not going to go near the worm, are you? He will kill you and eat you. That is no joke.'

'Trust me – I don't want to go anywhere near him,' Tyler said, which was true. 'I'm just making notes.' Ragnar's hard green eyes were full of doubt; Tyler began to regret having asked him anything in the first place. 'Okay, I have a sort of . . . bet with Colin Needle. That I can predict something better than he can. I don't want even to *see* Alamu; I just want to figure out where he goes. Honestly, it's nothing important . . .'

Just then Ragnar was called to help Mr. Walkwell with something, but Tyler knew he'd better stay away from the big man from now on – Ragnar suspected that something was up. That was certainly something they didn't teach you in school: how to deal with a suspicious Viking.

To his delight, Tyler discovered that little Pema, the young Tibetan woman who worked in the kitchen, had been paying attention to the dragon as well.

'I love to watch him fly,' she said, and he could see how much she meant it – her dark eyes were shining with excitement. 'When I was young my grandmother told me stories of the dragons – we call the country my family came from *Druk Yul*, the Dragon Land. So it is a great goodness to live so close to them now. And Alamu . . .' She blushed and smiled. She was older than Tyler had realized – not a girl but a young woman who just happened to be small. 'He is so beautiful. His wings are like hammered copper! The dragons are messengers of the gods, you know.'

Tyler wasn't certain what to say to that, but he was definitely interested in hearing more. 'Do you see him in the same place all the time?'

Pema shook her head. 'He flies past sometimes on his way out to the east.' She pointed over the gardens toward the distant hills. 'Sometimes he also flies over the garden, looking for things to catch – rabbits, other animals. But for some reason he does not like to fly above the garden this summer . . .'

Tyler wrote everything down. Pema was a careful observer, and the fact that she considered every sighting of Alamu to be a good omen meant she had plenty of information to share.

On his way out of the kitchen Tyler met Colin Needle. Colin was looking for extra blankets to help his mother prepare Gideon's new bed in the Snake Parlour, where she could nurse him and still keep an eye on everything else in her domain. Tyler was delighted to see that Colin was being kept on a short leash.

'Staying busy, are we?' he asked.

Colin glared at him. 'You'd better not be going anywhere, Jenkins. Everyone's supposed to stay around the house and help.'

'Oh, don't worry,' Tyler said. 'I *am* helping . . . in my own way.' He was enjoying Colin's discomfort. 'In fact, I should get going – and so should you. Don't want to keep your mother waiting.'

'You'd better not leave the house,' Colin almost hissed. 'You can't afford to get into any more trouble!'

'And who's going to stop me? You?' Tyler stepped around him. 'Run along now. Help your mother. Be a good boy.'

Colin just stared, as if he couldn't believe that Tyler

would dare to talk back to him. 'You . . . you have quite a big mouth, Jenkins, and one of these days . . .'

'Colin!' Mrs. Needle shouted from the Snake Parlour. 'Where are you?'

Tyler waved as he walked away. 'Enjoy your afternoon!' He made a point of sauntering out the front door in case Colin had doubled back to watch. It would drive him crazy to think that Tyler might already be going out in search of the nest.

*Dude, this is crazy,* Tyler thought. *Who would ever believe I'd be glad I took math?*

But his teacher, Ms. Shah, had taught him how to make a Cartesian Plane, which was basically a piece of graph paper with a big cross in the middle of it and a zero at the centre point and numbers going off in each direction so that they made a cross. Each number then became half of a coordinate, so Tyler drew the whole thing in pencil on a copy of an Ordinary Farm map from the Yokuts County Assessor's Office he'd found in the library and then began marking in everything the farm workers had told him about where they usually saw Alamu. When he'd finished with that he spread his newly marked map over his bed and studied it.

Tyler needed to find the place the male dragon went back to every time – that would probably be his nest. So if he marked every position where the dragon had been sighted, then drew a big circle around every mark, the place where the most circles overlapped should be a good central place to start looking for a nest . . . and in fact, Tyler thought he'd spotted a likely area: all of the dragon's favourite hang-outs seemed about the same distance away from the high hills on the western edge of the farm, an isolated area far from neighbours and roads.

*So let's have a look for that nest of yours, dragon-dude,* Tyler thought, *and all your shiny treasures. But not tonight – no way.* The idea of hunting for a dragon's nest in the dark frightened even Tyler the Impulsive. *No, I'll go tomorrow, when the sun's up and you're out making your rounds . . .*

The next day he raced through his chores so quickly that even Mr. Walkwell (who himself hardly ever slept or even took a break) suggested he might be working too hard. When he had finished he made himself a sack lunch, then waited to set out until Colin Needle was upstairs being lectured by his mother.

It took Tyler a good part of an hour to cross the farm and reach the hills where most of the Alamu reports seemed to overlap. According to his marked-up county map the tallest hill was called Miners Mountain; he decided that would be the best place to start looking, because even if he didn't find anything on the hill itself he'd have a good view from the top.

The late-morning sun was already baking the ground, and the dry grasses were buzzing with insect noises. Before Tyler reached the top (and had found

161

no sign of Alamu's nest) he'd emptied half his canteen; by the time he'd eaten his sandwich he'd drunk most of the rest. The scrubby trees on the hillside didn't provide much shade either.

An hour later he had finished the rest of his water, had watched the sun move across the valley like someone slow-wiping a window clean, and had stared through his binoculars until his eyes hurt, but still hadn't located anything that looked the least bit like a dragon's nest. He had also discovered that some of the bugs singing in the dry grass liked to bite people – liked it quite a lot, in fact. He was beginning to rethink the entire expedition when he noticed something glimmering in a fold of a hill near Miners Mountain.

Even with the binoculars he couldn't make out much more than a glint in the undergrowth, so he didn't leap up; he had already been fooled a couple of times by other shining things, discarded bottles, glass insulators from power lines. But though he stared and stared through the expensive binoculars his father had given him as a guilty late-birthday gift, this particular bright spot remained stubbornly mysterious.

Tyler finally decided that although it was mid-afternoon already, he should go down Miners Mountain and climb the other hill now. Who knew when he'd get this much free time again?

Tyler didn't know the name of this second hill, but discovered quickly that although it was not as tall as Miners Mountain it was actually a much more difficult climb, with no obvious trail and the way up blocked by tangled undergrowth and outcrops of layered stone that looked like haphazard piles of books. Each outcropping had to be either climbed or avoided, and by the time Tyler had got near the top even more of the afternoon had slid away and the sun was hurrying down the sky like an animal going to ground. For the first time Tyler started to worry. He didn't want to have to climb down the rocky, dangerous slope in darkness, and he had left the house so early he hadn't even thought of bringing a flashlight.

*Lucinda's right – I really do stupid things sometimes,* he told himself angrily.

He clambered up over the last large bulge of pale stone and into the shade of a tangle of oak and madrone trees, where he crouched to catch his breath. He forced himself to get up again after only a couple of minutes and climbed the last hundred feet of the uneven slope, then stepped out onto the flat, windswept summit of the hill. And there it lay in front of him – not just a single object, but a shining, sparkling line several feet long snaking through a trail of trampled grass. He'd found it!

Tyler's heart sped in triumph. He hurried toward the glittering track, then slowed, looking high and low to make sure that no one, scaly or otherwise, was watching him. Heart pounding, he paused beside his discovery . . .

. . . And found that it was nothing but a few

dozen bottle caps strewn across the hilltop like confetti.

'Huh?' Tyler stared, disbelief rapidly turning into fury. What was this crap? Was this *it*? The thing he'd been searching for all day – the grail he had climbed two high, hot hillsides to find?

'Crap,' he said, kicking at one of the shiny things. 'Look at me,' he shouted in disgust, 'Oh, yeah, I'm a hero! I've found *the famous hoard of ancient bottle caps*!'

And they weren't even that ancient – most of them looked as if they were from regular modern pop bottles. So they weren't even worth anything.

Tyler reached for his canteen, then remembered it was empty. Was this pathetic scatter really Alamu's secret hoard of treasure? Bottle caps, a couple of shiny pennies and a few bits of foil? Disgusted and very tired, Tyler was about to admit defeat and head back down the hill when he noticed the bottle caps weren't just scattered, or at least they didn't look completely random, but lay in a rough line. In places the line stopped completely, but as he squinted his eyes against the afternoon light he could see that they did form a kind of trail across the hilltop, as if something had dropped them from a clumsy, toothy mouth . . .

*On the way to . . . where . . . ?*

He squinted harder, doing his best to follow the almost invisible line, which petered out at the top of the slope facing away from the distant farmhouse. Then he looked down and saw another flash of reflected light in a clump of undergrowth about twenty yards down the steep slope – something very much larger than any bottle cap. He almost lost his balance several times as he hurried down the slope, racing the dying afternoon. As he drew nearer he saw that it was not an aimless growth of shrubs and small trees but a pile of trees and sticks and branches almost fifty feet wide, the sticks covered with brown leaves and the whole mass propped between the twisted trunks of several madrone trees growing at an angle on the hillside.

It was a nest. A very big nest.

*I found it!* he thought. *I was right! I did it all by myself!*

Tyler began to make his way down the slope, leaning so far backward to keep his balance that half the time he just gave up and slid down on his butt. Alamu, whether from brains or instinct, had built his nest on the far side of the hill from the farmhouse, out of sight, with nothing but the trail of bottle caps on top to lead whoever it was supposed to impress . . . Meseret, pretty obviously . . . to where the real thing was hidden just below the crest.

As he got near the thicket Tyler realized he was making a lot of noise and settled into a crouch. There hadn't been any sign of Alamu, but he couldn't see the whole nest because of the trees and the angle of the hill and he certainly didn't want to encounter an angry dragon on this naked hillside . . .

The wind changed direction, and as the animal stench of the dragon's nest struck him he realized he had been upwind of it all this time: if Alamu had been home, he would have smelled Tyler a long time ago. He could almost hear Lucinda asking him whether he *wanted* to get eaten.

The closer he got, the stranger and more impressive the nest appeared, a huge shape wedged between the madrone trunks like a bushy flower-head. It might be hidden from the farmhouse, but Alamu had still built it right out in the open, with all the arrogance of his position at the top of the food chain, and then filled it with his scavenged treasures – hubcaps, bicycle wheels, a crutch, wire fencing, aluminium garden furniture, all things that had glittered once, though many were rusted now. Tyler wondered how long it had taken the dragon to collect so much junk with no way to carry it but claws and jaws. The variety was amazing – there was even an artificial Christmas tree like a toilet brush made of tinsel. If Alamu had indeed stolen the Continuascope, then this had to be the place to find it.

He looked around for the dragon once more, then climbed carefully down into the nest, which swayed in a very alarming way: Tyler had to grab onto a huge tangle of baling wire to keep himself upright. Several seconds passed before he was sure that the whole thing wouldn't slide down from between the trees and take him tobogganing down the hill in a pile of jagged rusty metal. How did it support the dragon, which must weigh something like a thousand pounds?

Tyler eased forward like a man crossing a frozen but thawing river, stopping at each unusual sound or movement beneath him, and as he moved he sifted cautiously through the dragon's hoard, bits of pipe, chrome from cars, the rusted remains of a giant ceiling fan as big as the propeller of an ocean liner. Tyler couldn't even imagine where Alamu had found *that*.

Not only was he becoming more and more desperate to find the Continuascope before the light failed, the bottom of the nest had proved itself little more than a loose weave of madrone branches, so he kept his head down as he moved.

*'Owww! Rotten lizard and his stupid trash!'*

The sudden sound of a human voice was so startling that Tyler almost lost his grip and tumbled through the bottom of the nest. Colin Needle's pale face appeared before him, sucking on a bloody finger. When the older boy saw Tyler a flurry of emotions passed over his face – surprise, a little fear, but most of all, triumph.

'You! You creep!' Tyler shouted up at him. 'You followed me!'

'Really? You figured that out, did you, Jenkins?' Colin rubbed his finger on the sleeve of his shirt, leaving a bloody smear. 'So what? I would have found it myself if my mother hadn't made me do all those stupid chores.'

Tyler began to clamber across the mat of branches and junk, heading straight toward the older boy.

'Yeah? Well, she'll have a chore of her own – putting your face back on after I beat if off you!'

Colin's eyes widened. 'Stop! Right now!'

'Why?' said Tyler. 'You going to stop me?'

Colin looked more terrified than dangerous. 'Just . . . stop, Jenkins. I'm serious. Behind you . . .'

'Oh, nice one . . . !' Tyler began, then a huge shadow fell across him and he whirled to see Alamu sweeping down from the hilltop, wings spread. Tyler tried to throw himself forward to where Colin crouched at the edge of the nest but he could not make it. He heard Alamu's deep rumble of fury as the gliding dragon darted its long head at him and just missed by inches, then the orange-and-bronze monster swept past, wheeled in the air, and hurtled back toward him again, little pennants of fire trailing from its open mouth. Tyler tried to scramble out toward Colin Needle, but before he could reach the edge of the nest the part beneath his feet suddenly shuddered and then collapsed and Tyler tumbled into a chaos of broken branches and rusting metal.

# CHAPTER 18

## ANGEL WITH A FIERY SWORD

With Gideon downstairs in the Snake Parlour all of the house staff had been tiptoeing in and out to have a look at him, thrilled to have the master of the farm home again, but when Lucinda saw him it shook her badly. Her great-uncle was sitting up and eating broth from a spoon, but he didn't quite *look* right, although she wasn't certain exactly why. It was obviously Gideon, and he was still able to talk – she heard him grumbling a warning at Pema when the nervous young woman almost spilled some water on him – but his eyes were sunken and bloodshot, and he looked at almost everyone who came close as if he suspected them of trying to harm him. Yes, she realized, that was it – Gideon Goldring looked like one of his own less pleasant animals, peering out of its cage at its captors.

Mrs. Needle seemed to think everything was as it

should be, though, and it was true that he didn't make those faces at *her:* instead, Gideon looked up at the witch like a trusting child. She even made encouraging little noises as he slurped his broth or drank water, which made Lucinda feel sick to her stomach. She wondered whether Gideon had suffered some kind of stroke or something really bad, but no one was telling them.

*Well,* she thought, *if they're trying to hide it from us, maybe they shouldn't move his bedroom downstairs where we all have to see him . . .*

'Where are you going?' Mrs. Needle asked as Lucinda sidled toward the door. 'I might need you to run an errand for me.'

The last thing Lucinda wanted to do was spend all day here in this room, under the cold, watchful eyes of Patience Needle. 'Oh, I'll be back really quick,' she said. 'I just wanted to . . . to pick some flowers in the garden. To brighten the room up.'

'The garden,' said Gideon, nodding, his eyes not quite focused on anything. 'We lived in the garden once.'

'Huh?' Lucinda took a step back. 'What did you say, Uncle Gideon?'

'The garden.' Her great-uncle spoke as though it was an ordinary conversation, but what he said next showed that it wasn't. 'We had to leave. Angel . . . an angel chased us out. With a flaming sword. You saw him, didn't you? Or was that the serpent . . . ?'

'Hush, Gideon, you're confused,' Mrs. Needle said, which seemed a bit of an understatement. 'Just finish your broth.'

Suddenly the old man seemed to see Lucinda for the first time. He leaned forward, fingers outstretched as though he might grab at her, but she was well out of his reach. 'But listen . . .' He looked around as though worried about eavesdroppers, then turned his red, staring eyes to Lucinda once more. *'We can go back. Yes! We can sneak past the angel and get back into that lovely garden again . . .'*

Lucinda could not bear to listen to any more of Gideon's crazy ramblings. She turned and all but ran for the door.

*I know he wasn't talking about this place, not* this *garden,* Lucinda thought as she made her way down the rows, *but this part of the property still creeps me out sometimes.*

The huge garden spread down from the slightly higher spot where the house stood, or at least where the main and largest part of the house stood, and stretched across what would have been at least a city block back home, most of it overgrown and neglected. Only Mrs. Needle's herbs and Sarah's vegetable patch, both of which covered quite a bit of space at the end nearest the kitchen, looked as though they were regularly tended. The rest of the sprawling garden, with its rioting plants, overgrown paths, vine-choked arbours, and corroded greenhouse almost buried in vegetation, looked more like the remnants of some ancient civilization that the jungle had reclaimed.

It took a while for Lucinda to find the rose bushes she had been thinking of – the garden, like the farmhouse itself, could be a slippery place to find your way around – but she located them at last along a wooden fence some ten or eleven rows on from the old greenhouse. Lucinda thought it was a little strange that although the roses looked completely untended, the stems tangled in each other and many of the blooms brown and withered, the rose arbour had a smell as if someone had been putting fresh fertilizer on it, a pungent stink that made her want to hold her nose. Then, as she went down the length of the rose bed clipping the stems of the flowers that had just started to bloom, she stepped on something squishily unpleasant.

It felt so wrong that she was reluctant to lift her shoe, afraid to find she had trodden on a slug or some kind of animal dropping. When she finally worked up the courage to look, it was even worse – she had stepped on a dead mouse.

Except it was still moving.

Lucinda leaped back with a cry of disgust and horror. The dying mouse's legs paddled weakly, as though it was trying to swim, then slowed and stopped.

She stared at it from a safe distance. Whoever heard of a mouse being slow enough for a human to step on? What if it had rabies? The very thought made Lucinda's toes curl. She yanked off her shoe and scraped it on a wooden fence post until she thought she would be sick, then pounded the sole in the dirt, trying to make sure every last bit of the mouse was gone, but suddenly in her mind she stood in a cloud of invisible rabies germs. Didn't people say there was no cure? Or was that something else? What would her mother say? What if she had to have rabies shots . . . her friend at school had told her they injected them *in your stomach* . . . !

The unexpected sound of voices made her jump, but it was only Pema and Azinza laughing as they picked vegetables from the kitchen garden. She looked back down at the mouse carcass and for a disturbing second thought she saw it moving again – some kind of unkillable zombie mouse – but then realized that the movement was fleas and other small creatures deserting the corpse.

'Gross,' she said out loud. There was a daddy-long-legs struggling away too – surely *that* hadn't been on the mouse. But in fact many different kinds of bugs were all walking and hopping in the same direction, like a tiny parade. Horrified but fascinated, Lucinda bent and followed them along for several feet.

'But why would they all do that?' Several roly-polies joined the little procession. It was beginning to look like some kind of bug protest march. She poked with a twig at one of the roly-polies, which curled into a ball until she stopped, but then it got right back up and trundled after the others toward the back of the garden.

Lucinda followed the procession for several more yards as it was joined by other streams of tiny creatures, beetles and spiders and pillbugs. She also discovered that it was not the only such line – several other streams were winding through the leaning rows and tangled plants, all seemingly headed in the same direction. Lucinda was beginning to wish she had Tyler with her, or even Colin Needle, but both boys had left the house hours earlier.

She saw a lump lying only an inch or two away from the little procession she was following. *Ick*, she thought – *a dead bird. But they're all just walking past it! Don't bugs, like, eat dead stuff? Where are they going?*

She straightened up until she could see where the lines seemed to be converging – the old greenhouse, which loomed from the tangle of wild plants like a rock in an angry sea. Its high, peaked roof and all the glass made it look a bit like an abandoned church. The iron frame, once painted green, that held the glass had long ago become a ghostly rust-coloured skeleton, except for the roof and the ornamental weathervane, both mostly scorched black. In some places the bars had even melted and changed shape, sagging like taffy. It almost looked as though there had been a fire here, like the one in Gideon's lab that so obsessed her brother. But it didn't only smell like a fire: Lucinda was still very aware of the sweet stink she had noticed earlier,

174

as though something much larger than any mouse or bird lay rotting nearby. Was that what was drawing all the bugs, some big thing like a dead raccoon in the ruined greenhouse? But that didn't make sense – if all the little creatures wanted was to scavenge on a dead animal, why had they marched past the bird as if they didn't even notice it?

A dead cat, lying sprawled at the base of the greenhouse as though it had fallen from a great height, nearly made Lucinda turn around and head back to the house, but instead of clearing up the mystery it only made it stranger, because it was surrounded by the bodies of dozens of smaller creatures, mostly insects and birds, while the streams of bugs and other tiny creatures wound through this accident scene without even slowing, vanishing at last into cracks in the greenhouse glass or holes in the ground at the base of the old structure.

'What the heck is *in* there?' Lucinda asked, talking out loud again because she was badly spooked. She stepped over the bodies, most of which seemed quite recent, until she had nearly reached the dusty glass of the greenhouse. If she hadn't been able to hear Azinza singing something only a hundred feet away, with Pema shyly chiming in, she might have turned and bolted. Just the smell was beginning to get to her, but she also knew Tyler would look at her like she was the girliest girl in the world if he found out she had retreated without even examining the greenhouse.

Still, she wasn't going to be stupid about it. She turned and shouted to the two women at the other side of the garden.

'Hey, Pema, Azinza!'

Tall Azinza turned, shading her eyes. 'Hello, Lucinda!'

'There's something really strange about this greenhouse,' she called. 'A funny smell . . . and there are all these dead animals . . . !'

'What?' Azinza said something to Pema. 'I can't hear you!'

Lucinda was struck by a sudden worry. Was Mrs. Needle making some kind of witchy *poison* in there? But surely she would have done a better job hiding it . . . 'Could you come over here and look?' she called to the two kitchen women.

'We come to you!' Azinza called back, then led little Pema toward the space between the rows. From a distance and despite the different colours of their skins, they looked like a mother and child.

As she waited for them Lucinda stared at the scorch-marks and the charred husks of vegetation that lay around the base of the greenhouse like a shadow. How could you have a fire just here but not have it affect the plants growing *inside* the greenhouse? As Azinza and Pema came down the garden toward her she leaned closer to the greenhouse and tried to see through the dirty glass. The inside was so full of leaves that she couldn't make out anything, as if a crowd of green people were covering the panes with their hands to keep outsiders from looking in. Just beside where she stood, one of the panes had been pushed a little way out of its paint-flaking iron frame by the exuberant plant life inside. Without thinking she reached out to push the square of glass back into place and it tilted and fell out, breaking into two pieces on the ground.

For a moment Lucinda could only stare at the pale, wispy plume that snaked out of the opening – was it smoke? Was something *burning* in there? Then the wind changed direction and swirled the powdery cloud into her face. She gasped in surprise, accidentally sucking some of it into her nose and mouth – dusty, gritty, *itchy* . . . Her skin felt as if it was on fire. 'Oh, God,' she cried, but could barely force the words from her throat, 'my face! Help, my face . . . !'

'We are coming!' Azinza shouted, but the African woman seemed to be getting further away, not nearer. Eyes streaming with tears, cheeks burning, Lucinda blindly reached out her hands. Why wouldn't anyone help her?

She fell to the ground. Hands pulled at her, trying to drag her back to her feet, but Lucinda barely noticed them. Her throat was on fire, and her thoughts were drifting away into the darkness like dying sparks.

# CHAPTER 19

## WHAT TO DO WITH AN ANGRY DRAGON

The first thing he realized was that something was holding him by one arm in mid-air, like a giant about to grind his bones for bread. Dizzy, he opened his eyes and squinted up through the swirling dust, but whatever had him was not the dragon – something was pinching his wrist quite painfully. He kicked his feet but there was nothing beneath him, and no matter how he stretched he couldn't find anywhere to perch – he was caught like a fish on a hook. And where was the dragon? Tyler was still in one piece, so it clearly hadn't been able to reach him. Was it sniffing silently around for him even now?

It'll be dark soon, he realized. If he didn't get himself down before then, nobody was going to find him – nobody but the dragon. *Colin was here*, he abruptly remembered. *That little cheater followed me!*

He wanted to call out, but he didn't dare make that much noise.

Whatever held him seemed to be wrapped around his wrist. Instead of trying to get his feet onto something, he used all his strength to pull himself up with his trapped arm until he could reach his free hand above his head and try to find something else to grab. He had never tried to do a one-handed pull-up, and it was all he could do not to scream in agony at the effort it took, but at last, after some desperate scrabbling, he found a horizontal fence post in the tangle; once he could pull with both hands he lifted himself up until he could get his feet onto one of the madrone branches that held the nest. When he had regained his breath he took his weight off the arm that had held it so long and managed to twist it loose from whatever had grabbed it. Only when he had done this did he understand that what had saved him was the unicorn-hair bracelet Jeg had tied around his wrist. He reached out again and eased it loose from the old-fashioned television antenna on which it had caught. He wasn't going to leave such a good-luck charm behind, especially when he still had to find a way to exit the nest without the dragon getting him.

Something shifted above him, making the clutter of junk bob and groan a little, and for a terrifying moment Tyler felt sure Alamu was looking for him there, but the shape above his head was much smaller than the winged monster – in fact, it was only a bit bigger than Tyler himself.

'Is that you, Needle? Come down here so I can slug you.'

The shape moved and the tangle swayed a bit, so that Tyler had to shield his face from a cascade of small metal objects. 'Oh, yeah, Jenkins,' said Colin's voice. Tyler still couldn't quite see him. 'And why don't you shout a little louder to make certain the dragon hears you?'

'You little snot. You followed me!'

'I already told you, Jenkins, I would have found it first if you hadn't got a head start . . . !'

'Liar! Where's the Continuascope?'

'You didn't find it?' Colin sounded surprised by Tyler's question – in fact, he seemed genuinely pleased.

'You know I didn't. You probably climbed down and looked while I was knocked out.'

Colin snorted. 'Not likely. First of all, I can't even *see* you . . .'

A wide shadow flicked by overhead and they both looked up. 'Oh, man,' Tyler said, 'he came back – the dragon came back! Crap!' He did his best to work himself further down into the shifting heaps of dragon treasures without dislodging anything major, especially anything that might be keeping him from falling out the bottom of the nest. It was painful – a dozen things dug into him or stabbed him as he forced himself down into the clutter – a kettle, old cans, a bent and chewed cookie sheet . . .

Alamu landed with a sudden crash that set the entire nest rattling and swaying and almost made Tyler shout in terror. The dragon-stink, musky and harsh as ammonia, got right into his nose and made it hard not to cough or sneeze. The beast roared, then roared again, so close it made Tyler's skull rattle. As the echoes rolled down the valley it was all he could do to cling to a bouncing branch as bits of the stacked hoard tumbled away beneath him. He began to clamber as quietly as he could toward a safer place, ending up perched at last in an awkward hammock of rusted cyclone fencing.

A moment later the dragon's snout abruptly stabbed through the junk above Tyler, coming up a only couple of feet short. The fencing tipped and slid downward until Tyler was hanging on by his fingers, eyes shut tight; any moment he expected to feel the creature's scorching breath, to be toasted like a boy-sized marshmallow, but instead after a few more moments Alamu retreated, huffing with frustration. Tyler could hear the creature scrunching back and forth above him, a predator almost the size of a small plane. He stayed as motionless as he could but his arms were aching and his sweaty fingers were losing their grip. Then Alamu stopped moving. A long silence followed.

*He's listening,* Tyler thought, pulse pounding in his temples. *What if he can hear my heartbeat . . . ?*

Alamu's snout suddenly smashed down through the scrap metal once more, his long crocodilian jaws snapping only a foot away from Tyler's head. For a horrible, endless instant he stared right into the dragon's orange eye as Alamu stretched toward him, but the creature's neck was wedged between the remains of an office chair and a shopping cart – where the heck had Alamu found a *shopping cart*? – and the deadly jaws couldn't quite reach him. Tyler swung his body as far to one side as possible as Alamu snapped at him again, but for the moment the tangle of madrone branches and junk kept the monster from reaching him.

'Colin!' he screamed. 'Help me! He's right on top of me! Colin! Colin . . . ?'

Nothing. If Colin was still there, he wasn't going to advertise the fact.

Alamu pulled his head back. The shopping cart came loose and slid down a few feet to fill the space. The mass above Tyler shifted once more and he had to swing to the other side and grab a branch, then find something to put his feet on, because a moment later the entire length of cyclone fence he had been sitting on earlier tore free beneath Alamu's weight and fell to the ground below, bouncing and slithering a short distance down the hill and almost taking the dragon with it. Alamu clambered heavily to another part of the nest, hissing in irritation.

'Colin, please, get help! He almost got me . . . !' But

still there was no reply. Had the older boy just run away and left him? Or was Colin Needle himself lying somewhere on the hill below the nest, unconscious or dead? 'Colin . . . !'

Then just as Alamu again made his way across the swaying nest toward Tyler, something began screeching from the hillside down below, a terrible, painful sound like an animal caught in a horrible trap – for a terrible moment Tyler felt certain that Colin hadn't just fallen but had fallen onto sharp rocks and was loudly dying. Alamu hissed and his head snapped back. Then the dragon leaped into the air. The nest pitched violently at his departure: it was all Tyler could do to cling where he was. The screeching noise echoed once again from below, then was drowned by the dragon's angry, bone-shuddering snarl.

Tyler felt cold all over – that first scream had been one of the most terrible sounds he had ever heard. If it had come from Colin, the dragon must have found him quickly, because now the hillside had gone ominously silent.

Tyler struggled through shifting junk until he could see down to the ground. For a moment he thought he could make out something moving through the trees much further below, something that could have been the pale blue of Colin Needle's shirt, but it was impossible to tell for certain. Tyler called softly but no one answered.

*What if he's dead? Even if I get out of here myself, how*

*will I explain what happened to Colin? Gideon will kill me! Not to mention what the witch will do to me for letting her son get eaten by a dragon . . .*

Junk shifted a few yards away. A can worked its way loose and plummeted out of sight. A few more things moved and settled. Something was getting closer. He almost called out, hoping it was Colin, safe after all, then realized it was much more likely to be Alamu trying a more stealthy approach. Tyler braced himself as best he could and held his breath, but nothing could stop his heart from pounding, pounding, pounding . . .

'Tyler,' someone whispered. 'You are here?'

'Ooola!' He didn't think he'd ever been so happy to hear someone's voice in his entire life. 'Oh, man, Ooola, what are you doing here? Did you see what happened to Colin? Is the dragon gone?'

She stuck her head down between a casserole dish and a discarded paint can so he could see her. 'Me – I made a noise,' she explained. 'Animal noise. Did you hear?'

'That was you? The dragon went right after it.'

'Yes, he chase, but not see me. I throw rocks, he chase more.' Breathlessly she grinned at him. 'I save you?'

'Save me? Yes!' Tyler tried to find a more secure place to hang on – the nest was still shifting in a very disturbing way. 'But we have to get out of here before the dragon comes back. Do you understand? We have to go *now.*'

'Understand.' She stuck out a dirty hand.

'Can't reach you from here,' he said. 'I have to climb up.' He began working his way upward through the clutter. 'How did you know I was here?'

'Was looking for you. Followed Colin because I thought he looked for you.' She frowned. 'But when I come here, he is running back to house instead. I hid – he not see me. Then I come to see where is Tyler.'

'Running back to the house, was he? Thanks a lot, Needle, you creep.' With the girl's help he managed to scramble up one of the heavy tree branches that supported the nest – she was at least as strong as Tyler himself, although she was a good few inches shorter. 'Wow. You really saved my life, Ooola.'

'Me, you,' she said simply. 'You, me.'

Tyler hoped she just meant she had returned the favour he'd done for her, not that she was going to follow him everywhere from now on. He clambered down out of the tree with shaking legs and made his way carefully down the slope, examining the dozens of pieces of the hoard that had worked their way loose from the nest and tumbled out. Nothing that looked anything like a Continuascope was on the ground or visible in the parts of Alamu's chaotic hoard he could see, nor had he run across anything like it while he was in the nest. 'We'd better get out of here,' he said at last, trying not to be disappointed. He was lucky he wasn't dead or crippled. He didn't think he'd be bragging much about *this* adventure. 'I'm sure not going back in there to look some more.'

'You lose?' Ooola asked. 'What is gone?'

'Nothing really. But I came here looking for something and I didn't find it . . .'

Ooola nodded as if she understood something now. 'Shiny thing. Like this.' With her arms she made a circle the size of a basketball hoop.

'Yes, as a matter of fact. What do you mean?'

'Colin. When I see him run down hill, he carrying shiny thing.'

Tyler stared at her. '*Shiny* thing . . . ?'

She moved her fingers in a series of vague shapes, as if trying to draw circles and spokes and protrusions in the air, but 'shiny thing' was the only way she could describe it.

Despite his aches and pains and numerous cuts and bruises, Tyler took off down the hillside path at a trot, scarcely even keeping an eye out for Alamu any more. Ooola caught up with him within a short distance. 'Why you run? Help sister?'

'Because I have to catch Colin. He has something of mine.' He slowed for a moment as he finally processed what she'd said. 'Why would I run to help my sister?'

'Because she very sick. That why Ooola come find you.'

'What?'

'Your sister Lucinda very sick. Fall down in garden,

186

not talk. Ragnar carry her to bed. She white face, make bad noises.'

'Oh my God!' Tyler now hurried downhill even faster, his pace so brisk that several times he almost slipped and hurt himself badly, but now he was not just furious with Colin Needle, he was also terrified that while he had been out taking stupid risks, something really bad had happened to Lucinda.

# CHAPTER 20

## TAKING TEA WITH DESTA

Lucinda was in a cave that was also the farmhouse, sitting on one side of a table set in the middle of a room full of photographs. On the far side of the table, teapot held in a clawed foot, sat the young dragon Desta, smiling kindly.

'It's really rather simple,' Desta explained. 'You've been eaten alive. It happens all the time. My mama tells me that sometimes it's easier just to swallow a deer or a cow whole than struggle with carrying it back to the nest. More tea?'

Lucinda nodded, although she did not remember having had any tea in the first place.

'It's made with roses,' Desta said, pouring for them both and then picking up her own cup. 'Very good for girls. Girls like roses. You like roses, don't you?'

Lucinda couldn't remember whether she did or

didn't, but she nodded anyway. 'Oh, yes, of course. Lovely roses.' But it was hard to talk – her tongue felt huge and her face was very hot. The walls and ceiling of the cave-parlour were covered in a green paper with plant designs that actually seemed real, curling stems and dark, spiky thorns that hung all around. Lucinda wondered if Desta might even have made the tea from those wallpaper plants – the back of her throat felt very prickly and thorny indeed. 'When did you learn to talk so well?' she asked.

Desta had another sip of tea, her wing raised to her mouth, her smallest foreclaw protruding. 'I've always been able to talk. You had to learn how to listen.'

'But I thought dragons didn't like humans. Why are you being so nice to me?'

'Because you're probably dying.' She nodded sombrely. 'So if we don't have this conversation now, we probably never will, and I wanted to tell you that Azinza was right.'

Lucinda was confused and sad. She didn't want to die. 'Azinza?'

'About the monster. Something with a very long reach. Very, very long . . .'

'What do you mean? I don't understand!'

'*Lucinda!*' The dragon's voice grew cold and sharp. '*You must sit up.*'

'But I don't understand!'

'*Sarah, make her sit.*'

Lucinda couldn't understand where the cook had

come from, or why she couldn't see her, but before she could ask about it someone clutched her with strong hands and pulled her up out of her chair. As Lucinda fought against the invisible attack her tea spilled on her face.

'You stupid girl!' the dragon's voice said . . . but it wasn't the dragon's voice any longer. 'See what you've done – you've spilled it all! Now I will have to make more!'

Lucinda opened her eyes to find herself in the Snake Parlour, stretched out on one of the old couches. She could dimly make out the bulk of Gideon's bed, pale as a ghost-ship on the other side of the room. Sarah the cook sat over her, mopping her forehead with a damp cloth. Lucinda sat up. Not just her forehead was wet – she was sweaty all over. 'What . . . ?'

'You must not struggle, Lucinda,' Sarah told her, but her voice was kind. 'You have your medicine spilled all around. She goes to make more.'

'What happened to me?'

'It is not sure. Pema and Azinza brought you in from the garden – they say you fell down and that you were very sick. Mrs. Needle gives you medicine to make you better.'

Before Lucinda could ask any more questions the slim figure of Mrs. Needle swept back into the room, a cup in one hand. She laid her thin, hard arm against Lucinda's chest to hold her firmly in place. 'No more playing up, now, child. Drink this.'

Lucinda didn't have the strength to fight. *Besides,* she thought, *if she wanted to poison me she could have done it already.* Still, she smelled the dark liquid carefully before she drank it. It had a slightly musty taste, but had been sweetened with honey; Lucinda managed to drink it without much trouble. When she was finished Mrs. Needle leaned over her, looking carefully at Lucinda's face, her delicate nostrils flaring as she sniffed for odours. She pulled back Lucinda's blanket and began a painful examination of her belly.

'Spleen,' Mrs. Needle muttered as her long hard fingers dug in just below Lucinda's ribcage. 'Kidneys.' The Englishwoman seemed to be feeling as many different organs as she could – it was a dreadfully intimate sensation, but Lucinda was too weak to resist.

When she had finished, Mrs. Needle wrote a few notes in a small book. 'No harm to the organs,' she said.

'What happened to me?' Lucinda could only remember being in the garden, looking at the dead and dying animals. Beyond that she had only images – the greenhouse, the tangled roses – but it all seemed foggy and uncertain, as though it had happened to someone else.

The housekeeper gave her a cold look. 'Who can say, child? The garden is full of medicinal plants – dangerous things. You have been told that many times. Only a fool would go touching things she knows nothing about. You are lucky you are not dead.'

'I swear I didn't do anything wrong!' But was that

191

true? She wasn't entirely certain. 'I would never touch any plants I didn't know about . . .'

'Really?' Mrs. Needle was not going to be stopped or even slowed. 'So well behaved, are you? So reliable? Only days ago you insulted me in front of those Spanish people, child, those Carrillos – as much as suggested I was trying to . . . to *murder* Gideon! Last summer it was some madness about sending animals to spy on your brother, so you'll forgive me if I find your protests a bit suspect!'

Lucinda turned to appeal to Gideon, but he seemed barely aware of what was going on. The old man stared at Lucinda with his red-rimmed eyes as though he'd never seen her before, mouth moving as though he was chewing – or talking in a voice no one could hear. Just looking at him made Lucinda feel queasy and strange.

No, she realized, not just queasy – she was downright feverish. Her head was hot and seemed too large for her shoulders, and all her muscles ached. She swayed a little. She didn't want to argue any more – in fact, she didn't want to have to be here with pale, witchy Mrs. Needle or Uncle Gideon another second. And as she thought these woozy thoughts, the parlour door suddenly thumped open.

'Where's Lucinda? What happened?' It was Tyler, with Ooola and Pema and Azinza right behind him in the doorway. Ooola was actually trying to hold her brother back. 'Luce,' he said, 'are you all right?'

She did her best to smile, but her head was really pounding now. 'I've been better. Something in the garden made me sick for a while.' But she was *still* sick, she realized – worse, if anything: her headache more painful by the second and something burning at the back of her throat and in her nose.

'What is the meaning of this intrusion, Master Jenkins?' demanded Patience Needle. 'This is Gideon's sickroom, but you burst in here as though it were a barn and you were some kind of caterwauling animal. And look at you, dirty and tattered! I suppose it's unimportant to you that someone else will have to repair those clothes!'

Tyler knelt down beside Lucinda, looking her up and down. He felt her forehead. 'Wow, you're really hot! You should be in bed instead of here, Luce.'

'Yes, that's exactly where she should be,' said Mrs. Needle. 'And you, boy, should also be somewhere else so that your great-uncle can rest. Go on, all of you – out!' She waved her pale hands at Ooola and the kitchen women, but though they all retreated they did not go far, stopping to watch wide-eyed from the entry hall.

'No, send *her* out, Uncle Gideon,' said Tyler. His voice sounded too loud to Lucinda, but everybody else sounded loud too; each word made her skull throb. 'I need to talk to you about Mrs. Needle and her son.'

As she turned toward her great-uncle, Lucinda thought she might be dreaming again: Gideon was looking more and more like a dragon sitting on top of a hoard. Not a young dragon like Alamu, but an ancient dragon who had no allies, only enemies. He was looking at Tyler, but his mouth was pursed like he'd eaten something horribly sour. He looked nothing like the Gideon she knew – he barely looked human to her.

*It's the fever*, she told herself, *making me see things. It must be the fever* . . .

'You are a terrible, wicked boy,' she heard Mrs. Needle say.

'It's your son who's wicked!' Tyler was almost shouting. 'He tried to kill me – or at least he left me to die.'

Lucinda turned her heavy head away from Gideon and saw that Colin Needle was now standing in the parlour behind the kitchen women, his eyes wide and his face white with shock. What Tyler was saying must have upset him, although Lucinda couldn't make much sense of it. In fact, she could barely remember where she was.

*What's wrong with me* . . . ?

'As everyone here knows, Gideon is not well and I am nursing him,' said Mrs. Needle loudly. 'Do you want me to go out, Gideon? You have only to tell me and I will leave. Gideon? Do you want me to leave?' She finally caught the old man's attention. He looked at her vaguely for a moment, then shook his head. 'There. Do you see?'

'That's . . . that's . . . !' Tyler could hardly find the words.

'If you have nothing else to offer besides these horrid accusations, please leave this room and let your great-uncle rest,' said Mrs. Needle sternly. 'We will discuss your . . . astonishing behaviour some other time—'

'No way! I could have been killed! I was in Alamu's nest and the dragon came back! Colin left me there to die! All so he could steal the Continuascope for himself!'

The women in the doorway gasped in shock. Lucinda couldn't see Colin any more. Had he run away? Were the things her brother was saying true?

'The Continuascope, is it? Which has been missing since before Colin was even born?' Mrs. Needle looked as if she was ready to dive in front of Gideon to protect him from Tyler. 'And what is your proof of this absurd accusation?' She looked up. 'Where is Colin?'

'Probably ran off to hide the evidence,' Tyler said.

Mrs. Needle was so pale and her face so angry that she looked more like a vengeful spirit than a witch. 'In other words, you have no proof of any of this.'

Gideon suddenly sat up in bed, his face twisting with annoyed confusion. 'What's going on here? What's going on?'

The door swung wider as Ragnar stepped into the room, big as a tree and clearly unhappy about something too.

'Gideon,' the Norseman said, his booming voice filling the small darkening parlour, 'once again Hector Carrillo is at the front gate.'

'Send him away,' said Mrs. Needle quickly.

'Send him away,' Gideon echoed a moment later, but without much interest.

Ragnar shook his head. 'No. Not again. This is a debt of honour – something you used to know about, Gideon Goldring, when you were a true thane. Carrillo and his family need answers from you. They have been offered much money. If they sell to that man Stillman, our home here – your farm, Gideon – will be in great danger. You have repaid Hector Carrillo by ignoring him for weeks. No more.'

'What are you talking about, you impudent Dane?' Mrs. Needle was so furious now that little spots of red had appeared on her cheeks. 'You have no right . . . !'

'I mean that Hector Carrillo is waiting at the inner gate,' Ragnar said calmly. 'I brought him through and he is there now.'

'At the *inner gate*?' Mrs. Needle's voice was close to a screech; Lucinda had never heard her so enraged. 'You brought him onto the farm property? Have you lost what little wit you had?'

'Perhaps,' said Ragnar. 'But I value my honour. Gideon is well enough now to talk with him. Don't fear,' the big man said, turning to the others. 'Carrillo has seen nothing but the house – no animals. But I will not send him away again . . .'

Patience Needle turned to Gideon. 'Do you hear what this fool has done, Gideon? Brought strangers onto your property, given away your secrets! And these cursed children whom you so kindly invited have also slapped you again. The boy is completely out of control, and now even the girl has been meddling with things in the garden that are none of her business—'

'That's a lie!' cried Lucinda. She tried to get up, but she was dizzy and her head felt like a blob of wet cement: she would have fallen if Azinza's strong hand hadn't caught her.

'Enough of your nonsense, witch,' Ragnar growled. 'Let Gideon speak for himself.'

But Mrs. Needle was like an opera singer in the middle of her big scene – she was building up to her big conclusion. 'Gideon, do you understand – the boy has been meddling in the *dragon's nest*! God Himself cannot say what will come of that – you know how dangerous Alamu can be when he is disturbed. You really must do something, Gideon. These children bring only trouble and now a stranger is on your land even as we speak, looking . . . spying . . . !'

'Spying? You and your creepy son are trying to *steal* this whole farm!' Tyler shouted at her.

'A stranger . . .' Gideon peered out from beneath his bushy eyebrows as though he had only finally heard what was being said. His sallow face stretched in a grimace of distaste. 'Here? On the farm . . . ?'

'Yes,' said Mrs. Needle, almost triumphantly.

'Strangers! Our secrets will be uncovered. We will lose the farm – and you will lose Grace once and for all.'

'She lies, Gideon,' said Ragnar. 'Just come and talk to Carrillo. He is an honourable man. He only wishes to speak about . . . about Stillman, and other things . . .'

Gideon sat up straighter, struggling and quivering so that he looked like something being born out of the tangle of blankets. 'You . . . brought . . . a stranger . . . here?'

'It is Hector Carrillo, your neighbour!' Ragnar protested. 'We owe much to him . . . !'

'Banish them,' hissed Mrs. Needle. 'Send them away. They are traitors, all of them – Ragnar, the boy, the girl. They are *all* trying to steal the farm from you!'

'Steal my farm?' Now Gideon was fighting to get out of bed, his face almost purple with rage as he waved his arms like a drowning man, but he seemed bleary, slow, as if he truly was underwater. 'Out! All of you, out! Out of my room, off my farm! I trusted you, but you betrayed me!' He turned his mad, staring eyes on Tyler and Lucinda. 'And you children,' he said with what looked shockingly like actual hatred, 'have done nothing but try to destroy what I'm doing here. Go away, all three of you traitors – get out of my sight! *And never come back to Ordinary Farm!*'

# CHAPTER 21

## A SURPRISE MEETING

Automatic lights all over the farm were flickering on as the sunset dwindled, their orange glow only a shade lighter than the sky. Tyler stood in the front doorway, his heart beating so fast he felt dizzy, wondering if he would ever see this wonderful, shocking place again, as Ragnar appeared from the Snake Parlour carrying Lucinda cradled in his arms like a small child.

'How is she?'

The big man shook his head. 'I do not know. Not well. We will ask Hector Carrillo to help us.'

'Hear that, Luce?' Tyler asked. 'The Carrillos will help. Everything will be okay.' She opened her eyes and did her best to smile, but it was not the most convincing show of confidence Tyler had ever seen.

Pema and Sarah thumped down the stairs, each

199

dragging one of the children's suitcases. Both women were crying.

'Everything is in them,' Sarah told Tyler. 'Pema swept under your beds and your closet.' She suddenly began to sob again.

'Where will you go?' Pema kept saying. 'Where will you go?'

'To the Carrillos, I think, if they will have us.' Ragnar nodded, considering. 'At least for one night. Lucinda must have rest and a comfortable bed.'

'What if they don't want us?' Tyler asked, worried by Lucinda's pale, listless features. 'Mr. Carrillo was pretty mad at us the last time we saw him.'

'Not at you,' Ragnar said grimly. 'Mad at Gideon, and the witch who gives him such bad counsel.' He scowled. 'Where is Simos? I wish I could speak with him before we go.' He turned to Sarah. 'Tell Walkwell what has happened. He will know what to do.'

'But what's going on?' Tyler felt as though the world had abruptly turned upside down. 'Why is Gideon acting so strange?'

'I know not,' Ragnar said. 'All is strange today. This is like the day that was my death-day.' He waved to Sarah and the other women, then to Caesar in the kitchen doorway, before he led Tyler out of the front door. The sky was a curtain dark as pencil lead.

'Death-day?' It took Tyler a moment to understand. 'The day you almost died, but instead you came here to our time? But Gideon saved you. You didn't die!'

'I was ready. I had sung my death-song.'

They were silent as Ragnar led Tyler across the property to the nearest automatic gate. Mr. Carrillo was parked on the other side, his truck running, belching little puffs out of its tailpipe. He looked up as they approached. 'Where is Mr. Goldring?'

Ragnar stopped beside the truck. 'Gideon is not coming. In fact, he has thrown me and the children off the farm.'

'What?' Hector Carrillo stared at Lucinda where she lay, limp and barely conscious in the big man's arms. 'What's wrong with her?'

'No one knows – something in the garden made her sick. But she needs a safe place to rest.'

'My wife will know what to do,' Mr. Carrillo said. 'Get in. You too, son,' he told Tyler. 'I'll call her when we're off the property – I can never get a good signal here.'

A few moments later they were bumping slowly across the open spaces beyond the farmhouse and inner buildings, the two men in the front, Tyler and his sister in the back seat. Lucinda was half-asleep, leaning on Tyler's shoulder.

'Did all of this happen because you let me onto the property?' Mr. Carrillo asked.

'It is not the cause,' said Ragnar, 'but it is a part.'

They stopped at the gate that led out of the middle zone and into the outer part of the farm. Ragnar got out and walked to the control box, then punched numbers into it. Nothing happened. He frowned, then did it again.

'Did they change the codes already?' Tyler asked. 'That's pretty stupid – we won't even be able to get out . . .' But even as he spoke something long and low and as big as a tiger stepped out of the shadows only a few yards from Ragnar. When it turned its pale, hairless face toward them, Tyler saw the orange smoulder of its eyes reflecting the truck's headlights.

'Oh, jeez,' he said. He was having trouble getting his breath. 'R-Ragnar! On your left, it's one of those . . . those . . . !'

'Manticore,' said the Norseman softly. 'Hammer of Thor, that thing should not be out of its pen so early – someone has made a mistake. Keep your voices calm, and none of you move.'

Mr. Carrillo squinted through the windshield. 'What in hell . . . what in *hell* . . . ?'

'Quiet,' said Ragnar. 'Drive away, Hector. Drive back to the house.'

'I don't know how to get back through the other gate,' said Mr. Carrillo. 'And I'm not leaving you here.'

The sound of his voice clearly excited the manticore: it sat up straight and swivelled its dead stare between Ragnar and the truck.

'Does either of you have a knife?' the Norseman asked.

'A knife?' Mr. Carrillo didn't quite understand. 'Not in the truck . . .'

'Here.' Tyler pulled out his jackknife. His heart was pounding like a marching band, a thousand terrified thoughts ping-ponging through his mind. He slowly rolled down the window and tossed it toward Ragnar. At the movement the manticore let out a strange bark and jerked back a step. The knife bounced in the dirt and landed near Ragnar's feet.

'A very small blade indeed –' the Viking frowned as he slowly crouched and picked it up – 'but that can't be helped.' The manticore watched him intently, its tail rattling back and forth through dust and dead leaves like a hissing snake. It was all Tyler could do not to shout for help – but who would hear them anyway?

'Get back in the truck, Ragnar!' Mr. Carrillo said.

The bearded man only shook his head. 'No. If I move he'll come after me – he will strike soon in any case. Get the children away.' He began moving in a wide slow circle, trying to pull the manticore's attention away from the battered pick-up.

Lucinda stirred beside Tyler. 'I'm sick,' she moaned. 'I want to go home.' She didn't seem to have any idea of what was happening. An instant later the manticore struck at Ragnar, reaching for him with a speed that utterly shocked Tyler. Ragnar was barely able to avoid the creature's clawed fingers – as he danced back the front of his shirt flapped open, torn to tatters.

'Drive, curse you, Hector!' Ragnar shouted. 'Get these children away from here . . . !'

But even as he spoke the manticore leaped toward

him, snarling in a curious, high-pitched way. Ragnar fell back but the thing was faster than he was, and although he hacked at the creature with Tyler's knife, whatever blow he dealt it did not stop it or even slow it down. Man and monster went down in a struggling heap, arms and legs and lashing tail. A moment later one of them rose. The snarling noise had been replaced by something else, something closer: Mr. Carrillo was desperately trying to restart the stalled truck, but the engine turned and turned without catching.

The manticore, limping and snarling, began to circle Ragnar's motionless body, examining him before beginning to feed. An instant later the pick-up's engine fired.

*Bwam!* Tyler and Mr. Carrillo both shouted in terror as something smashed down on top of Mr. Carrillo's truck, a huge impact as if a car had dropped out of the sky. The windshield spiderwebbed and sagged inward. What was it? Tyler felt as if he couldn't breathe. Another manticore . . . ?

Alamu's crocodilian face appeared as its long, slender neck dipped down from the top of the car just outside Lucinda's window.

*First the manticore – now this . . . ?* was all Tyler had time to think, before the dragon opened its jaws wide and let out a bellowing screech that made his skull rattle. Lucinda woke up, took one look out of her window and started screaming; Mr. Carrillo was shouting words in Spanish that Tyler couldn't understand.

The dragon leaped off the truck and landed on the ground with enough force to kick up packed earth. The security lights made Alamu's scales shine light flecks of gold, but he was not posing to be admired, he was coiling to strike. An instant later he spread his wings and launched himself at the manticore.

Alamu hit with the full force of his body, then his wings bellied with air and pulled him up into the air, knocking the surprised manticore away from Ragnar's motionless body. An instant later Alamu dropped back down again. Even as the manticore reared up, the dragon seized the beast's head in his long claws and forced his enemy to the ground beneath his greater weight. The manticore thrashed but could not escape, the end of its spiny tail pounding the ground like a mace.

'Why the hell are these things trying to eat us?' screamed Mr. Carrillo in English. 'Where did they *come from*?'

'Tell you later.' Tyler was so frightened he thought he was going to pee himself.

Mr. Carrillo got the truck into gear at last and it leaped forward across the dirt. For a moment Tyler thought they were going to crash through the fence, but then the truck spun, dirt flying, back to the spot where the two impossible beasts were locked in a screaming death struggle. When they reached

Ragnar's motionless body, Mr. Carrillo stood on the brakes and they slid to a halt. Then he opened the door and leaped out.

'Help me get him in!' he called to Tyler.

Every second out of the car felt like death was at Tyler's shoulder – he was fighting back tears of terror. Ragnar's body was terribly heavy, but at last he and Mr. Carrillo managed to heave the big man over the tailgate and into the bed of the truck. Ragnar groaned but did not open his eyes.

'Go!' Tyler screamed to Mr. Carrillo as he jumped into the back seat next to his sister. Lucinda's eyes were open and she looked as if she wasn't certain whether she was awake or having a nightmare. 'Go, go, go!'

The truck threw dust as the wheels churned, then it skidded and slalomed around the two creatures' struggle, which seemed to have suddenly entered a new and less violent stage, the dragon bending over the smaller manticore almost tenderly, sniffing at it as it twitched on the ground.

'I think the electric fence might be off,' Mr. Carrillo shouted, 'but don't touch the doors of the car, just in case – don't touch anything!'

'What?' How could they avoid touching the seats they were sitting on?

Tyler didn't have long to wonder: a couple of seconds later the pick-up truck hit the fence and smashed through, collapsing it into a tangle of wire mesh and broken poles. For a second the truck threatened to get stuck, but then it jounced over the wreckage and they were out into the open spaces beyond.

'Head for the main outside gate,' Tyler said as he looked back. Alamu was watching them, but to his relief showed no signs of following. The dragon stretched his head up on his long neck to observe them, then bent once more to the crumpled, motionless form of the manticore.

# CHAPTER 22

## A THING OF GEARS AND STARS

Patience Needle watched from the front door as the Mongolian herdsmen went past with wheelbarrows filled with manticore parts. The dead creature was too massive to move easily in one piece, but Mr. Walkwell had some kind of superstitious objection to burning it, so they were trundling the body off to bury it somewhere in the hills.

'One of Gideon's most foolish, dangerous ideas, those animals,' she told Colin. 'I told him, but he wouldn't listen. "They'll kill someone," I said, and I was quite nearly right. It still may happen.' She shook her head. 'Such a pig-headed man.'

Colin Needle had stopped watching the clean-up – the blood made him feel dizzy and sick to his stomach, and of course more than a bit guilty because of his own involvement. This should have been his moment of triumph, now that the Jenkins children and the Viking bully had been thrown off the farm, but for some reason Colin didn't feel as happy as he thought he should. 'How is Gideon doing?' he asked, peering into the parlour. The old man was sleeping, or appeared to be, his mouth wide open and his eyes shut. 'Any better?'

Mrs. Needle's mouth tightened a little, but she did her best to smile, an effort Colin appreciated because he saw it so seldom. 'I think so. I'll have him up and about soon.'

Colin felt his chest loosen. When she talked about Gideon, it was with real puzzlement and concern in her voice – that proved his illness couldn't be anything to do with her! He wanted to celebrate this happy state of affairs in some way, but both he and his mother were going to be very busy today. Already she had made several calls to Gideon's lawyer, Mr. Dankle. 'I am not pleased, Mr. Dankle – not pleased at all,' he heard her say at one point. Dankle was out of town, apparently, and whatever she wanted from him would have to wait. Some legal question that needed answering because of Gideon's illness, Colin guessed, or some insurance thing. He didn't really care too much.

And why should he? His enemies had been driven from the field, and Colin Needle himself was now the boy with the best toy in the whole wide world.

*

In fact, Colin knew he had been very lucky. When he heard Tyler Jenkins shouting about the dragon's nest and Gideon's precious Continuascope he had been certain that things were going to get bad quickly. He had only used his computer to open the manticore cage to cause a distraction – how was he supposed to have known that Carrillo fellow from next door was waiting outside the inner gate, right in the monsters' way? It had been sheer dumb luck that only one manticore had got out, and even greater luck that Alamu had been close enough to notice the ruckus and judged the escaped manticore nasty enough to be a challenge. Colin knew that the creature's death was a terrible loss – one of only six in the world! – but he also knew that Walkwell and the rest could dispose of a dead manticore. A dead Hector Carrillo would have been a lot more difficult to hide. In fact, it chilled him how close he had come to getting somebody killed.

*But I'm fighting a war to save this farm,* he reminded himself. *In wars, there are casualties. And the prize – the prize is worth it!*

Including, of course, the best prize of all: the ability to use the Fault Line, and everything that would come with it – and that ability was now Colin Needle's.

The Continuascope was still where he had left it in the library the evening before on his way back from the dragon's nest, stashed unceremoniously beneath one of the dusty chairs. Colin lifted the device up to the morning light that streamed through the high windows. It was a beautiful thing even if you didn't know what it could do, a complicated but graceful arrangement of golden celestial rings, starry pale crystals, and shiny gears in many sizes, some big as salad plates, others smaller than the tip of Colin's finger. Everything in him longed to try it out, but he knew he wasn't ready.

In the past year he had managed to hunt down more of Octavio's journals, scattered in the oddest places in the house; it had taken much persistence, but as he had tracked down piece after piece the search had also given him new insights into Ordinary Farm's creator. Something had clearly made the old man more than a little paranoid about his discoveries, enough that he seemed to have intentionally hidden his writings. Either that or he had been senile at the end and had just forgotten where he had left them. But even after close study of all the material he had so proudly managed to assemble, Colin had barely begun to understand the ideas in Octavio's work, let alone anything relating to how to use the complex instrument that was the Continuascope.

*Patience.* It wasn't just his mother's name, it was Colin's word to live by. No point in getting himself lost in the Fault Line by being in a hurry. The Jenkins kids were gone now, after all. He could take his time.

He began by cleaning every inch of the Continuascope gently and thoroughly with a soft cloth, Q-tips, and alcohol, and, for some of the very hard-to-reach places, a little canister of compressed air that he kept for cleaning keyboards and computer parts. Considering the time it had been in the dragon's nest, Octavio's device seemed to be in amazingly good condition; under the dirt it appeared largely undamaged.

When he got hungry Colin trotted back across the grounds to the kitchen and helped himself to some leftover dinner rolls, as well as some pickles and slices of ham from the refrigerator. He also grabbed a pitcher of cold milk, then carried it all back to the library so he could keep working.

It was early afternoon by the time he finished cleaning. Colin touched the crystals in their tight baskets of coiled golden wire. They might have been a little warm to his touch, but that might also have been his imagination because he was very excited. After so long, after so many nights hunting for journals and information, and after the mind-numbing fight to understand the things Octavio Tinker had written – and after he had risked his life too, searching the dragon's nest – all that work, and now here he was, holding the actual article in his own trembling hands.

*The most powerful thing in the world – and it's all mine.*

Colin surprised himself – it was as if someone else had thought it, not him. But it was true, wasn't it? Governments around the world would pay mill-ions – no, billions! – for this thing, and even more for Ordinary Farm itself. Look at that crook Ed Stillman – he had brought half a million just to buy what he thought was a live dinosaur egg. How much would he have been ready to pay if he had known it was from a real, live dragon . . . ? And what would he give for the ability to travel to any time in history . . . ?

*No.* Colin did his best to clamp the lid on such thoughts. Maybe later, when he had assumed real control of the farm, he could think about all the different possibilities; now he had more important things to do. He would study and study and study, and when he was ready he would take the Continuascope and then he, Colin Caiaphas Needle, would make the Fault Line his own.

# CHAPTER 23

## AT CRESTA SOL

Ragnar groaned and straightened up in the seat. Tyler was frightened by the blood on the Norseman's face and chest, but Ragnar felt himself carefully, then declared, 'Nothing but swipes.' He touched the back of his head. His hand came away bloody. 'But that thing rattled my brains against the ground. What happened?'

When Tyler told him, Ragnar grinned through the drying blood. It made him look frightening and fierce. 'Then the worm saved my life, because the manticore would have had my guts. I had never thought to owe a dragon thanks, but I do.' He looked at Lucinda. 'Your sister?'

'I don't know. She's sick.'

Ragnar leaned over to touch Lucinda's forehead, nodded, then saw the mess he had made of the seat behind his head. 'I apologize, Hector Carrillo,' he said. 'My blood is in your car.'

Mr. Carrillo didn't say anything, but Tyler could see the man's eyes were still wide with fright and he was hunched over the wheel as he drove as if the devil himself might be chasing them.

Tyler didn't understand how sick his sister really was until they reached the Carrillos' farm. As Mr. Carrillo pulled up in front of the house, Lucinda, who had been leaning on Tyler's shoulder for most of the trip, began to slide off the seat. He clutched her arm and shook her but she was out cold, although 'cold' was the wrong word to use – Tyler could feel the heat coming off her like a light bulb that had been burning for hours.

'She's really hot,' he said, struggling to keep her sitting upright, but Lucinda was as limp as a rag doll. A very heavy rag doll. 'She's got a bad fever!'

'The Carrillos will see that she has what she needs,' said Ragnar, but he didn't sound very convinced. It was strange to see the huge Norseman at a loss for what to do, but it was also frightening.

Tyler was so busy trying to get Lucinda to wake up that he hadn't noticed Mr. Carrillo had got out of the car until he returned with his wife, Silvia. Mrs. Carrillo looked almost as worried and frightened as Tyler felt, but she took control quickly. 'Lift her out and carry her inside,' she told Ragnar. 'Hector, get me some water and some towels.'

As they brought Lucinda into the house the Carrillo children came running to see what was going on.

'Is she all right?' Carmen asked. 'What happened?'

'Your father said she's got a fever. Go get a pair of your pyjamas and a bathrobe,' her mother said. 'She's going to need a change of clothing – everything she's got on is soaking wet.' When Carmen was gone and Ragnar had put Lucinda down on the couch Mrs. Carrillo wrapped Lucinda's head in damp towels, then stuck a thermometer in her mouth.

'You couldn't warn me?' she asked her husband.

'Phone never works over there.' He frowned. 'Should we take her into Liberty?'

Mrs. Carrillo scrutinized the thermometer. 'A hundred and one. Not too bad. I'll sit with her. If it goes up any we'll take her in.'

Lucinda's eyes fluttered open. She looked around but it didn't seem as if she could focus. 'Tyler . . . ?' Her voice was a cracked whisper.

'I'm here, Luce. You're going to be okay. We're at the Carrillos' house . . .'

'Something . . . in . . . g-g-g . . .' She closed her eyes, defeated for a moment, then tried again. 'G-Green . . . house . . .'

'We know. You were out in the garden near the greenhouse when something made you sick. Do you know what it was?'

'*Greenhouse . . . !*' she said, almost crying. The effort

seemed to exhaust her. She closed her eyes and seemed to fall asleep again.

Tyler held his sister's hot, damp hand. Seeing her like this frightened him, and for the first time in a long time he wanted his mother. 'Man,' he said to no one in particular, 'what *happened* over there?'

It got worse before it got better. Lucinda had to be carried off to Carmen's room twice during the evening to have her sweat-soaked clothes changed. She moaned and thrashed for much of the evening, sometimes talking to a Tyler who wasn't there (instead of the Tyler who was sitting next to the couch watching worriedly); other times she seemed to be speaking to the dragons – once she even asked Desta to pass the tea. And a few times she seemed to be talking to something else entirely, something that frightened her badly. 'No!' she kept saying. 'Don't want to! Don't want to go!' During those moments it was all Tyler could do to hold onto her slippery hand.

At last Lucinda's skin began to cool and her sleep became less disturbed. She also stopped talking.

Mrs. Carrillo examined the thermometer. 'Just under a hundred. I think she'll be okay. You kids, off to bed. Steven, get Tyler a sleeping bag and an air mattress out of the garage – and don't forget to shake out the spiders!'

Tyler laughed. 'I'm so tired I could sleep in a whole nest of spiders.'

Grandma Paz, who had been helping Silvia Carrillo nurse his sister, crossed herself hurriedly. 'Don't say such a thing – you will bring the *susto* on yourself.'

'A *susto*'s kind of like a curse or something,' Steve whispered. 'It comes from being scared.'

'As it is, I will have to sweep your sister,' said Paz. 'You too, maybe.'

'What does *that* mean?' Tyler whispered to Steve. 'I don't want to be swept.'

'Don't worry about it,' Steve told him quietly. 'You just lie down and she waves a broom over you. But don't let her near anything bleeding. I fell off the monkey bars at school once and my leg was all bloody and she wanted to put powdered rattlesnake in the cuts.'

In fact, now that it seemed as if Lucinda was going to be all right, Tyler was beginning to be aware of all his own cuts and bruises from his time in Alamu's nest: every inch of his body seemed to have been scraped or poked; but Tyler's idea of medicine did not include any kind of poisonous snakes. 'So, yeah,' he told Steve. 'That's really interesting, about your grandmother and everything. Maybe I'll just sleep in the front yard tonight.'

He didn't, of course. In fact, Tyler woke up several times during the night, frightened for his sister, but each time he went out to check on her she was sleeping more or less peacefully on the couch, with either Grandma Paz or Mrs. Carrillo asleep in

Mr. Carrillo's big armchair beside her. At last, some-time before dawn, he was able to fall asleep for good, but his dreams were full of tangles and snags and the sounds of something large trying to find him.

Tyler stood out in front of the Carrillos' house and stared across the valley, but of course he couldn't see anything of Ordinary Farm from here except the hills that surrounded it. Lucinda, who for the first time in two days had felt well enough to get off the couch, stood beside him wrapped in a blanket even though the day was a hot one.

'I'm telling you, there's something in that greenhouse, Tyler. It was like smoke, or like . . . I don't know. But it got into me and made me sick!'

'You just know that witch is growing poison apples or something in there,' Tyler said. 'You're lucky you're alive.'

'It wasn't just poison though,' his sister said, shivering and pulling the blanket closer. 'It was . . . like something got inside me. Into my head. I can't explain. I can still feel it a little . . .'

'Better be careful or Grandma Paz is going to get out her broom again.' Tyler squinted. 'Anyway, you're better now, so forget about it.' He picked up a dirt clod and flung it as far as he could. 'The real problem is Colin Needle.'

'Oh, Tyler, he's not that bad . . .'

He turned on her. 'He *is*, Lucinda. He is. And he's got the Continuascope, I just know it.'

'Well, that's good, isn't it?' She was pale and distracted, still nowhere near her old self. 'It's been missing a long time and Uncle Gideon really needs it to look for Grace. Who cares who gets the credit . . . ?'

'That's not the point!' At least Tyler was pretty certain it wasn't. 'I don't care about the credit, but don't you understand – Colin has the Continuascope! He can use the Fault Line! And if his mother gets hold of it, *she* can use the Fault Line. They could go back into the past and make it so we were never born!' Something at the corner of his eye was distracting him, an odd shape flitting toward them across the pale blue sky.

'Colin wouldn't do that,' Lucinda said.

'He'll do anything his mother tells him to do,' Tyler said stubbornly. 'She was probably the one who sent him after it in the first place . . .' He narrowed his eyes against the sun. 'What *is* that?'

For half a moment he almost convinced himself it was Alamu streaking toward them down the sky like an avenging demon, but although it drew rapidly nearer, the shape did not grow much larger and his heart began to slow to normal. Then he recognized it.

'Zaza!' He laughed and clapped his hands together as the little creature glided down toward them. 'Look, Luce, it's Zaza!'

'That's nice. But I have to go lie down again.' She

turned and made her way unsteadily back into the house. Tyler hardly noticed her go because the little winged monkey had landed on him and was climbing around on the top of his head, tugging at his hair and chattering softly, seeming as pleased to see him as he was to see her.

'Good girl! Heya! Good girl!' He laughed at the little tickling fingers. 'Hi, Zaza! Whatcha doing? You came all the way over here, did you?' In other times he would have been terrified that the Carrillos would see – Silvia and Paz were only a dozen yards away in the kitchen, making dinner – but if they hadn't said anything about the manticore and Alamu, he didn't think they were going to make much of a deal about Zaza. 'What brings you here, Z?'

It was strange that the little monkey should come so far to see him when she had hardly spent any time with him at all this summer. The year before they had been almost inseparable, but this time she had stayed away except when Tyler was out on the edges of the farm. Why would she come to him out by the reptile barn or all the way over here at Cresta Sol but never call at the window of his room as she used to almost every night?

He sat down and let her climb all over him, petting her and playing with her, enjoying the softness of her velvety wings and her funny, inquisitive noises. She looked him in the face and pulled on his nose with her little fingered hands until he began to believe she wanted him to follow her, maybe even back to the farm.

'I can't,' he said. 'I got kicked out. But I sure wish you could talk like Lucinda's dragons. I bet you'd tell me what's going on back there.'

At last, puzzled and a bit distressed, Zaza flung herself into the air, circled Tyler's head once, twice, chattering loudly, and then sped away back toward Ordinary Farm.

'Okay,' Tyler said to the Carrillo kids, 'what's going on with your folks? It's been three days. Why haven't they said anything about what happened?'

'About what happened where?' asked Steve without looking up from his GameBoss screen.

Tyler rolled his eyes. 'Come on, man! Your father was driving the car – we had a manticore chasing us and a dragon on the hood. We almost died! Why haven't they said anything about *that*?'

'I know,' said Carmen. 'It's scary. It's like it never happened.'

'No.' Little Alma shook her head, her expression solemn. 'It happened. You can see it on their faces. They're just not talking to us about it.'

'But why?' Carmen flopped down on her bed, bouncing Lucinda, who was resting there in a sleeping bag.

'Stop,' Lucinda groaned. 'My head hurts.'

'Sorry. But your brother's right – why haven't they said anything? It's creeping me out!'

Steve Carrillo stood up. 'Dude, there's a simple solution. Let's go ask 'em.'

They could hear Hector and Silvia Carrillo arguing in quiet but strained voices as they approached the kitchen. '. . . to deal with it,' Hector was saying. 'It's pretty clear we have to do something . . .'

'Do something?' This was Mrs. Carrillo. 'What are *we* supposed to do? You might as well try to do something about . . . about a volcano!'

Carmen knocked on the closed door. 'Mom? Dad? What's going on?'

A moment later it swung open. 'We'll talk to you kids later,' Mrs. Carrillo said, peering out. 'Your father and I are having a discussion.'

'About the stuff we want to talk about. So why don't you have the discussion with us?'

Mrs. Carrillo stared at the children for a moment. 'All right,' she said at last. 'Meet us in the living room.'

'Well,' Mr. Carrillo said when they were all settled, 'as you may have guessed, this business with the Tinker farm, with those . . . dragons, or whatever those things were . . . didn't come as a complete surprise to your mother and me.'

'Huh?' Steve looked stricken. 'You mean you knew? About the farm and . . . and the kinds of animals they have there?'

'But how?' Carmen asked.

'Because . . . well, because your great-grandfather

knew Octavio and helped to build that farm,' said Hector. 'And . . . there are some other things you haven't . . .'

Suddenly the front door rattled and banged open. Grandma Paz pushed through with two hefty bags of groceries, which she deposited on the floor, then turned around and closed the door firmly. 'He's coming again,' she told them. 'That man. He was right behind me the whole way in from town.'

Hector Carrillo turned to Tyler and Lucinda. 'You two stay out of sight or he might ask questions,' he warned, then turned to his own offspring. 'Go with them.'

'Who are they talking about?' Tyler whispered as he and the others pushed down the hallway into Steve's room.

'Who do you think?' Steve told him. 'That crazy Stillman guy – the billionaire. He comes by every few days.'

Tyler heard the doorbell ring and the door open. He was curious – he had never seen Stillman in real life – and opened Steve's door just a crack, but he couldn't see anything of the living room. He could hear voices though, and heard an unfamiliar one say, 'I find it hard to believe you won't take twice the market price for this place, Mr. Carrillo.'

'And I find it hard to believe you won't take no for an answer,' said Hector.

They spoke for a minute or so more, but their voices

became quieter and Tyler could make out only a few words. Then the front door was firmly closed.

'Why does he keep trying to buy our house, Papa?' Alma asked when they were all back in the living room. 'We told him we won't sell it.'

'Because he's the kind of man who thinks he can always get what he wants just by throwing money at it,' Hector said, but the lines between his brows deepened. 'I'm beginning to think he might be right.'

Silvia Carrillo sat on the sofa pinching the bridge of her nose. Tyler, horrified, looked from one to the other and said, 'You're not really going to sell to him, Mr. Carrillo, are you? Not to Stillman. He's Uncle Gideon's worst enemy!'

'I don't know what I'm supposed to do if Gideon Goldring won't even talk to me.' Hector Carrillo banged his beer down on the little round table. 'How many times can I beg the man to talk to me? How many times do I have to let him treat me like a dog?'

'But it's not really Gideon's fault!' said Lucinda. Everyone turned to look at her.

'What do you mean?' Tyler asked.

Lucinda shook her head. 'I'm not sure – but it's not! I mean, there's something really wrong with him . . .'

Grandma Paz chose this moment to emerge from the kitchen with a glass of tomato juice and plop herself down on the couch next to her daughter. 'So,' she asked, 'have you and Hector told them about *la Mina Frecuentada* yet?'

'Mother!' Silvia Carrillo almost screamed it.

'Whoa! Doesn't that mean "ghost mine" or something? asked Steve. 'Sounds like an amusement-park ride. What are you talking about?'

'Nothing,' said his father sternly. 'Your grandmother just likes to tell crazy old stories.' He gave Paz a very hard look. 'It's her age.'

Silvia stood up, an expression of pain and weariness on her face. 'Enough for tonight,' she said. 'Have you all forgotten about the evening milking? The cows must be full to bursting. It's time for work! We'll finish this later.' But she looked as if she hoped they would never, ever return to that particular subject.

# CHAPTER 24

## MR. KOTO'S LETTER

Days passed at Cresta Sol without anything changing. July turned into August, the end of their summer vacation loomed, and still Lucinda and Tyler remained banished from their great-uncle's house and land. Ragnar met with Mr. Walkwell at the Cresta Sol property line every few days, but according to the ancient Greek things had not improved: Gideon Goldring was still sickly and still doing pretty much whatever Mrs. Needle told him. She did not even allow the exiles' names to be mentioned in Gideon's presence.

Ragnar slept in the Carrillos' dairy barn and helped Hector and Silvia with the farm. Lucinda and Tyler hung around with the kids. It was fun to have time with Carmen and the others, but Lucinda was beginning to feel like the old Ordinary Farm had been a dream and now they had woken up.

*I could have been spending all this time getting to know Desta, learning how to really talk with the dragons,* Lucinda thought. *Is anyone giving her carrots? She enjoys them so much! Haneb must be so busy with us gone, especially Ragnar – will he have the time to pay her some extra attention . . . ?*

Tyler flopped down beside her. He looked around the empty living room as if there might be spies hiding behind the sofa cushions, but it was late afternoon and everyone was out of the house doing chores or running errands. 'Grandma Paz – she knows a lot more than she's telling,' he said in a dramatic voice.

'Well, duh.'

'What does *that* mean?'

Lucinda sat up carefully – her head sometimes still pounded if she moved too quickly, but otherwise she was feeling better, although she still had no idea what had happened to her that day in the garden. '*Everybody* around here knows more than they're telling – except us kids. That's the whole point. The place is full of secrets.'

'Well, I'm going to find out what she's hiding. You can tell she's dying to tell somebody . . .'

Lucinda sighed loudly. 'And then what? You'll ride Eliot the sea serpent up Kumish Creek, throwing hand grenades until Colin Needle and his mother surrender?'

'What is your problem? Why are you being like this, Luce?'

Tears came into her eyes. 'Because I'm tired of listening to you talking about all the things we're supposed to be doing when we're *helpless*. I wish we'd never learned about this stupid place. It's all been just . . . trouble. And scary, dangerous things. I want to go home.'

Tyler stared at her as if she'd announced she didn't want to have Christmas any more. 'You're crazy, Luce.'

'Well, I'm tired,' she said, 'and I still feel lousy!'

'But you're totally in love with those dragons—'

'You don't get it, Tyler. I don't care any more! *It's too hard!* Even the grown-ups can't make this work – what are we supposed to do? We're kids!'

'But the grown-ups can't make things work *because* they're grown-ups!' Tyler shouted.

Lucinda rolled her eyes and said, 'I'm going to go take a nap.'

Tyler followed her down the hall to Carmen's room. He was angry now too. 'So you're just going to give up? We've got a few days of our summer left – that's *all*. And you want to let the Needles have the farm and all the animals and do whatever they want while we go back home – while we go back to *school*?'

'What else can we do?' Lucinda knew she was being hard on her younger brother; he wasn't feeling ill like she was, so of course he was frustrated. But she really did feel exhausted – whatever had caused the strange fever was not entirely gone. Suddenly it was all she could do to stumble to her bed.

When Lucinda woke up it was mid-afternoon. The sheet stuck to her sweaty skin and the air in the Carrillos' house was hot and close. She wanted to take a shower, but she needed fresh things to put on afterward or getting clean was pointless. She rummaged through her jumbled suitcase for unworn socks and underwear until she had emptied it completely, but she still couldn't find anything clean. Because she had been sick she had let everything go, but now it seemed she would either have to find out how to use Silvia's washing machine or just wear dirty stuff. She began to search through the suitcase's various zipper pockets, hoping a clean pair of underpants might have strayed into one of them somehow. To her surprise, she found something in one of them, but it wasn't underwear.

She lifted out an old, yellowed envelope with a Madagascar postmark. It was one of the letters she had been holding when Mrs. Needle burst into her room their first night back on the farm, the night Tyler found the box mailed to Grace Goldring. Lucinda had tried to gather up all the letters when Mrs. Needle came in, but several had fallen onto the floor. This one must have gone under the bed or something, and Pema and Azinza had found it when they were packing her suitcase and just stuck it in.

She climbed onto the bed. The envelope was still sealed – the letter had never been opened, and Grace had never read it, which was a strange thing to think about. Did the person who wrote it wonder why she had never replied? Lucinda couldn't help wondering what Doctor Grace Goldring had really been like. In all those pictures in the memorial parlour she looked very calm, very pretty, very smart – exactly the kind of woman Lucinda wanted to grow up to be. Now here in Lucinda's hands was an unopened letter addressed to the woman, sent from half a world away, in a box of biological specimens from Madagascar. She held it up to the light to read the now-faint handwriting. *13 July 1989*, it said, sent by someone named Fabien Koto.

Her heart beating faster, she slit the envelope carefully with scissors from Carmen's well-organized desktop and pulled out the yellowing paper. The letter was printed but looked old enough and strange enough that she guessed it had been written on a typewriter.

*Dear Dr. Goldring,*
*I send you my best wishes! The weather here has been good – Antananarivo is a very pretty place in the spring and I hope you and Gideon will come here some day! It would be a great pleasure to show you around! In the meantime, I send you the fruits of my last trip to the market. The* Chamaeleo belalandaensis *would have been a much more exciting find if it was still living, but even the dead ones are seldom seen these days, and this is well dry and I think not too unpleasant!*

*You were right that it is the people of the southwestern coasts that come across the strangest discoveries, things often found floating on logs or root-system rafts. I am not sure I understand your argument as to why that precise spot at Moromboke should prove such a nexus for biological oddities and events, but I am very happy to report the fruits of my success! That is to say, I indeed found myself overwhelmed by the diversity of new botanical specimens. And am herewith sending many back to you.*

*I have a funny feeling they are not all Madagascan. Sorting through and understanding what we have here will take time and study. However I do wish to draw your attention to the prize of the group (as far as I am able to tell!) It is a fungus completely unlike anything I have ever known. I have included a small piece for you, but in the safety of a glass tube! Again, it is not native to Madagascar, but enough have landed on the shores over the years that the Mikea tribes have incorporated it into their myths, naming it what is best translated as 'Call-You Spirit Plant'. Their tales claim that the thing is something like the Sirens or Loreleis of the esteemed ancient poet Homer! Many tribal stories tell of people summoned to die by the 'Call-You' fungus, and how they are helpless to fight against it – as if their will was no longer their own. My tests suggest it is simply a fungus, although a highly complex one! Anyway, I*

*send it to you, learned Dr. Goldring, with the hope
you may find it as interesting as I did . . .*

The letter was signed, '*Your friend and colleague, Fabien
Koto.*'

Lucinda put the letter down, her heart beating wildly.
An entire box of rare and unknown specimens had
been sent to Ordinary Farm – to Gideon's wife Grace, a
scholar and a scientist trusted with the handling of rare
and possibly dangerous specimens. But instead they had
been hidden away for twenty years and now had fallen
into the hands of Patience Needle. Had the specimens
been labelled? Lucinda knew that Mrs. Needle and her
son, unlike the rest of the farm's workers, actually knew
how to use a computer. Had Mrs. Needle been able to
find out something about the dangerous secrets that
had been lurking in that box all these years? Had she
decided . . . to grow some of them?

Several things clicked into place in Lucinda's mind
all at the same time. On the night they found the box
Tyler had said the tubes were full of seeds and bits of
plants. Mrs. Needle *loved* things like that. She was an
expert in these things – botany, herbology. And the
logical place to try to grow unknown tropical species
would be . . .

The old greenhouse.

And if the witch was going to plant one of those
weird specimens, which one would she want to grow?
Lucinda knew the answer to that one too.

'Many tribal stories tell of people summoned to die by the "Call-You" fungus,' Fabien Koto had written, 'and how they are helpless to fight against it – as if their will was no longer their own.'

*Those spores – it must have been the 'Call-You' that I breathed at the greenhouse!* she realized. *I'm so lucky I only got a tiny bit . . . !*

And what better way to control someone's mind than with the mysterious Call-You, which even most doctors would never have heard of? What better way to make sure that Gideon Goldring behaved the way Mrs. Needle wanted him to behave? And what better time to do it than just as he was about to change his will to leave Lucinda and Tyler the farm?

*And once the witch is certain she's figured out how to use it, she could use it on anyone . . . or on everyone.* Then it wouldn't be just mice and birds and bugs dying outside the greenhouse, pulled helplessly by the Call-You, it would be any victim Mrs. Needle chose.

The thought of what had almost got her, and what was probably still lurking inside her, made Lucinda feel ill all over again.

# CHAPTER 25

## VALLEY OF THE WHIRLWIND

'We have to do something, Luce!' said Tyler before he had even finished reading Fabien Koto's letter. 'This is terrible! Colin's got the Continuascope and his mom's brainwashing Gideon with some kind of zombie mushroom – we have to get back to the farm!'

'What good would that do?' Lucinda shook her head. 'As long as she's got Gideon under her control she can just throw us out – she can have us arrested for trespassing if she wants to. She could claim we stole something . . . !'

'They can't arrest us without calling the police. They're not going to do that,' Tyler said. 'The Needles don't want strangers on the property any more than Gideon did.'

'I don't know. We have to talk to Ragnar about this.'

'He's not here, Luce. He snuck back over to the

farm to help Mr. Walkwell with the unicorns. A lot of them are sick.'

His sister frowned. 'Wow. Maybe it's because of that fungus. I mean, if it poisoned all those birds and bugs in the garden . . .'

Tyler waved his hand. 'It doesn't matter now. We can't wait any longer. We have to do something!'

'No! We can't do anything until we figure out what it is we should do,' Lucinda said.

Tyler sighed and shook his head. His sister just didn't get it. 'If you don't want to get involved,' he told her, 'then just leave it to me.'


Grandma Paz was in the yard behind the house when he found her, throwing out food for the chickens from a plastic bin.

'Layer food it's called,' she told him, as if he had asked. 'Nothing to do with layer cake. It means like laying eggs.'

The little old lady, Tyler was beginning to discover, liked to tell stories about everything, not just Ordinary Farm. At dinner she would often share long and occasionally funny tales about one of her relatives getting into trouble or making an embarrassing mistake. Sometimes she even talked about her Indian grandmother and the more distant past, but she never said anything about the stuff Tyler really wanted to hear, and he had been waiting for a chance to talk to her on his own.

He followed her around the yard as she scattered the chicken feed, which pretty much looked like ordinary birdseed to Tyler. 'In Australia they call them "chooks",' Paz said, exactly as if he'd asked that too. The birds scuttled after her, heads bobbing, making happy little *purple-purple-purple* noises in their throats.

Tyler took a breath. 'The other night, you said something about . . . about a haunted mine.'

'Ah, you heard that, did you? I was wondering when one of you would ask. You are the one who always wants to know, aren't you? You must get in lots of trouble.' She laughed.

Tyler did his best to share her amusement. 'Yeah, I guess that's me. Is there really a place like that around here?' Ever since he had heard the phrase he had been thinking about it – it sure sounded a lot like the Fault Line. And if anyone around here had made it clear they knew some strange things about Ordinary Farm, it was Grandma Paz.

'*La Mina Frecuentada*. That's what my father and *mi abuelo* used to call it. Steven is right, it means "the haunted mine". But they didn't go there. Too many stories. The whole place had too many stories.'

'Like what?' Tyler hoped he didn't sound *too* interested – that was a sure way to scare off a grown-up. They started thinking, *What if this kid gets into trouble? It'll be my fault!* Then they clammed right up. 'Ghost stories?'

'Sometimes.' She was halfway around the pen now,

the hens and chickens crowding along the fence near her feet like tourists looking up at a plump Statue of Liberty. 'All kinds of things, child. Monsters. These hills have had stories since long before my *abuela*'s day. I told you about the Indian man who found the Land of the Dead, right . . . ?'

Tyler remembered well, but it was rare to get her alone and talking. 'Tell me again.'

'Don't play with me, boy. I told you once, that's enough. He went to bring back his dead wife and made it all the way to the Place of the Spirits. That was in these same hills – *las Lomas Embrujadas*, the old folks called them when I was a girl: the Witching Hills.'

'Witching Hills?'

She straightened up. Tyler hadn't really started to get tall yet, but he could easily look her in the eye. It was hard just now though, because she was staring at him like he had called her a name. 'I said, don't play with me, boy. You know about these things. I can tell by how you look, how you listen – the questions you ask. You have the same look as old Octavio when he first came.'

'You knew Octavio Tinker?'

'Knew him? Men in my family built most of that crazy house of his. I was a young woman when Octavio first came, so I remember him very well, yes. He was always asking my grandmother for stories like you ask me. Her people were from the Yaudanchi tribe . . . but

I told you that already too.' She smiled again. 'Yes, you are a lot like him – you even look a little like him. He loved that name, *las Lomas Embrujadas*. And just like this rich *ladrón* Stillman, Octavio wanted to buy the old mine and the land around it to add to what he had already bought. But my grandfather wouldn't sell, no. Ha!'

Tyler had already started to ask another question when he suddenly realized what Grandma Paz had said. 'Hang on. Octavio wanted to *buy* the mine from your grandfather? You mean the haunted mine you were talking about?'

'That's what they called it, yes. I didn't say it really was haunted.' She frowned, as if wishing she hadn't started the conversation. 'But . . . way back then, my grandfather let some men dig there for the silver. He didn't sell the mine to them, he just . . . how do you say it . . . ? Leased it. But those men didn't stay long!' She laughed. 'No, not long at all! That's where it got the name! They were scared like rabbits! Never came back!'

Tyler shook his head in confusion. 'Wait You mean there's a piece of land *here*, on this property, that has a haunted mine? A place where people see ghosts?'

'They used to. Nobody goes there any more. Too dangerous.' She nodded. 'And not just ghosts. All kinds of things. Magic animals.' She shuddered and crossed herself.

'But you're saying it's on your property. Not ours –

I mean, Uncle Gideon's?' It sounded like she was talking about the Fault Line. He couldn't make sense of it.

Grandma Paz stared at him again. 'You've been here two summers and you still don't know which are the Magic Hills?' She pointed away from Ordinary Farm to a line of hills some miles away to the west, blanketed in purple and brown shadows as the sun sank behind them. 'Those are *las Lomas Embrujadas*,' she said. 'And down at the bottom of the biggest one is the place they tried to make their mine.'

'But I thought all the magic places like that were on *our* farm – you always say what a dangerous place it is!'

'It is! Where you live – *Valle del Torbellino*, it's called, Valley of the Whirlwind – my grandmother's people said that in the old, old days, Whirlwind broke open the ground there to find his lost son, and that was how the opening was made into the Land of the Spirits!'

'So you have an opening like that on your land too? Then why did you say all those bad things about Ordinary Farm?'

She shook her head in disgust. 'Octavio's land, Gideon's land, is very bad *all over*. Our land here is fine as far as you can see. Only out there, in the north –' she pointed to the distant hills – 'are there bad things. We don't go there, so no problem. The cows are happy, the milk is sweet, and the ghosts don't bother us. That is why we live here. That is why I would *never* live where you live.' She nodded her head as if she had proved a difficult and unlikely mathematical theory.

Tyler turned to head back to the house, his head full of complicated and confusing thoughts.

'Don't step in the chicken poop!' Paz cackled.

*So the Carrillos have had haunted tunnels in their hills all along* . . . A sudden thought made him stop and hold his breath. He was so stunned by the idea that the world around him seemed to have suddenly gone silent.

*Does that mean that their haunted mine is . . . is connected to the Fault Line somehow? Underground? Which would mean it's connected to Ordinary Farm too.*

That put everything in a different light. Everything.

*The Haunted Mine. The Witching Hills. The* – what had Paz called it? – *the Valley of the Whirlwind. The whole place is weird – the whole valley! If Octavio didn't want outside attention, it's no wonder he started calling these places things like 'Standard Valley' and 'Ordinary Farm'* . . .

Because this place had *never* been ordinary.

# CHAPTER 26

## BEASTS AND BALONEY

In the evenings after dinner Lucinda liked to lie on her air mattress in Carmen's room and listen to the warblers and bluebirds flitting through the trees that shaded the Carrillos' backyard. Their chiming songs soothed her and reminded her that although she might not be where she wanted to be, on Ordinary Farm, she was still in a very nice place, surrounded by friends like Carmen and Alma and the rest of their family. But today the birds were silent, as if the distant thunder that had begun half an hour or so ago had frightened them away.

'What, another storm?' Carmen looked up from the laptop she had to share with her brother and sister, the subject of much power-struggling among the three Carrillo kids. 'This has been the wettest summer in, like, *forever.*'

'It never rains very hard,' said Alma. Carmen's little sister was stretched out on the floor, drawing with crayons. 'And it smells so good afterward. Like growing.'

'As long as I don't have to go out in it.' Carmen frowned. 'Speaking of annoying things, where did Steve and your brother go, Lucinda? They ran off after dinner while they were still chewing.'

Lucinda made a face. 'I think they're doing something in the garage. Last time I went past I heard a lot of banging and clattering.'

'Building a spaceship out of old drink cans, probably,' Carmen said.

'No,' Alma corrected her, 'I think Steve said they were getting stuff together to . . .' She paused and looked up as the door of her room opened.

Silvia Carrillo leaned in.

'Carmen, *m'hija*, your father and I promised we'd go have some dessert with the Sotos. We'll be back about nine thirty, but if we're not I want you getting ready for bed then and you can read till we get here, okay? Grandma Paz is in her room watching television if you need her.' She shut the door and a moment later they heard the front door open and close.

Lucinda had been trying to read but she was feeling distracted. Maybe it was the smell and feel of the coming storm, but she hadn't been having much luck with *The Lion, the Witch and the Wardrobe* anyway. Those kids were in a magical place too, but everything seemed to come pretty easy to them, and when things got bad the wonderful 'Jesus lion' (as Carmen called him) always showed up and fixed things.

*I wish we had a magic Jesus lion,* she thought. *I'm tired of trying to figure out all the answers by ourselves.*

Mr. Walkwell wasn't Aslan, of course, but he was the closest thing they were going to get – after all, Lucinda thought, he was practically a Greek god! From what she'd learned on the internet and in books it seemed he was a faun, a kind of Greek forest spirit, but every time she thought she had worked up the courage to ask him more about his background, one look at his weathered face and his dark, watchful eyes made the words clog in her throat like lumpy porridge. There was so much she would have liked to ask him – were the gods real? Had there really been a Hercules? And a Jason and the Argonauts, like that funny old movie Tyler loved so much? But this afternoon, as she had stood with Ragnar at the fence between Cresta Sol and Ordinary Farm, she didn't even consider asking him. There were far too many other things to think about – serious things. Life-and-death things.

'You should not risk coming back, Ragnar,' Mr. Walkwell said. Here at the edge of the property and in broad daylight, he was wearing boots to hide his hoofed feet, and he was plainly uncomfortable: he shifted from one leg to the other as they spoke, the stuffing that made the shoes fit crinkling and crackling. 'At the moment things are no worse with either Gideon or the witch. We should try to keep them that way . . .'

Ragnar shook his head. 'But Simos, look at you – you are exhausted. You did the work of ten men even when I was there . . . !'

Mr. Walkwell snorted. 'So now I do the work of ten and a half. I will manage.'

Ragnar smiled at the joke, but Lucinda knew he didn't approve of Mr. Walkwell taking on so much. 'I have never seen him this way,' the Norseman had told her that morning. 'He almost seems old.' Which was a strange thing to say, considering Mr. Walkwell must have been around for at least a couple of thousand years, but now, looking at the old Greek's bony face and dark-ringed eyes, she understood Ragnar's concern.

'It is not me who needs your pity,' Mr. Walkwell told them. 'Every time the witch brings Gideon out to have him give orders he seems slower, weaker, and more stupid, like a tree that does not get enough water. I fear for him.'

The idea of her great-uncle growing sicker and sicker at Mrs. Needle's hands made Lucinda's heart race with fear. 'It's the greenhouse! I know there's something in there! I can give you the letter I found if you want to see it – there's something really bad in there and I'm sure it's what Mrs. Needle is using to control Uncle Gideon!'

Mr. Walkwell only looked at her, not as though he didn't believe her but as if it didn't matter.

Ragnar shook his head sadly. 'If I could simply break the witch's neck, I would,' the Norseman said. 'But the gods only know whether we would ever get Gideon back afterward. The same if we simply took him away from her. As long as he is in her power, she knows we dare not do anything.'

'Ragnar speaks the truth, child,' Mr. Walkwell told her.

'But what about the thing that got Gideon – and me?'

'I will not let anyone go near the greenhouse, that you need not fear.' Mr. Walkwell turned to look over his shoulder, back toward Ordinary Farm. The wind was changing – even Lucinda could feel that. 'Another storm coming,' he sighed. 'By Olympus, what next?'

'That settles it,' Ragnar said. 'I am coming with you. The sick animals will have to be penned. You cannot get it done in time on your own.' The big man vaulted the fence with the ease of someone a quarter his age. 'I know it is hard for you to wait, Lucinda, but I will come back this evening and tell you everything I have seen. Go back to the house now. This storm may bring lightning.'

'*Will* bring lightning,' said Mr. Walkwell darkly. 'And only the *Moirae* – only the Fates themselves – can say what else will come with it.'

### Carrot Girl!

She could hear it as clearly as if someone had spoken it into her ear – the name (or more precisely the

246

idea) that the young dragon Desta used for Lucinda. The sound that was not a sound came again: *Carrot Girl – help!*

Lucinda had fallen asleep on the air mattress in Carmen's room – in fact, she realized, she was still at least half asleep, but she didn't dare open her eyes for fear of losing touch with the frightened dragon. She had never dreamed the creature's thoughts could reach her this far from the farm. *I'm here, Desta. What's wrong?*

*Too much wrong! All wrong! Frightened!*

And it wasn't just herself the young dragon was worried about. *Meseret* – Lucinda felt it as an image, not a name, the huge, warm shadow-thought that represented Desta's mother – *she hungry too! Other animals – escape! Growling! Scaring Desta! Others running and shouting!*

And even as these ideas fluttered and whirled through her mind like panicky bats Lucinda could feel something else as well – Desta was trying to fly. Lucinda could sense the young dragon straining at her harness, struggling to let her wings pull her up into the air.

*She's ready!* Even in the midst of so much confusion and fright, Lucinda felt a swelling of excitement. *She's ready to fly!*

*Tell me what's going on, Desta. What's happening?*

*Everything bad. Bad-smell animals out hunting.* For a moment she could almost see what Desta saw – a slouching four-legged shadow, a pale, orange-eyed face peering into the reptile barn – and a cold shiver ran down Lucinda's spine, even though she was miles away.

One of the manticores was out.

Lucinda sat up. Carmen's room was empty and dim, the light of the dying evening turning the long window into a glowing violet rectangle. She could faintly hear the television in Grandma Paz's room down the hall. Outside the trees thrashed in a strong wind and a few raindrops were already spattering against the window.

The dragon's thoughts suddenly vanished from her head.

*Concentrate*, Lucinda told herself. *Desta? Desta, can you still hear me?* The moment of contact now felt slippery as a piece of soap at the bottom of a bath or a watermelon seed squirting across a plate each time she tried to close her fingers on it. *Concentrate*. And there it was, but only for a moment, the last, dwindling perceptions that came from the terrified dragon . . .

*Running things*. The ideas flitted across Lucinda's mind like shadows on a window shade. *Wind and growing darkness. Warm rain making all the smells strange. And the hunting things still lurking outside the reptile barn but working up their courage to come in – there was more than one of them now, and they were barking to each other, excited chuffing noises like an axe biting into wood . . .*

Lucinda's skin went cold. Was all that really

happening? Could it possibly be just some kind of dragon-nightmare? But in her heart she knew it was all too real. Since the first moment she had seen Gideon's new watchdogs, the manticores had terrified her. But how had they gotten out? And more importantly, if it had taken Alamu to kill just one of them, how on earth would anybody at the farm be able to get all the rest back into their cage . . . ?

Tears of worry running down both cheeks, Lucinda leaped up and sprinted down the hallway.

'*Tyler!*' she shouted as she burst out the back door and headed for the garage. She saw that the boys had set their tent up inside it – the canvas was lit from within but she couldn't hear them. 'Tyler, it's the farm! Something's really wrong on the farm!'

No reply. No movement.

'Tyler, don't play games!' She yanked back the flap and leaned in. 'I just . . . Desta just –' She stopped when she realized it was pointless. The tent was empty, but for a clutter of comic books and video-game magazines. Tyler and Steve weren't there.

With Carmen and Alma – and, when she finally understood what had happened, with Grandma Paz as well – Lucinda turned the Carrillos' house upside down but found no sign of the boys anywhere.

'Where could they be?' cried Paz. 'Are they playing a trick with us?'

Carmen came out of the kitchen. 'No, they're really

gone. They took food with them. Baloney sandwiches. And of course they didn't put anything away – not even the mayonnaise!'

'At eight o'clock at night?' Grandma Paz was irritated at the mere thought. 'What for? They both ate like pigs at dinner . . .'

'Because they're not coming back right away,' Lucinda said, suddenly feeling queasy. 'They're . . .'

Alma came back into the house, hair dripping, carrying a piece of paper in her hand. 'I found a note in the tent.'

Paz grabbed it from her. Lucinda and the girls leaned over her shoulder to read.

*Were out doing important things and well be back soon. Dont worry about us were fine.*

'My brother is allergic to apostrophes,' Alma said, but she looked really frightened. 'Where do you think they went?'

'Why would they go out somewhere?' demanded Grandma Paz. 'Those *pinches*! And in a storm!'

'Oh. Oh, no.' Lucinda suddenly remembered Tyler's excitement over what Paz had told him. 'It's Tyler. I bet he and Steve are going to try to get back into Ordinary Farm.'

Carmen looked shocked. 'How can they do that? There's an electrical fence! Even my brother isn't *that* stupid.'

Lucinda slumped down onto the living-room couch. 'I don't think that's the way they're going.' She turned to Grandma Paz. 'Tyler said you told him there was a tunnel or something that might connect this property to Gideon's . . . some underground way?'

The old woman's eyes opened very wide. 'Oh, goodness, they wouldn't go there, would they? To the old mine? That's a terrible place!'

'Which is exactly the kind of place my brother would go.' Lucinda wanted to be angry at him but she was terrified. What would she tell Mom? 'He loves stuff like that . . . Oh, Tyler, you *idiot*! All because he's so worked up about Colin Needle and the Contin . . .' She suddenly realized Paz was still standing there. 'Never mind. What do we do? Where is it? How do we get them before they get themselves killed?'

'I'll get my car,' said Paz. 'I know where it is, and if they haven't been gone too long we can beat them there. You girls get your jackets and shoes on and get in the car. *Diós mio*, those two! I am going to tan their little *culos* . . . !'

As Carmen and Alma ran off, Lucinda told Paz, 'I'm not going. Someone has to stay here to tell Ragnar what's happening – he's coming back soon. If they beat you to that mine or whatever it is, then Ragnar will have to be the one to go and get them.' *And if he doesn't already know about the manticores being out*, she thought, *well, that's something else that has to be dealt with*. She wanted to cry but couldn't afford to waste

251

any more strength on tears. This was shaping up to be a horrible, horrible night.

Grandma Paz threw her hands up in surrender. 'What am I thinking? I have to call Silvia and Hector too, tell them what those little *idiotas* have done. They'll come right back when they hear, so you won't be on your own long.'

A scant three minutes later Lucinda stood in the driveway watching Grandma Paz's big old car bump down the gravel driveway on its painfully slow way toward the Cresta Sol front gate. The drizzle had stopped but the sky was cloudy and the moist warm breeze tugged at her hair.

'Hurry up!' Lucinda called to them, but all that came back to her was the sound of the rising wind.

# CHAPTER 27

## WEIRD SCENES INSIDE THE SILVER MINE

'So, not trying to criticize or anything, but is this your *actual plan*?' Steve Carrillo was a good-sized kid; with his parka billowing in the wind and the clanking of canteen and flashlight and various other implements dangling from his backpack he looked as if someone's camping tent had pulled up stakes and escaped. 'I mean, like us walking about a zillion miles in the rain? And the mud? And it's getting dark? And did I mention that it's raining?'

'Just be glad it's summer – at least it's warm,' Tyler told him. 'And we'll be out of the rain soon.' At least he hoped so. He didn't really know much about Grandma Paz's abandoned silver mine except for where it was on the map, and he certainly didn't want to think about what they were going to do if they got there and couldn't get inside. He could already imagine what

Lucinda would have to say about this latest idea of his, and it wouldn't be, 'Good thinking!'

Steve had started the adventure full of his usual good humour.

'Shouldn't we be bringing a gun or something?' he asked as they set out in the hot grey-blue evening between waves of summer storm. 'Y'know, in case there are any . . . monster-type things? Dragons? Stuff like that?'

'A gun?' Tyler was shocked and a little intrigued by the idea. 'You don't have a gun, Carrillo.'

'Not really, but my uncle has a rifle he uses to shoot at crows. I could get that. And I've got my paintball rifle. Dude, you *know* how good I am with that.'

Tyler snorted. 'Yeah, and if we need to splatter yellow stuff on a dragon, you're my first choice. But we're just going in some tunnels. There's probably nothing down there but gophers.'

'And snakes. And spiders. And more snakes.' Steve stopped. 'Maybe we should think of some different way to do this, Jenkins. Grandma Paz says that place is haunted!'

Tyler shook his head. 'It's not haunted. It's connected to the Fault Line, like I explained. So every now and then something weird probably comes out of it, like back at the farm. But I know how to deal with the Fault Line, dude! I can totally go in and out. I've done it!'

'Yeah, and I was there. And it sucked.' Steve

shuddered. 'Dude, some crappy monster made out of old rags or something tried to *eat* me the last time I went anywhere with you.'

'That wasn't the Fault Line, that was the other side of the mirror. That's . . . different.' Although he didn't really know if that was true. It wasn't like he could look it up online or in a textbook or anything.

'I don't care if the things with teeth that want to kill us come out of a mirror, or a hole in the ground, or a box of cereal,' Steve said forcefully. 'Things with teeth equal *bad idea*.'

'Anyway, you went into the mirror by yourself – *I* was the one who got you out, remember?' Still, Tyler couldn't really disagree with Steve Carrillo's basic point. Walking across the dark fields toward the looming hills, he was growing less and less fond of his own plan every minute.

Tyler hoped it was a good omen that once they reached the foothills they found the little road leading to the mine pretty easily. With their flashlights cutting a bright path through the flurrying raindrops, they hiked uphill another mile or so until they reached the mine entrance, a frame of old timbers surrounding a hole in the hill just at the base of a rocky cliff. Someone had nailed some ancient grey slats across the front of it as a barrier, but there were no signs reading KEEP OUT! THIS MEANS YOU! or anything else Tyler had expected from Saturday-morning cartoons. A board over the entrance might once have proclaimed the mine's name, but rain and wind and sun had scrubbed the wood clean long ago. All they had to do was duck beneath it and they'd be inside.

Thunder boomed in the distance. 'Oh, hellz no,' Steve said, eyeing the mine entrance with dismay. 'Oh, come on, look at that! That's like where zombies live. We're going . . . in there?'

'Zombies don't live. But yeah, that's where we're going.' Tyler put down his backpack and took a swig from his canteen. 'You can stay out here if you like. Your folks have probably called the sheriff's office by now. They'll give you a ride home.'

'If they even find me alive. You're a knobweed, Jenkins. I'm not sitting out here waiting for the wolves and bears to eat me.'

The thunder rumbled, closer now. Tyler was beginning to see flickering smears of brightness over the distant hills on the other side of Standard Valley, beyond Gideon's farm. 'So, the police or wild animals. Or the lightning could fry you,' said Tyler. 'That's always a possibility too.'

Steve stretched his round face into an expression of extreme disgust. 'I hate you so much, dude. I hate you worse than homework.'

'Yeah. I'll go first.'

The first part was the easy bit – it was all stairs. They went carefully down the rough shaft on a succession of rickety old wooden ladders and steps until Tyler guessed they had descended about the depth of a four- or five-storey building. Steve's grandfather and his workers (or whoever) had done their work well; the old structures creaked and swayed, but Tyler never felt like they were at serious risk, although Steve Carrillo seemed to think they were only moments away from plunging helplessly into the Earth's core.

'Look,' Tyler said, pointing his flashlight downward, 'you can see the bottom. It's like climbing a tree. Just pretend this is all 64-bit.'

'Does that mean there's a giant gorilla out there somewhere who's going to start throwing barrels at us?'

'Ho ho.' Tyler had reached what seemed to be the beginning of the main shaft. He flashed his light around. The final ladder ended in a natural cavern tall enough to stand in, although the three tunnels he could see opening out from there looked a lot less spacious. 'Which way do you think we should go?'

'Hey, sure,' said Steve, 'I'll just release my cyborg tracking hound . . .' His fingers rapidly flurried the A and B buttons of an imaginary video-game controller. Then he turned and frowned at Tyler. 'Seriously, dude – that part is *your* job.'

Tyler crouched at the base of the ladder for a moment to consider. He cocked his head, even took a sniff of the warm, damp air. If this had been a movie he would have felt something or heard something and made a brilliant deduction, but this was not a movie. He flicked his flashlight beam along the walls.

'Batteries don't last forever,' Steve reminded him, but it was the fearful undercurrent in his friend's voice that made Tyler more uncomfortable than the words. Maybe Lucinda was right. Maybe he did jump into things. Maybe he shouldn't have dragged Steve Carrillo into this crazy plan . . .

He did his best to think calmly. If this cavern was connected somehow to the Fault Line a mile away at Ordinary Farm, he reasoned, then maybe he could feel the air moving in one of the tunnels. He licked his fingers and gently moved them from side to side, then turned and did it again.

'There has to be a better way onto your uncle's farm than this, Tyler. I'm serious,' Steve said. 'It's not like that English lady is going to *kill* him or anything. She needs him!' He liked this thought. 'So we might as well go back to my house. Maybe my folks even know some place we can get into the tunnels closer to your uncle's property . . .'

Tyler ignored him. He was doing his best to remember what he had felt when he had found the Fault Line the first time. It had been frightening, but it had also been a feeling unlike anything he'd ever had before. After a moment he walked to the first tunnel opening and stood in front of it with his eyes closed and his palms held out, then moved to the second and did the same.

'What're you doing?' Steve asked. 'Asking the spirits to help you? *"Eenie, meanie, chilli beanie . . ."*'

'Shut up, dude. I mean it.' The third tunnel at first seemed no different, but after a few moments Tyler began to feel what seemed like a faint stirring of the air. It was enough to make up his mind. It had to be – the only other way would be trial and error. 'This direction,' he said, then ducked his head and headed down the tunnel. He could hear Steve trudging after him, murmuring darkly to himself.

'How long have we been down here?' Steve had been trying to edge sideways through a narrow spot in the tunnel, but he and his backpack had stuck. Tyler loosened the straps so he could slip out of it. 'It seems like days,' Steve complained. 'This goes on forever!'

Tyler looked at his watch. 'It's ten. We've been down here about an hour.'

'No way. Only an hour?' Steve started to hoist the pack back onto his shoulders, then sighed. 'I forgot about the dark.'

'What do you mean, you forgot?'

'Going along in the pitch dark is real creepy, man. Even with flashlights.'

'Yeah. It's like being in another universe.'

'Don't say that out loud!' Steve dropped his pack and swore. 'Seriously, I need a rest. How about a snack break?'

Tyler nodded. 'When we get out of this tunnel into the next open cave.'

Whoever built the mine had mostly dug tunnels to connect a complex of natural caves – low, angular spaces walled with grey shiny stone that looked a bit like melting ice cream – but in several places they opened out into chambers of various sizes, a couple of them larger than a small house. Both boys were glad not to have seen much in the way of snakes or spiders, but they had discovered that the caves housed plenty of bats, so when they reached the next large chamber Tyler had to look around for a while until he could find a place for them to perch without having to sit in too much bat guano. The atmosphere didn't seem to spoil Steve's appetite though: Tyler had only taken a couple of bites from his sandwich when the last of Steve's was disappearing.

'So sue me!' Steve said when he saw Tyler's expression. 'All this exercise – I was hungry.' He took a huge, gurgling swallow from his canteen. 'And thirsty!'

'Slow down on that water. I don't know how long it's going to take us to reach the farm.' Tyler was feeling better about his choice of tunnels now – the simple fact that they had been walking so long (when they weren't crawling and dragging their packs through some of the tighter passages) suggested he had picked the right tunnel to reach Ordinary Farm.

'You never told me what we're going to do when we get there.'

'I totally did.'

'You totally did not. It was all, "We have to find out what they're doing!" Like a cartoon. Like *Agent Aardvark*.' He frowned. 'Which makes me Muggsy Meerkat. Crap.'

'Well, we *do* have to find out what they're doing – Colin Needle and his mother.'

'Dude, you know you're a little obsessed, right?'

'I'm not! He's got the Continuascope, which means if he learns how to use it he can travel in time! And his mother's got Gideon totally under her control. Hypnotized! Which means they can do anything they want with the farm.'

Steve gave him a look that clearly said: *Trying to keep crazy person calm*. 'So we're supposed to mess with them? What if she puts a spell on us? What if they go back in time and kill our grandfathers or something?'

Oh, Lord. Did they have to start thinking about what Colin Needle could do to change things *that* way? In science-fiction movies, that was where things always started to go really wrong, and then afterward civilization was destroyed and everyone turned into killer mutants. So Colin Needle and his crazy, nasty mother might not just steal Ordinary Farm – they might accidentally or even purposely *destroy the whole world*. 'Oh, *great*!' Tyler said, and slapped his hands on his thighs, disgusted he had not thought of this earlier. The sound echoed in the small high cavern

261

and reverberated down the tunnels in either direction: he could see nothing of this and hear everything.

The echo carried on repeating, far longer than it should have. The smacking sound seemed to have become something else now, something a little quieter . . .

'Wait,' Tyler said quietly. 'What's that?'

'What's what?' Steve looked from side to side, but the erratic flash of his light revealed nothing but the stone around them. 'Don't do that – you're freaking me out! What's *what*?'

The noise was getting louder.

'That. Sounds like . . . footsteps.' A slow patting sound, scratch and flap, scratch and flap. 'Ssshh.' Tyler lifted his hand. 'Someone's coming.'

'Dude!' Steve looked about five seconds from a heart attack. He was struggling to keep his voice a whisper – his eyes were so wide the whites were almost glowing. 'You're joking, right?' But Steve could hear it too now. 'It must be someone following us – my dad, maybe . . . !'

Tyler said, 'No, listen. It's coming from the wrong direction.'

'Oh, man, no way!' Steve made a lunge back toward the tunnel through which they had come, but Tyler grabbed his jacket sleeve and held on, even as the other boy nearly pulled him off his feet.

'Steve, don't move!'

The footfalls came again . . . *tap* . . . *skritch* . . . *tap* . . .

*skritch.* Tyler turned his flashlight toward the further tunnel. Something was moving there, an angular shadow. Tyler's heartbeat stuttered and jerked. A moment later the dark shape stepped out into the cavern and the glare of the flashlight.

A bushy-haired old man in a black suit stood only a few yards away from them, blinking and trying to shield his eyes from the light. He had a huge moustache like in schoolbook pictures of Mark Twain and a day's growth of white whiskers on his chin. His face was familiar – extremely familiar. Tyler could only stare with his mouth hanging open.

Steven Carrillo sounded like he had something the size of a football stuck in his throat. 'Dude, I've seen that guy! In the library at your farm – in that picture!' He sucked in air, his whispered words helium-squeaky. 'But . . . but I thought he was dead!'

'He is,' said Tyler, backing away from the apparition. His heart felt like it was going to jump out of his ribcage. 'He's totally, *totally* dead.

'Steve – that's Octavio Tinker!'

# Chapter 28

## Strange Allies

Lucinda had been pacing back and forth across the Carrillos' living room for the last half an hour. She couldn't concentrate enough to read, couldn't find anything to watch on television – in fact, she was too worried to do anything but listen to the thunder of the summer storm and the rain drumming on the roof.

*Why doesn't Ragnar come back? We need him! Tyler must be soaking wet if he's out in this,* she thought, but she felt a lot angrier with her brother than she felt sorry for him. *How could he do this! Doesn't he know how dangerous it is?* It wasn't just going down in an old mine, although that had Tyler-Strength Stupidity written all over it, but even if he made it back onto Ordinary Farm, what was he going to do there? It was night-time – dangerous animals were free and roaming, and, according to Desta, not in their right places at all . . .

Suddenly she wasn't angry, she was just frightened – really frightened. It seemed like Tyler, the farm, the dragons – everything was at stake tonight, and here she was waiting for Ragnar to come back. But what if he didn't?

Lucinda threw herself back down on the couch and again tried to read her book but it was almost impossible to keep her eyes on the page – the words kept swimming away from her like frightened fish.

She almost didn't hear it at first because of a particularly loud thunderclap that sounded like it was just overhead, but when the thunder died away it still felt like the whole house was shaking. *Knock knock knock!* Whoever was at the Carrillos' front door wasn't taking it easy: *knock, knock, knock, knock, knock!* Lucinda jumped off the couch, but then stopped in front of the door.

'Who is it?'

'*It's me,*' said a man's voice, and for a moment just the fact that it wasn't Ragnar or anyone else she knew made her heart lurch. '*We had an appointment, remember?*'

Lucinda made certain the chain was on before she opened the door. As she peered out she could see trees whipping in the wind and rain flying in front of the yard lights. The visitor was a handsome older man in an expensive-looking windbreaker, his grey hair swirled all around by the storm.

'Who are you?' she asked.

'Who are *you*?' he snapped back at her. Lucinda didn't think that was very polite. 'I'm here to see Silvia and Hector Carrillo.'

'They're not here.' There was something familiar about him that nagged at her. 'You'll have to come back some other time . . .'

'Like hell I will. I'll wait.' His eyes narrowed. 'Hold on. I've seen you before.' His pale eyes widened in surprise. 'I know who you are. You're one of the Jenkins children.'

'I don't know . . . I don't know what . . .' But Lucinda had suddenly realized who this was and was trying to close the door, but the man blocked it with his foot.

'Don't.' His voice was flat – he wasn't asking. 'There are a couple of large men in that car.' He nodded toward the sleek black vehicle parked in the driveway. Even when the lightning flashed again, Lucinda couldn't see through its windows. 'If I call them they'll kick this door down and things will get unpleasant very quickly. Now, are you going to let me in, young lady?'

'You're Edward Stillman, aren't you? The one who wants Uncle Gideon's farm.' She didn't know what to do. It would be crazy to let him in, wouldn't it? But the Carrillos did know him and had talked to him – she'd heard them say that several times. At last she slipped the chain off the latch and stepped back.

'Very sensible.' Stillman stepped inside and brushed the water from his hair and shoulders. 'First intelligent thing anybody from Ordinary Farm has done in a long time.' He looked her up and down, thankfully not in a creepy, dirty-old-man way, but not like a normal, nice grown-up either. 'Your name is Linda, isn't it?'

'No. Lucinda.'

'Ah, yes. And your brother's name is Tyler. Where is he? And why did you have to stay home on what should be your big night, Cinderella? Don't you know what they're doing tonight over at your great-uncle's place?'

She had no idea what he was talking about, unless he somehow knew about the manticores getting out, but that didn't seem likely. 'My brother's not here. The Carrillos aren't here either, and I think you should go. Otherwise I'll . . . I'll call the police . . .'

Stillman laughed. 'What, you mean the Yokuts County Sheriff's office? On a night like this they'll be down at Rosie's interrogating a piece of pie and some coffee, congratulating themselves on being indoors.'

'Then I'll call nine-one-one . . .'

He shook his head. 'Don't be stupid, child – I'm not going to hurt you. I'm not some . . . *villain*, you know. Your Gideon . . . he stole that place from *me*. And now I suspect he's trying to put it out of my reach forever. But I'm not going to let him do it, you see.' Stillman pulled out a slim phone, not much larger than a few playing cards in a pile, and pushed a button. 'Did you reach anyone there yet?' he asked the person on the other end; a moment later he growled in disgust. 'Then keep trying! And try Dankle again too.' He shoved the phone back in his breast pocket.

Lucinda, who had been looking around the room trying to decide whether she might be able to escape out the back door, suddenly looked up. 'Dankle?' she said. 'I know that name. That's the lawyer guy.' The one Kingaree had met in the park on Fourth of July. Had Stillman set the whole thing up?

The billionaire gave her a look of annoyance. For a man with a nice face, Lucinda thought, he didn't make many nice faces. 'Of course you know him – don't play stupid with me, young lady. He's your great-uncle's lawyer, the one who's going to put you and your brother in Gideon's will to inherit the farm. You damn bet you know him.'

'Uncle Gideon's lawyer . . . ?' Lucinda suddenly felt as though the ground had begun to crumble beneath her feet. 'Dankle is Uncle Gideon's lawyer too? The same guy?'

'Same . . . ? What are you trying to pull?' Stillman pointed her toward the couch. When she was sitting he took a chair across from her. The rain was still drumming hard on the roof but the thunder seemed to be getting further away. Stillman's stare was hard and without kindness. 'Talk. What do you know about the lawyer?'

Lucinda took a breath. 'No. You first, unless you're

going to beat me up or something. You tell me what this is about or I'll just shut up and wait for the Carrillos to get back. Which will be any minute!'

Stillman stared at her – she could almost see his mind humming like a calculator, thinking up and discarding a hundred different possibilities in a few seconds. He was smart – she needed to remember that. He was smart and mean and rich.

At last he sat up straight. 'All right, kiddo, you win. Instead of turning this into the Inquisition, we'll bargain. I'll tell you something, you tell me. Deal?'

She tried to keep her voice more confident than she felt. 'Deal.'

'We'll start with the lawyer,' Stillman said. 'Barnaby Dankle. An ambulance chaser from over in Liberty. Gideon's used him for years – mainly because they're both cheap, but also because Dankle's willing to bend a few rules, look the other way to pick up a few extra billable hours. In other words, he can be bought. And I know, because *I* bought him too.' He laughed harshly. 'Yes, I've known all of Gideon's legal business for a couple of years now. Dankle tells me everything. That's how I found out a few weeks ago that Gideon was planning to change his will so that if something happened to him, you and your brother would inherit Ordinary Farm.'

So it was really true; Ordinary Farm was meant to be their inheritance. Lucinda's heart soared, but at the same time a great fear clutched her. How could a couple of kids possibly make something as crazy as Ordinary Farm work? How could they succeed where Gideon himself was failing?

'But changing the will didn't happen,' said Stillman. 'Until tonight, that is. Dankle took a cab to your farm half an hour ago. He was expected. They let him inside.' Suddenly his voice, which had been calm, grew tense. 'Your turn, kiddo. Are they changing the will tonight? And why aren't you there?'

And suddenly things began to make sense – an evil, evil kind of sense.

'I think they *are* changing the will,' Lucinda said slowly. 'But it doesn't have anything to do with me or my brother now. It's Mrs. Needle. It has to be!'

Stillman gave her a sceptical look. 'What? The housekeeper? I told you, child, don't lie to me. I know too much.'

'You don't know anything!' Grown-up men, she was learning, could be just as wrongly sure of themselves as her little brother. '*She's* the one you're fighting – she's your real enemy, not me and Tyler. We're just kids!' And it was true: there was very little she could do. But there was a *lot* that Ed Stillman could accomplish.

She told him what she and Tyler had overheard in the Liberty city park when Dankle met with slave-trader Kingaree, although obviously she didn't mention Kingaree's connection to the Fault Line. 'Whatever they're doing, it must be tonight.' Lucinda could not keep her fear inside any longer. 'Kingaree must be working for her. Mrs. Needle, she's . . . she's brainwashed Gideon somehow. Drugged him. He's been really sick for weeks. And now I'll bet she's changing the will so that she and her son get the farm!' Lucinda knew she was right – she could feel it. Suddenly she was desperate to find some way to get to Ordinary Farm. 'Tonight!'

Stillwell's expression had become less angry but no less intense. He looked at her like a piece of equipment he was considering buying, one that might or might not do the job. 'Tonight, is it?' he said at last. 'Well, that two-faced shyster Dankle is going to get a shock – and so's this Needle woman if she really thinks she's going to steal something that rightfully belongs to Edward Stillman.' He stood up and headed for the door.

'Take me with you!' Lucinda cried, hurrying after him. She couldn't just sit here reading on the couch while the world came to an end. 'I can help you get in. I know the place.'

Stillman laughed at her as if she'd told him she could lend him money. 'You're joking, right? *You* help *me*?'

Lightning flared outside the window. 'My brother's on his way there! He's trying to sneak onto the property. I have to find him.' She hated doing it, but she let her feelings into her voice. She was pleading with the man who might be the farm's worst enemy. 'Please help me – *please*!'

He considered for a moment, then showed a small, crooked smile. 'All right. Get a jacket. It's pouring.'

That was almost like a normal human being, Lucinda thought, but she didn't let it fool her. 'Thank you. But I have to leave a note.'

'Hurry up, then!' His moment of amusement was over.

She scribbled a quick note – *I'm okay, will be back soon, Lucinda* – and followed Ed Stillman out the door with her jacket pulled over her head and water splashing all around her feet. The front yard was turning into mud. The rear door of the big car swung open as they approached. Stillman pushed her inside, next to a large black man.

'Make room, Deuce – we have company.' Stillman swung himself in beside her, then called to the bulky white man in the driver's seat, 'Go. Tinker farm.' He turned to stare out the window as the driver swung them out onto the main road. 'God, this is a hellish night. And it's only going to get worse . . . for somebody.'

On Lucinda's other side Big Deuce laughed, a man cheerfully looking forward to some serious unpleasantness. His arms were as big around as Lucinda's waist. She huddled down in the soft leather seat and began to wonder whether this had really been such a good idea.

# CHAPTER 29

## THE AMAZING NEEDLESCOPE

Colin made certain that nobody was near any of the windows at the front of the house before making his way across the driveway toward the silo. His mother was conveniently busy with something – she had hardly spoken to him all day, and her face had that tightly drawn look that meant he should be glad about that – but he didn't want to take a chance someone else would see him and mention it either to her or Mr. Walkwell. Fortunately the old Greek monstrosity was occupied noon and night trying to make up for Ragnar Lodbrok's absence.

Colin paused at the silo door for a last scan of the perimeter, then used his copy of the padlock key to let himself into the empty silo. He liked to think of his adventures as military missions, everything planned down to the last detail; on one of the trips to Standard

Valley he had made his own set of keys for just such occasions. It was another example of why he should be the master of the farm someday, and sooner rather than later.

He opened the lock on the hatch door, then made his way down the ladder and into the outer section of the Fault Line cavern, unvisited as far as he knew since Simos Walkwell had come here weeks earlier, searching for Gideon.

Colin set down his powerful flashlight and sat beside it on the cavern's stony floor, then carefully lifted the Continuascope out of his pack. It had felt quite heavy when he was carrying it down the hill from Alamu's nest and even when he had held it in the library, but here, so close to the Fault Line, it suddenly seemed much lighter. He even fancied he could feel it trembling a little, like an animal longing to be let down to run.

He reached up and flicked on the headlamp he had ordered from an internet camping store, then held the Continuascope out before him. He had assembled many pages of Octavio Tinker's musings about how to design and build a tool that would allow him to navigate the Fault Line – a time machine, Colin had come to understand with a tickle of wonder and fear – and had studied them carefully, but he still wasn't certain he could make it work. Tyler Jenkins might be able to find his way back out of the Fault Line by some kind of sheer dumb luck, but Colin didn't think the same would be true for him.

The first thing he wanted to check was whether the thing could open the Fault Line at all – worrying about navigating the countless different 'temporal strata', as old Octavio had put it, would have to wait. From the information he'd gathered, the Continuascope seemed to work a little like a crystal radio: it could be adjusted to measure different energy frequencies. In fact, Octavio Tinker's greatest invention was not that much different from a radio tuner, with each frequency it could locate being a route to a different time and place. The Fault Line gave anyone who stepped into it access to those routes, but they were basically infinite in number: only with a Continuascope could anyone who didn't have Octavio's own bizarre natural gift locate a particular destination or find their way back home with any accuracy.

Colin made sure all the parts were in their starting position. One of the most fascinating things about the Continuascope, he had discovered, was that it worked without external power – no cord, no batteries. Instead its mechanism was based on vibration, and was set into motion by a collection of springs and gears much like those of a huge and extremely complicated pocket watch.

With all the vibrating coils tuned to their most basic setting, Colin gave the winding stem a dozen brisk turns, as Octavio's papers had suggested. As soon as he let go of the stem the Continuascope began to vibrate softly in his hands, pulling ever so subtly from one side to the other like a spinning gyroscope. Some of the smaller rings had actually begun to spin at various speeds within the curve of the Continuascope's main frame, and others were beginning slowly to revolve. It was a strange sensation: when he held the shiny mechanism close he could hear a quiet hum, but he felt its trembling quite strongly in his teeth and the bones of his head.

Colin got up and walked further down into the cavern until he reached a spot that he knew was where the Fault Line commonly opened. He left the coils at their loosest setting – what in a radio would be the dead air at one end of the dial –  and then pulled back a small lever on the frame and released it. A tiny striker hit a tuning fork, which sent its vibrations up and out of what looked like a little halo of nasturtiums or tiny trumpets at the end of the golden spine that traversed the instrument. A moment later the air in front of him and the darkness that filled it both began to part, like a zipper being pulled in midair. When he could see the light of a pale, overcast day leaking in, Colin Needle shouldered his pack, took a deep breath, and stepped through into the Fault Line clutching the Continuascope to his chest with both hands.

He shivered for a long time after he stepped back through into his own place and time, and even after he kicked the ice and snow from his shoes his feet still felt like they had been frostbitten, but he was full of triumph. Not only had he successfully entered the Fault Line and come back out again, but unless he was completely mistaken he had stepped out into the very moment in the ice age that had spewed out that troglodyte Ooola and her rescuer, Tyler Jenkins! In fact, he had even seen what he felt sure were their two pairs of footprints leading toward the spot where he had stepped out, although fast disappearing under falling snow. If it was true, he had learned something else – that on its own the Fault Line itself did not necessarily change time or location all that often. Ordinary Farm had apparently been connected to this particular ancient glacial valley since last summer, and even the moment on the far side did not seem to have changed.

Which was all good – very good. Had he ever taken the initiative back from Tyler Jenkins now! But unlike Jenkins, Colin was going to experiment carefully and scientifically until he could make the Continuascope – and the Fault Line itself – do just what he wanted. In fact, he could imagine the day would come when everyone would just call it 'the Needlescope.' No, maybe 'the Amazing Needlescope', because he was going to do things with it no one else had even considered. And what better way to ensure that control of Ordinary Farm stayed where it ought to stay, with Colin and his mother?

He supposed he ought to thank Tyler Jenkins for helping him, not only to find the Continuascope in the first place, but by being stupid enough to get himself and his sister thrown off the farm, leaving the field clear for Colin Needle.

He laughed out loud, a strange sound in the empty cavern, the cold in his feet and fingers offset by the warm glow of triumph. He was going to do great things now that the Fault Line was his to command. He was going to make everyone sit up and take notice. In fact, he was going to do more than that – he was going to make them all bow down and admit the farm should be his.

*Needle Farm!*

# CHAPTER 30

## TINKER BLOOD AND BONE

'Dude,' whispered Steve. 'Tell me again – why are we giving water to a ghost?'

'Because he's not really a ghost.' Tyler watched Octavio Tinker empty the canteen, then wipe his mouth with a wrinkled hand – a hand of flesh and bone. 'I think he came out of the Fault Line . . . from the past.'

'No way,' said Steve. 'Really? I mean, dude, that's *awesome*.'

'What's that?' The old man looked up, staring at Tyler with bright, sharp eyes. 'What did you say?'

'The Fault Line, Mr. Tinker – we know about it.'

'Hmmm. And you seem to know my name too.' Octavio handed back the empty Cub Scout canteen. 'Thank you for the drink. How do you know me, boy?' The old man looked to be eighty if he was a day, but his wits seemed sharp. Tyler didn't want to lie to him and didn't even know how to if he tried.

'I know you because . . . because you're from the past. Our past. You're in the future now – your future, that is. At least I think so.' He looked from the inventor to Steve Carrillo, who was watching events with total absorption. 'That's the only way I can make sense of it. I'm guessing you've been experimenting with the Fault Line and you've come out in the future.'

The old man raised a bushy eyebrow. 'Truly? That wasn't my intention. What year is it?' When Tyler told him he raised the other eyebrow too. 'Hmmm. You're right – this is some twenty years and more ahead of when I entered the Breach.' He smiled, looking like a child with a secret. 'So it opens both to the past *and* the future! My theory was correct! But you said "Fault Line". Is that what it's called these days?'

Tyler shrugged. 'I guess. It's still a secret. You used both names in your . . . notes. Your granddaughter's husband calls it the Fault Line . . .'

'Gideon?' The old man shook his head. 'Hah! I should have known he'd manage to hang onto the place somehow. I hope Grace is keeping him in line . . .' He trailed off and suddenly a stricken look came over him. 'Oh, Lord, I forgot! Have you seen her? That's who I'm here hunting for – my granddaughter Grace!'

Tyler felt pretty sure he had, but not in the way Octavio Tinker meant. 'No, sir. Not here. Not today . . .'

'Damn.' The old man seemed ready to wander off again, but hesitated. 'Can you tell me if I'm going to find her . . . ?' he began, then suddenly stopped and then waved his hands. 'No! No, forget I asked. Don't want to know about the future. Too many chances for paradox. Don't tell me anything more about what's in front of me, boys. *Nothing!*'

Tyler, who had already been worrying about what he should or shouldn't say to the inventor of the Continuascope, felt a wash of relief. What could he tell him anyway? He didn't know what day it was in the old man's time – Gideon's grandfather-in-law might have five years left to live or five days. All Tyler knew for sure was that he would wind up dead beside his car in the Ordinary Farm driveway on the night Grace disappeared . . .

*Whoa,* Tyler suddenly thought. *He said he's looking for Grace. What if . . . what if that's the night he came from?* The night his granddaughter, Gideon's wife, vanished forever? The night she somehow wound up in the mirror world where Tyler had met her? 'You're looking for your granddaughter, you said. What happened to her?'

'That's just it,' said the old man unhappily. 'I don't know! I came back from an errand into town and she was gone! She was here by herself when I left, but there's no note to say where she's gone, and the Contin—' He stopped abruptly, looking from Tyler to Steve with sudden suspicion.

'I swear I don't know anything, sir!' said Steve quickly, holding up his hands, backing off. 'I'll go sit right over here and you don't have to touch me with your Time Hands or anything.'

Tyler couldn't help rolling his eyes. 'You were going to say "the Continuascope",' he told Octavio. 'We know about it already. I live on the farm during the summers and . . . and I know a lot about you and the Fault Line, Mr. Tinker. Don't worry – your secrets are still safe.'

Octavio looked him over for a moment, then nodded. 'Good. But I didn't realize I'd actually crossed over into the Fault Line. Must have been caught in a fluctuation.' He pointed to Tyler's flashlight. 'I've been lost in the dark for a long time, son. Help me look for Grace and I'll tell you what I know. Maybe between us we can make some sense out of this.'

Tyler couldn't quite figure out Octavio Tinker. Half the time he seemed as sharp as anybody, but at other moments, like when he stood at the intersection of two mine tunnels calling brokenly for his lost granddaughter, he seemed to be what Tyler's mother would have called *pretty much loopy*. Was the old man in shock – had he suffered a trauma? Or was he just getting senile, someone whose grasp on the outer world was slowly growing dark?

They walked for a long while. Sometimes, when Tyler was leading, he could sense something strange, a faint pressure or resistance down some of the passages.

Other directions felt almost welcoming, as though instead of having a cold, strong wind in his face he suddenly had a balmy breeze at his back. Caught up in these observations, it was some time before he noticed that he and Octavio Tinker were taking turns at the front, and that both seemed to understand without speaking when it was the other person's turn to lead.

'You seem to have the knack, young man,' old Octavio said, as if he had been thinking the same thing. 'Do you know what I'm talking about?'

'You mean . . . finding my way around down here?'

'The knack for travelling the Fault Line, yes. I have it too, as you've probably noticed, although it's a fuzzy sort of science at best. But for most people, their first trip through here would be their last. It's all much easier with the Continuascope, of course – or at least much more precise – but I can make my way around a little bit without it. You can feel the Fault Line in front of us, can't you? That's what you're heading toward.'

'I . . . I guess.'

Octavio Tinker turned to study his face. 'Are we related, son? Or are you someone Gideon's brought in to experiment with?'

He didn't want to lie to this fierce, clever old man, especially not if Octavio Tinker might be doomed to die soon. *Twenty years or more ago*, he reminded himself. *But for him, soon* . . . 'Yes. I am related to you.'

The old man seemed very pleased by this. He clapped Tyler on the shoulder with a hand like a bundle of fragile sticks. 'Good! Ah, that's good news. So I've left behind some kind of a legacy, after all!'

'Oh, you've left a lot, sir.' He wondered if there was some way to bring the old fellow back to the present-day Ordinary Farm. Even Mrs. Needle wouldn't be able to dispute with Octavio himself! But of course something like that would probably create even worse problems in the long run – problems that could affect a lot more than just who controlled an obscure farm in the foothills of the Sierra.

Reluctantly Tyler put the idea aside. Thinking about all of the science-fiction angles to travelling in time, though, had made him wonder about something else.

'Why don't you have the Continuascope?' he asked.

The old man looked a little startled. 'Eh?'

'The Continuascope. You said it makes finding your way much more precise. Why did you go into the Fault Line without it?'

'Because Grace took it – she must have; it's gone from the place I keep it. That's why I had to come in here after her.'

'Really?' That didn't jibe with what Tyler knew. Hadn't Gideon told them last summer that the Continuascope had been found lying beside the Fault Line entrance on the night his wife disappeared? 'Are you certain?'

'Why do you ask? Do you know something I don't . . . ?' Octavio, who had been leaning forward, suddenly and violently waved a hand in Tyler's face.

'Wait! No, don't tell me! I don't want to know!' A moment later he smiled, almost embarrassed. 'Sometimes I feel as if I negotiate with the Creator every day for the wonders that He allows me to see. I don't want to ask too much and have Him take His business somewhere else.'

Tyler was still waiting for Steve, who had slowed to a slug-like pace. 'Okay, Mr. Tinker, sir, here's another question: there's only two places to get into the Fault Line, right?'

Octavio paused also. 'That's my working hypothesis. But since one of them's at the bottom of the Indian Ocean, I'll likely never have a chance to test it.'

'Indian Ocean?' Tyler had no idea what he meant.

'Yes, south of Madagascar. It's the opposite side of the earth from this Fault Line opening here – the other pole, as it were. The fifth-dimensional energy, you see, is drawn in there and erupts here. Of course, over the aeons there may have been polar shifts . . .' Octavio broke off to take a pad and ballpoint pen from his pocket and scribble some notes. Tyler held his flashlight close, but could make no sense out of the old man's strange symbols. 'See? Polar shifts,' Octavio said with satisfaction, closing his notebook.

Somewhere behind them Steve Carrillo groaned.

'That wasn't quite what I meant,' said Tyler. 'I mean, the two places to get into the Fault Line from here. There's the Fault Line itself, of course, but also that washstand mirror in the library.' He wondered how much he could get away with. 'Maybe Grace went in through *that* instead.'

Octavio gave him a baffled look. 'The what?'

'In the library – the big library on the farm. There's a little room with a bed in it, and a sink.'

The old man nodded. 'A retiring room, we'd call it. I sometimes have a bit of a nap there if I'm in the middle of some research. But there's no washstand mirror in there, just a little low table with a bowl on it.' He frowned, thinking. 'No, no mirror. No mirror at all.' He looked at Tyler quizzically. 'What makes you think there's an entrance to the Breach in the library's retiring room? No offense, young fellow, but I'm sure I would have noticed . . .'

'Can you please slow down?' called Steve Carrillo from a dozen or so yards behind.

Tyler was stunned – how could Octavio not know about the washstand mirror? – but before he could ask any more questions the old man suddenly stopped in the middle of the low tunnel and raised a bony hand.

'Ah! There – can you feel it?'

Tyler felt a strange tingle on his skin, the softest impression of fresh air on his face. 'I think so.'

'Feel what?' said Steve, trudging up behind them. 'Can we take a break? Are we . . . are we nearly at the Fault Line?'

'It feels like it,' Tyler said.

'I'm glad you think so, because I can't feel anything,'

said Steve, fumbling out his canteen. 'Except pain. And hunger.'

Gideon clapped Tyler on the shoulder. 'Oh, yes, that's it. You're Tinker bone and blood, lad, there's no doubt about it!'

'Me, I'm regular-person bone and blood,' said Steve, wiping his mouth. 'And I'm glad you guys are having a good time with your Tinkerpalooza thing, but me, I'd like to get *out* of here.'

'And I suddenly realize that you must be Ignacio's grandson or great-grandson – my neighbour from next door,' Octavio said with a whiskery smile. 'You have his eyes. His mouth too. A friendly fellow, if a little too fond of talking when people are trying to concentrate . . .' He pointed. 'It's close by now. Follow me, lads.'

He plunged forward, walking like a younger man, as if the nearness of the Fault Line gave him energy. He led them into a larger space, a natural cavern where the tunnel they had been following became a sort of *T*, but instead of turning down one of the new directions, Octavio Tinker only pointed at the featureless stone wall. 'Do you feel it?'

Tyler nodded. In fact the new sensation was making him feel a bit dizzy – as though he stood swaying on the edge of a very high cliff with nothing in front of him but air. 'I feel . . . something.'

'Umm, no offense,' Steve began, 'but what the heck are you two talking about? Because that's, like, solid stone.'

'Here.' Octavio pointed. 'Touch it.'

Steve took a few steps forward and extended his hand. It passed through the stone as though nothing real was there. 'Dude! That's amazing!' He plunged his hand in and pulled it back over and over. 'That's so spooky!'

'Precisely!' Octavio Tinker laughed, sounding far younger than his age, and Tyler wished he could have got to know the old man in real life instead of in this timeless netherworld. How different from Gideon, with his moping and his suspicions! 'But I'm afraid it's time now for us to go our separate ways . . . or rather, our separate *whens.*'

'Maybe we could . . . go with you,' Tyler said. 'Help you find Grace.'

'No way!' Steve sounded horrified. 'My folks must already be seriously pissed at me. How are they going to take it if they find out I went into the past? Not good, that's how.'

The old man shook his white head. 'No, no, no. Your friend is right – it's not a good idea at all, lad. You have your future and I have mine – even if it *is* your past. I feel sure it's only in places like this that we can even dare to mix them for a short while.'

'Really?' Tyler was disappointed.

'Yes, really. And one of these days, if we meet again in some not-place, I'll explain it to you. But for now I have a granddaughter to find, and you have whatever lies before you . . .' He extended his hand. 'By the way – what is your name, young man?'

'Tyler.' He reached out and allowed the old man to take his hand. He couldn't have imagined this moment in a million years.

Octavio gave it a firm shake. 'A pleasure,' he said. 'I wish you well, whatever your future endeavours may be.' For a moment a puzzled look crept onto his face. 'I never asked you what you were doing down here, did I? Ah, probably just as well, just as well . . .' The old man made a stiff little bow, then stepped back toward the stone and vanished.

'Dude, we did not see that,' Steve said. 'He really was a ghost. He really was!'

'No, he just went back into the Fault Line.' Tyler felt strange and empty. He missed the old man already. 'And now we have to do it too.'

'But we're not going to the past! He told you not to!'

'No, and we're not going to,' Tyler said. 'But we're not really in our time either right now. I can just tell.' And he could. As Octavio Tinker had said, they were in some kind of *when* that didn't belong to any of them – a not-place in not-time. 'So if you want to get back to where we were, we're going to have to step through too.' He reached out his hand. Steve looked at it with mistrust. 'It's nothing weird. You have to be touching me.' Again, he didn't know how he knew it, he just knew it.

'It's not that, man,' said Steve. 'It's just . . . you promise, no raggedy ghost things?'

'I'm not promising anything. I hardly know what's going on myself. You should know that by now.'

Steve swallowed, then stretched out his hand and squeezed Tyler's in his damp fingers. 'If you get us killed, Jenkins, I'll *totally* kill you back . . .'

And then Tyler took a step toward the stone and darkness swallowed them, and they fell out of the damp tunnels into a hot, crackling void.

# CHAPTER 31

## ELECTRIFIED

Lucinda knew she had been in less comfortable places than the back seat of Edward Stillman's expensive car, wedged between him and the large, frowning man named Deuce, but off the top of her head she couldn't think of any that didn't include live dragons.

As they slid onto Springs Road in the growing rainstorm, Stillman broke the long silence. 'You know, I'm not as bad as Gideon makes me out to be,' he said. '*He's* the interloper, after all. And now that I think about it, if you're related to Octavio then you're far more closely related to me than you are to Gideon Goldring.'

'Yeah, whatever.' Lucinda didn't really want to talk. Her stomach was so nervous and jumpy that she was afraid she might throw up at any moment.

'Please. I despise the way children talk today,' he told her. '"Whatever" – a lumpish word for lumpish ideas. Show a little respect for your elders, child. You might learn something.'

She had asked him to bring her, Lucinda reminded herself, and now she was stuck with him, so maybe it would be better not to make him too angry. 'Sorry, Mr. . . . Mr. Stillman, I'm just really worried. Are we really related?'

'Your grandfather was Octavio's great-nephew. Your grandfather was also my cousin.'

'Okay, we're family, I guess. But why do you want to hurt Gideon?'

Stillman made a noise of disgust. 'Haven't you been listening? He's the one who hurt me! He stole what was most important to me in the whole world – Grace Tinker. Oh, and also my access to Octavio's papers. Can you even *imagine* how frustrating it is for a scientist like me not to have access his own great-uncle's groundbreaking work?'

Lucinda didn't know what to say. 'Yeah, that does sound . . . very frustrating.'

'I grew up spending summers here, just like you and your brother. The farm was mine . . . or it should have been! Then Gideon Goldring came along and started weaselling his way into everything.' Stillman was angry now, his eyes narrow and his lips pale. 'Do you want to see something?' He didn't wait for an answer, but took out his phone and touched a button, then held it out to Lucinda. 'Look. Look at this! Do you know who that is?'

It was a photograph of four people walking, two in the background and two in the foreground, all of them on the gravel driveway in front the main house at Ordinary Farm, a spot she could recognize easily even in an old picture. The two in the back were talking and looked very stern and businesslike – a younger version of what could only be Uncle Gideon and an older version of Octavio Tinker than she was used to seeing in the library portrait. There was something else strange about the picture as well, some nagging detail she couldn't quite put her finger on. 'Which one . . . ?' she asked.

Stillman's finger stabbed the screen. 'There. Right in front. With Grace Tinker.' And indeed, now that she paid more attention to the foreground couple, Lucinda recognized Gideon's lovely, brown-haired wife from the pictures she had seen in the parlour. The long-haired man walking beside her and apparently making her laugh was young and fit, dressed in slacks and sandals and a Hawaiian shirt . . .

'You,' she said quietly. 'That's you walking with Grace.'

'It certainly is,' said Stillman. 'We were good friends since her childhood, and would have been more one day, but Gideon stole her from me.'

'Eww, wasn't she like your cousin or something? That's disgusting!'

He gave her an extremely cold look. 'Cousin once removed. Perfectly acceptable. Do you want to know what's *truly* disgusting, little girl? Gideon married her, then when he knew he could secure the farm for himself, he got rid of her.'

Lucinda thought of the misery she had seen on Uncle Gideon's face when he talked about his lost wife. 'I don't believe he hurt her – that he did anything bad to her. He really loved her!'

'Hah.' Stillman shook his head. It was strange to look from the face in the picture to the face beside her. Ed Stillman was still slender, still handsome. Except for his grey hair he might have been the man in the picture, escaped from the past and dropped into the present like something out of the Fault Line. 'Gideon Goldring never loved anyone but himself,' he said angrily. 'If he cared for her so much, where is she? And why did he do everything on God's green earth to keep the police from properly searching that property?'

Lucinda knew: because they would have found a lot of things no one had ever seen before. They would have found a hole into the past. They would have found monsters . . . 'I don't know,' she said. A thought had suddenly occurred to her: if Ed Stillman had truly been a favourite of old Octavio and his granddaughter, why didn't he know about the Fault Line? Octavio Tinker would have had to work hard to keep it secret from a regular visitor, but he obviously had done just that. Had Octavio decided a long time ago that Stillman wasn't trustworthy? 'Gideon probably had his reasons to keep the police out, because I know he really loved Grace.'

Stillman looked at her in disgust. 'He truly has you children brainwashed, doesn't he? Oh, poor old Gideon! Everyone's out to get him!' He stared at the screen of his phone and his face changed, softened. 'So many years ago – Good Lord! I was here more than I was at my parents' house – a lot more . . .'

Another thing that had puzzled Lucinda suddenly revealed itself to her. 'Who took that picture?'

'What?'

'If all of you are in the picture, even Octavio, who took it?' Because that had been back in the days before Mr. Walkwell or any of the other Fault Line people, hadn't it? Had it even been a farm then, or just Octavio Tinker's crazy house?

Stillman looked at her as though she had asked him to explain Santa Claus. 'Who took it? What does that matter? Dorothea, probably – Grace's cousin from back east. She lived on the farm for several years. There were always lots of people around in the old days – it was a joyful place, full of music and good conversation. Before Gideon took over.'

*There are still lots of people there*, Lucinda thought but didn't say. *It's just they're from the ice age and ancient Mongolia and places like that . . .*

The driver now pulled over to the side of the road. The windshield wipers swooshed back and forth, but the rain was coming down so hard it didn't make much difference. Lightning blanked the sky for a long moment. Lucinda could dimly see the front gate of Ordinary Farm appear a hundred yards away, but it had disappeared by the time the thunder finally came.

'We're there, Mr. Stillman,' said the man behind the wheel. 'Do you want to call the house again or something?'

'Call? What am I – a stranger?' Stillman laughed. 'No, we're going in, Cater. Drive through the gate.'

'It's shut,' the driver pointed out.

'So?'

Cater gunned the engine.

'But there's an electrical fence!' cried Lucinda, suddenly terrified.

Stillman laughed even louder. 'Oh, goodness, do you think an electric fence is going to hurt us? In *here*? Girl, you could hose down this car with an AK-47 from close range and barely scratch it . . . !'

The car leaped forward and smashed against the front gate in a grinding explosion of metal poles and snapping wires. There was no shock, or at least none that Lucinda could feel, and an instant later they were through the outer perimeter, a few strands of fence still tangled in the bumper and dragging in the gravel as they headed toward the inner gate, where the trick would no doubt be repeated.

*But what if the animals get out?* she wanted to shout. *What if the manticores get loose?* It terrified her to think of those things with their long claws and weird, manlike faces roaming the countryside. But what could she say about it? She tried, 'Gideon has watchdogs, Mr. Stillman – big, dangerous ones! If we . . .'

Ed Stillman smiled and reached into his jacket, but this time instead of bringing out a cellphone he produced an ugly squared-off pistol, so flat and unreflective in the dim light of the car that she could hardly even see it. Still, it drew her eye like an evil magical object from a fairy tale. 'I wouldn't worry too much about the watchdogs, young lady,' Stillman told her, 'unless it's *their* safety you're worrying about. Because the explosive bullets in this baby would kill a rhinoceros. '

'We don't have any rhinos on Ordinary Farm,' she said faintly as they swerved and spun through gravel, hurrying toward the farmhouse and whatever terrible craziness she'd set into motion.

'Well, that's lucky for the rhinos, then,' said Edward Stillman, slipping the gun back into its holster, 'because I'm in a bad, bad mood.'

# CHAPTER 32

## MARCH OF THE BUTTHEADS

'Okay, Jenkins,' Steve said as they staggered out into wider spaces of the Fault Line cavern, 'I definitely have to give you one thing – some interesting stuff happens when I hang out with you.'

Tyler flicked the beam of his flashlight around until he located the ladder and the hatch door above it and the tightness in his chest eased a little. They were in the right time, anyway, or at least it looked that way. 'Sorry, what?'

Steve just went on as though Tyler hadn't said anything. 'I mean, whoa, I wish I knew you when I was little. "Mom, can I have a play date with Tyler? We're going to go through the mirror and we might meet some ghosts and then we're going to play with the dragons . . ."'

'Crap.' The feeling of having made a mistake – of

having made a *lot* of mistakes – suddenly crashed down on top of Tyler. 'Crap, crap, crap.'

'What's wrong?' Steve suddenly looked serious, darting his own flashlight all around the rocky chamber. 'What is it?'

'I totally forgot – it's locked.' Tyler smacked at his leg in frustration. 'I'm such an idiot! There's a padlock as big as your head on the other side of this thing. We can't get out this way. Shoot!' He climbed up the ladder and shoved at the hatch to show Steve what he meant, but to his astonishment the trap door not only moved, it popped right open.

'Guess they don't make those padlocks like they used to,' Steve said. 'Can we just get out of here now?'

'But . . . but . . .' Tyler pushed the hatch open and lifted his head. The silo was as empty and cobwebbed as it had been the last time. *Wow, I can't believe most of the summer's gone by and this is the first time I've been here!* he thought. He had been dreaming about the Fault Line most of the year, but this summer had been crazy. To emphasize the point, rain was drumming hard on the silo roof, as if this was not August but February. 'There's another lock too – on the outside of the silo door . . .'

'Yeah, well, check it before you waste too much time telling me how it's as big as a horse or something,' said Steve. 'Y'know, just in case it's open too. Then let's go get something to eat.'

Tyler wasn't as surprised this time when he pushed

on the door and found it unlocked. He peeked outside just as lightning whitened the sky, then let the door fall closed again as thunder followed only a second or two later.

'Let's go, already!' said Steve. 'Onward to snacks!'

Tyler glared at him. 'You do know that we have more important things to do right now than feed you, right?'

'Says the man who doesn't have to keep this magnificent physique of mine constantly fuelled.' Steve patted his belly. 'Your suggestion is considered and rejected.'

Tyler couldn't help smiling. 'I'll try to steal you something if we go past the kitchen.'

'Where *are* we going now that we're here, anyway?' Steve had settled in on the silo floor and was patting his pockets as if hoping he'd find a candy bar or something he'd missed. Tyler thought that was pretty unlikely since Steve had been doing the same thing every few minutes for the last several hours. 'Because you never told me.'

The reason Tyler hadn't told him was that he hadn't really thought about it much. His only real goal had been getting back onto Ordinary Farm. He needed to . . . no, scratch that, he *absolutely had to* stop Colin Needle from pulling off some kind of game-changing trick with the Continuascope, making everybody think that he was the one with all the answers. And of course, if Lucinda was right about all this spores-and-fungus business, Tyler knew he should probably try to do something about that too.

*Gideon.* If Gideon was confused, then what was more likely to bring him back than to see his beloved Grace again?

'We're going to the house,' he told Steve, opening the door of the silo as thunder again crashed overhead. What he didn't say, but could have, was that they were going right into the witch's castle without even a bucket of water to throw over her.

They had taken only a few steps when Steve suddenly let out a noise of surprise and disgust and scrambled back into the shelter of the silo's front door. 'Dude, I just stepped on something disgusting!' He trained his quivering flashlight beam at the muddy ground. 'Ooh, it's like a giant salamander. With two heads . . . !'

Tyler looked at the confused creature, pale and shiny in the rain as it waddled away from the harsh glare of the flashlight, limping slightly. The false head in the rear appeared to watch them reproachfully as the animal hurried on. 'It's one of those things from the reptile barn,' he said. 'Can't remember the name – amphibunnies, something like that. Me and Lucinda always just call them "Buttheads" because they have another head on their butts . . .'

'Amphisbanae,' Steve said. 'Wow. They're real.'

Tyler turned to look at his friend. 'What are you talking about? How do you know that?'

Steven Carrillo scowled. 'Dude, I am only the best Dungeoneer in my school. I have run so many games that people just say, 'We're going to play some Steve today.' Something flipped past his face, wiggling slightly, and he flinched back. 'But I have *no* idea what *that* just was . . . !'

'Flying snake.' Tyler watched it splash gently to the ground and wiggle away in the same direction as the two-headed lizard, apparently headed toward the far end of the farmhouse. As he watched, he noticed for the first time that quite a few crawling things were moving through the rain-spattered mud. 'Whoa, why are all these snakes and things here? It's like they all got out of the reptile barn . . .' A sudden thought struck him. 'We have to get going.' He grabbed Steve's arm and shoved him off the steps of the silo and toward the distant house.

'What are you doing . . . ?' Steve was hopping and skipping over the mud in what would have been a very comical manner, but Tyler was not feeling very humorous. 'You'll make me step on these things.'

'Doesn't matter. Keep going.' He had just realized that if this parade of buttheads and flying snakes meant the reptile barn was open, they might be meeting up with the bigger reptiles any moment – not just basilisks and cockatrices, but dragons too.

They hurried across the open space between silo and house. The summer storm seemed to home in on them as though it had eyes – Tyler could have sworn

302

the rain was harder where they were than anywhere else. Lightning cracked and this time he could see it, a shimmering, shivering bolt that zigzagged down from the sky on the far side of the house; for a moment the weird profile of Ordinary Farm jumped out against the glare like a theatre set. In that instant of black house and white sky he saw something sliding across the heavens, a shape like one of the flying snakes but a hundred times bigger. 'Okay, just run!' he shouted, yanking Steve so hard they both nearly fell.

Twenty seconds later, slipping like skaters on bad ice, they reached the gravel driveway. They dug across it to the porch at the kitchen end of the house where Tyler pulled Steve into the ornamental bushes.

'Ssshh,' he said, shaking his friend until he stopped groaning. 'Shut up! You'll get us killed!' The lightning flashed again, but to Tyler's great relief there was no longer anything dragon-shaped in the sky. He looked back over his shoulder at the house. The lights were on in the dining room and kitchen areas, but all the curtains were drawn: there was no way to tell who might be working in there, if anyone was. 'We'll go around to another door. Come on!'

But even as they crept along beside the house, keeping the front garden hedge between themselves and the driveway, Tyler heard an unexpected sound, the rumble of car tyres on the gravel. He stuck his head above the ragged hedge and saw a long, low black car, the kind you might see pull up in front of a

Hollywood premiere, except Tyler was pretty certain no famous actors or actresses were going to be making an appearance here tonight.

Steve popped up beside him. 'Who's that?'

'I don't know.' He hesitated for a moment, but he couldn't imagine anything good coming out of that car. Animals loose, strange visitors – what was going *on* here? 'Just forget about it. We have to get inside fast.' *Before something eats us*, he thought but didn't say.

They crawled the rest of the way around the kitchen end of the house on hands and knees like commandos moving in on a well-defended enemy position. Thunder boomed like artillery.

'Hey, Jenkins,' gasped Steve. He paused to shake a newt off his hand – a newt whose skin, despite the heavy rain, flickered with tiny yellow flames. 'Do you think the world's going to end tonight? Cos I have to say, it kind of feels like that to me . . .'

# CHAPTER 33

## A SNAKE MADE OF SMOKE

'Deuce, Cater, you gentlemen stay here,' Edward Stillman told his men as the car slid to a stop a hundred feet or so from the front door of the farmhouse. 'I'll call you if I need you – but I don't think I will.'

'Ummm . . . cellphones don't work very well here,' Lucinda said.

Stillman rolled his eyes and patted his coat where his shoulder holster was hidden. 'I've also got a gun. *Those* work here, don't they?'

*What was I thinking?* She suddenly felt certain she'd made a terrible mistake, but it was too late to back out now. How would Uncle Gideon feel when he found out she'd brought his worst enemy onto his property?

*But Gideon's not himself,* she thought, a*nd the farm is in terrible trouble, so I'll have to take my chances.* She stepped in front of the billionaire. 'No! No guns! You have to be careful. Innocent people live here. Animals too.'

Stillman showed her a cold smile. 'I'll do my best to remember that, young lady.'

She led him down the driveway in the warm, heavy rain, then around to the kitchen's back door.

*So far so good,* Lucinda thought as he followed her inside: *We're in the house and Stillman didn't see any of the animals or anything else he shouldn't.* But how long could such luck last?

She bypassed the kitchen and took him up a flight of stairs instead, then along one of the back corridors that led past Mrs. Needle's rooms, but an unexpected noise nearby in the pause between thunderclaps frightened her – someone on the steps? Maybe the witch herself? – and she hurried along to the end of the hall, then down the stairs there and into the ground-floor hallway and rooms that ran behind the Snake Parlour. Gideon was probably still sleeping in there, which made it another likely spot to run into Mrs. Needle, something Lucinda didn't want to do until she had a better idea of what was going on. But what *was* she going to do? What was the plan? She was always mad at Tyler for running off without thinking things through, but she had just done the same thing and she was beginning to realize how dangerous it was to be roaming this huge, confusing house, full of people, in a summer thunderstorm, with Ed Stillman and his gun.

In fact, what if Mrs. Needle and Stillman just went into business together? Why should the billionaire help Gideon when what he really wanted was to get *rid* of Gideon? *No*, she realized, *this was a stupid idea and it's getting worse by the second!*

She turned to Edward Stillman. 'I think I took the wrong way,' she said quietly. 'This place can be really confusing – you probably remember how big it is. We'd better go outside and look for another way around . . .' If she had to she could run from him, hide somewhere – he hadn't been here in so long that she must know the place better than he did. And after that? Well, surely Mr. Walkwell wouldn't let Stillman and his bodyguards just wander around on the property!

'No.' Stillman grabbed her arm in a surprisingly strong grip. 'No, I don't think so, young lady. I can hear voices on the other side of this wall.' He looked at a wide cabinet with pegs for hats and scarves and umbrellas that stood against the wall – a hall tree marooned here, far from any entrance. 'And there's a door there behind that.'

'The door's nailed closed,' whispered Lucinda. That was the truth – she'd tried to open it once from the Snake Parlour side and found out it was impossible.

'Very likely, but there's a little fanlight window over the door. If I stand on that –' he indicated the hall tree – 'I can look into the other room and see who's in there.'

He climbed up before she could think of a reason

for him not to. He pressed his face against the glass and his eyes widened. His voice was a hoarse whisper. 'Well, I'll be a son of a . . . !'

'What is it? What?' She was so frustrated she wanted to shout at him, but of course she didn't dare. She ran and got a chair from further down the hallway and carried it back, then climbed up onto its seat to peer through the window. She didn't like standing this close to Stillman, smelling his lime-scented aftershave, but she desperately wanted to find out what was happening in the Snake Parlour.

A second later she began to think she would have been happier not knowing.

Gideon's bed was still at the centre of the room and Gideon was still in it, but beyond that everything looked more like a horror movie than another evening at the farm. Skinny old Gideon had been tied to the bed, his wrists knotted to temporary aluminium rails like someone being restrained. He wasn't exactly struggling to get free, but his shadowed eyes were fixed on Mrs. Needle with an expression of animal fury.

Or maybe it wasn't Mrs. Needle he was staring at, Lucinda abruptly realized. Maybe it was the tall man in the dark hat and coat that made him glare that way. Lucinda could understand that – seeing that face again made *her* feel short of breath and sick to her stomach too.

Jackson Kingaree was back in Gideon's house.

'I should kill him . . . the traitor,' Stillman murmured.

'You know Kingaree?' Lucinda was horrified. Were they *all* working together?

'Who?' Stillman looked angry enough to chew his way through the wall with his teeth. 'No, I'm talking about that little weasel Dankle.' And indeed, the lawyer had just moved up out of the shadows and into the light where Lucinda could see him. He was pale and sweaty, and looked almost as frightened as Lucinda herself.

Dankle was pacing back and forth beside Gideon's bed. When he spoke, Lucinda could barely hear him through the glass. '. . . It's just . . . it's just that this will never hold water,' he said, hands flapping. 'Legally speaking, I mean. Just look at him! Mr. Goldring is plainly not in his right mind!'

'But you're going to say he *is* in his right mind, lawyer.' Kingaree's voice was deep and rough. Lucinda pressed closer to the window. 'That's why you're here. And you're in it a sight too deep to back out now.' He smiled. It wasn't pleasant. 'Or am I wrong, Mr. Dankle?'

'I'm not . . . I'm not saying . . .' The lawyer was flustered. He moved closer to Mrs. Needle as though she could protect him. From this angle Lucinda could see the room's big stained-glass window, but it was dark on the other side and the details of the design were murky, the serpent a mass of dark coils like billowing smoke.

*A snake made of smoke*, was Lucinda's fearful thought.

*That's like Mrs. Needle – full of poison, but you can never catch her, never pin her down . . . !*

'But people are going to talk, you know,' Dankle went on, 'especially if one of the witnesses benefits from the change in the will.'

'Damn!' said Ed Stillman, a little too loud for Lucinda's comfort. 'You were right, girl. She's trying to change the will in her own favour!'

'It won't be me, though; it will be Colin,' Mrs. Needle told the lawyer, her voice soothing and reasonable. 'A boy Gideon has raised for years as if he was his own son – raised to be his heir. And you can clearly see that Mr. Goldring is no longer fit to manage the place, Mr. Dankle. It's terrible, but he's completely lost his mind. He wouldn't want the place to fall apart just because he is . . . unwell.'

'But . . .' The lawyer shook his head but could not meet her eye. 'That's all well and good, Mrs. Needle, but if the will is ever contested . . .'

'And who would do such a thing, Barnaby?' she cooed, leaning close to the flustered Dankle. 'The Jenkins children? Those distant, distant relatives whom Gideon himself has thrown off the property?' She eyed the lawyer. 'Mr. Kingaree, would you do me a kindness? I left Mr. Dankle's *rather generous* retainer in an envelope on my desk upstairs. Would you go and fetch it so we can get on with things? Gideon will need his rest soon.'

To everyone's surprise, Gideon himself spoke in a

strange, guttural scrape, like someone with a mouthful of dirt. 'Have . . . to . . . want . . . to . . . it *hurts* . . . !'

'Poor dear thing,' said Mrs. Needle, stroking Gideon's head like he was a sick dog. 'Will you go do that for me, Mr. Kingaree? You can see he needs his sleep.'

As the tall man walked out of the parlour Lucinda felt her hands curling into fists. That Needle woman really was a witch in every way! Lucinda had never wanted to hit anyone so much in her life. She was so angry that for a moment she didn't even notice Ed Stillman shifting and sliding on the hall tree next to her. 'What are you doing?' she whispered.

'What do you think?' he snarled back. 'Ending this charade right now, *that's* what I'm doing!'

In a couple of seconds Stillman had stepped down off the cabinet and headed back along the hall toward the kitchen end, moving much more quickly than she would have guessed of a man near Gideon's age; by the time she could scramble after him he was gone.

*What's he going to do? Is he going to shoot somebody?* For a moment she hoped the house would defeat him as it did so many newcomers, but then she remembered that Stillman had spent lots of time here when he was younger.

As Lucinda reached the stairs she heard the creak of the old wooden floorboards – Stillman getting away, or someone approaching? Kingaree? Panicked by indecision, she at last clambered into a broom closet and held the door closed. The footsteps paused near her hiding spot, and Lucinda could hear nothing except the hammering of her heart. Then whoever it was moved on, climbing slowly but heavily up the squeaky stairs. As soon as the noise had faded Lucinda poked her head out to make sure the hallway was empty, then scampered for the kitchen. As she stepped through the swinging door she almost knocked over Azinza, the kitchen's African princess.

'Lucinda!' The tall woman stepped back, raising her hands as if to defend herself. 'What are you doing here? You are not supposed to be in this house. Go away before she finds you!' Her forehead wrinkled. 'How did you get here?'

'Never mind.' Obviously Azinza hadn't seen Stillman. Lucinda went up onto her tiptoes to throw her arms around the tall woman and kissed her on the cheek. 'Oh, I missed you so much! Pema and Sarah too!'

Azinza smiled and started to say something, then stopped, head cocked to one side. 'Someone coming. Might be *her*. You go on now – hurry!'

Lucinda didn't argue. She waved to Azinza, then trotted across the kitchen toward the back door. She paused for a moment, startled by thunder, and stared out at the dark ocean of the garden and, though she couldn't see it, the lonely island that was the ancient greenhouse.

*Never. I'm never going near that place again.*

Something floated to her through the rumble of the storm. It took a moment to realize it was inside her head.

*Frightened! Carrot Girl help – frightened!*

In all the frightening time with Stillman she had almost forgotten about the young dragon.

*I'm here,* she thought as clearly as she could. *Desta, I'm here! I'll come as soon as I can!* But not now, Lucinda told herself. It would be crazy to start across the huge farm in the dark, with no idea of who or what might be out there. No, as guilty as it made her feel, the young dragon would have to wait.

She made her way instead along the front of the house, in and out past the window boxes, dodging from one sheltering part of the complicated facade to another. She could hear strange animal sounds floating across the distance on the rainy wind, and the ground at her feet was boiling with bugs and snakes and even uprooted worms toiling across the earth, heading for the far end of the house as if they had all been invited to some gala party. It was like what she had seen near the greenhouse, but now it was happening here, hundreds of yards away!

*Stop, Lucinda,* she reminded herself. *One thing at a time. Right now you've got Man with Gun, Dangerous Witch, and Brainwashed Gideon – that's enough to deal with.*

Water drizzled from overflowing roof gutters as she crept from one hiding spot to the next, but for the moment the lightning and thunder had died away. At last she reached the Snake Parlour's front window and crept up close to peer through a lighter-coloured panel near the bottom of the stained-glass window. She could hear voices through the old, thin glass. Mrs. Needle was there, her pale face rigid and expressionless. Dankle the lawyer stood beside her, looking in every way like a grown man who was about to wet his pants. That was no doubt because of the third standing figure: Ed Stillman, gun in hand and anger plain on his face.

Stillman was inspecting Gideon Goldring, who looked even worse from this angle, his face like a wax dummy's, mouth agape and deep-sunken eyes focused on nothing. Lucinda felt a sudden fire of hatred inside her. Patience Needle had done this to him – had turned their great-uncle into this pathetic old *thing*.

'What have you been doing to him, woman?' Stillman demanded. 'Poisoning him? That seems a bit old-fashioned.'

'You are a trespasser, sir,' said Mrs. Needle so calmly that if it had been anyone else Lucinda would have admired her courage. 'And you have threatened us with a gun. I don't care who you are, Mr. Stillman, you are now a criminal. And Mr. Dankle here is an officer of the court.'

The lawyer raised his hands like a man trying to keep friends from disagreeing. 'Now, Mrs. Needle, let's not—'

Stillman laughed. 'Then call the police. Go ahead! Dankle, you should know the number.' He looked around. 'Nobody in much of a hurry, eh? I thought not. Obviously Gideon's got something going here that you think is valuable – isn't that right, my lady? And you thought you'd like to have it for yourself.'

'See here, Mr. Stillman,' said Dankle, stuttering a little from nervousness, 'we're all civilized folk. Please put the gun down and we'll talk this out.'

'Oh, really?' Stillman suddenly turned and pointed the gun right at Barnaby Dankle. 'You mean you're going to tell me the truth about your little double-cross – or is it a triple-cross? Are you cheating her too? Because you've certainly put the screws to your other employers: me and poor old Gideon.'

'This is . . . It's a misunderstanding . . . !' The lawyer began to back away from him. 'You see, it's . . . it's just that . . .'

Lucinda didn't hear the rest because at that moment something sharp and icy cold pressed against the side of her throat and a hard-callused hand covered her mouth.

'Don't make a sound and you might live,' said a quiet but horridly familiar voice. 'Well, well, well . . . who's this sneaking around in the dark?' Jackson Kingaree's mouth was so close to Lucinda's ear she could feel his hot breath. 'Didn't I tell you we'd meet again, little girl? *Didn't I?*'

# CHAPTER 34

## A Snowball's Chance

Colin Needle climbed the ladder from the cavern up into the silo. There were footprints on the dusty floor that he didn't remember being there before, and for a moment he froze in fear, but he hadn't seen anyone in the Fault Line cavern, and the silo itself was obviously empty, so he decided he just hadn't noticed the tracks on his way in.

Besides, why would anyone be messing around near the Fault Line on a night like this, anyway? The Jenkins kids were gone, Gideon was sick, and Mr. Walkwell had plenty of work to keep him busy.

Colin closed and locked the hatch behind him, then slid out of his backpack and set the Continuascope down on top of it to keep the brass he had so carefully buffed and polished from getting scratched again. He reached into the pocket of the jacket he had chosen to wear for his experiment – a far, far heavier garment than anyone else would be wearing even on a stormy night like this – and took the handkerchief out of his pocket before unwrapping his souvenir.

There it sat, the symbol of his triumph, glistening in the beam of his flashlight like a Christmas ornament, but it was both far more plain and far more wonderful than any mere decorated glass ball.

*A 20,000-year-old snowball,* he thought to himself. But what made the snowball really special was that it came not just from the ice age, but from at least a day *before* Tyler Jenkins had entered that snowy world. Colin knew that because he had set the Continuascope carefully, and this time when he stepped out of the Fault Line in the same place he had visited in his first experiment, there were *no* footprints – not his, not Tyler Jenkins's.

*I made the Continuascope work!* Colin wanted to laugh and dance in triumph. *I set it and it took me right where and when I wanted it to go!* Even old Octavio himself would have had to admit that Colin Needle deserved to be the Continuascope's new owner!

But as he stared at the tightly packed white sphere he saw that the handkerchief was darkening around it: the snow was starting to melt, and that would never do. He meant to keep it in the freezer as a symbol of his conquest of the Continuascope – his first step toward taking his rightful place as the master of Ordinary Farm.

He wrapped the snowball in his handkerchief once more and placed it carefully back in the pocket of his jacket, then headed up the stairs.

The rain was pelting down as he left the silo, making his hood bounce above his eyes as he headed back to the house, but beneath his jacket Colin was already sweating – the coat had been good for the ice age but was way too warm for even a rainy summer evening in Standard Valley. Still, he barely noticed. He was already trying to decide where he would go next – or *when*, more likely, since he had a better grasp on how to set the time coordinates than those that seemed to control location. Would he have to compensate for how the earth changed position over time? That might mean he'd have to create or find some complicated computer program. Of course, if it meant he could travel back to ancient Egypt to see the pyramids being built, or to the walls of Troy to watch Achilles fight Hector, it would be worth it.

He was just wondering whether he could take a video camera with him to the past, and if there was a way to make money from that – a feature-length movie of real dinosaurs, maybe, which he could claim he animated – when he realized that something was wrong. The worst of the lightning and thunder had passed, although he could see flashes and thunderheads beyond the western hills and headed toward them, but the expanse of ground between the silo and the driveway was empty but for a tractor deserted when the storm got bad. As he stared he noticed a rather curiously large number of crawling shapes scuttling across the mud as though the rain had flooded all the small animals out of their tunnels. It was a strange, lonely scene, but that didn't explain why he had the distinct and disturbing feeling that something was watching him.

He stopped, squinting at the distant house, but although he could see lights in the window and what might even have been shapes moving behind the curtains in a couple of the rooms, he couldn't imagine anyone being able to see him out here in the dark. He took a few more steps, then the wind changed, and suddenly a new scent swept over him, sharp and sour as vinegar.

Startled, Colin turned and looked back toward the silo. Something was coming around the tall old structure, walking toward him on all fours with slow, measured steps. An animal. A really big animal. Its head lifted even as Colin stood staring, as though it had not noticed him until now, and the lights from the distant house reflected orange in the lamps of its eyes, as if they were windows and some terrible flame burned inside the low, slanted skull.

One of the manticores was loose.

Colin whimpered in terror, then turned, taking a few running steps toward the house, but he was overbalanced by his backpack and the clumsy coat.

He skidded in the mud and tumbled to his knees, then could not get up for a moment as he thrashed helplessly in the muck. He looked back, certain he would see that pale, horribly humanoid face right on top of him, but the manticore had not increased its pace, as though it knew he could not outrun it. And the monster was right – it was a hundred yards to the house at least and Colin couldn't possibly outrun the thing. He whimpered again. The creature kept coming, but now he could see something wasn't right about it. Its head trembled a bit from side to side, like Gideon's after he took Colin's mother's medication, and its steps seemed awkward, as if it had hurt itself. Despite this, though, it continued toward him, slowly but relentlessly. Colin scrambled to his feet and began to run again, but he stepped on something that burst wetly beneath his foot, and he fell again. His backpack with the precious Continuascope slid down around his arms and he had to shrug it off, still making little noises of terror. When he had finally freed himself the monster was only yards away. Colin tried to get up but knew it was no use. Even if he ran now, the thing would be on him in a second. The house waited, but far out of reach, an impossible distance away.

Lightning flashed, and the manticore's eyes flashed too. 'Help!' Colin screamed. 'Help! Mr. Walkwell! Mother!' But the thunder drowned his cries. He scooped up a handful of mud and threw it at the beast, but it only spattered harmlessly against its already mud-smeared legs. As it drew nearer he could see the foul yellow teeth in its drooling mouth, the weirdly ape-like nostrils flaring as it inhaled his scent.

'Go away!' he shrieked. 'Leave me alone!' His hand settled on the wrapped snowball and he threw it, handkerchief and all; it struck the manticore square on the snout and burst in a puff of white. The thing's head and neck continued to shake and tremble, but otherwise it showed no sign of having noticed. The handkerchief caught for a moment on the creature's bristly cheek, then slid off and fluttered away in the rising wind.

Jaws grinning, eyes glowing like a jack-o'-lantern's, the beast slouched toward him.

# CHAPTER 35

## GONE SOUR ON THE OPERATION

Lucinda didn't think she had ever been so scared in her life, and she was a girl who'd been dangled upside down in mid-air by an angry dragon. But the night she had been tangled in Meseret's harness had been so absurd, so crazy, that even at the time it hadn't felt entirely real. This was different. A bad, bad man was holding a knife against her throat – a man who she knew wouldn't hesitate to kill her if it would benefit him. And on top of everything else, he smelled *awful*, rank with sweat and stale tobacco, as though he had been wearing the same clothes for days: she was terrified she might be sick, might startle him by gagging. 'Please don't hurt me,' she whispered. 'I'm not going to scream or try to get away.'

'That's good,' he told her just as quietly. 'Because I want to hear what that little Patience is saying.'

*That little Patience* was Mrs. Needle, of course, who was facing Stillman and his gun across Gideon Goldring's sickbed on the other side of the window. Gideon was struggling in his restraints but his eyes were unfocused and he hardly seemed aware of what was going on right in front of him. Dankle the lawyer – *everyone's* lawyer, it seemed – cowered against the wall beside the door, doing his best not to be noticed.

'God,' Lucinda could hear Stillman saying, 'I almost feel sorry for Gideon Goldring, and that's something I thought I'd never say. What must it be like having a viper like you as an employee, Mrs. Needle? Challenging, I'm sure.'

'I have done nothing but sacrifice for Gideon and his needs.' Mrs. Needle was very carefully not looking at Stillman's gun. Lucinda wondered how much the witch knew about modern weapons – she had been born five centuries ago, after all. For a moment Lucinda half hoped she would try something foolish and get shot. 'But it has come to the point where Gideon has put the farm at risk too many times,' she went on in her calm, precise voice. 'Some of us . . . some of us have nowhere else to go.'

'Yeah, that's sad. You should find somebody who cares and tell him about it.' Stillman waved the gun around as if it was a laser pointer, as if they were in the middle of nothing more serious than a boardroom dispute. 'This farm belongs to my family – which means it really belongs to me. The polite fiction that

Gideon's wife ran off somewhere doesn't hold water. I knew Grace Tinker since she was a little girl. She loved Gideon, astonishing as that might be. She wouldn't have gone anywhere.'

'Our aims are not so different, Mr. Stillman.' Mrs. Needle still wasn't looking at the gun, but she was looking at Edward Stillman with an intensity Lucinda had never seen – almost like some hypnotist in an old movie. 'You want what is best for this place. So do I. Perhaps . . . perhaps we could work something out . . .'

Outside the window, Kingaree tightened his grip on Lucinda, then leaned even closer until his lips touched her ear and tears of fright formed in her eyes. 'Listen to that little earwig getting ready to sell me out,' he snarled. 'Oh, she's fine to look at, but she is rotten all through. I should have known she would never make good on all those promises.'

Thunder boomed just overhead, near enough to make Lucinda gasp. More fat drops of rain began to fall. One of them splashed down her forehead, but she didn't dare move with the sharp blade at her throat.

Stillman laughed. 'What about your cowboy friend, whoever he is? Have you already got everything you want out of him?'

'Please, Mr. Stillman . . .' began Barnaby Dankle, but no one was paying attention to him.

'Kingaree? He's nothing,' said Mrs. Needle. 'A bravo, a common criminal. I only brought him in to

324

make certain neither Gideon nor Mr. Dankle turned tricksy . . .'

'Oh, she is the queen of deception!' Kingaree hissed, and the knife pressed deeper. But even in the midst of her discomfort and growing fear Lucinda wondered whether she was the only one watching Gideon: her great-uncle, still seemingly oblivious to all that was going on around him, had worked one of his skinny arms out of its restraint and was plucking at the other one, his mouth hanging open, his face screwed up in a grimace of pain or frustration or both.

'Um, Mr. Stillman . . . !' Dankle had just noticed Gideon's escape attempt. 'Mr. Stillman, I think . . . !'

'Shut up, lawyer!' But Edward Stillman's angry words were half buried in a new, louder crash of thunder. Lightning turned the sky above Lucinda white for a moment, then the thunder came again, so loud that for that instant she forgot every other danger.

Then many things happened, one after the other. The first was that the house blew up.

Lucinda realized afterward that it was only a lightning strike and it had done nothing worse than find the lightning rod on top of the house's highest turret and race down the ground wire into the earth, but the crack was so loud and the rush of hot air so powerful that it felt more like a bomb exploding.

All the power suddenly went off – the lights in the Snake Parlour and in the rest of the house and the utility lights hung on wires between farm buildings, all gone in an instant as blackness wrapped them round. Lucinda heard Stillman shout something inside the pitch-black parlour and Mrs. Needle shouting too, but she couldn't make any of it out because Jackson Kingaree was dragging her back from the window, filling the darkness with curse words she had never heard before as well as a few she had. Lucinda saw a flash on the other side of the window and heard a loud bang, then the sound of a man shrieking in pain.

'Where's Gideon?' cried Mrs. Needle, not in fear but in something more like indignation. 'You fools! He's got away!'

Out in the darkness Kingaree froze in place like a hunting animal, his arm still around Lucinda's neck. 'Don't you make a sound, girl, or by God I will cut you,' he whispered. 'You are my ticket out of here . . .'

He never finished. A horrible clatter and the sound of more shouting arose from the darkness near the end of the driveway, somewhere near where Stillman had left his car and his bodyguards. The thumping and scraping noises and men's terrified voices got even louder – it sounded as if a mob of angry peasants had attacked the car with pitchforks and baseball bats. A series of flashes and pops like exploding firecrackers snapped through the air.

*Oh my God,* was all Lucinda had time to think. *Stillman's bodyguards are shooting at something – is one of the manticores here? Or is it Alamu . . . ?* Then another loud *bang!* blew out the parlour window. She had no idea whether it came from inside or outside, but Kingaree dropped down onto his hands and knees. Lucinda didn't know whether he was ducking or had been hit, but she grabbed her chance.

She bolted away from the house and into the dark, scrambling on all fours until she could get upright, headed away from the guns and whatever had attacked Stillman's bodyguards, sprinting as fast as she could across a patch of untended dry lawn now half drowned by puddles. Stems smacked against her shins as she ran.

She had gone only a few steps when she heard Jackson Kingaree crunching over the gravel drive, trying to cut her off. She didn't think she could outrun him in the open but she was terrified that he would slash her for trying to escape, so she cut between two seldom-used drying sheds and headed for the farm road that led out across the property toward the reptile barn.

'*Mr. Walkwell! Ragnar! Help!*' she screamed. Silence didn't matter now – the murderous Kingaree was only a dozen steps behind her. '*Help me!*' But all she heard was crashing and hoarse screams and animal growling from the dark driveway behind her. Whatever had found Stillman's bodyguards was now apparently tearing pieces off his expensive armoured car.

Lucinda realized as she emerged from between the sheds that she had misjudged the length of open space

327

she would have to cross: there was no protection and no cover for hundreds of yards along the farm road, and nobody in sight to help her. Kingaree was close behind her as Lucinda turned and headed toward the cyclone fence that guarded the levee where Kumish Creek passed through this part of the property. She jumped up onto the wire and began to climb. Kingaree came slowly toward her, confident now that she couldn't get away.

'You know I can swing over that fence in a hot second, so you might as well come back now, child. It's a terrible bad idea, making me angry.' He stopped a few feet away as she began to pull her other leg over. His eyes were slits, but he was doing his best to smile. 'Now, hold on. We need each other. I need you to help me get out of here – see, I've gone sour on this whole operation. Jack Kingaree's not going to get myself shot for that two-timing Needle baggage. So you get off that fence and the two of us'll parley.'

'No.' The storm had slackened a little. In the intervals between thunderclaps Lucinda heard strange noises from several different directions, muffled shouts and the squeals of frightened animals. She inched further away along the top of the fence, trying to keep some distance between her and her pursuer. The lights were still out all over the farm, but there was enough moonlight to see Kingaree's long, pale face and the gleam of his knife, which he was making sure to keep in view. 'No,' she said again, louder. 'I'm not coming down. *Mr. Walkwell!*' she shouted. '*Ragnar! It's Kingaree! He's here!*'

The tall man laughed. 'Neither of them two are coming, and I ain't afraid of either of them anyway. Walkwell's wiry enough, but he won't hurt me... because I'll have *you*!' At the last word he strode forward and leaped up onto the fence, his coat flapping like dark wings. Panicked, Lucinda tried to jump down, but one of her feet caught in the diamond space between the fence wires. As she struggled to free herself the man in the long black coat climbed toward her as quickly and easily as a spider on a wall. He snatched at her; for a moment his grasping fingers closed on her shoe, but it came off and she was just able to swing her leg over and jump down on the creek side of the fence. She kicked off her other shoe and ran along the levee beside the dark water. Kingaree swung himself down onto the concrete and began to lope unhurriedly after her. 'You can't outrun me, child. I'm twice your size and strong as vinegar!'

She was hemmed between the creek and Kingaree. The levee extended a long way before her, but she knew she could not outrun him on open ground. She stopped and turned to face him, so frightened of the man that she could barely breathe. Better to give up, she told herself. He wouldn't hurt her – he needed her. But her speeding heart didn't entirely believe that.

'Now that's a good girl,' he said, slowing to a walk,

approaching her along the concrete levee with the knife hand at his side and his other hand out.

'Stop there,' she said. 'Why should I trust you?'

He stopped and cocked his head to the side. He had lost his hat somewhere and the rain had plastered his black hair close to his skull. 'Trust me? Trust got nothing to do with it.' He shook rain out of his eyes. 'You're going with me until I'm safe off this property, and you're going to mind me just how I say or I'll cut you. I don't have to kill you to make you wish you'd never crossed me, you know.'

Lucinda's attention was distracted by movement in the shadows behind Kingaree, something rising out of the darkness of the creek. As she stared, trembling with cold and terror, she saw a large shadow separate itself from the rest. For a moment Lucinda thought that the reeds and long grasses and weeds of Kumish Creek had uprooted themselves and crawled up onto the levee, until she saw two huge eyes glinting in the moonlight, circles as big as softballs rising behind the unsuspecting Kingaree like twin moons until they hung a full half a foot above his head, the only glimmer in a dark, dripping mass like a moving haystack.

*Uncle Gideon's river monster*, she thought. *With the crazy name.* Then she remembered. *Bunyip.*

Kingaree's wet face wrinkled in puzzlement. 'Why are you staring like that? That's an old, stupid trick, child. There's nobody behind . . .' Then he heard a noise and turned. Jackson Kingaree didn't even have a chance to cry out before the huge shape was wrestling him backward into the tall reeds. He found his voice at last, shouting in raw-throated horror as he stabbed at the sodden mass over and over. The two of them, man and mythical beast, fell and rolled down the side of the levee as Kingaree's terrified curses peppered the air; then they splashed into the dark creek.

Lucinda did not wait to see what happened. She climbed back over the fence as fast as she could, ignoring her cuts and scrapes. She slipped getting down, landing so hard that for a moment she thought she'd broken her ankle. The sky went white and thunder rolled again as she forced herself to her feet. The struggle was still going on behind her, but the weird, intermixed noises of Kingaree and his attacker fell away as she limped back toward the house across the dark, rainy farm.

# CHAPTER 36

## NEHCTIK

Steve looked up the dark stairway in horror. 'What are you talking about? Why should we go up there? You said the witch's rooms are up there!'

In another part of the house, nearer to the front door, unfamiliar voices were raised in loud argument. Tyler's heart was beating hard: at any moment someone might walk in and find them. 'That's where the mirror is now,' he said with quiet urgency, and pushed again, but Steve Carrillo was big enough not to be moved if he didn't want to. 'I'm serious! Mrs. Needle took it. Gideon's wife Grace is stuck in there just like you were, and we have to save her.'

'That's *totally* different from what you said before,' Steve accused him. 'You told me we had to stop Colin – that he had this Continnyscope thing and he was going to take over the earth or something if we didn't

332

get back here and stop him. That he could destroy time like some kind of supervillain.'

'Exactly!' said Tyler, shoving him again. 'So we have to get Grace out of the mirror and then Gideon will . . . I don't know . . . it'll snap him out of whatever's wrong with him! We need Gideon to get well so he can stop Colin.'

'What? That totally doesn't make any sense at all! Forget it – I'm not going *near* that mirror. It's crazy in there, and I felt like I was in there for years last time!'

'Nobody's going to make you go in the mirror. You can wait for me.'

'Yeah, great. Wait around in the witch's room in your big old scary farmhouse. Good plan. No way, Jenkins.'

'Look, if we stay here, the witch will *definitely* find us.' Thunder boomed outside, and as it died away Tyler heard the loud voices again. One of them sounded like Patience Needle's. 'There she is now. Let's get the hell up there!'

Steve Carrillo moaned in protest but allowed Tyler to hustle him up the stairs. Tyler slipped in through the open door of the witch's office, then turned to beckon Steve after him. The room was tidy, as it usually was, everything on the desk and in the tall stand of apothecary shelves neatly stacked, potted plants arranged along both edges of the desk in rows with each pot carefully labelled. The only thing that didn't seem to fit was a pile of papers scattered carelessly across the desk as if a powerful wind had swept through the room and touched nothing else. On the far side of the little room stood the hand-carved wooden washstand and the tall, shiny rectangle of the mirror.

'It really is here,' Tyler breathed. He felt a kind of fierce joy, as if he had been rewarded for a stubborn defence of the truth.

'I told you,' Steve began, 'I'm not . . .'

All the lights went out.

'Wh-what . . . ?'

'It's okay,' said Tyler, but he was shaken himself. 'I'm still here!'

'What's going on?' Steve Carrillo sounded as if he was working up to a major panic attack. 'What's happening?'

'The power went out, that's all,' Tyler said. 'We've got flashlights. It's okay.' He flipped his on and swept the light around the room. The noise of the storm seemed louder now in the deep shadows, the witch's room larger and even more unsettling. Tyler leaned over the desk, sweeping his light back and forth across the scattered papers, but they seemed to be mostly ordinary, bills and other business documents.

*Bang!* The muffled explosion from downstairs made them both jump.

'That's a gun!' Steve said.

'Somebody knocked something over, that's all,' said Tyler.

'You are totally lying, Jenkins! Let's get out of here.'

Tyler also felt the very strong urge to bolt, but he had come too far to give up. 'I can't – I'm going in the mirror to get Grace,' he said. 'I told you.'

'You're not leaving me out here in the dark!'

'Then you can come with me.'

Another loud bang was quickly followed by a third.

Steve had just found his own flashlight. His eyes bulged. 'Don't try to tell me those weren't gunshots . . . !' His eyes widened further, until Tyler was afraid they would roll right out of his sockets. 'I hear someone coming!'

Tyler started to deny it, but there was no doubt – they could both hear rapid footsteps coming up the stairs. 'Oh, crap. Hide, quick!' He swung the flashlight around the room, but other than the dark space under the desk there was nowhere to go but into the mirror. Tyler knew he would never get Steve to follow him into it without a fight, so he grabbed the large boy's arm and dragged him toward the desk instead. 'Here!'

They had barely turned off their flashlights and crawled as far back under it as they could, wedged in by the backpacks they were still wearing, when the door of the room was flung open and crashed against the wall with a hollow thump.

'Traitor!' Mrs. Needle's voice hissed, cold and sharp as a piece of broken glass. 'I know you're here somewhere. You can't hide from me.'

The tiniest little whimper escaped Steve Carrillo's

mouth. Tyler grabbed his friend's hand and squeezed it as hard as he could. Mrs. Needle had not moved, which meant she was still standing in the doorway, listening. A moment later she strode toward the desk and Tyler felt his body turn cold, as though all the blood had leaked out of him at once. He squeezed Steve's hand again, as much to remind himself he wasn't alone as to keep his friend quiet.

Mrs. Needle was right beside the desk now: he could hear the swish of her skirts as she moved. 'If you can hear me, you had better come out,' she said. Only the fact that she didn't seem able to see in the dark, like a cat or a fox, kept him from crying out in fear. He bit his lip until he tasted blood. 'Come out, I said.' She raised her voice. 'I know you're here. You can't hide from me.'

Steve was shaking, his body moving as though he was crying without sound. Tyler didn't know what his friend was doing, but prayed he'd do it silently. At last Mrs. Needle moved away from their hiding place.

'If you are here and not answering me,' she said at last, 'I will give you cause to regret it, Mr. Kingaree. I swear I will teach you a very, very painful lesson.'

She paused as if waiting for an answer, then turned and stalked out of the room, pulling the door closed behind her. Tyler heard her move down the hall and open another door.

He flicked his flashlight on and dimmed the beam with his shirt. To his astonishment, Steve Carrillo was

336

kneeling beside him holding a long metal spike in his hand.

'I couldn't find my knife,' he whispered. 'I was going to stab her with the tent peg.'

'If it's not made out of silver it'd probably just make her mad,' Tyler told him. 'Come on, we have to get out of here before she comes back.'

Steve put the peg in his pocket. 'Where do we go? Downstairs?'

'Are you kidding? Didn't you hear? She's looking for Kingaree. That's the slavery guy I told you about! He's probably running around here with a gun, shooting at people.'

'Then where . . . ?' He suddenly understood. 'Oh, no. Oh, no, no, no.'

'Come on, dude. Do you want to be here when she comes back with a flashlight of her own?' Tyler pulled himself out from under the desk and climbed up onto the marble sink.

'No!' said Steve, tugging himself loose with a bit more difficulty than Tyler had. 'Not going – no way!'

'Suit yourself.' Without even wondering whether it would work, Tyler threw himself forward into the mirror, which parted for him like vertical mercury.

He landed in a clumsy heap, his backpack twisted halfway around his shoulders and head so that he fell over trying to get up. When he finally got it straight and could sit up and turn on his flashlight, he was stunned to discover he was in a different room than

337

the last time he had crossed through the mirror. For a moment it frightened him badly – had they fallen through into some even weirder and more dangerous place this time? – but then he realized why: the mirror wasn't in the library any more, so the Yrarbil was no longer on the other side of it. Instead he was in the mirror world's version of Mrs. Needle's office.

He crawled back to the washstand mirror and waved his flashlight so that Steve could see it on the other side. 'I'm okay, Steve,' he said, though he doubted his friend could hear him. 'Come on!' A few seconds later Steve Carrillo tumbled through the mirror's surface and crashed to the floor like a punctured parade float, backpack crooked and cup and canteen clattering.

'Let's go find Grace,' Tyler said. 'Maybe we can get back and get out before the lights come back on.'

Steve shuddered. 'Not me, dude. I don't need another visit to Spooktown. I'll wait right here.'

Tyler shook his head. 'Not a good idea. We don't know enough about how this place works – we might never find each other again. You'd better come with me.'

'Crud.' Steve said it with real feeling.

The corridor was empty outside Mrs. Needle's mirror room, but that didn't make Tyler feel much better. The real pictures on the real wall in this part of the house were creepy enough; the pictures in this mirror version were even more bizarre, photos of deserted, crumbling houses and ruined stone towers, fading images of people in clothing from times and places Tyler couldn't even guess at, places and things he'd never seen and never wanted to.

'Yeuch!' said Steve, peering into one dusty frame as they passed. 'Does that woman have some kind of giant grasshopper? She's holding it like a *baby* . . . !'

'Don't look at that stuff. Just keep moving.' Tyler was straining every nerve to listen. He was hoping that the ragged thing that haunted the library didn't come down to this end of the house – the Bandersnatch, Grace had called it, a name from the Alice in Wonderland books – but who knew what other nasty things might be crawling around in this ugly reflection of Ordinary Farm? He certainly didn't want to meet a mirror dragon or a mirror manticore.

Tyler could see the garden from the windows in the passage. That didn't look like a place he ever wanted to visit either. It was a stormy evening in the real world, but here there was only the bleak, depressing calm of a late winter afternoon, a tiny trace of silvery light still to be seen in the dark grey sky. The nearest part of the garden was a courtyard and lawn surrounded by a stone wall, empty but for a large black bird with a long thin beak and long thin legs that hopped slowly from place to place, hunting for something in the matted grass beside a ruined sundial. Beyond the walls stretched the rest of the garden, so overgrown and untended that it seemed more like a ghostly forest.

*Way too easy for something to sneak up on you around here*, Tyler thought.

'So where are we going?' Steve Carrillo was trying to sound calm but he wasn't entirely succeeding. 'Do you even know?'

'I've been thinking. The other time I was here Grace was hanging around the library, like you – but so was that Bandersnatch, that creepy thing that tried to get us.'

Steve looked a little sick. 'Oh, God. I remember that.'

'But Grace is a real person. She has to eat, and I didn't see anything like food in the library place, so I figure we should check the kitchen instead.'

'Great, Jenkins – if we had a map.'

'Well, there are signs, and since everything's kind of backward here, just keep your eyes open for one that says "Nehctik".'

Steve made a face. 'Neck Tick? What's that – a room full of giant bloodsucking ticks?'

'It's "kitchen" backward, you doorknob. Remember "Yrarbil" and "Rallec"?'

'Oh. Yeah.'

They found the stairs. The carpet was so old that it had been worn down to the wood in the middle of each step. Tyler held up his hand for silence and led Steve Carrillo downward until they had gone two storeys and were somewhere near what Tyler felt should be the kitchen. He led Steve down the hall until they came to a large double door, then cautiously pushed it open and peered inside.

It was the kitchen, but it took Tyler a few moments to be certain; the ceiling was several times higher than in the real kitchen, so that the room seemed almost like some kind of silo or tower, the looming walls covered with shelves that mounted up far above their heads, so high they could only be reached by teetering ladders.

Tyler saw movement and let the door fall shut a little further, narrowing the crack through which he and Steve were peering. Several small shapes were scuttling about the room, strange creatures with big eyes, not much face, and arms like long twigs, as if instead of Pema and Azinza and Sarah the mirror kitchen was staffed by huge pale beetles in old-fashioned dresses and bonnets.

'Oh, man, what are *those*?' whispered Steve. He sounded as if he was getting ready to bolt.

'Sshhh!' Tyler whispered back. 'Doesn't matter. We're just waiting.' It seemed to be near supper time – the little workers darted busily from place to place, skittering up and down the ladders to fetch ingredients, tending a huge boiling pot that seemed larger than the ancient wood-burning stove on which it sat, stopping only to argue with each other in voices like the swish and rattle of crumpled paper. Despite their clothes the kitchen creatures seemed as alien as crabs scuttling across the bottom of the sea. After a moment Tyler decided he didn't want to watch them any longer than he had to, and let the door fall silently closed.

'We're just waiting,' he told Steve again. 'Find a comfortable spot.'

It took almost an hour for them to finish their preparations, but at last all the kitchen creatures, nearly a dozen in all, trooped off to serve the meal, a chittering parade weighed down with bowls and trays as it made its way out of the kitchen by the far door. Some of the meals they carried were still moving, rattling the crockery as they tried to escape. One of the main courses, a mouse-like creature with a tail ten times its own length, caused a huge fuss when it leaped off its tray and ran up the sleeve of one of the beetle-workers. When the shrieking was over, the meal recaptured, and trays and crockery picked up again, the remaining cooks filed out of the room, leaving the Nehctik silent and empty.

'Finally!' said Steven Carrillo. 'My legs are killing me from sitting like this! Can we go back in now?'

Tyler shook his head. 'Not yet. Just stay there.'

'Why?'

'You'll see.' Tyler held his fingers to his lips. 'Remember, everybody's got to eat.'

Something stepped into the corridor behind them, filling the low hallway with cold, sighing like a windstorm. To Tyler's immense relief it turned away after a few moments and moved off in the opposite direction, rasping and scraping like a metal fireplace screen dragged across the wooden floor. Steve Carrillo flinched and trembled but stayed silent. Tyler was proud of him – he had been very close to running away himself.

'Yeah, everybody's got to eat, Jenkins,' Steve said in a shaky voice when the noise had finally died away. 'But I bet some of these things would be happy to eat *us*.'

# CHAPTER 37

## HORTICULTURAL ACTIVITIES

Lucinda felt like a rag doll that had lost its stuffing. Kingaree had terrified her, the thing that had *grabbed* Kingaree had terrified her too, and it had all left her as weak as when she had been suffering from the greenhouse fever.

In fact, she was beginning think the fever had come back: her head seemed swollen, too big and too heavy, and there were moments when the rumbling thunder and wailing winds of the storm sounded like voices calling to her.

She did her best to concentrate on just putting one foot in front of the other as she walked back to the house. She didn't even know what she was going to do when she got there. She couldn't hear them at this moment, but Stillman and his men might still be running around shooting at things. Lucinda knew she should have a plan, or at least a goal, but it was all she could do just to keep moving.

As she reached the broad, curving driveway she saw a man's shape appear in the front doorway; after a moment's swaying hesitation, the figure went clumsily across the porch and down the stairs, then past the Snake Parlour window and along the side of the house, heading toward her. It was Gideon, barefoot in his pyjamas and robe, stumbling through the hot, rainy night.

'Uncle Gideon!' she shouted.

He didn't even look up. He reached the end of the building and turned away from her, trudging slowly toward the garden and outbuildings like the last man in a chain gang.

Lucinda ran across the gravel but Gideon had already disappeared into the darkness. She hurried after him as best she could, but the ankle she had twisted jumping down from the fence was beginning to feel like it might be seriously injured and she couldn't go much faster than a limping trot.

After a moment she saw him again, staggering toward the dark rows of plants that bent and waved in the wind.

*The garden. He's headed for the kitchen garden.* A sudden chilling thought. *No – he's headed for the greenhouse . . . !*

Lucinda reached the old man's side just as he got to the outskirts of the garden. She tried to catch hold of his arm but he shook her off, moaning something over and over that sounded like '*Lennie, no! Lennie, no!*' It was only when she had grabbed him again that she realized he was trying to say 'Let me go,' but his mouth couldn't form the proper sounds.

Gideon was stronger than she had imagined he could be – it was difficult even to hold onto his arm with the way he was fighting her. 'Help!' she shouted. 'Somebody help me! Help Uncle Gideon!' But just as when she had been pursued by Kingaree, no one answered. The house was still dark, although Lucinda could hear shouting voices and an occasional bang that might have been gunshots or just shutters being slammed by the powerful winds.

Gideon shook her off again and put his bony old hands on her shoulder, then pushed her so hard that Lucinda slipped on the muddy ground and tumbled backward into a row of cornstalks. She struggled to her feet, soaking wet and half drowned in mud, but as she grabbed him again and begged him to stop he turned and she realized it didn't matter what she said: her great-uncle's eyes had rolled up until only the whites showed and his lips were skinned back from his teeth like the snarl of a frightened dog. As she stared in horror Gideon swung his arms, and one of his hands cracked against the side of her head and knocked her down again.

Lucinda lay sprawled among the broken stalks. Old as he was, he was still too big and strong for her. Not only that, but the voice that had been just at the edge of her thoughts earlier was growing stronger. She could understand it now, not words, not even concise ideas like Desta's thoughts: it was a *feeling*, something beyond language or even ordinary thought.

*Come. Come here. Come here now.*

But the most frightening thing was how strong it was – how much Lucinda wanted to yield to that simple, powerful demand.

*Come here.*

It was the greenhouse, she realized – or whatever was *in* the greenhouse. But even as she understood that, she also became aware that she was crawling through the rows of corn toward it and had been doing so for long moments already. She struggled against the pull, slowing herself, but Gideon, completely captured by it, was already several rows ahead.

*I can't worry about me*, she thought, dizzied by thunder and the pressure in her head. *I have to stop Gideon.* Instead of fighting the summons she climbed to her feet and staggered forward, letting the urge have its way, at least for a moment; when she caught up with her great-uncle she grabbed him around the legs and tumbled them both down into the wet garden.

*Stop fighting.* Wordless but clear, the voice still pulled at her. *Come here.*

Everything in her wanted to give in to that summons – everything except a tiny, thinking part that was still Lucinda and only Lucinda. It was like fighting against a rip tide: the muddy ground all around her seemed alive as creatures of a dozen different sizes – bugs, rodents, wounded birds – crawled and hopped toward the greenhouse and whatever it was that called them all. Meanwhile, Gideon was fighting to get up, flailing and thrashing like a wounded animal, and only his witlessness allowed her to keep him from succeeding.

The greenhouse was only a few dozen yards away now – she could see it looming above the wind-lashed plants like a ship on a stormy sea. Gideon squeezed out from under her, ripping at her skin with his bare nails, and in the fight she was rolled over and her head shoved down toward the mud. Lucinda found herself face to face with what had once been a rabbit but was now only a shrivelled sack of skin covered with little white bumps, pierced through and through with smooth, white, wormlike stems that had grown up out of the kitchen-garden soil. As she pulled back, gagging, she realized that she was surrounded by tiny corpses, dozens of insects and small animals snagged in white tangles.

The fungus. It really *was* a fungus, just as the letter from Madagascar had said, a fungus that could somehow infest a living creature and then draw it in toward the parent growth . . . the thing in the greenhouse . . .

'*Help!*' she shrieked, terror giving her strength. She held desperately to Gideon as though they were both caught in a whirlpool. '*Help us!* Help me! It's got

Gideon!' The rain washed her tears away before they reached her cheeks. 'Can't anybody *hear* me?'

'I heard you,' said a voice close to her ear. 'You can let him go.' Strong brown hands closed on Gideon and lifted him from her grasp as easily as plucking a dandelion. Mr. Walkwell carried Gideon back many yards, to the edge of the garden, then dumped him on the ground. The caretaker leaned down and flicked his finger at the back of Gideon Goldring's skull and the old man in the muddy bathrobe immediately collapsed in a heap.

'I did not want to do that to him.' Mr. Walkwell's hooves were plunged deep in the muddy ground. 'But the thing has enslaved him.'

'Oh, thank you, thank you . . . !' Lucinda began, but Simos Walkwell was already walking past her toward the greenhouse.

'Get the others. I will need help,' he told her.

She felt too exhausted even to stand. 'Where are they? Where's Ragnar?'

'He cannot come.' He waded through the greenery like a fairy-tale giant crashing through a forest. 'The manticores are out,' he called, 'and some of them are in the reptile barn.'

'The reptile barn . . . ?' No wonder poor Desta had seemed so frightened. Lucinda got to her feet, about to run back to the house, but saw that Gideon was already stirring and beginning to crawl toward the garden again. 'Mr. Walkwell! Wait . . . !'

The man with goat's hooves had almost reached the greenhouse.

'You must deal with it!' he shouted. Another flare of lightning blazed across the sky and lit up the entire garden. A huge cloud of what looked like white dust puffed out of the greenhouse, enveloping Mr. Walkwell like a fog. Thunder boomed, then lightning scratched across the sky again. Even as Mr. Walkwell waved his arms, trying to clear the powdery mass, countless white tubes or stems suddenly wriggled up out of the greenery to tangle and tie him like Gulliver on Lilliput's beach. Mr. Walkwell fought back, snapping many of the faintly luminous stems, but for every one he broke several more wrapped around him, lively and clever as fingers. Within instants he had become a wriggling, man-shaped mass of fungus strings, but his thrashing was already beginning to slow.

'Oh, God, somebody help us!' Lucinda shrieked.

Gideon was crawling back into the garden. She wrapped her legs around his waist and then threw herself down, grabbing at the thickest, most well-rooted plants she could reach, but she knew that her failing strength couldn't hold out long against the pull of the thing in the greenhouse. Rain splashed dirt into her eyes. 'Help us, please!'

Then, to her immense relief, she saw that somebody was coming toward her with a flashlight. She prayed it was Ragnar or one of the Mongolian herders, anyone who could help her keep Gideon from the greenhouse.

The flashlight played over Gideon's maddened face.

'Good God, what is that fool doing?' asked Ed Stillman.

'Help me!' Lucinda begged. 'Grab him!'

Stillman stood and stared for a long moment. 'You know,' he said at last, 'I don't believe I will. I've made sure no one's altering the will tonight. That's all I really cared about.' He looked out over the storm-whipped garden and the almost unrecognizable form of Simos Walkwell in his cocoon of white strands. 'Now if, as it appears, some botany experiment of Gideon's has gone badly wrong, I don't think I want to be around for the end . . . especially if my old friend is as determined to get himself killed as he appears to be.' He laughed and pointed his light at Gideon's face again; Gideon growled and snapped his teeth at the beam like a trapped animal. 'And I'm not interested in staying to answer police questions. No, I rather think that's up to you and the rest of Gideon's weird little cult . . .'

'You . . . you rat! We'll tell them you were here . . . !'

'Oh, I rather think you'll have trouble getting *that* to stick.'

Somebody else came stumbling toward them out of the darkness, a big, shadowy shape, but Lucinda's hope that Ragnar had finally arrived was quickly dashed.

'Mr. Stillman,' said the man named Cater, out of breath and frightened, 'something . . . something attacked the car!'

'Really?' The billionaire smiled sourly. 'And you two

with all those guns and the car with all that armour? What could possibly be the problem?'

'I don't know! But it ripped through the metal in a couple of places and it almost got Deuce! The power went out in the house and we turned the light on in the car, then it just . . . jumped on us. From nowhere!'

Stillman rolled his eyes. 'Fine. I was just thinking we should be leaving anyway – after all, we'll own all this soon enough. Come along – we still have to go collect that idiot Dankle and get him fixed up.' Stillman looked to Lucinda with a shrug. 'I shot him by accident. My God, the fuss he made! You would have thought I'd blown a hole in his chest instead of giving him a harmless wound in the fat of his arm . . .'

Lucinda was losing her hold on Gideon, who was as slippery-wet as a giant otter. 'Please, Mr. Stillman, please don't leave . . . !'

He shook his head sternly. 'You don't understand, little lady. Other people don't use me to get what they want – *I'm* the one who gets what *I* want. That's how it works.' He turned to Cater. 'Let's leave these folks to their . . . horticultural activities.'

Ed Stillman and his bodyguard turned and walked back toward the darkened house, visible only in the intermittent flashes of lightning.

'No!' screamed Lucinda. Gideon had his hand over her face now, pushing so hard it felt like her nose might break. 'Don't leave us like this! Don't do it!'

But only the storm answered her.

# CHAPTER 38

## COLIN'S CUNNING PLAN

In all the world there was only Colin and the manticore and the flashing sky. The orange eyes stared as the creature paced toward him. The weird, almost manlike face showed no expression, a pale, wrinkled leather mask with feral jaws agape so that he could see every terrible tooth. As it neared the smell of the thing struck Colin like a blow: instead of trying to run he collapsed like something broken that should never have been forced to stand in the first place. Then the huge shape loomed above him, blocking light and hope, choking him in that terrible sour smell as he waited for the end . . .

Then it stepped over him, and rain struck Colin's face again. Sky. The sky was above him once more. But where was the monster?

For long, long moments he waited, empty as a torn

sack, and in the screaming centre of his thoughts he wondered if the thing meant to play with him before it killed him, like a cat with a mouse. At last, when nothing but warm rain had touched him for long seconds, he cautiously opened his eyes.

Colin turned his head slowly, mud rolling beneath him, and saw with blinking surprise that the manticore was walking away from him, less like a stalking predator and more like a ship in a strong wind, lurching and swaying as it stepped onto the gravel drive. It turned and took a few steps toward the far end of the house, away from the kitchen, then it slowed, stopped, and began to shiver, a violent shake from tail to head and back again so that the creature seemed to be pulled between two invisible masters, one at each end. It staggered, overbalanced, and then collapsed to the ground where it lay kicking and twitching. Colin did not even consider moving: he lay peering at it through slitted eyes, holding his breath. As he had feared, the creature lurched to its feet again and took a few wobbly steps before finding its balance, but instead of turning toward him it resumed a slow, slightly unsteady march toward the space between the end of the house and the nearest outbuildings. Where was it going? The beast seemed have some terrible duty, something that would carry it forward as long as strength lasted.

As it vanished into the dark and Colin lay gasping, he realized that the tickling he felt on his feet and ankles and legs and wrists and fingers was not mud but what could only be termed a stream of snakes, frogs, worms, and other slithering and hopping things, all following in the path of the limping manticore.

He jumped up and shook the small things from his clothes and backpack. This seemed like a good time to head back to the house, and quickly: his heart had just begun to slow, and in the comparative calm he realized that several other manticores were still unaccounted for.

But what was that human-faced monstrosity doing in this part of the farm? Could the electrical storm have somehow sprung the locks on the manticore cage, or had someone let the things out on purpose, as Colin had once done himself? Could it have been Tyler? The Jenkins brat was always making mischief, but somehow, even in his most indignant certainties, Colin Needle couldn't quite convince himself that Tyler, horrid though he was, would deliberately let loose a killer like that.

When Colin reached the house he locked the front door behind him. The power was still out but his flashlight gave as much light as he needed to see that the house seemed deserted. The Snake Parlour next to the entry hall was a shambles and Gideon's bed there was empty. The smaller pieces of furniture had been thrown around, and Colin also saw what looked suspiciously like spatters of blood on the floor. He felt a sudden chill. What had happened here? Where was

Gideon? And more importantly, where was Colin's mother?

Azinza and Pema and Sarah were locked in the kitchen and wouldn't come out. Sarah shouted something about shooting and screaming but refused to open the door, as though Colin wasn't just as much of a victim as any of the women. He hurried up the stairs toward his mother's rooms; to his relief he could hear her voice as he stepped onto the landing, but her words were uglier than anything he'd ever heard from her before.

'The snake! How dare he? I will show him his own beating heart, freshly torn from his chest and still steaming . . . !'

'Mother?' He stepped into her office. Her desk and the floor around it were littered with papers. 'What happened?'

She looked up sharply at his entrance and just the sight of her face twisted into a grimace of pure rage was enough to make Colin take a step backward, hands raised as though to protect himself from a blow. His mother's expression froze, then relaxed into something less terrifying. 'Colin Needle, where have you *been*? I've been looking all over for you! You were supposed to be in your room!' Her eyes widened as she saw his backpack. 'Have you been *outside*? When I told you very, very clearly to stay in the house?' For a moment he thought she might cross the room and strike him, but then she shook her head, her mouth like a tightened string. 'Go to your room.'

'Where's Gideon? What happened?'

'*Not now.*' She turned back to the papers, rummaging through them frantically, as if the disordered pile was a haystack and she had dropped her last needle into it.

'Mother, stop! Everything's crazy! One of the manticores has got out, and it almost . . .' But she was no longer paying attention, as if her only child had suddenly ceased to exist. 'What were you shouting about when I came in, Mother? What are you trying to find . . . ?'

'*Not now,* Colin,' she snapped again.

'You aren't listening! One of the manticores is out – maybe all of them! We have to find Walkwell! He's the only one–'

She turned on him in fury. 'You have become a *very disobedient child.* Go to your room this moment and lock the door. That is an *order.*'

Such was the force of her voice and the nature of their long, unequal relationship that a moment later Colin was stumbling out of his mother's office and headed toward his own bedroom. He pushed through the door and dropped his pack on the floor, then shoved it under the bed with his foot. Whatever happened, he wanted the Continuascope safe. It was bizarre to think how excited he had been feeling only half an hour ago, how optimistic, how triumphant!

Then he saw that his laptop computer was open on his desk.

But Colin Needle never left his laptop open. He

hated the thought of the dust that floated through the ancient house, the residue of its moth-eaten carpets and uncleaned rooms, filtering down onto his keyboard. He *always* closed it. But who had been into his computer, then? And why?

As he stood, still wearing his dripping jacket and muddy clothes, he considered the possible guilt of the Jenkins kids, and even whether old Caesar might have left his laptop that way after some senile attempt to dust it, but he couldn't forget that earlier in the day his mother *had* told him to stay inside – several times and very forcefully, in fact. She had said she was worried about the storm, and of course Colin had ignored her, since the place he had planned to go was underground and would be unaffected by even the worst electrical storm. But now that he thought about it, she had been very insistent.

And other than Colin himself (and of course Gideon Goldring, who had been too sick even to talk much, let alone climb the stairs to play with Colin's laptop) the only regular resident of the farm who knew how to use a computer . . . was his mother.

No! He couldn't believe that his mother would have used Colin's own program to open the manticore cage – it must have been Tyler Jenkins! But no matter how hard he tried, he couldn't convince himself. His mother had been preparing feverishly for something all day. Had it been something she wanted to hide? Had she released those murderous beasts to keep Walkwell and the Norseman busy while she saw to her own business, whatever it had been?

And where was Gideon Goldring? Good God, could he be . . . *outside*? Had he worked himself free somehow? Maybe that was Gideon's blood on the parlour floor, and now he was wandering, confused and dripping blood, out where the manticores were hunting.

Colin hesitated, then grabbed up his flashlight and headed out into the hallway. He had promised his mother he would lock his door, so he did. From the outside. A few moments later he was downstairs. He took a heavy iron poker from the entry-hall fireplace for a weapon, but he was praying he wouldn't have to use it: Colin had no illusions that he could kill a mythical creature as big as a lion with little more than a metal back scratcher.

Despite the heavy winds the storm still hung just above the farm, a lightning-painted darkness, clouds black as ink. Colin stood in the ankle-deep mud and stared down at Lucinda Jenkins, who was wrestling what appeared to be a very dirty, very crazy Gideon Goldring. 'What are you *doing*?' Colin demanded.

Lucinda turned her face toward him. 'Oh, Colin, help me, please! There's something in that greenhouse, some . . . *killer fungus*! It gets into animals and then . . . I don't know, it *calls* them. Like they're hypnotized! They come and get tangled up – it even got Mr. Walkwell!'

She tried to point; he followed the line of her clumsy gesture and saw a tangled, manlike shape beside the greenhouse, something that looked like a struggling, upright sleeping bag made of faintly glowing white lace. 'It's trying to get Gideon too – he keeps trying to go to it! It grabbed Mr. Walkwell when he got too close, and I think I can feel it too, now. Oh, Colin, please help! I can feel it *pulling* at me . . .'

He stared at the greenhouse. The whole thing was moving – no, the greenhouse was stationary, but it was covered with pale tendrils and *they* were moving, thousands of threadlike things waving in the wind like the fronds of a coral reef. Was that what his mother had been searching for so desperately? For a way to kill such a monstrosity? But what could accomplish such a thing except a million gallons of weed killer? They didn't have anything like that on the farm.

Lightning flashed again, turning everything in the garden either flat black or glaring white. He looked down at the fire iron in his hand. *Electrical storm,* he suddenly thought. *Lightning . . .*

He threw the fire iron away. It spun through the rain and squelched down into the mud, but even as he watched it he suddenly thought of something – something crazy. Something *big.* Without a word, he turned his back on Gideon and Lucinda and ran toward the farmhouse.

'No! Where are you *going*?' Lucinda shrieked.

'Colin, come back or I'll hate you forever!' *I can't hold him any longer . . . !*

'You have to – just for a minute,' he called back over his shoulder, hurrying his words before the thunder would drown him out again. 'I'll bring back something to tie him with. Just hold on!' Because Colin had an idea.

*That's right,* he told himself. *I'm going to save Gideon. I'm going to save everybody. Watch Tyler Jenkins try to top that . . . !*

It took long seconds, minutes even, to find the big spool of wire left over from the installation of the electric fence: it had been buried deep in one of the sheds since the previous autumn. With the heavy spool in one hand and an old iron fence post, electrical tape, and a pair of clippers cradled in the other, Colin ran clumsily back across the property toward the house. He stopped beneath the part of the roof with the tallest turret – the one that held the house's lightning rod – and located the wire that led from the rod, across the roof and down the side of the house until it wrapped at last around a metal water pipe that grounded it to the muddy earth. Colin looked up to make sure no lightning was flickering, then swiftly cut the lightning-rod wire near the ground and spliced it to one end of his own wire, trying to make up for his clumsy, wet hands by wrapping several layers of black electrical tape around the splice. When he finished he clambered to his feet and hurried around the side of the house toward the garden, unspooling the wire behind him.

He was holding the spool by its plastic handle, but he knew that wouldn't help him much if a bolt struck the lightning rod now and tried to ground itself down the wire. *I'll be roasted like a Christmas goose,* Colin realized, suddenly breathless with terror.

He ran even faster until he had reached the garden and the rows of wind-whipped plants. Lucinda shrieked at him but he did not slow down to help her – if necessary, they could use some of the plastic-coated wire to tie Gideon up once the thing in the greenhouse was dead, but he couldn't worry about that yet. He dropped the fence post, unspooled another couple of dozen yards of wire, then stripped the insulation from the unused end of the wire and twisted it around one end of the metal post before tying it through a hole in the metal and then taping the whole thing securely. He stood up and hefted the wired post like a javelin. It was fairly well-balanced. The only problem was, Colin knew he couldn't throw it even half the distance to the greenhouse.

'Don't worry! This will work!' he shouted, doing his best to ignore Lucinda's distracting screams – apparently Gideon was on the verge of escape again. The whole scene was so daunting that Colin considered waiting until Ragnar appeared: the huge Viking could easily throw the piece of metal three times the distance Colin could, probably more. But the glory would then be Ragnar's, and Colin's own role might even be forgotten. No, something had to be done *now*. There could be no question of waiting for the Norseman.

Colin walked down the ends of the rows toward the greenhouse, carefully letting the wire fall behind him without getting tangled so that when he threw it the fence post would fly true. Mr. Walkwell had stopped struggling and his still form was only a dozen yards ahead of Colin now. He was almost close enough, almost, but another section of the storm was rolling in and he was holding bare metal in his hand – metal connected to the lightning rod on the house's tallest point. In a sudden panic he hurried the last few steps toward the spot he had picked out, pulling his arm back, but just as he had almost reached it something snagged his feet and ankles, tumbling him to the ground.

Colin looked down. Strange white strands like kite string had extended – grown? – from the sodden ground and had already begun to twine up his legs with amazing speed. Even as he watched they wrapped around him, tiny strands branching off and growing right through the fabric of his clothes, making his legs prickle and sting . . .

Thunder boomed again. His heart speeding so fast now he felt faint, Colin realized he was lying on top of what might at any moment become a live electrical wire connected to the rage of the heavens themselves. He rolled over and pulled his arm back to toss away the makeshift javelin, but something was tightening all along the length of his arm. He was snared by hundreds of pale strings as strong as ivy creepers. He fought, but it was already too late: the fungal strands wrapped his arm tightly just as they had already wrapped the rest of him, and before he could do anything his hand was bound to the naked length of iron.

He couldn't move. He was tied from foot to shoulder and holding a live electrical conductor in his hand. 'No!' he shouted, 'I'm stuck! Help me! Someone help me! *I don't want to die . . . !*'

But Colin Needle's cries were drowned out as another wave of the storm swept down from the far hills and across the farm, crackling with sparks of new lightning.

# CHAPTER 39

## NIHLOCK'S RETHUM

Tyler had been certain that finding the kitchen – or the Nehctik, as it was labelled here in the mirror house – would solve their problems, and he seemed to have been proved right.

One of the huge room's many doors opened a crack, but for long moments nothing came through. Tyler nudged Steve Carrillo. At last, a dark shape crept through into the kitchen, staying close to the floor and moving with the fitful stop-and-go of a spy advancing through dangerous territory. Wrapped in a billowing, dusty length of fabric that might once have been an ancient blanket or tablecloth, the interloper looked a bit like a four-legged ghost as it scuttled over to one of the shelves. Then a pair of quite human-looking hands emerged from the blanket's folds and began scrabbling in the jars and canisters.

'*Now!*' said Tyler, pushing through the door and into the kitchen.

The strange thing heard him coming and reared up in shock – he had a glimpse of wide, frightened eyes in the shadows of the blanket – then retreated toward the door, but the cloth tangled its legs so that it stumbled and nearly fell. It hurried away across the room making a strange frightened 'hoo'-ing noise.

'Stop!' Tyler called. 'Stop – we want to help you!' But the shrouded figure was already halfway out the far door. Tyler had to leap forward and grab at it, then suffer a few panicky but ineffective blows before the struggling subsided. As it fought him the blanket fell away from its head. Tyler found himself face to face with the old woman he had met before, her eyes wide with fear.

'Grace!' he said. 'Grace, it's me! You met me before, remember? You warned me about the Bandersnatch. Don't be frightened, Grace.'

She was still trying to pull away even as she watched him and listened, as though her body was not entirely under the control of her mind. In the midst of this faded fairy-tale castle her clothes seemed strangely modern, although tattered and threadbare and dusty, the kind of things a nice lady on a bus might wear. Grace had disappeared twenty years earlier. Had twenty years passed for her in this place, or had it seemed much more?

At last she stopped wriggling. 'You're . . . Grace?' she asked.

'No, no, you are.' He turned to Steve, who was staring nervously from the doorway. 'It's okay. This is how you were too. Help me with her.' He turned back to Grace. 'Don't be afraid. That's just my friend Steve. He was trapped here too. He got out. Now we're going to get you out.'

'Out . . . ?' she said slowly. 'What do you mean?' She wasn't fighting now, but it felt like she might begin again any moment. What if she cried out? If those bug-things here were the weird reflection of the sweet, friendly kitchen workers in the real Ordinary Farm, he definitely did not want to meet anything more unpleasant, like a mirror manticore.

'Out,' he told her, making his voice as soothing as he could. 'We're taking you back to where you came from, Grace. Don't you remember Ordinary Farm? The real Ordinary Farm, not this backward place? Gideon? Octavio?' None of the names appeared to ring any bells for her, which frightened him. Steve had taken a while to get his memory back. Maybe she had been here so long she never would. 'Do you remember anyone?' Who might be particularly memorable from Grace's days on the farm? 'Mr. Walkwell? From Greece?'

She paused in surprise, then nodded slowly. 'He's kind. Yes, I remember him, he's kind.'

Relief flowed through Tyler. 'Well, he's there –

he's waiting to see you again, Grace. And so is your husband, Gideon.'

The woman's expression suddenly turned worried. 'Gideon. He's angry with me. Shouted. I remember.'

'He's not angry any more. He wants you to come back. Really.'

She allowed herself to be manoeuvred toward the door, but when she saw the stairs she balked. 'No! Not up there. The White Lady . . . the one with the eyes . . . !'

That didn't sound very nice. 'Don't worry – whoever she is, she's not there now because that's where we came from. Come on, it's okay!'

But as they finally coaxed her up the last set of steps toward the passage leading to the room where the mirror waited, they heard a rustling and the air was suddenly full of the scent of ashes, the cold, acrid stink of something that had burned long, long ago. Tyler, who was bringing up the rear, looked down as a shapeless head surrounded by tattered grey filaments peered up at them from the depths of the stairwell.

'It's that thing from the library – the Bandersnatch!' Tyler called, trying to keep his voice low even as his mouth and throat went dry with terror. '*Run!*'

He put his hand in the middle of Grace's bony back and pushed, almost lifting her up out of the stairwell and onto the hallway floor. Steve was tugging her arm so hard Tyler hoped he didn't damage her, then thought, *No, God no, better a broken arm than to get caught by* that *thing . . . !*

Tyler knew he shouldn't look back but he had never been very good at doing the sensible thing. *Curiosity may have killed the cat, Tyler Jenkins,* a teacher had once told him, *but if it had also been as stubborn as you it would have quickly lost the other eight lives as well.* He snuck a glance back over his shoulder.

He had seen the otherworldly thing chasing them the last time he came through the mirror, had even seen a little of its terrible, vague face, but this time he recognized something in the dead grey features. Whatever it had become, the Bandersnatch had once been some version of his great-uncle Gideon Goldring.

Steve slowed to a trot in front of him as they burst out into an open hall.

'What are you doing? Keep running!' Tyler said. He almost ran into Grace, who was suddenly stumbling.

'Where are we?' Steve spun in a circle, his eyes wide with terror. 'I don't recognize any of this!'

Tyler was about to shout at him, but he realized a second later that he didn't either.

'Oh, man,' he said. 'You're right. How did we wind up here?' The hall was broad and high, with flickering lights perched in cobwebbed chandeliers and the floors covered with dusty carpets thrown haphazardly across each other. At the far end a stairwell spiralled up at strange angles, and a single door led out from either side of the hall.

'I don't know, Tyler, but I can hear something back there . . .' Steve was bouncing in place like a kid who needed to use the bathroom. 'Where do we go?'

Something was telling Tyler that he should choose the left-hand door, but that didn't fit with his memories and sense of direction – surely they had descended for some time to find the kitchen? And just as certainly he remembered that the Gideon-thing, the Bandersnatch, made its home in the lowest parts of the mirror house. He glanced at pale Steve and the exhausted, frightened old woman. Lucinda was always telling him not to be so impulsive, and there was nothing about the left-hand door to recommend it except a vague feeling.

'We go up,' he decided. 'The stairs – hurry!'

Without inviting discussion he caught at Grace's arm and pulled her forward across the dusty hall. Steve groaned but followed. As they ran, shadows passed across the high windows, winged shapes that seemed far too large to be birds.

The stairs were much harder to climb than he would have guessed, leaning at treacherous angles. At the top they pushed through a doorway onto another landing, this one smaller and better kept – the dust only lightly frosted the surfaces instead of lying in drifts like snow – but from this smaller entry hall there was only one way out, up another set of narrow stairs like a dimly lit tunnel.

*Up*, he thought to himself, although some dim feeling was still urging him to turn around and take his chances with whatever might be below. *Up is the only thing that makes sense. We'll either find the way out or we'll find some light.*

'I want to get out of here, Tyler,' Steve said, huffing up the stairs behind him. 'I really want to go home, man. My parents must be going crazy . . . !'

Tyler shook his head, not to deny what Steve said, but because he barely had the strength to climb and pull Grace – he couldn't talk at the same time.

They spilled out into a room that was the cleanest and best-lit they had yet seen, but still dim and dusty by most standards. Something about it seemed familiar, although Tyler knew he'd never been there. It was some kind of sitting room, with chairs and small tables and sideboards. Photographs in frames stood on every surface – Tyler thought there must be a hundred or more – and as he moved into the centre of the room he realized they were all of the same woman, her face always blurred by shadow but her slender, upright figure and graceful bearing recognizable in each likeness, no matter how strange the other things in the pictures.

*It's like that place Lucinda told me about,* he realized. *The parlour in the real house with all the pictures of Grace – 'the Shrine', Luce called it.*

He watched the real Grace moving between the pieces of furniture, oblivious to the faded photographs, and wondered why they meant so little to her.

Then something screeched.

The cry was so loud and harsh that for a crazy instant Tyler thought it must be one of the shadow-birds he had seen outside the hall windows, loose in the house and swooping toward them. *'Rethuuum oot muk!'* it cried. *'Reed, rethum oot muk!'*

Tyler and Steve looked at each other in shocked surprise, but it was Grace who seemed the worst affected. She let out a whimper of fear and fell against one of the tables, sending the pictures crashing to the floor.

'It's her,' she moaned. 'The White Lady! She'll catch us now for sure!'

Something heavy was coming nearer, something strange and clumsy dragging and bumping toward them. Then lights brighter than any of the house's flickering bulbs flashed in the corridor outside the picture parlour.

*'Nihlock!'* the thing cried, and the edge in its voice grew sharper, more jagged. *'Nihlock, oo-ee ra rrrehw?'*

'Oh, man – it's talking backward!' said Steve. *'Nihlock, nihlock* – it's yelling for *Colin!'*

*'Oo-ee ra rrrehw, Nihlock?'* the thing howled, and something crashed against a wall and broke.

Now Tyler knew who it was, if not *what* it was. He also knew that with the horrid sounds getting louder each moment they had only one hope. 'Run!' he shouted. 'Back down the stairs!' He reached over and gave Steve a shove in the back. 'Hurry!'

As they pelted down the stairs Tyler did his best

to keep Grace upright. Her legs kept moving but she seemed barely conscious, murmuring as though caught in a terrible dream and trying to wake herself up.

They reached the bottom of the crazy-curving staircase. Steve tumbled onto the floor but got up quickly. 'Which way?' he shouted.

Which one had been the left-hand door? They were facing the other way now, so it had to be the one on the right. 'There – go!' Tyler was furious with himself: instead of trusting his instincts he had tried to do what someone else would have done – he, Tyler Jenkins, explorer of the Fault Line and navigator of the Mirror World – and it had almost got them killed. *In fact,* he thought as he half-carried Grace after Steve, *it still might.*

As they sprinted across the hall toward the door something big came down the stairs behind them, something tall and stretched with long, waving arms, a twisted figure wrapped in billowing white like a misshapen bride. Twin beams of brilliant light stabbed out from the place where its eyes should have been, their glare obscuring the thing's face as its gaze raked the walls of the great hall and then fell on Tyler and Steve.

'*Meth ees I!*' it cried. '*Nihlock, mooorlob huth nih!*'

Tyler could only pray as he slammed through the doorway that they wouldn't have to meet the mirror Colin too.

They ran and ran. For a while they could hear the

mirror Needle clumping along behind them, and then could only make out the steam-whistle shriek of her voice. Finally they got beyond even that. Tyler now all but shut his eyes, relying on his sense not of where they *should* be, but of where the mirror was, a sensation like a warm glow at the edge of his thoughts.

It seemed as if they had been running for half an hour when they found themselves getting near the Nehctik again. Of course – he had stupidly forgotten that the washstand mirror was in a different place, in the mirror version of Mrs. Needle's office. Did that mean they were entering the mirror-Needle's territory again? He shuddered, but realized that maybe they had done themselves a favour, leading her away from her office.

At last he reached a door that felt right. Tyler swallowed deep as he turned the knob, but when he saw that it was indeed the mirror office he gasped in relief. He dragged Steve and the white-haired woman through, then slammed the door and grabbed the handle tightly. The mirror was waiting, all alone in a pool of faint, dreary light.

'Go!' Tyler said. 'Help her through, Steve. I'm going to hold the door just in case.'

Steve Carrillo guided the exhausted Grace through the frame of the mirror and pushed her through the reflection, then clambered wearily up onto the mirror washstand himself. 'Jenkins,' he said. 'I gotta tell you something . . .'

'I know,' said Tyler as he pulled himself up beside him. He could hear something moving in the hallway just outside, and the angry murmur of backward speech. 'I know – *never again*. And I totally agree.'

As the knob began to turn on the office door they plunged through the unsolid glass, Steve first, then Tyler right behind him.

# CHAPTER 40

## CARROT GIRL NOT NICE

Lucinda didn't even know why she was still trying to hang onto Gideon. She was out of strength, while he, deranged by the call of the greenhouse-thing, was still fighting as hard as ever. Colin Needle had tried to help but had failed completely and instead put himself in deadly danger. Even Mr. Walkwell had succumbed to the thing. Ragnar, the only person left who might conceivably help, was on the other side of the farm. It was hopeless.

*Yes, surrender*, a voice urged her, although not in words: the words were all Lucinda's, as if she was talking to herself, a soothing, reasonable version of her own inner voice . . . *Come here. Join. Become.* An impression of completeness beckoned to her, a promise of joy in belonging so powerful it wasn't even an emotion but a state of being – so wonderful that words couldn't even describe it. *Come. Become us . . . !*

*Carrot Girl! Help! Scared!*

The new voice in her thoughts, that of young Desta, startled her back to herself. She realized she had almost lost her grip on her great-uncle and she grabbed his muddy bathrobe tighter.

*Desta? Desta, can you hear me?* But Lucinda's thoughts seemed to drift up and be snatched away as if by the wind: nothing came back to her.

Another lightning flash made the rain seem to hang in mid-air. Shiny white strands of the monster fungus were rising all around the greenhouse, bursting through the soil and reaching toward the sky as if worshipping the storm, and even as these hundreds of strands twined upward, the main fungus body was growing larger by the moment, swelling like rising dough, pressing against the dirty greenhouse windows. Panes of glass began to burst out of their frames, shattering with sounds loud enough for Lucinda to hear them even above the rising winds.

*Carrot Girl . . . !* The dragon's thoughts were growing fainter. *Help! Scared! Bad animals!*

*The reptile barn! Mr. Walkwell said the manticores were loose in the reptile barn!* Remembering was like another painful blow. *Oh, poor Desta!* She did her best to push all the other thoughts away – struggling, deranged Uncle Gideon in her arms, that thing like a pile of rotted marshmallows swelling and oozing out of the collapsing greenhouse, and helpless Mr. Walkwell and Colin Needle . . .

*Oh, God, Colin! He's trapped holding that piece of metal, and there's lighting everywhere . . . !*

. . . and against all that painful clamour in her thoughts, she turned her mind back to the young dragon.

*Desta . . . ?* It was so terribly hard to concentrate . . . ! *Desta, can you hear me? I'm here. Here!* She thought she felt a momentary touch of the dragon's thoughts, like a burst of radio music through a roll of static. *Desta?*

*Carrot Girl . . .* And with the faint call came a sort of vision, as if she was seeing what the dragon saw – shapes scuttling across the floor of the reptile barn, the weird, barking noises the manticores made as they hunted – but there was something strange about it too. If she was truly seeing what Desta saw, the young dragon seemed to be looking down on the scene from above, perhaps perched on one of the catwalks near the roof of the vast structure.

*What are you doing up there?* Desta's wings had barely been strong enough to lift herself off the ground when Lucinda and Tyler had been banished. *Did you fly up there?*

Y*es. Yellow Man let me out.* That must be Ragnar because of his white-shot golden hair.

*Smart,* Lucinda thought. *Gives her a better chance of staying safe – the manticores can't fly.* And then something else occurred to her. *Is Yellow Man still there?* she asked.

*Yelling. Running with stick. Fighting bad animals.*

For all his strength and bravery, the Norseman hadn't been able to beat one manticore at the gate – what could he do against several? *And are there other people with him?*

*Turn-Face and Hat Men.*

That would be Haneb and the Three Amigos, she knew – Desta was always trying to steal the herdsmen's fur-lined hats. She hoped the farm workers would be able to hold off the manticores on their own, because she needed Ragnar. *Bring Yellow Man to me,* she told the dragon.

*?* What came back was confusion.

*Bring him to me, Desta. You have to bring him to me. It's important!*

*No – bad animals hurt Desta. No!* The fear in the mess of jumbled ideas was very real – the young dragon was terrified of the manticores.

*You have to. I need you. Carrot Girl needs you.*

*No.* It was the panicky, absolute refusal of a child. *No!*

In the rainy garden across the farm, Lucinda wrapped her arms tighter around Gideon's skinny chest as she did her best to fall into the dark, calm place where she could not just speak to the dragon but feel her – and be felt by her. *You have to. I need you. If you don't, I won't give you carrots any more . . . !*

379

But no bribe or even threat was going to coax Desta down from her perch in the rafters of the reptile barn. Lucinda realized she would have to do on purpose what she had done by accident that day when Desta tried to steal the bracelet.

*Desta,* she warned, *if you don't do what I want, I'm going to make you.*

*No!* The young animal was beyond reason. Lucinda reached out until she could feel Desta's thoughts, feel Desta whole. She applied pressure to those thoughts, imagining as carefully and thoroughly as she could what it would feel like for Desta to jump down. At first she did her best to make it seem that it would feel good to do what Lucinda wanted, but the dragon was either too frightened or – somehow, despite her age – too strong to be manipulated by kindness. A cold, miserable feeling settled over Lucinda, a feeling of pure need.

*I'm so sorry* . . . she thought, then reached out and squeezed Desta's thoughts, hard.

*No* . . . *! Hurts* . . . *!*

Horrible, it was just horrible – Lucinda had never done anything that made her feel worse; it was using sharp spurs on a horse that was already doing its best, like spanking a child who didn't know what she had done wrong. Even in the midst of all the other crazy, overwhelming sensations, what she was doing made her feel sick, but there was no other way to save Gideon, Mr. Walkwell, and Colin. Time had run out.

380

*Let go!* It was a silent but agonized shriek of pain and betrayal. *Carrot Girl bad!*

Pushing and squeezing at the dragon's most sensitive feelings, Lucinda did her best to concentrate, to ignore the sense of betrayal flowing back to her along their connection like poisoned air as she forced Desta to spread her wings and leap down from the rafters, then clung to the dragon's thoughts as the creature flapped in an awkward spiral and hit the upper-floor landing with a painfully hard thump. Desta's misery was a throbbing ache in Lucinda's own heart, but she couldn't afford to let go.

*Now get Ragnar. Pick him up. Bring him to me.*

Desta's resistance had become as thoughtless as that of any wounded animal, but no matter what the dragon did, she couldn't free herself from Lucinda's control. Desta climbed onto the railing and then sprang out into the air to glide on trembling wings across the upper part of the barn. One of the Three Amigos looked up and shouted a warning, but Desta abruptly dropped down and caught Ragnar by the shoulders of his thick white overalls, then lifted him several feet in the air and glided toward the open front door of the reptile barn. The young dragon had the wingspan of a small plane but it was still hard for her to lift the Norseman. Lucinda felt the big man fighting back, fighting hard, and within a few yards of escaping the barn Desta had to drop him.

*Get him again!* Lucinda couldn't afford to think

about what she was doing, about the pain she was causing Ragnar and this beautiful, one-of-a-kind animal. *Grab him. Bring him to me.*

The Norseman turned to hurry back into the barn but Desta caught him from behind, grabbing him by the reinforced collar of his safety suit, then beat her wings so hard that within only seconds she had lifted him a hundred feet in the air, where Ragnar recognized the futility of further resistance. He stopped struggling and even reached up to grab the dragon's legs and take some of the weight off the claws that must be digging painfully into his body through the heavy canvas.

*I'm sorry, Ragnar,* Lucinda thought, but of course he could not hear her thoughts as the dragon could. Now she just wanted the nightmare to end, one way or another. *I'm sorry, Desta, I'm so sorry . . . !*

A painful, hard thump against her forehead brought her attention back to the reality of the garden and the storm. Desta and Ragnar suddenly disappeared from her mind's eye. Her great-uncle Gideon was trying to push away from her, his mouth opening and closing with a clack of teeth as though he was trying to say something, but his eyes were as empty as a department store mannequin's. One of his flailing hands struck her on the jaw so hard it felt like a tooth came loose, then he was dragging her through the mud in the chaos of thunder and lightning flash.

Something dropped from the sky beside her and

landed in an awkward jumble of wings and arms and legs and raspy protest. Ragnar rolled out of the thrash of dragon-limbs and stood up, ready to defend himself if Desta attacked again. The young dragon's snaky head whipped from side to side, hissing; when she saw Lucinda she backed up in alarm, as if unable to reconcile the Carrot Girl before her on the ground and the cruel mistress in her head who had forced her to come here. For half a moment Lucinda could feel the animal's rage so strongly beating out at her like the heat from an opened oven door that she thought Desta might simply bound across the ground between them and snap her head off.

*Carrot Girl . . . !* The thoughts bombarded her, slapped at her – the dragon equivalent of shouting. *Carrot Girl bad! Hurt us!*

Desta leaped into the air with a loud slap and thrash of wings and flew off over the top of the farmhouse. For a single, lightning-painted instant she reappeared further along the sky, then vanished again.

Ragnar stumbled toward Lucinda and dropped to his knees, then grabbed Gideon in his strong arms and imprisoned him. The master of the farm continued to resist, but with no more luck now than a babe in arms. 'What happened?' the Norseman demanded in a voice made hoarse by shouting. 'Did *you* send that wormling after me . . . ?'

'We're in trouble!' She quickly told him as much of

383

the story as she could. 'You have to help Colin! Help Mr. Walkwell!'

The Viking looked at the greenhouse and made a face. 'Baldur's blood, that is the ugliest thing I've ever seen . . . !' He turned back to Lucinda. 'Master Needle had a good idea for once – set the cursed vegetable on fire.'

'What?' In the midst of her struggle with Gideon she hadn't even grasped exactly what Colin had been planning. Now, as if thinking had awakened his resolve, the old man began squirming once more in Ragnar's arms.

'I ask your pardon,' the Norseman said.

'What?' Lucinda was so exhausted that nothing made sense. 'Why?'

'Not yours, child.' He lifted a fist big as a beef roast and struck Gideon sharply on the back of the head. The old man slumped and lay still.

'Now I go to get what I need to kill this demon,' he said, and loped off toward the farmhouse. 'Don't fear,' he shouted over his shoulder. 'I will come straight back!' Rain swirled, blown almost horizontal by the wind.

Freed from Gideon, Lucinda crawled across the wet ground to Colin, who had long since stopped struggling and lay silent and still in his net of fungal threads. She pulled at the aluminium fence post in his hand, but although she could break any single one of the little white fungus threads easily, each time she

384

did several crept back in to take its place and she could not break them in bunches. Lightning leaped down from the sky only half a mile away, making a dazzle on top of a nearby hill, and even as she watched the shrieking wind was rolling more black clouds toward them like a steamroller.

Colin opened bleary eyes. 'Don't let me die,' he begged her. 'Please, don't let me die. I'm sorry I took it. I'm sorry!'

She had no idea what he was sorry about, nor did she care. 'I'm trying to help you!' Her wet fingers kept slipping off the strands. 'Oh, God, I'm trying, Colin!'

'Stand away, girl!' Ragnar came crashing back through the garden toward them, something heavy swinging in each hand. He set down the two large cider jars and wrenched the aluminium post out of the boy's hand, shredding hundreds of fungal threads with a horrid ripping and popping noise as Colin let out a screech of agony.

Ragnar straightened up, took a quick couple of steps, and flung the metal fence post toward the greenhouse. It wobbled through the air, trailing its wire like a giant threaded needle, but was pushed sideways by the powerful wind and fell to earth several yards short of the wall of dead and dying creatures that had piled up at the structure's base.

'The gods curse it!' The Norseman turned to Lucinda. 'I must go closer, but then the demon will be able to reach me as it caught Simos – unless I can set it burning. That will give me a few moments, I think!' He lifted and uncorked first one of the gallon jars, then the other. The smell of gasoline blew past her on the wind. Ignoring another cry of pain from Colin, Ragnar tore the sleeve off the boy's wet shirt and crammed it into the mouth of the jar. He did the same thing with the other sleeve, prompting a weaker cry of pain and protest. Colin looked as if he had all but fainted.

'Do you have fire?' Ragnar asked Lucinda. 'Or any way to make it?'

She stared at him for a long, confused moment, then shook her head. She searched Colin's pockets; he was in so much pain he scarcely seemed to notice. 'He doesn't either,' she said.

He smiled a grim smile. 'Then I have no choice but to try to wade through those griping demon-fingers. If Simos could not do it, then I cannot, but I must try.' He reached out and patted her cheek with his gasoline-stinking hand. 'I ask for your pardon, Lucinda.'

She flinched. 'Are you going to hit me?'

Ragnar shook his head. 'I ask pardon because I cannot sing my death-song well in your tongue, Lucinda Jenkins. Still, it must be sung so it can be heard by those who listen, and they say the gods understand all tongues!' He set the jugs down beside her and trotted through the rain toward the greenhouse. 'This will be the second time I have sung it!' he shouted over his shoulder. 'Let us hope that again it will be in vain!'

386

Lucinda didn't know what he meant.

The monstrous thing inside the ancient greenhouse had long since forced out all the windows and was oozing out of every opening in the corroded metal cage, its uppermost extensions stretching thirty feet or more into the air and branching into hundreds of shapes as weird and alien as snowflakes. As the Viking approached, the starry profusion of shapes shuddered and the entire bulk of the fungus began to swell and rock.

The Norseman's voice rose, each word loud and heavy as a great stone.

*'It gladdens me to know that Odin sets out the*
*benches for a banquet . . .'*

he sang, or rather chanted in a deep, booming voice.

*'Soon we shall be drinking ale from cups of horn!*
*A hero who is ushered into Odin's hall does not*
*lament his death, and Ragnar Leather shanks shall*
*not enter Old One-Eye's hall with words of fear*
*upon his lips . . . !'*

Shiny white strands began to climb the tall Viking's legs, more and more of them coiling around him until he staggered to a halt several dozen yards from the greenhouse, not far from the motionless, cocooned shape of Mr. Walkwell.

*'I have fought against foes in many battles . . .'*

he sang, louder now to best the mounting thunder.

*My sons are gone, and their sons after them,*
*I myself brought an ending to many men*
*And now I am a king out of his time!*
*But I never imagined pale serpents like these*
*Would be the ending of my life . . . !'*

Ragnar bent and ripped away as many of the strands as he could, then forced himself a few steps forward, tearing the pale root-like strings out of the earth as he went, snapping dozens of them with each stride. He took a step. He took another step. Against all odds, he was still moving toward the thing, but each step was slower and more laboured than the last.

Colin raised his head, clutching his arm against his belly as he spoke through chattering teeth. 'Is he . . . is he g-g-getting close to it . . . ?

Lucinda watched a moment longer and then shut her eyes in despair. Rain warm as blood ran down her face. 'No. It got him. It's . . . it's tangling him up like Mr. Walkwell.'

'It's my fault . . .' Colin said. 'I should . . . I should have told you . . . that there was something weird . . . in the greenhouse . . .'

'Lucinda!' It was a new voice. 'Lucinda! Where are you?'

She opened her eyes. 'Here, Tyler! Over here!'

Something was crashing toward her through the garden rows like a charging elephant; a moment later her brother tumbled onto the muddy ground beside her.

'Lucinda! What's going on? And what's *that*?' He stared at the horrible white thing swelling from the greenhouse like rising bread dough. 'This is crazy!'

Even as she tried to form the words to explain, Steve Carrillo came staggering up behind him. Steve doubled over, gasping for breath, and lifted a hand in a shaky sort of wave. 'H-hi, Lucinda.'

'You're too late, Jenkins,' said Colin bitterly. 'You and your dumb friend. We've already lost.'

'Ragnar said we needed to burn that thing.' Lucinda spoke quickly before the boys started to fight again. 'There's a pole with a wire on it over there, attached to the lightning rod. That was Colin's idea, but Ragnar couldn't throw it close enough. Then Ragnar made some gasoline bombs, but we didn't have anything to light them with.' For a moment she felt a sudden twinge of hope, foolish as it was. 'Do you have something? Matches?'

Tyler thought hard, his face twisted in worry, then shook his head. 'Sorry, Luce.'

She felt as though she was about to dissolve, as if the rain had been beating down on her for so long she was about to become water herself and flow away. 'Oh, Tyler, where were you? How could you run off

389

like that? There were guns . . . and the manticores are loose . . . and I think that thing is going to *reproduce*!' She pointed to the impossible thing growing out of the greenhouse. The strange, tentacle-like shapes extended from the main body like tiny chimneys, hundreds and hundreds of them, each one ending in strands that waved in the wind like seaweed. 'That's what it does! But if it puts out spores with all this wind and rain, it's going to take over *everything*!'

'Hey, *I* have a lighter,' said Steve Carrillo.

'*What?*' Lucinda and Tyler both shouted it at the same time, so loud that Steve shied back.

'Sure,' he said, looking a little shamefaced. 'I borrowed it from my uncle. You can't make a fire on a night like this without a lighter or some matches, and I wanted to make s'mores. Heck, I thought we were going *camping*.'

He had scarcely produced it from his jacket pocket before Tyler snatched it away, pulled the cider jars close and applied the flame first to one of Colin's torn-off sleeves, then to the other. The fabric was wet, but gasoline had soaked up into it from the jar and after just a few seconds both wicks caught and burned with a blue-yellow flame. Lucinda cowered away, fearing that they might blow up any second.

'Don't worry – that's not how these things work,' Tyler said. 'At least I don't *think* so. Steve, you grab that one.'

'Me?'

'No, the other Steve. Look, my sister can barely sit up, and Needle looks like his arm's broken. Come on, dude. Hero time.' But although he spoke bravely, her brother looked pale and frightened, his lips almost blue in the weird storm light.

'Don't do it,' Lucinda told him. 'It already got Ragnar and Mr. Walkwell!'

Tyler only shook his head. He stood up, holding one jug away from his face; after a moment, so did Steve Carrillo.

'If we live through this,' Steve said, 'I'll need to use your phone to call home. My folks are probably really pissed.'

And then he and Tyler went loping down the rainy garden rows, slowed by the weight of the heavy jugs.

'Lift your feet,' Lucinda heard Tyler yell. 'Don't let those white things get a grip on you!'

Lightning flashed so bright that for a long moment everything before Lucinda's eyes went black, even as the thunder made her very bones shudder. Then she dimly saw the lights of the two jugs bobbing near where Ragnar had stopped.

'You're too close!' she screamed, but Tyler was also shouting.

'Throw it high, dude!' her brother called to Steve. 'They have to break!' And he swung his own by the ring at the neck, spinning himself and the jar round and round like an Olympic hammer-thrower, then let it go. It flew up and then plopped down into the

391

mud without breaking, a foot short of the pile of dead animals clustered against the greenhouse's iron structure. The flame was still burning, though it guttered in the rain, and as gasoline spilled out of the jar it made a growing but unimpressive pool of blue fire.

'No . . . !' Tyler shouted in despair. 'Steve, you have to do it! You have to hit the greenhouse!'

Steven Carrillo stared for a moment as another lightning flash turned the entire garden into a kind of stage set, rows and rows of flat pictures, each set in front of the next – garden plants, the greenhouse itself, mountains, and sky. Then he bent down. For a moment, Lucinda thought he was going to set the cider jar down and simply walk away in defeat, but he was bending for balance. He spun, surprisingly nimble, holding the jug in both hands, and then let it go. It flew end over end, flaming wick rotating like a Catherine wheel, its arc not as high as Tyler's but a little longer. Lucinda's heart rose – it was going to reach the greenhouse!

It thumped against the uppermost part of the structure without breaking, the impact deadened by the pale, doughy globs growing out of the frame. For an instant it teetered there and it seemed the monstrous thing would simply draw in the jug itself like a sea anemone snatching a fish, but it was too heavy and too delicately balanced. It fell away, rolled down the mound of dead creatures at the base, and smashed into the other jug, breaking them both. Flames spattered up the sides of the greenhouse and the pale, doughy flesh where it had oozed through the broken panes. More fire spread across the ground. The white tentacles spasmed in shock and what could only be pain.

*!!!!!!!!*

The greenhouse-thing's screaming thoughts, if anything so primitive could be called that, ripped through Lucinda, knocking her flat on the ground and leaving her dizzy, unable to make her arms or legs work. It was the worst thing she'd ever felt in her head, a convulsion of fiery agony that seized her and shook her like the jaws of some great beast. When the worst had passed she could only lie still for long moments with rain splashing her face, until finally she found the strength to drag herself upright again, although the fungus-monster's sensations of alarm and pain still battered her.

The part of the white thing that wasn't on fire was stretching even further into the sky now, mouth-like holes gaping in the pale spongy mass as if a thousand voices screamed at once, but all Lucinda could hear above the storm was the whistle of escaping gases. In its pain the creature had lost control of much of its network of threads, and Ragnar was busily tearing himself loose. As soon as he could move his legs again he staggered over to Mr. Walkwell and yanked him free, but the farm's overseer did not move and

Ragnar had to carry him away from the burning greenhouse: Simos Walkwell, who could lift the farm wagon with one hand, looked as shrunken and lifeless as a withered turnip, but at least he was free. Beside Lucinda, the fungal strands fell away from Colin Needle and withdrew into the ground.

But suddenly, just when it had seemed they had destroyed their terrible enemy, the mass of the main fungus body began to split open above the places where fire was blackening its flesh. A transparent ooze began to flow from these cracks, extinguishing the flames that had been scorching the thing's surface. The echo of its power still pulsed in Lucinda's head, its single-minded need to spawn, its mindless determination to spread itself to the winds. The thing was not beaten.

Lightning flashed again.

'Everybody, back!' Ragnar shouted. 'Quickly!' He bent and picked up the fence post from where it had fallen short and advanced toward the greenhouse like a knight marching into a dragon's cave. Lucinda could barely hear him over the thunder and a bizarre whistling noise that was coming now from the thing, but she did as he had said, pulling Colin by his good arm until the boy finally managed to crawl on his own. She turned to look for Tyler and Steve hurrying after her, and saw something behind them she would never forget, although she would wish for the rest of her life that she could.

The charred white and black mass was stretching

wider now, its strands quivering with the spores they were about to release, but the truly horrible thing was that for a moment she could see something of Gideon's own face and shape forming itself out of the main body's moving white surface, as if the fungus had tasted her great-uncle so deeply and so long that it wanted to *be* him.

A blinding flash of light whitewashed the sky. Ragnar threw the fence-post spear again and this time it shivered through the air and thumped into the thickest part of the monstrous fungus, the wire trailing like a row of silver sparks. Thunder boomed and boomed again, very close, then the sky exploded in a monstrous flash, so powerful that the ground lurched, knocking her off her feet again. Blue fire crackled and arched where the fence post stuck out of the ground, and white strands curled into blackened threads all around the ruined greenhouse.

The body of the thing, a grotesque and unstable copy of Gideon, swelled and began to grow bigger – for a mad moment Lucinda thought it would pull itself out of the greenhouse wreckage and walk – but then burst into gouts of dripping fire. The monstrous Gideon face twisted in agony or fury, then fell back into bubbly nothingness. Spores poured out but caught fire and disappeared in clouds of burning sparks, popping in the air, vanishing like the falling fireworks at a Fourth of July show. Inky black smoke curled from the melting wreckage and was swept away by the wind.

Lucinda felt a hand on her arm, then one on the other side. It was Tyler and Steve Carrillo lifting her out of the mud.

'We're alive,' was all she could say. 'Alive.'

Tyler nodded, shook his head, then nodded again. 'Yeah,' he said. 'We're alive.'

'Don't worry about me,' she told him. 'You guys have to carry Gideon. Ragnar knocked him out, but that thing had him really bad.'

With the boys awkwardly cradling the unconscious Gideon, they all turned their backs on the smouldering greenhouse and began to make their way across the garden toward the house. Colin was staggering along under his own power, holding his arm against his chest. Lucinda moved up to offer him some support, but he turned away from her and continued to make his own slow way. Ragnar was carrying Mr. Walkwell. The sight of the old man's closed eyes and limp form frightened her.

'Is he all right, Ragnar? He's not . . .'

'Simos is alive,' the big man told her. He didn't look as though he could claim much more himself. 'But he is in a bad way.'

'We won, didn't we?' she asked, but she said it quietly, mostly to herself.

'Oh, one thing, Luce,' Tyler said from behind her, grunting a little as he tried to balance his share of their great-uncle. 'If you were going to go and lie down? There's . . . there's kind of someone sleeping in your room.' She turned to look back. Tyler had a funny expression on his face, a little nervous, but also quite proud. 'You remember Grace? Gideon's wife?'

Lucinda had no idea what he was talking about and was so battered and exhausted that she didn't think she could string two more words together, so she opted for just one.

'Whatever.'

# CHAPTER 41

## LIKE A ROLLING SNAKE

Steve Carrillo's parents came to pick him up about noon, and as they pulled up to the front gate in their pick-up and got out they looked as though they hadn't got any more sleep the previous night than Tyler and Lucinda and the rest of the folk at Ordinary Farm.

'By the time you get done being grounded,' Mr. Carrillo told his son, 'you're going to be ready for the retirement home.'

'It was all my fault, sir,' Tyler said. 'It was my idea. Steve was just helping me . . .'

'Helping himself to a big punishment,' said Mrs. Carrillo sharply. Behind her, Alma and Carmen, who didn't know yet what had happened, made mocking faces from the back seat. Tyler gave them an embarrassed wave.

Hector Carrillo turned to Ragnar, whose visible

skin was covered with stripes of purple bruises. 'And how are you all?' Mr. Carrillo asked. 'You said on the telephone that Gideon had a relapse.'

Ragnar nodded. 'But he will be well, I think. The crisis has finally passed – for good, this time. He is being tended.'

'You didn't take him back to the hospital?' said Silvia.

Ragnar shrugged. 'He did not wish to go.'

'He still needs to talk to us,' said Hector, and Tyler realized that the man's anger had not all been directed at his son and Tyler Jenkins.

'This time he will, I promise,' Ragnar said. 'Things will change. You have my word on it.' He extended his hand and Hector Carrillo took it. They shook, then Hector asked, 'Where's Simos? He usually comes out to say hello.'

'He . . .' Ragnar's face grew sombre, but all he said was, 'You must forgive him. He had a difficult night.'

'Hey, Jenkins,' Steve shouted to Tyler from the rear window of his father's truck. 'If you get a chance, come see me before you leave. You don't have to call first. I mean, it's not like I'll be going anywhere . . . thanks to *you* . . . !'

Tyler couldn't help smiling as they drove off. Steve was a good guy – a real friend. 'Is Gideon really going to talk to them about their property? How's anyone going to make him?'

The Norseman was still looking grim as he opened

the gate. The power to the fence was off and had been since the electrical storm. The remaining manticores were safely padlocked in their adobe-brick barn. 'Things will change around here. They must.'

Only one more day remained until Tyler and Lucinda took the train back home, and Ordinary Farm was as sharply divided as ever, with most of its residents on one side and the Needles on the other. Nothing had been resolved, of course: Gideon no longer seemed to be brainwashed but he had only been conscious for short stretches and had been too tired even to sit up, let alone deal with the weighty matters that needed his attention; Mr. Walkwell was not much better, and was being nursed on the couch in the same room as Gideon, so that Sarah and her helpers could watch over both patients at the same time. Tyler didn't know what the greenhouse monster had done to him, but Simos Walkwell had only woken up for the first time the previous evening, and still hadn't said much more than a few words, although Sarah said he seemed better this morning. Interestingly enough, Tyler had also discovered that there were now several gunshot holes in the Snake Parlour walls. Obviously events that night hadn't only been happening beyond the mirror and out by the greenhouse.

Although nothing permanent could be accomplished until Gideon was back in charge, Ragnar and Sarah had at least managed by sheer stubbornness and threats of force to chase Mrs. Needle away from Gideon's bedside and the Snake Parlour in general, so the witch had retreated behind the locked door of her part of the house. Colin spent most of his time with her, or at least in his room, which was about what Tyler would have expected.

The previous summer the Jenkins kids might have stayed silent about things and wouldn't have expected to receive any useful answers even if they had asked questions, but now something had changed, not least of which was how Tyler and Lucinda felt about things. Even if they hadn't become the heirs to the farm (despite all the chaos of that night, it didn't seem as though anybody had actually managed to change Gideon's will) Tyler knew that their great-uncle had at least been planning to do it. The way he figured it, they had a *right* to know what was going on. And he was pleasantly surprised to find out that Ragnar Lodbrok, at least, seemed to agree.

Tyler found the Norseman examining the wreckage at the back of the garden. It was still hard to believe what had happened out here only a couple of days before, but as they stood looking at the melted ruins of the metal greenhouse and the yards-wide crater of blackened vegetation and scorched animal carcasses, the evidence was right in front of him. It looked as if someone had firebombed the place.

'We will haul away the metal bars,' Ragnar said. 'They have a furnace in Liberty where they melt old metal. That will make sure the seeds are dead.' He poked with his foot at a part of a bird lying on the ground. Tyler had no idea what kind of bird it had been. 'The rest we will bury. If I knew a priest I would bring him to bespell the demon's grave.'

'It wasn't really a demon, was it?' Tyler asked. 'More of a big mushroom, really.'

Ragnar looked at him with disbelief. 'If that thing was only a mushroom, then the Fenris Wolf himself is just a pup and the Midgard Serpent no more than an eel.'

Tyler couldn't think of anything to say to that. 'What's going to happen with the farm?' he asked after a while. 'After Lucinda and I go home? You can't just let Mrs. Needle get away with everything she did, can you?'

'It is not so easy, Tyler Jenkins,' said Ragnar. 'They are like Gideon's kin. And would you have us kill her and leave her son an orphan?'

'You could kill him too.' Tyler saw the look on Ragnar's face. 'I'm just kidding!'

'I do not much like the boy, but his crimes are nothing like his mother's,' the Viking said. 'It would be hard to imprison her, but possible.'

'Why don't you just throw her out?'

'So that she is out of our sight and reach, like that terrible man Kingaree?' Ragnar and others had searched up and down Kumish Creek but had found no body or any other sign of Jackson Kingaree.

'Should we send her out to roam the world with all of Ordinary Farm's secrets in her head, plotting mischief against us? Against Gideon?'

Tyler frowned. Put like that, it really wasn't very simple. 'But she can't get away with what she did! What she *tried* to do! She could have killed us all!'

'I know,' Ragnar said. 'And when Simos is well again, we will do our best to make a plan to keep her from doing evil.'

'What are you going to do?'

The Norseman shook his head. 'I have not talked to Simos, so I will not share my thoughts yet. Gideon is still master of this place and still my thane – not you, young Tyler. Not yet.' He looked at Tyler's outraged expression and a trace of amusement crept over his broad bearded face. 'What, do you hate secrets so much? Don't you have a few of your own, boy? What about the woman hidden in your sister's room?'

Tyler flushed. 'Grace? But that's different – that's a *good* secret. And I'll share it with Gideon as soon as he's well enough to know what's going on. Besides, she's barely been awake herself.' Much to Lucinda's irritation, of course, since it meant she had to share her brother's room. Grace seemed to be sleeping off the effects of her years of fugitive existence in the mirror house, waking only to take a little nourishment and peer around in confusion before going back to sleep again. The kitchen women had been nursing

403

her (when they were not ministering to Gideon and Mr. Walkwell) with Ooola the ice-age girl taking the lead, perhaps fascinated by someone even newer to the modern world than herself.

'Remember, you are not a grown man yet . . .' Ragnar began, as if Tyler didn't already know that, but the Norseman was interrupted by a flutter of wings as a small shape swooped down out of the hot, bright sky. (The lightning storm and the rain had passed with that terrible night and already seemed as distant as an old nightmare.) A second later Tyler was laughing and trying to keep tiny hands from pulling off his eyebrows and poking up his nose.

'Zaza! You're back! I missed you, girl – I've hardly seen you all summer!'

Ragnar watched the winged monkey climbing on Tyler's head, then looked to the misshapen blob of metal and charcoal that had once been the greenhouse. As he stroked his beard another faint smile curved his lips. 'Animals know much we do not, Tyler Jenkins. If the little ape will come to this place again, perhaps we do not need a priest after all.'

With Zaza riding shotgun on his shoulder, Tyler followed Ragnar out to the reptile barn, where the Three Amigos and Haneb were clearing up the wreckage left by the manticores' break-in. Lucinda was there too, standing a few yards away from Desta's pen. The young dragon was pointedly ignoring her, and Tyler thought his sister looked miserable, like she had a crush on some high-school big shot who didn't even know her name.

The manticores had caused a great deal of destruction in the huge barn, tearing open metal cabinets and scattering feed bags and canisters everywhere, terrorizing and killing some of the smaller or slower animals (Tyler was glad those remains had already been cleaned up) and generally creating as much havoc as an entire herd of elephants. Tyler could still see one of the stepladders hanging from a beam thirty feet overhead, but couldn't begin to guess how it had got there.

Only two of the manticores had survived that terrible night – the fungus had lured and destroyed two, and a third had apparently come too close to Meseret's pen: only a bloody stump of tail was left behind to show what had happened. After the way the first one had attacked Ragnar and the rest of them at the gate, Tyler didn't feel sorry for the manticores, but he was happy to know the last pair were back safe in their cage. They were rare, amazing things, there was no question about that – he just didn't ever want to see one again.

As Tyler surveyed the damage, Lucinda walked over to him, a baby amphisbaena looking around confusedly from the palm of her hand. At least, Tyler *thought* it was looking around, but it might also be waving its tail in the air: even near the end of their second summer he found it hard to tell which end of an amphisbaena was which.

'How are Gideon and Mr. Walkwell this morning?' his sister asked.

'Sarah said Gideon's doing better. Eating a little. Talking. Making sense, even.' He reached out and stroked the little creature on its nearest end. It was the front, he could now see, although its implacable stare didn't give much away. 'I think I'm going to bring Grace down to him this afternoon. Mr. Walkwell's a little better too, she said.'

Lucinda carefully put the lizard back into its cage. 'Are you sure? He's not very well.'

'This will make him feel better. Besides, we're leaving soon.'

'It is too bad you cannot get advice from Simos first,' said Ragnar from a short distance away. 'He is very wise, and he was here before I was – before any of us who came from the Fault Line. In fact, he is the only one of us who knew Gideon's wife. Perhaps he knows something about the two of them that you do not, young Tyler Jenkins.'

'You know how much Gideon misses her,' Tyler said. 'What could be better for him than having her back . . . ?'

He was distracted by a sudden whoop of noise from Kiwa and Jeg. The two of them were chasing a hoop snake, which had got loose from its pen and was bowling across the floor just out of their reach, tail in its mouth as it rolled like a wheel. Alarmed, Zaza leaped from Tyler's shoulder and flapped off into the upper reaches of the massive barn where she hovered, shrieking indignantly at them all.

'There he goes, over there, under the sprayer! Don't hurt him!' shouted Ragnar, laughing as he went to help them. 'But remember, he can give you a good nip!'

As the third herdsman and Haneb joined in, the comic scene became even more frantic. Tyler turned to look for Lucinda. His sister was observing the chaos with all the joy of someone watching homework assignments being written on a blackboard. A moment later she turned and walked out of the barn.

'Luce!' he shouted, but she didn't acknowledge him.

He didn't hurry after her – it was too much fun watching everybody trying to catch the swiftly rolling snake. The chase had excited and upset many of the other residents of the reptile barn, the basilisks hissing and the tiny cockatrices spattering the insides of their enclosures with venom, until even Meseret lifted her massive head above the edge of her pen to have a look. Zaza got so excited she peed on one of the Amigos from mid-air, which only added to the shouting.

*Wow*, thought Tyler, enjoying the chaos – *just look at this crazy place! Is there anywhere cooler on the entire planet? And me and Lucinda saved it again!*

# CHAPTER 42

## AN INTERRUPTED MOMENT

Colin Needle had walked around for two days with his head full of unpleasant thoughts, but no matter how he had considered things, no matter how he tried to explain them to himself, he couldn't make the worst one go away.

Tyler Jenkins had been *right* – Colin's mother had been the one who had made Gideon sick. And in trying to change Gideon's will, or whatever she had been up to on the night of the storm (he was still piecing the story together), she had also used her son's computer, as well as the security system Colin had so painstakingly set up, to let the manticores out, bringing deadly danger not only to the other residents of the farm, but to *her own son*.

But how could she do such a thing? Colin had always known his mother was difficult and temperamental, even that she had a cruel streak, but this was different. She had told him so many times that her excesses were on his behalf that he had believed it in the same way he believed rain was good for plants. Now his life seemed to have been twisted into a completely different shape, one that he had never seen before and had no idea how to use.

As Colin reached the bottom of the stairs he met Caesar coming out of the kitchen with what looked like Gideon's lunch, a tray with soup and bread and a sparkling white napkin rolled up and held in a silver ring. Colin nodded as Caesar went past, and Caesar nodded politely back, but suddenly Colin felt certain that there was something other than politeness in the old man's dark brown eyes – contempt? Outright hatred, hidden only by his polished manners?

Little Pema was dusting the furniture in the entry hall, and she too nodded to Colin as he passed, but despite the demure, downward cast of her eyes he fancied he could see her shrink back as if she did not want even his shadow to touch her. He knew the kitchen women did not like him, but he had always supposed it was because of his bad temper or the way he sometimes spoke without thinking, dismissing things he felt were plainly stupid. But was it more? Was their dislike of his mother deeper than that most workers felt for unsympathetic managers – did they really hate and fear her? Did that mean they hated and feared Colin Needle as well?

These were new thoughts, quite new, and Colin didn't know exactly what to do with them. For most of his life he had known that the other farm residents didn't like the Needles, but he had managed to convince himself that much of it came from the dislike the weak always felt for the strong – his mother was nothing if not strong. Sometimes her strength even scared her own son. Why shouldn't it make others nervous?

But one day while Gideon had been missing, Colin had found a few envelopes from the Madagascar crate near the old abandoned greenhouse and had wondered why his normally so-careful mother would bring those foreign seeds and spores to the garden, where the risk of them causing mischief in an entirely new environment was so great. Why wouldn't she simply raise them under controlled conditions? Later, when Lucinda had been overwhelmed by the spores from the greenhouse, Colin had begun to be suspicious, but still hadn't been able to make sense of it. Only when Lucinda told him what kind of spores they were and he thought about Gideon's mysterious disappearance and return did it all begin to make a kind of terrible sense. It wasn't her experiments with the exotic plants and fungi his mother had needed to hide away from the house's inhabitants, it was who she had been experimenting on – Gideon Goldring himself. His mother must have been hiding the old man out in the garden. Somehow his mother, Patience Needle, had knocked Gideon out and dragged him to the greenhouse all by herself, only to have him escape on the Fourth of July.

*Witch.* It was a word that came up out of the darkest places inside Colin like a belch of foul gas from the bottom of a deep pool. His mother was a witch, and not the good kind. It wasn't the first time he had heard it, or even the first time he had thought it himself, but it was the first time he had really let himself feel what it meant.

*My mother is a witch.*

Colin Needle had never felt so alone.

He stood in the shade of the porch, sweat dripping down his face and making his clothes stick to his skin. Although the storms had passed, the sky was just cloudy enough to make the day as close as it was hot. He was thinking he might go and look at Eliot the sea serpent, whose silvery splashing sometimes gave Colin a feeling of freedom that very few other things did, when a movement in the distance caught his attention.

Lucinda Jenkins was walking slowly toward the farmhouse, trudging through the shadow cast by the tall grain silo that stood over the Fault Line. He didn't know what he was going to say to her, didn't know if he could think of anything *to* say, but she looked as if she didn't feel any better than he did, so at least he wouldn't have to try to make cheerful conversation. Colin knew he wasn't very good at that.

He waved awkwardly as she climbed the steps to the porch. 'Hi.'

She looked up at him and smiled, but he felt sure it was the same smile she would have given any stranger on the street. 'Oh. Hi, Colin.'

She had paused for a moment but now she looked as though she was going to continue past him into the house. He suddenly didn't want to be on his own again. 'Ummm,' he said, as if it actually meant something. 'Ummm. You . . . do you want some lemonade? I think Sarah just made some.'

Lucinda looked at him again, more closely this time. After a couple of seconds she seemed to relax, although she still looked sad. 'Yeah. Sure, that would be nice.'

'Just wait and I'll go get it.'

When he came out again a few minutes later with two glasses she was sitting in one of the rocking chairs. He handed her one of the glasses and let himself down into the other one, careful not to spill. Just for once he didn't want to do anything clumsy, didn't want to embarrass himself.

'So . . .' he said as she drank. 'You're going home tomorrow, huh?'

She nodded. 'Yeah. I guess it's just as well. Desta hates me.'

It took Colin a moment to put it all together. 'Oh, the little dragon. Well, don't feel too bad – they've *always* hated me.'

She gave him a slightly annoyed look. 'You do know that's your own fault, right, Colin?'

For a moment he wanted to argue, loudly if necessary – didn't anyone understand that he was trying to make important things happen? – but just as suddenly as the need had filled him, it leaked out again. He took a deep breath and let it out. 'Yes. Yes, I suppose you're right. I've certainly done my share of stupid things. Selfish things.'

She lifted an eyebrow. Lucinda Jenkins was really quite pretty, he noticed again. Not flashy like the oldest Carrillo girl, who dressed like someone you'd see on a teenage TV show, all jangly bracelets and complicated hairstyles, but very nice nonetheless, her hair straight and shiny, her serious face, so pale a few weeks ago, now quite tanned. 'You really mean that, Colin?' she asked. 'Or are you trying to butter me up for something?'

He shook his head. 'I've been . . . I don't know. I've been wanting to talk to you. About a lot of things.' He suddenly realized that one of the things he wanted to tell her was that he *liked* her, liked her in a way that was different from anyone else he knew, but starting that particular conversation seemed as terrifying as diving out of a moving airplane at night with a parachute that might or might not work. 'Talk about what's been going on here. About some of the things you said. Because some of them . . . some of them were right . . .'

'What do you mean?' Her weariness had been set aside. She looked interested, even sympathetic, and for the first time since the night of the storm Colin felt as though things might not be as wretched as they seemed.

'Well . . .' He hesitated, suddenly overwhelmed by all the thoughts in his head. What could he tell her? That he agreed his mother was dangerous – that he was beginning to be really frightened of her, not just in the old ways, but in entirely new ones? After all, Lucinda and her brother were leaving: it was Colin who would be stuck on the farm with all these people who already hated him. What if his mother found out what he had been thinking, these disloyal thoughts? What if she found out he had been talking to the Jenkins children about her?

On the other hand, what if he said nothing and next time something *really* bad happened . . . ?

But before he could speak again, a shout rolled across the open spaces beyond the driveway. '*Hey! Hey, Luce!*'

It was Tyler Jenkins, jogging toward them, shirt untucked, baseball cap sideways, looking like the perfect model of a stupid American middle-schooler. Colin felt his insides twist with disappointment and resentment.

As he reached the porch Lucinda said, 'Hi, Tyler.' Did Colin fancy he heard a little disappointment in her voice too? If so, that almost made the intrusion worthwhile. 'Hang on a second – I'm just talking to . . .'

At first Tyler didn't even look at him. 'You should have seen it, Luce – it was totally epic! One of the hoop snakes got out, then Zaza got spooked and she got into Haneb's hair, and he was screaming and jumping around trying to get her off . . .' He slowed, then stopped, staring at Colin. 'What's your problem, Needle? Can't I talk to my own sister?'

Colin swallowed an angry reply. 'Go on, Jenkins, say what you want to say. Nobody's stopping you.'

'Really? You're sure acting like you wish *you* could. Was I interrupting something?'

'None of your business.' He heard the sound of his own voice, cold and angry, and at that moment it was just how he wanted to sound.

'Tyler!' said Lucinda. 'We were just talking. Don't be a jerk.'

'What?' Her brother turned toward her, face red. 'Why is it *my* fault? He's the one sitting there looking like he wants to punch me . . .'

Colin stood up so abruptly the rocking chair's skids squeaked on the porch boards. 'Forget it! Just forget it! Enjoy yourself, you two. Really a pity you'll be leaving tomorrow – it breaks my heart to think of it.'

And without even listening to what Lucinda Jenkins was saying – because what kind of fool had he been to think she would ever understand anyway? – Colin turned and banged through the door into the house. He almost knocked down little Pema as he stormed through the entry hall, heading for the stairs and the security of his own room, but the thought of apologizing to her never even crossed his mind.

# CHAPTER 43

## SAVING GRACE

'Are you still mad at me? Come on, I didn't even do anything this time!'

That was mostly true – after all the fights her brother had picked with Colin Needle he hadn't really been too bad this time – but Lucinda was frustrated at how close Colin had been to opening up to her.

'Don't you get it? He was telling me that we were right about everything, stupid!' She bent to pick up Colin's lemonade glass, abandoned on the porch.

'So? We were!'

'We could have had him on our side!'

Tyler made a disgusted face. 'Like anyone would want him on their side!'

'Forget it. You're impossible.' She carried the glasses into the house. The door to the Snake Parlour was closed, which probably meant Gideon was having a nap. He was supposed to be getting better. Lucinda hoped they'd get a chance to see him before they left.

As she rinsed the glasses in the kitchen she tried to figure out why Tyler crashing into the middle of the conversation like a runaway truck upset her so much. It wasn't just because she and Tyler were going to leave tomorrow and things seemed even more confused than they had last year. It hadn't even been because for a moment it had seemed like they had a chance to make an ally of Colin Needle, although that would certainly make things a lot easier – Lucinda had a feeling the fight for Ordinary Farm was going to get really, really nasty before long. No, it was something else.

Colin had seemed almost . . . nice. That was what bothered her. He had been lost and confused and scared and looking for help and he had turned to Lucinda. She had seen something in him she had never seen before, the Colin that was separate from his scary witch of a mother, the Colin that was more than just a strange nerdy kid who dressed badly and had been raised in a crazy place without any other kids around. For a moment she had thought she was seeing the real Colin . . . then Tyler had stomped in and the moment was lost – maybe forever . . .

Azinza swept into the kitchen with a tray full of crockery. 'Gideon is feeling better and he's going to talk to us!' she announced with great satisfaction. Pema and Sarah came in just behind her and the wide room was suddenly full of noise and movement.

'What? Who?' Lucinda realized she had been standing over the sink for several minutes, lost in thought.

'Gideon, girl! Caesar is giving him a bath and dressing him!' Azinza put the tray down so hurriedly that the cups and bowls rattled. 'Which means he will also be told your brother's secret! A happy day! I will bring some flowers for his room.'

'Just a few!' said Sarah. 'The parlour will be full of people. I don't want anyone to knock over the good vases.' But the cook was clearly excited too. All the women had been helping take care of Grace up in Lucinda's room and they were all agog to see what would happen when Gideon and his long-lost wife were reunited.

'Whoa.' Lucinda felt a sudden pang of worry. For some reason, she just couldn't imagine that Ragnar and Mrs. Needle would both stand quietly by without telling Gideon what had been going on during his illness. Ragnar would tell the truth, of course, but Mrs. Needle would have to lie, and then things would get very, very difficult . . .

'I have to go talk to my brother,' she said abruptly, and headed for the door, leaving Sarah, Pema, and Azinza to look at each other in surprise

It was a slightly weird scene upstairs, in what had been Lucinda's room until the night of the storm: Grace was sitting on the bed with Ooola kneeling behind her, brushing Grace's thin white hair. (The ice-age girl, after a lifetime of bear-grease and tangles, had taken to clean hair and brushes with joy and would sit for hours happily tending the hair of the other women. Lucinda had been amused at how many times Ooola had asked Tyler to let her brush his hair as well, and how adamantly her brother had always refused.)

Tyler was pacing back and forth in the middle of the room like the producer of a Broadway show just before opening night. 'What is it?' he asked. 'Is Gideon up yet?'

Lucinda could only shake her head. 'Why are you making such a fuss of this? Why have you kept it a secret from Gideon?'

'Because he's been unconscious most of the time. Duh!'

Grace had looked up at the mention of Gideon's name, her eyes mild and slightly anxious. 'Do I know you?' she asked Lucinda.

'Yes.' It was hard to connect this frail, blinking creature with the beautiful, bright young woman in all the old photos. 'I'm Tyler's sister – this is my room, remember? Gideon's our great-uncle.' She turned to her brother. 'We should have taken her to a hospital, Tyler. There's something wrong with her.'

'Nothing that seeing Gideon again won't fix,' he said stubbornly.

'Gideon.' Grace shook her head. 'Will he . . . will he be mad at me? For coming back?'

'Are you kidding?' Tyler said. 'He'll be thrilled!'

Lucinda was not so certain – mad at her for coming back? What did that mean? But before she could ask any more questions Azinza appeared at the door. The young African woman had put on her best dress, a wrap of cotton cloth in bright browns, yellows, and reds that draped her tall slender form all the way to the floor. She really did look like some kind of royalty.

'He is ready for us,' she announced. 'Come down!'

Tyler turned to Ooola, who was making a few last adjustments to Grace's hair. 'You wait with her at the top of the stairs. I'll call you when it's time. Understand?'

Ooola nodded at this great responsibility with a solemn, almost worshipful expression. Lucinda liked the cavegirl just fine, but she thought that someone who listened to her brother that seriously had to be a bad influence on him. Sometimes Ooola acted as though Tyler had shown up in the ice age on purpose just to rescue her, rather than by messing around with something he should have left alone, which was what had actually happened.

She felt a moment of regret for this hard thought as she went down the stairs. Yeah, but if he hadn't done something stupid then Ooola would probably have been eaten by that bear . . .

'Just please don't do anything too dramatic and embarrassing,' she begged Tyler quietly as they reached the bottom of the stairs. The rest of the farm

421

folk were filing into the entry hall, murmuring quietly among themselves.

He gave her an irritated look. 'You'll be thanking me when this is all over, just watch. You'll be calling me Mister Genius Dude.'

'If you say so.' She was too worried even to tell him what an idiot he was sometimes.

The Snake Parlour was a good-sized room, but it would have been crowded just with all the farm folk in it. With Gideon's bed taking up the centre of the space, it felt to Lucinda as if she was elbow to elbow with the other passengers on a crowded train, which reminded her how soon she and Tyler would be on their way back home again.

Both Gideon and Mr. Walkwell were sitting up, although for once Lucinda thought she might have picked her great-uncle in a race, or even a wrestling contest between the two of them: Simos Walkwell looked weirdly pale and frail, while Gideon, although not at his strongest, was obviously healthier than he'd been for weeks. As usual, his hair stuck up in unruly wisps – it was clear that another of Caesar's attempts to tame it with a comb and water had already failed.

'Uncle Gideon, it's good to see you,' Lucinda told him, and she meant it. From the expression of his eyes and face she was pretty sure they had the old Gideon back. 'I'm glad you're feeling better.'

He nodded and smiled at her, but he was listening

to something Ragnar was telling him; when he did lean away from the big man it was to wave to the Three Amigos, who had stopped in the doorway and stood shyly, their hats in their hands. 'Please, come in,' Gideon told the herders, and his voice was so mild that for a moment Lucinda was frightened that she might have been wrong, that her great-uncle might still be some kind of brainwash victim. Then Gideon frowned and waved emphatically. 'For heaven's sake,' he said in an irritated tone, 'I said come in, already!' Lucinda was relieved.

The nervous Mongolians scuttled forward and squeezed in behind Ragnar and Haneb and the kitchen women.

As she went past him, Lucinda stopped beside Simos Walkwell.

'How are you?' she asked. 'I came to see you yesterday but you were sleeping.'

The ancient faun looked at her with weary eyes. Even the stubs of his horns seemed dull. 'That thing had me for a long time,' he said slowly. 'Like you, I breathed its poison seeds, but I breathed them for nearly an hour. I saw . . . terrible things.' He shook his head. 'A world where that demon was the only living thing left on the earth. I dreamed that it was reaching up to conquer the very heavens them-selves . . .' Mr. Walkwell trailed off, then lifted an unsteady brown hand to pat her on the arm. It was strange and disturbing for Lucinda to see him this

423

way. 'Forgive me, child. It is a long time since I have been brought so low. Go and sit. There is much to discuss today.'

All the farm's inhabitants seemed to be present now, even Colin and his mother, who had come in last and arranged themselves at the foot of Gideon's bed where they stood with stony faces like mourners at a funeral.

'Well,' Gideon said, 'it's a pleasure to see you all – more of a pleasure than you can guess!' He smiled as if at a private joke. 'There have been times in the last few weeks when I didn't think this would ever happen again – you, me, all of us here together on the farm. Needless to say, I am grateful for the extra work you all did during my illness, but I am even more conscious that much of the confusion was my own fault.' He nodded his head. 'Yes, my fault. I am an old man and I hold the safety and happiness of many good people in my hands – you people. I cannot afford to be so careless.'

Lucinda was impressed. Was Gideon actually going to admit for once that he might not have all the answers? But that still wouldn't solve the farm's worst issues. She snuck a glance at Mrs. Needle, the farm's most dangerous problem as far as Lucinda was concerned, and caught Colin looking back at her with an odd, unreadable expression on his face. When he met Lucinda's eyes he quickly dropped his gaze.

'So what I wanted to tell you,' Gideon went on, 'is

that I'm going to make things a lot clearer about what happens if I'm not around . . . no, let's be honest – *when* I'm not around. Because I won't live forever.'

'Don't say this!' Sarah the cook crossed herself vigorously. She sounded genuinely frightened, and little Pema looked as though she might burst into tears.

Gideon laughed. 'Come, come, my dears. We all die someday, and we all have a responsibility to be ready for whatever changes will come. After all, if it weren't for you and Patience nursing me so ably over these last weeks, I might not have been here today to give you this little speech!' He chuckled, but the rest of the farm folk looked at each other or glanced quickly at Mrs. Needle. 'No, I've been doing a lot of thinking the last few days about all of this,' Gideon went on. 'Lucinda and Tyler, would you come here, please?'

Her brother jumped like he'd been pinched. 'What? Us?'

'Just go,' Lucinda whispered. She grabbed his elbow and pushed him toward Gideon's bedside. Their great-uncle smiled at them like a weary department-store Santa Claus greeting his last two clients at the end of a long day.

'Caesar, help me sit up a little, will you?' When the pillows had been plumped again behind him, Gideon nodded. 'Better. Thank you. Ah, you two,' he said to Tyler and Lucinda. 'How you've shaken this old place up! It wasn't very long ago that I was wishing I'd never brought you here – but that's not the way I feel any more. A place like this needs more than just a legal owner; it needs to belong to someone who cares about it – who loves it. I think I know the answer, but I want to hear it for myself. Do you two really love Ordinary Farm?'

'Yes!' said Tyler, so quickly and so loud that Gideon jumped a little.

'Yes, Uncle Gideon, of course! We really, really do.' Lucinda thought of angry Desta and what she'd had to do to that poor little dragon to protect the farm. 'More even than you know.'

'That's what I wanted to hear.' Gideon reached up a shaky hand to clasp Tyler's hand, then Lucinda's. It frightened her how fragile his bones felt beneath the skin. 'And here's what I want to say. I am going to make a new will. I haven't changed the terms of my old one since my wife's . . . my wife's disappearance.'

Lucinda couldn't help looking right at the Needles. Colin still wouldn't meet her gaze, but Mrs. Needle stared back as if daring Lucinda to say something. Didn't Gideon know that the witch had been trying to change his will only a few nights ago? Why hadn't Ragnar or someone else told Gideon about that? Did they expect her and Tyler to do it?

'You see,' Gideon continued, 'I understand now that it's not just my farm – it belongs to everyone in this room. In fact, most of you have nowhere else to go. None of you came here by choice – not exactly –

and without the farm, your existence here in this world, this time, would be difficult and maybe even impossible. Not to mention all of our animals that can only survive here, where we've learned how to take care of them.

'So here is what I'm going to do. After much thought, I am making Lucinda and Tyler my heirs. When I'm gone Ordinary Farm will belong to the two of you – but only if you agree to abide by my terms and honour all the responsibilities that go with it.'

Even in the midst of such an amazing moment, something about what he said nagged at her. 'Responsibilities?' Lucinda asked. 'Like feeding the animals? Of course we'll take care of them just like you have, Uncle Gideon. We know all about that.'

'Not quite.' The old man held up his hand to hold back more questions. 'No, part of what it means to own Ordinary Farm is to protect Ordinary Farm – and all the people on it. If you agree to be my heirs, you must also solemnly promise me that everyone here will always have a home at Ordinary Farm.'

'Everyone?' asked Lucinda, astonished. 'No matter what they do?' Even if they try to brainwash or kill people? she wondered. How could she and Tyler promise to let Patience Needle stay when they already knew she would go to any lengths to take the farm for herself and Colin?

'Ummm . . . ummm . . .' Tyler was fidgeting like someone who needed to use the bathroom – it was clear he was feeling a painful need to share his own secret. Lucinda hoped he'd keep his mouth shut about Grace until they could find out whether Gideon really meant what he'd just said.

'You mean even if we're in charge someday, we can't ever kick out anybody here?' She avoided looking at Patience Needle, but everyone in the room except Gideon knew who she was talking about. 'No matter what they do? We can't say yes to that, Uncle Gideon.'

'Come, come,' he said, frowning. 'I'm not asking you to do anything I haven't done myself. It's simple, child – do you promise to abide by my rules?' His displeasure turned to surprise. 'Tyler, what are you doing? Where is he going? Come back here!'

But her brother was already slipping between the Three Amigos, hurrying out of the parlour. Once again, Lucinda wished Tyler would think before he acted. Now she had only a few moments before he showed up with Grace, and that would probably be the end of any real conversation for the day.

'I'm very unhappy with your brother's irresponsible behaviour,' Gideon said. 'And speaking of irresponsible, what on earth are you trying to say? I'm offering you an amazing gift – nothing like it has ever existed before. Why can't you just do as I ask?'

She cleared her throat. 'We're really grateful, Uncle Gideon. It's just that some of us . . . feel that not everyone here on Ordinary Farm . . . has your best

428

interests . . . the farm's best interests . . .' She turned to Ragnar, Sarah, and the kitchen women. 'Isn't anyone else going to talk? Hasn't anybody told him anything . . . ?'

But before another word could be said Tyler burst through the doorway leading his surprise. She was dressed in a simple dress from twenty years or more ago and her hair was brushed and shiny.

'Look, Uncle Gideon,' Tyler said, half tugging her toward the old man's bedside. 'Just look who we found for you while you were sick! Look who's here! It's Grace!'

Gideon looked at her, his face slack with confusion and growing wonder. Then it somehow slid right past wonder and back into pure confusion. 'What? Who is this?'

'It's Grace, Uncle Gideon!' Tyler was almost jumping up and down in his worried excitement. 'Your wife!'

Gideon stared at the woman for a long moment, then turned to Tyler. 'What are you talking about? That isn't Grace.'

Tyler was clearly getting panicky now. 'Just look at her again, Uncle Gideon! It's been twenty years and she was stuck in a real bad place – but it's her!'

Gideon looked again at the white-haired woman, who seemed nervous just returning his gaze, blinking and leaning away from him. He shook his head. 'No. Not my Grace.'

Tyler turned to Ragnar and the rest. 'Maybe he doesn't recognize her because he's been sick . . . !'

'No, Gideon speaks the truth,' said Mr. Walkwell from the couch. 'I am the only other person here who knew her.' He shook his head wearily. 'That is not Grace Goldring.'

# CHAPTER 44

## THE PRICE OF PEACE

If Colin Needle hadn't been in such a miserable mood he would have taken a great deal of pleasure from the expressions on Tyler Jenkins's face as it became clear that no amount of insisting on his part was going to turn this confused old woman into Gideon's long-lost wife.

Even better than that, the younger Jenkins had completely distracted everyone just when Lucinda had been about to tell Gideon about the things Patience Needle had done. Colin might have his own doubts about his mother, but he couldn't imagine anything good could come from her being denounced in front of everybody. Still, the danger was by no means gone, just delayed, and Colin could sense something behind his mother's carefully composed features that he'd hardly ever seen in her before: a shadow of distress or even fear.

This new realization struck Colin like a blow – his mother *didn't know what was going to happen next*! The situation here was actually beyond her control. He had never imagined such a day might come and he didn't know whether to be excited or terrified.

'But if this lady's not Grace,' Lucinda suddenly asked, bringing a little quiet to the noisy room, '. . . then who is she?'

While everyone else had been arguing, Gideon had been staring at the newcomer. Now he blinked and sat up straighter in his bed. 'My goodness,' he said, 'I've just realized . . . I think it's Dorothea! She used to live here with us. Dorothea, is that you?'

'Dorothea?' asked Tyler, as deflated as Colin Needle could ever hope to see him. 'Who the heck is Dorothea?'

'Grace's cousin, Dorothea Pence – but she left and moved back east years ago! What's she doing here?' Gideon leaned toward the woman. 'Dorothea, is that really you?'

She at first only looked confused, but at last she nodded. 'Dorothea. Yes, that's my name. I . . . I had forgotten . . .'

'But where did she come from?' Gideon demanded. 'Did she just wander onto the property? Dorothea, when did you come back?' He turned to Mr. Walkwell. 'Simos, do you know anything about this – no, you've been sick too. Ragnar?'

The Norseman spread his hands. 'Tyler found her. As he said, he . . . brought her back.'

'Tyler?' Gideon's voice had an edge now. 'And you brought me Grace's necklace too, didn't you? Told you found it in the library. Well, you'd better tell me everything – and this time I want the whole truth, boy.'

'I . . . but I don't . . .' Tyler hesitated, then looked at his great-uncle in a pleading way. 'Really?'

Sweat dripped down the back of Colin Needle's neck. His guts felt heavy, and it was all he could do not to look over at his mother. If Tyler Jenkins started talking, who was to say where he'd stop? Did anybody in this room really want Gideon Goldring to know the whole truth?

'The mirror on the washstand?' Gideon seemed astonished. 'The antique washstand that was in the library, in Octavio's retiring room? That mirror?' He turned to Mr. Walkwell. 'What do you think of that, Simos? Strange, eh?'

Mr. Walkwell was sitting up on his makeshift bed, paying close attention to everything being said, but he didn't reply.

'And it's upstairs now?' Gideon asked, his voice stern again as he turned to Mrs. Needle. 'In your room, Patience? Is that true? What's it doing there?'

The housekeeper spoke slowly and precisely, as if she had started considering her answer long before

Gideon asked the question. 'I thought it seemed an unusual, interesting piece of furniture, too nice to be hidden away. I had it brought to my office because . . . well, because I liked it.' She nodded. 'Isn't that right, Colin?'

Colin nodded too. He felt as though everything was balanced on a knife-edge – that things could still go back to the way they were, but could just as easily tumble over into something completely unknown and unpredictable.

'And so that's where the locket came from too.' Gideon had taken it from his neck and held it draped across the palm of his hand. 'I remember now – Grace gave it to Dorothea when she left for Providence.' He turned toward Dorothea, who was sitting on a chair beside his bed. 'When did you come back from the east coast?'

The woman shook her head. 'I never left. I got to Los Angeles but I couldn't bear to leave Grace behind. She seemed so downhearted! So I called the people I was going to stay with in Providence and told them I'd changed my mind. Then I took the train back to Standard Valley – I didn't tell anyone I was coming until I got there because . . . well, because I thought you might be upset, Gideon. Uncle Octavio drove out to pick me up – I was worried because he was getting along in years, but he got us back to the farm with no problems . . .' She trailed off, staring at her water glass. 'But I don't remember what happened after that.' She looked up, and now it was clear to Colin and everyone else how upset she was, her eyes red-rimmed, her expression almost haunted. 'I don't remember anything . . . except nightmares . . . !' Tears began to roll down her cheek. 'Oh, what's happened to me? Why am I so old?'

Gideon waved his hand; he looked uncomfortable. 'There, there, dear. You're safe now. We'll explain everything soon.' He looked around a little desperately. 'Dorothea's still tired, I'm sure – she may remember more when she's recovered. Sarah, why don't you take her back to her room . . . ?'

'I do it,' said Ooola, jumping to her feet. She led Dorothea out of the Snake Parlour. In the quiet that followed their departure, Gideon turned back to Tyler Jenkins.

'Why did you lie to me, boy? About my wife, of all things?' He crossed his arms over his chest and glared. 'About my wife!'

As happy as Colin was to see his enemy get a tongue-lashing, he was worried about what Tyler might say; a moment later his worries were confirmed.

'Why? I had to, Uncle Gideon. Everybody lies to you.' Most of the people in the room sucked in their breath at the same time. 'Last year, this year – everybody!' Tyler smacked his hands together in frustration. 'People try to let you know what's going on around here, but you never want to hear it!'

'That's nonsense!' Gideon's face darkened. 'Are you

saying you tried to tell me that the mirror from the library was some kind of miniature Fault Line – but that I wouldn't listen?'

'No, that's not what I'm talking about.' Tyler turned to his sister. 'It's way more than the mirror. Luce, help me out. Tell him about the witch – tell him what Mrs. Needle did to him.'

Now Lucinda Jenkins stepped out beside her brother. Colin felt dizzy and sick, but he did nothing to stop either of them, as though he was in one of those dreams where he couldn't make words come out of his mouth. 'He's telling the truth, Uncle Gideon,' Lucinda said. 'Can't you remember anything that happened to you? Mrs. Needle nearly killed you – she's been trying to take the farm away from you. And last summer she almost killed Tyler . . . !'

She hadn't even finished before Colin's mother stepped forward, her face white and her brows like slashes of ink. She pointed her trembling hand at Lucinda and the girl shied back as if it were a gun. 'How . . . how dare you!' she spat at the girl, then whirled to face Gideon. 'These children have treated me dreadfully since they first came – but this is utter madness! Tried to kill you, they claim! Me, who went nights on end without sleep to nurse you during your illness – as anyone else in the house will confirm!'

'But you caused his illness!' Lucinda Jenkins was clearly frightened of his mother, but Colin could see she would not give up so easily. For a moment he forgot

436

all his own fears in a sort of fever of admiration – but only for a moment. 'Everybody knows what you do, Mrs. Needle!'

'She tried to kill you with a fungus, Uncle Gideon!' shouted Tyler. 'And she sent this . . . this devil-squirrel thing after me last year . . . !'

Lucinda turned to the other farm folk, but many of them actually shrank back from her as though she might grab them and drag them into the fight. 'What's wrong with you all? Isn't anybody going to speak up but Tyler and me . . . ?'

Sarah's plump face was red and her eyes teary, but a determined expression was hardening her features. She opened her mouth as if to speak, but Mrs. Needle turned and glared at her so fiercely that the cook snapped it shut again.

'Do you really credit any of this?' Colin's mother demanded, turning back to Gideon. 'Do you hear the nonsense these children spout? Of course that boy would take his sister's side. Of course he would swear to the truth of her demented tales. Did you hear him? Poison fungus? Devil squirrels?' She was breathing so hard in her fury (and, yes, in her fear) that Colin had a sudden picture in his head of his mother tied to a stake, surrounded by jeering peasants. 'Will you sit there and let them call me a witch when you know that I have done nothing that was not by your own orders?'

Now it was Gideon who looked caught between two enemies. 'Now, Patience,' he said, 'I'm sure the children are exaggerating . . . It's a misunderstanding, that's all . . .'

'No, Gideon.' The deep voice surprised everyone. 'The children are not exaggerating.' Ragnar stepped forward. 'Will you listen to me? Does my word mean something to you?'

Gideon gaped at him. 'Ragnar . . . ?'

'And I must speak too, Gideon,' said Mr. Walkwell from his couch. 'The children are right – the woman is a poison, Gideon. She means us all harm. She wants everything for herself.'

'Liars!' Colin didn't even realize until everyone turned toward him that it was his own voice screaming. 'Don't! She's not . . . !' And then he turned and stumbled from the room, uncertain at first where he was going except that he had to get away from those accusing faces, away from his mother as she was slowly surrounded like a cat treed by a pack of baying hounds.

'Colin!' His mother's voice was piercing. 'Colin, where are you going? Come back here!'

But suddenly he knew what he had to do. He hurried toward the stairs that led up to his room.

Less than a minute later, his backpack now clutched against his chest, Colin jumped down the last few stairs and shoved his way into the Snake Parlour. People were shouting, even his mother, who seldom raised her voice even in the grimmest circumstances.

'You have had too many chances already, witch!'

438

Ragnar bellowed, his voice loud enough to drive nails.

'Close your mouth, you Norse peasant!' his mother cried.

'Peasant?' Ragnar's voice became, if possible, even louder. 'I was a king . . . !'

'Stop!' shouted someone else in a ringing voice.

Gideon had thrown back the covers and put his feet on the floor, and was now lifting himself up to a standing position with some help from Caesar. 'Stop, all of you! I won't have this kind of behaviour in my house!' He turned and saw Colin in the doorway. There wasn't much kindness in the old man's face. 'It's a good thing you came back, boy, because clearly we all have a lot to talk about. A lot of serious, serious things to talk about . . . !'

Colin's heart now felt as stone-heavy as the rest of his innards. He could tell by the look on Gideon's face that there would be no turning back to the way things were, no sweeping this under the rug. Colin pawed at the strap on his backpack, trying to get out the Continuascope. 'Hold on, Gideon, hold on. I have something to show you . . . !'

The old man wasn't having it. 'No! I said I want to talk, boy! I want answers!'

'No, you need to see this . . .' Colin couldn't get the buckle open. 'My . . . my mother figured out where this was – she sent me out to get it . . . !'

'No way – no way!' screamed Tyler Jenkins, rushing

forward. He grabbed the backpack and tried to yank it from Colin's hands. 'You total liar! You followed me – I found it!'

'Tyler! Colin! Oh, for goodness sake,' said Gideon, for the moment more irritated than furious, 'will someone just stop these two and their cursed wrangling? I need people to start talking sense around here! Ragnar?'

But even as the big Norseman stepped up and reached for the backpack that held the Continuascope, his hand so strong and his arm so solid that Colin knew he could take it away easily even if Colin hung on with both his own, Gideon Goldring made a strange noise. Ragnar stopped, staring, the backpack forgotten. Everybody else in the room was staring too.

Gideon Goldring had opened his mouth to say something else, but nothing came out but a weird rasping. He tried to suck in more air and only made a horrible thwarted noise in his throat. He opened his mouth wide as if to scream, but still nothing would come. He turned bright red, then his face began to darken into an even more frightening colour, grey-blue as a bruise, and he suddenly crumpled to the floor.

'Oh, no!' Lucinda Jenkins shouted over the cries of the others in the room. 'He's having a heart attack! We have to get him to a hospital!'

Ragnar let go of Colin's backpack and in a moment was kneeling by Gideon's side. The old man was still struggling, but his movements were growing weaker.

He kicked his legs feebly, bending and straightening like a fish yanked from the water.

'He can't get his breath!' Tyler shouted. 'Call an ambulance!'

'It'll take forever for them to get out here,' said Lucinda, her face white with shock and horror. 'Is there a helicopter or something – a medical helicopter?'

'Ragnar, take him!' cried Simos Walkwell from his couch. 'Take him in that terrible machine and drive him to the town! Swiftly!'

'If he's having a heart attack,' Tyler said, 'he needs help now! We should take him over to the Carrillos' . . .'

Suddenly Mrs. Needle was standing beside Ragnar and Gideon, whose hands and head were the only things that still moved, although it was little more than twitching. 'It is not his heart, you fools,' she said in a voice hard and clear as glass. 'And the cure is very simple.'

'What are you talking about, witch?' Ragnar looked as though he would be happy to tear her head off with his bare hands.

'Quiet, Norseman. Get back and I will help him.' When Ragnar didn't move, she stared at him, then looked around the room. 'Fools. Do you really want Gideon to die instead of letting me cure him?'

Mr. Walkwell's voice cut through the sudden hush. 'Let her try to heal him, Ragnar. You go and bring the car around to the front door.'

Mrs. Needle smirked. 'No car will be needed.' She

reached into the pocket of her apron and pulled out a tiny glass vial as black as her skirt. She unstopped it, then let a couple of drops fall into Gideon's open, gasping mouth.

'What are you doing to him . . . ?' Lucinda demanded, but Colin's mother ignored her, staring at Gideon as though the old man lying on the floor fighting for a breath was the most interesting thing she had ever seen. Colin clutched his backpack tight, suddenly more frightened than he'd ever been in his life.

A moment later the agonized, stretched lines of Gideon Goldring's face began to ease. The blood-bruise colour receded almost as quickly as it had come, and a few seconds later the harsh gasping abruptly stopped as well. Gideon's mouth closed and then opened again so he could suck in a long draught of air. It very quickly became clear he was breathing easily again.

'*Gott wird gepriesen!*' murmured Sarah. 'Praise to God!'

'You poisoned him!' Lucinda accused Colin's mother, frightened and angry in equal measure. This time Colin didn't move or say anything because he had been thinking much the same thing himself. 'You poisoned him just so you could give him the antidote!'

Mrs. Needle actually smiled, though it was not a pleasant expression. 'Oh, nonsense, child. This is a problem Gideon developed this summer when he was recovering from his illness—'

'You mean the fungal spores that you dosed him with?' Tyler demanded. 'That illness?'

Colin's mother kept her smile but the rest of her face was as stiff as a mask. 'You really should learn to respect your elders, Tyler and Lucinda Jenkins. Your rudeness is going to get you into serious trouble someday.' As Ragnar helped Gideon back to his bed, Patience Needle turned slowly toward Mr. Walkwell, as if he was the judge to whom she was making her case. 'These children may spout any madness they please, but I'm sure you understand, Simos. You are Gideon's oldest friend here. You understand that he has this very serious condition, that I and I alone have the medicine to cure it – or to keep it at bay entirely. So which will it be, Simos? Would you have a needless war between us, or will we all pull together to keep Gideon well – and take care of this farm for the dear, dear Jenkins children, who will inherit it someday?' Her smile abruptly pulled into a line thin as a knife-slash. 'If they live that long, of course. Life is uncertain even in this brave new world.'

Mr. Walkwell stared at her, his face a study in sorrow, anger, and weariness.

'Don't do it!' Tyler Jenkins said, as if he sensed what was coming. 'We'll take Gideon to a hospital! Don't let her have her way!'

'Nobody is having their way, child,' said Colin's mother, but she still kept her eyes fixed on Mr. Walkwell. 'We are making . . . a compromise. Doing what is best for all parties. And Gideon will agree, I promise you.' She looked over to Gideon. He was conscious again, but like a frightened child he did not look up to meet her gaze. 'Yes, dear Gideon has always understood where his best interests lie.' She lifted an eyebrow. 'Well, Simos? Is it to be peace between us?'

Ragnar stepped away from Gideon and stood over her, looking down with his hands knotted into broad fists. Each of his arms looked almost as wide as Colin's slender mother. 'Just tell me what you wish, Simos,' the Norseman said through clenched teeth. 'I will stand by you.'

Mr. Walkwell slowly shook his head. 'I must think of Gideon – and the farm,' he said. 'So we will have peace.' He looked from Colin's mother to Colin himself, and his eyes suddenly seemed so dark that Colin gasped. 'But remember, we will have peace only as long as Gideon and these two children remain healthy.'

Mrs. Needle laughed. 'As you say, Simos – peace. For now. Come along, Colin.'

Colin Needle had been about to give up the Continuascope to save his mother, but now he didn't even want to go with her. His prize was still hidden in the backpack, still his secret, safe from all others. He would hide it again, even from his mother. What else did he have that was truly his?

'Colin, I'm waiting.'

He didn't want to follow his mother, but he did,

because that was what he had always done. But after today how could anything ever be the same? He needed to think about that, Colin realized as he trudged up the stairs. He needed to think about that very, very carefully.

# CHAPTER 45

## HIGH AS THE SKY

'Okay, I admit it,' said Tyler as the horse pulled the wagon up the long driveway toward the Carrillos' house. 'I don't get exactly what happened yesterday. Did we win or did we lose?'

Ragnar snorted. 'He is changing his will for you. It is happening, and that is very fortunate for you.'

'I know, I know. But didn't Mrs. Needle just get away with it again? Am I stupid or something? She's a witch! I thought that the bad guys were supposed to get punished.'

'It's not that simple, Tyler . . .' Lucinda began, although she had been worrying too. After yesterday's weird events in the Snake Parlour, the evening had been long and quiet, more like the gathering after a funeral than the festive time they had shared with the Ordinary Farm folk before their departure the previous year.

'But in one way your brother is right,' said Ragnar. His expression reminded Lucinda of the thunderclouds of last week. 'We have failed to dislodge that woman from Gideon's hearth. In that way, she *has* won.'

'Because she poisoned Gideon,' Lucinda said bitterly. 'Because she's blackmailing everyone.'

'Yes, but she is like a serpent – she strikes best from cover,' Ragnar told her. 'Now she must come out where all can see her. Don't fear, you two – Simos and I will no longer be silent. We will make sure the Needle woman never has so much power on the farm again, or so much freedom. Yes, from now on the fight will be in the open, and Gideon will not be able to hide his eyes behind his hand to avoid it.'

That made Lucinda feel a little better, but another thought occurred to her as the door of the Carrillos' house swung open and Steve, Alma, and Carmen all crashed out into the front yard. 'But what if she tries to hurt you guys? Tyler and I won't be here! We won't even be able to help . . . !'

Ragnar's big hand patted her back. 'I was a king and Simos was counsellor to several kings in his day.' He grinned. 'We may smell like farmers, but there is more to both of us. Don't fear, child – we will not be caught by surprise again so easily.'

'Time to go,' Ragnar said after what seemed far too short a time with the Carrillos.

'No, don't!' said Carmen. 'Just a little longer . . . !'

'The train will be at the station in an hour and the road is slow and muddy after all the rain,' the big man said. 'You children know I am right.'

'Are Mr. and Mrs. Carrillo still mad at Uncle Gideon?' Lucinda asked.

Ragnar shrugged. 'Gideon is himself again and understands he cannot ignore this matter any longer. I told them he has promised he will come here in a few days, when he is strong enough. Together they will work out something – Gideon does not want to lose such good neighbours.' His smile was gentle this time. 'You have too many fears, young Lucinda. Things are not perfect, but they will be better now.' He gently shook the reins and Culpepper clip-clopped toward the main road.

Even Ragnar the Viking, big as he was, shrank quickly into the distance and vanished as the train pulled out of Standard Valley station, but there was time for Lucinda to climb up on the seat and shout one last thing out the window at him.

*'Don't make us wait until next summer to come back! We get holidays off school, you know!'*

'Whoa!' said Tyler, plugging into his GameBoss. 'Everybody's staring, Luce. Maybe you should sort of chill out a little.'

To her embarrassment, he was right. Half the people in the passenger car had turned to look. She saw a conductor coming toward her and quickly slid down to a sitting position once more. The man in uniform frowned but continued past.

Tyler was already deep into something called 'HAMSTROMANCY'. Lucinda couldn't understand how he could just do that, disappear into some game as if he didn't have a care in the world. She settled back and closed her eyes, trying to calm herself enough to read or look at the scenery, but thoughts were swirling in her head like startled birds and they wouldn't stop. What was going to happen? If they were going to be the heirs of Ordinary Farm, wouldn't their mom have to know sooner or later? Would she come to the farm with them? What if she totally freaked out?

But what was bothering her most of all, Lucinda realized, was the strong feeling of unfinished business. There were still so many questions!

'You're not the only one who doesn't get it,' she said to her brother.

She must have spoken louder than she meant to, because Tyler heard her even through his earbuds. 'Get what?' he asked without looking up from his hamstering.

'I don't know. Take those off, will you?' She waited. He grunted and turned off his game. 'A lot of stuff,' she said. 'What was that witch really trying to do to Gideon with that fungus? And why didn't *I* turn into a zombie too – was it just because I didn't get as much of the spore stuff as he did . . . ?'

Tyler looked at her, all innocence. 'I think you

mean, "Why didn't I turn into more of a zombie than I already am?"'

She gave him a hard shot on the leg to focus his thoughts. 'Cut it out. We know from the letter that the fungus thing came from near Madagascar. Didn't you tell me Octavio said something about Madagascar too?'

'Yeah, he told me it's on the opposite side of the earth from the Fault Line here. That's what I think he said, anyway. That the two places were like the North and South Poles. But it was pretty scientific.' He shook his head. 'Okay, giant Madagascar Fault Line fungus. I have a question too – how did Gideon get away from it? Why was he wandering around on the Fourth of July?'

'I have a theory.' Lucinda put a piece of tissue in her book to mark her place, then slid it into her backpack. 'When I was at the greenhouse the day I got . . . spored, I guess, some of the metal of the greenhouse was melted. I think it must have got hit by lightning in that first storm.'

'So?'

'So that's almost for sure where Mrs. Needle was keeping Gideon, and then the lightning hit the place and then . . .' she shrugged, 'then somehow it freaked out the fungus or something. Anyway, I think that's when he got out, because there was that storm, remember, and then the next day was the Fourth, when we went to the Carrillos' and Gideon suddenly showed up.'

Tyler nodded. 'Okay. Sort of makes sense. But what about the other stuff? I know Colin's got the Continuascope. What if he starts messing with the Fault Line?'

She shrugged. 'There's nothing we can do about it right now. You warned Ragnar and Mr. Walkwell. They'll keep their eyes open. They said they'd find it if they could, or at least keep him out of the Fault Line.'

He scowled. 'That guy is such a creep.'

For once Lucinda didn't bother arguing. 'And the mirror, the washstand mirror – they said Gideon was going to take that back from Mrs. Needle, so that's good too, right?'

'I guess. But how come Octavio didn't know anything about it? How could it be sitting right there in his house and the guy who knew *everything* didn't know?'

Lucinda still found the idea of Tyler meeting old, long-dead Octavio Tinker in a spooky tunnel under the ground something she didn't really want to think about too much. 'Hey,' she said, 'I brought Uncle Gideon's worst enemy onto the property and lived to tell the tale. Everything about Ordinary Farm is crazy.'

Tyler laughed. 'I can't believe you did that, sis. You were awesome!'

Looking back on it now, the whole thing with Stillman terrified her. What had she been thinking?

But what was done was done. It had turned out all right. No use getting all worked up about it.

*Wow*, she thought. *That's almost like something Tyler would say.* Suddenly, she was glad to have a brother. 'I hope everything's going to be okay. And I really want to go back there soon – maybe over Thanksgiving!'

Tyler laughed again. 'That girl who was saying all last summer, "I want to go home!" – wasn't that you?'

'Yeah, and that kid who was saying, "Gee, Lucinda, sorry I kept getting you into trouble" – wasn't that you? No, wait, it wasn't, because you *never* say that.'

A year before, Tyler would have snapped at her, or just plugged back into his GameBoss and ignored her. 'Well, *somebody* has to make things happen,' he said. 'That's my job.'

'Oh, and you're good at it too, Tyler Jenkins,' she told him, smiling despite herself. 'Way too good.'

They stopped talking after a while and Tyler went back to guiding his hamster-wizard through its perilous quest, but Lucinda kept losing track of the words in her book, and looking out the window didn't cheer her up either. She was still miserable at how things had ended up with the dragons. After all that Lucinda had done that summer, all her kind, slow, careful attempts to build a connection with the dragons, and especially with little Desta, the whole thing had gone *ka-boom* in a matter of moments.

*But I didn't want to do it! I didn't want to upset her!*

*I had to do it to save the farm . . . to save Gideon and everyone else, including the dragons . . . !*

The hurt was so sharp that for a moment she could almost feel what she had felt that night, the storm of Desta's furious, terrified thoughts and how she had forced herself to ignore them. Thinking about it made Lucinda feel as if she had a chunk of ice in the middle of her chest where her heart should be. *I'm so sorry,* she thought. *I'm so sorry, Desta . . . !*

*Carrot Girl sad?*

It surprised her so much she gasped. *Desta? Is that you?* The dragon-thoughts were faint, like a voice you could hear only when the wind was blowing in the right direction, but at the moment that was the direction it *was* blowing. *Desta?*

*Sad why?*

How could she explain such things to a dragon – and a young dragon at that? Especially when they might only have moments. *Carrot Girl is sad because . . . because she made Desta sad. Didn't want to. Had to. But still sad. Carrot Girl sorry. Carrot Girl so very, very sorry . . . !*

There was a long pause, and Lucinda was certain she had lost the fleeting contact. Then:

*Carrot Girl make better.*

*What? How? What can I do to make it better? I'm going away now for months and months!* Lucinda did her best to convey the feeling of time – moons waxing and waning repeatedly. *Gone long. What can I do?*

*Come back soon.* The thought came with a tickle of dragonly amusement. *Next time bring more carrots – millions of carrots!* The thought was of a pile as high as the sky.

Laughter like a stream of warm, smoky bubbles floated through her mind. Then the touch was gone and Lucinda Jenkins was alone in her own head once more.

# THE
# DRAGONS
## OF
# ORDINARY FARM

## by Tad Williams and Deborah Beale

'The plot is clever, the characters interesting and mysterious and best of all, it has dragons! I can hardly wait for the next page-turning adventure.'
*Christopher Paolini*

Tyler and Lucinda have to spend the summer with their Uncle Gideon, a farmer. They think they're in for lots of sheep, horses and pigs. But when they arrive they discover that Ordinary Farm is, well, no ordinary farm.

The bellowing in the barn comes not from a cow, but from a dragon. And the thundering herd in the valley? Unicorns. Plus, there's a flying monkey, a demon squirrel and farmhands with strange powers.

The place seems like an adventure. But when darker secrets surface and Uncle Gideon and his creatures are threatened, Lucinda and Tyler must act. Will they be able to save the dragons, the farm – and themselves?

£6.99, available from all good bookshops